OF ASHES AND DUST

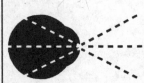

This Large Print Book carries the
Seal of Approval of N.A.V.H.

OF ASHES AND DUST

MARC GRAHAM

WHEELER PUBLISHING

A part of Gale, a Cengage Company

GALE
A Cengage Company

Farmington Hills, Mich • San Francisco • New York • Waterville, Maine
Meriden, Conn • Mason, Ohio • Chicago

LIBRARY OF CONGRESS CIP DATA ON FILE.
CATALOGUING IN PUBLICATION FOR THIS BOOK
IS AVAILABLE FROM THE LIBRARY OF CONGRESS

ISBN-13: 978-1-4328-4750-0 (softcover)

Published in 2018 by arrangement with Arcadian Dreamscapes, LLC

Printed in Mexico
1 2 3 4 5 6 7 22 21 20 19 18

He has cast me into the mire, and I have become like dust and ashes.

— Job 30:19 (NKJV)

For my father, Lou Graham, who always had a story to share, and who never missed an opportunity to tell his family he loved them.

ACKNOWLEDGMENTS

Writing is chiefly a solitary activity, but the refining and editing of a story are best done as a team sport — albeit one that sometimes feels like full contact. Many lovely souls and sharp minds have contributed to the inception and improvement of this novel, and I'm grateful to each of them. Any remaining deficiencies are entirely my own.

Dee Lynch facilitated my introduction to this story and reinvigorated my passion for writing.

Len Douglas and Dr. Andrew May provided insight into the history and development of the Transcontinental and Western Australia Railroads.

Pamela King Cable, Golda Fried, Dena Harris, and Edmund Schubert comprised my first literary critique group and helped me to learn what I didn't know about writing.

Melissa Fike and Rob Payo are dear

friends who slogged through a hefty first draft and helped me to find the kernel of the story.

No writer should journey into the dread realm of publication without experienced guides. There are many trailblazers, and they are to be found among writers groups. Of profound help to me have been Backspace Writers, Historical Novel Society, Pikes Peak Writers, and Rocky Mountain Fiction Writers.

My partners in Highlands Ranch Fiction Writers are Lynn Bisesi, Deirdre Byerly, Claire Fishback, Nicole Greene, Michael Haspil, Chloe Hawker, L. S. Hawker, Laura Main, Vicki Pierce, and Chris Scena. Their collective spirit and insight make a sometimes daunting journey one to be savored and treasured, and they make me a better writer. Because magic.

Tracy Laird, Sharon Kendrew, and Jeanette Schneider are beautiful and brilliant co-conspirators in our scheme for literary world domination. *See you at Arno's!*

In the course of developing my writing career, I've had the privilege of meeting and interacting with a host of great authors who have been beyond generous with their time and insights. Among the many are Tracy Brogan, Stephen Coonts, Bernard Cornwell, Margaret George, C. W. Gortner, Kevin Hearne, Brad Meltzer, and Boyd Morrison. For class and talent, they set high bars, and I'm indebted to them.

Tiffany Schofield, Alice Duncan, and Erin Bealmear guided me into the world of publication with grace and wit. My eternal gratitude goes to them and to the entire Five Star family.

Finally, my bride, Laura. She is my first reader, toughest critic, loudest cheerleader, wittiest brainstormer, and greatest love. She makes the journey possible and worth making. *ILYWATIA.*

PROLOGUE

So this is what it is to die.

Sunlight drenches the earth and washes the clouds from the sky, all but drowning a stubborn half moon that peeks through the midday glare. I stand on a rocky hilltop and stare at the valley floor a half mile away, where a bluish glow flows from the lugs of a detonator into its attached cable. Part of my mind insists this can't be real, that the detonation should happen in a fraction of a second.

Heedless of that fact, the radiance traces the cable up the slope, around scrub brush, over small outcroppings and loose stones, to the summit of the pass. The glow splits where the terminals splice into the cable and follows the several branches, one of which passes between my feet. I try to turn, to follow the path of the glow, but I can't move, not even to rub at a bit of dust that tickles my nose.

Nearly forty years of striving, scratching, clawing out an existence in a world indifferent, and it all comes down to this: to die alone on a barren pass on the underbelly of the earth. Did any of it matter? Did I make a difference? Without pausing to answer, the radiance continues along each branch to its end. Like a drove of rabbits, the glows dive into the mouths of the boreholes that dot the hilltop.

I'll be damned.

But nothing happens. Hope flickers in my breast and all my senses fire. Salty air teases my tongue, and my skin twitches under sweat-stiffened muslin and denim. Life is a dust devil dancing, swirling about me.

Then the ground moves.

Ripples stir from the boreholes as from pebbles tossed in a pond. The waves grow and merge, their energies focused on me. Like a hammer blow, the shock wave pounds into me, followed by the roar of a hundred cannon, surrounding me, penetrating me.

Then I am weightless, soaring high above the bleak landscape. The ground rushes up to greet me, and my world is ringed about by a horizon of pain.

CHAPTER ONE

Crawford County, Arkansas — May 1846

The pain faded as quickly as it began, and I rubbed my backside.

"You know it hurts me to do that." Mama hung the switch on its peg by the fireplace and smoothed the folds of her skirt. She wiped a tear on her sleeve before turning to face me.

"Yes'm," I said, my eyes cast down, my chin tucked.

"You're a good boy, Jimmy. You just need to act like it."

"Yes'm," I repeated with a catch in my throat.

I couldn't quite remember what I'd done to get this whipping, which was maybe why I got so many of them. But I kept my head down and looked sorry all the same.

Mama knelt and pulled me to her, the hug made clumsy by her swollen belly. She

15

shuddered with a sob, and snuffled in my ear.

"Now you run along with your chores," she said, "while I clean this up."

"Yes'm," I said yet again.

I turned and saw the muddy floor, then remembered Mama always telling me to take my boots off before I came inside. I felt a little sorry then, seeing the mess I'd made. Not quite six years old, I made plenty of messes. I never meant to be bad, though. It just . . . Well, it just happened. I limped and rubbed my backside again as I trudged toward the door, then lifted the latch, stepped outside and pulled the door shut behind me.

Then I ran.

Ran with abandon, my arms stretched wide as the cool breeze brushed my cheeks and swept through my hair. I breathed deeply and tasted fresh rain and sweet clover on the spring air. Winter had dragged on and on, and it wasn't my fault the rains had come just when it was warm enough to play outside.

I ran through the fallow field behind our cottage until the slope of the land hid the house from view. Thoughts of wood to be stacked and eggs to be gathered flew away like the crows that flapped up ahead of me.

The birds cawed at me and I squawked at them, still running, until I reached the woods at the far side of the field.

In the refuge of the trees, I slowed and caught my breath. Fog skimmed the ground and danced about the bases of the trees. I picked my way through the underbrush, following game trails when I could find them, until I came to the edge of May's Branch. The usually quiet stream ran fat with rain and snowmelt and babbled away as it raced toward the Arkansas River.

I followed the bank upstream, the wind in my face. Moving as quietly as possible, I was rewarded by the sight of a doe and her twin fawns grazing on water grasses and drinking from the creek. The little family drank their fill, then retreated into the woods. I thought of following them, but was distracted by a raccoon that scrabbled up from the bank in front of me and disappeared in the brush.

I chased after the masked bandit, not caring how much noise I made now. After a few minutes of crashing through the trees, I stumbled into a mossy clearing with a fairy ring at its center. I walked around the ring of toadstools, remembering the stories I'd heard from Zeke, a slave boy from the neighboring farm.

"Take you to the fairy world, you step in one," he'd told me. "That, or make you a twin, so's you can be two places at once."

He hadn't said how the things worked, but my waiting chores made a twin sound pretty good. I stood at the edge of the circle, closed my eyes and jumped in.

Nothing.

I stepped back out and tried again, this time thinking of the wood shed as I jumped. Still nothing. I ran sunwise about the circle, then the other way. I tried spinning around until I was dizzy, walking on my hands, jumping in backwards. Nothing worked, but I kept trying until my growling belly reminded me that breakfast was long since past.

I kicked at one of the worthless toadstools, then hightailed it home, splashing in every puddle on the way. As I came to the rise in the field, I saw a figure running toward our cottage from the road. By the dark skin and easy gait, I knew it was Zeke. I set off across the field to beat him to the door.

"Miz Robbins, Miz Robbins," he shouted as he reached the porch ten strides ahead of me. He bent over to catch his breath, hands on his knees.

"Beatcha," I said as I leapt over the step and onto the porch.

My muddy boots slid across boards still slick from the morning's rain, and the door opened just as I would have crashed into it. I skidded into Mama and almost pulled her off her feet.

"James Douglas Robbins."

I was JD to most folks, Jade to the slaves, and Jimmy to Mama — usually. When she called me by my full name, I knew I'd soon hear the whistle of the switch. Mama's face flushed as she grabbed my wrist, set me on my feet, and shook clay and mud from her blue calico dress.

"Miz Robbins," Zeke said again, delaying my punishment.

Mama turned toward him, her hand still tight about my wrist.

"It's Marse Robbins, ma'am," Zeke said. "He hurt, and Marse Barnes say to come fetch you right quick."

Fear of the switch turned to something else as a cold hand squeezed my belly. The blood drained from Mama's face. She let go of my wrist, hitched up her skirts and set off toward the Barnes farm. Zeke and I chased after her but, even with her pregnant belly, she outpaced us on the mile-long run.

We reached the farmyard to find slaves milling about the porch. Mister Barnes — sleeves rolled up and hat pushed high on his head — stepped through the crowd of black faces, took Mama by the elbow and helped her up the steps.

"Keep him back, Zeke," he said.

"Yes, suh," Zeke said. He put his hands on my shoulders and steered me away from the porch.

"I wanna see him," I said.

"Ain't nothing for a child to look on," he said, assuming the air of an adult — never mind that he was just a few years older than I. "Nor grown folk, for that matter. Your pappy gonna be fine, but he don't need you gawking at him right now."

Zeke led me toward the back of the big white house while, behind us, harnesses jangled and clamshells crunched. Just before we turned the corner, I caught a glimpse of Doc Aubry's buckboard racing up the drive, followed on horseback by Bull, Mister Barnes's chief slave.

"Oh, Marse Jade." Belle, Bull's wife, waddled down the back steps and picked me up, muddy boots and all.

My fear drained away as she squeezed me against her full bosom and carried me to the kitchen porch where lemonade and fresh cookies waited.

"He's a mess," Angelina Barnes said as Belle set me down. The girl was just eight but seemed in an all-fired hurry to be grown up.

"Hush, child," Belle said.

I reached for a cookie, but Angelina snatched it up and spun away. Her fiery red hair fanned out behind her as she yanked open the screen door and let it slam shut behind her.

"Aw, don't mind her," Matty Barnes said around a mouthful of oatmeal cookie.

We were the same age, and best friends. The chubby boy had red hair like his sister. Where hers flowed long and wavy, though, his sprawled about in bushy curls.

"How'd you get so muddy, anyway?" he asked. "You fall down?"

I shook my head and bit into a ginger snap.

"Your pa fell down," he said as he wiped lemonade from his chin onto his sleeve, "right under a barrel of tobacco."

"Did you see it?" I asked.

"Nah, but I heard it. *Bam.*" He clapped his hands together, forgetting about the glass he held. Lemonade splashed into his face and down his shirtfront. "Oh, Belle," he whined.

"Hush now, Marse Matty," Belle said as she wiped away tears and lemonade with her apron. "You run on up and change 'fore

21

your mammy see you, y'hear?"

Matty rubbed his eyes with pudgy fists and nodded. He took another cookie from the tray, grabbed my hand with lemonade-sticky fingers and led me inside.

"C'mon, JD," he said. "I wanna show you my new soldier."

I wiped my feet as best I could before being dragged across the threshold. I followed Matty into the kitchen where Ketty, Belle's daughter, sat on the floor humming to herself and polishing silver. Matty pulled me through the kitchen, down an echoing hallway, up the stairs and across the landing to his bedroom. The Barnes house always made me uneasy, and I walked on tiptoes, stuffed my hands in my pockets, even held my breath lest I somehow soil the place.

The room seemed big enough to hold our whole cottage, and I wandered to the open window while Matty rummaged through a pile of toys. The sheers rustled and swayed on a light breeze that carried a murmur of voices from the front porch below. Worries for Pa niggled at me, and I strained my ears to make out the words, but Matty's excitement dashed my efforts.

"Papa bought it off the Jew," he said, holding up a tin cavalryman suspended by a string through its campaign hat. "It moves, see?" Matty bounced horse and rider on the string, and the charger's legs moved in a parade gait. "Take that, you dirty Messicans," he shouted, swinging an imaginary saber. "You wanna try?"

"Sure," I said.

I took the toy and bounced it through a few paces before Matty snatched it back.

"Charge," he shouted.

Matty skipped around the room, smacking his hind end as he followed Rough-and-Ready Taylor into battle. I didn't have much stomach for taking on the invisible Mexican army, so I ducked through the window and crawled out on the balcony.

". . . should be able to save it," I heard Doc Aubry say as I crept to a knothole Matty and I had discovered. I put my eye to the hole and looked down on the porch.

Mama knelt beside Pa, holding his hand. If she was pale, he was paler still, his face covered with sweat that plastered thin, brown hair to his forehead. His jaw muscles bulged and flexed as he clenched his teeth together.

"I have to reset the leg," Doc Aubry continued. "Ben, Bull — hold him steady."

Master and slave moved to either side of Pa and placed strong hands on his shoulders. My throat tightened as Mister Barnes moved and revealed a white spur of bone that stuck through Pa's right shin.

"Drink this, Jim," Doc said as he pulled a bottle from his bag, unstopped it and held it to Pa's lips.

Pa took a small sip, then spat out the medicine.

"What is it?" Mama asked.

"Laudanum," Doc said. "It'll dull the pain and keep him still so I can set his leg proper."

Mama stroked Pa's hair and whispered to him. He started to argue, but gave in and let her put the bottle to his mouth. After a few pulls, his eyes glazed over, his jaw went slack and his shoulders sagged under the hands that held him.

"Easy, now," Doc said softly as he tested his grip about Pa's ankle.

Without warning, he yanked on Pa's leg, and the bone slid beneath the flesh. Despite the laudanum, Pa screamed and fought as Bull and Mister Barnes tried to keep him down. His thrashing flung Mama against the porch rail, and her face went from white to grey.

"Hold him," Doc ordered, and the men struggled to obey.

Pa let out a moan, and his eyes rolled back as he went still.

"That's the trick. Well done," Doc said. He poured a different medicine where the bone had poked through, then began splinting the busted leg.

"Sarah?" Missus Barnes said. She moved to Mama's side, gently shook her and patted her cheek. "Doctor," she cried.

"Just a moment, Charlotte," he said.

"Now," she insisted, as a dark pool of blood spread beneath Mama's dress.

CHAPTER TWO

Britton, Arkansas — August 1852

"Get me that one, Jimmy."

Becca's nose pressed against the display cabinet. Her breath fogged the glass while her fingers left narrow smudges.

"You sure?" I asked.

"Uh-huh," she affirmed, and licked her lips hungrily.

"Two licorice sticks, please," I said to the storekeeper.

Becca handed me her penny — the reward for having lost her first tooth — and I slid it across the counter. The grocer handed over the candy, and Becca clapped her hands and hopped in anticipation.

"Make it last," I cautioned her, and she nodded as she grabbed the treat.

We stepped outside into the sticky August air. Becca bit off a piece of licorice, made a point of slowly chewing it, then stuck her tongue out at me, wide-mouthed so I could see the black mush. I grinned back at her with a bit of the candy plastered to my front teeth.

"You look just like me," she lisped through her gap.

"You two 'bout ready?" Pa said, grit in his voice.

He stood with Ma and Doc Aubry across the street from the general store. The black oak in the doctor's front yard provided shade, but offered little comfort against summer's sweaty grip. Ma fanned herself and dabbed a handkerchief at her perspiration, while Pa just looked hot and annoyed. His green eyes sparkled a little when Becca ran to him and leapt into his arms.

After he'd had his accident and Ma lost the baby, Becca's birth a couple years later was the first time I could remember him smiling. She could always lighten his mood, but his usual scowl returned when he looked at me. His face darkened even more as his gaze fell on my sling.

"Let's see that arm," Doc Aubry said.

He eased my right arm out of the sling, then tested all my finger, wrist and elbow joints. I did my best to mask the pain, but couldn't help taking a sharp breath and grimacing when he stretched the busted arm a little farther than it wanted to go.

"That's fine," he judged as he settled the sling back in place. "A few more weeks and you'll be right as rain."

"A few more weeks and it's harvest time," Pa pointed out, more a reminder to me than the doctor.

"True," Doc said, "and I expect the boy'll be able to help out just fine."

Pa grunted at that.

"We'd better get, if we're to make home by dinnertime. Thanks, Doc," he said, patting the bottle-shaped bulge in his pocket.

Doc's face clouded over.

"I need you to try cutting back on the . . ." He glanced down at Becca and me. "On the medicine. If the leg's still giving you pain after all this time, maybe there's something else we can do about it."

Pa set Becca down, shifted the gnarled hickory cane to his left hand and extended his right to shake the doctor's hand.

"This'll be the last one, I promise," he said. "We'll have the rest of the payment for you soon as we can, once Lefty here gets back to work."

He looked pointedly at me with that last bit, and I turned my head away.

"Don't you worry about that, Jim," Doc said. "You'll get it to me when you get it to me. And you, young man," he added, pat-

28

ting my shoulder, "stay out of any more trees for a while."

"Yes, sir," I mumbled, then turned to follow Pa and Ma toward home.

Becca grabbed my left hand, but I shook loose and curled my arm beneath the sling, folding in on myself as I gave in to self-pity.

It wasn't as though I'd meant to fall from the tree. The Barneses had us over on Independence Day for a picnic, and the great black walnut tree was too tempting for a boy to ignore. Matty and I had shinnied up the trunk while our parents and sisters relaxed on blankets in the shade.

Matty stopped at the first branch — just a few feet off the ground — when Missus Barnes cried that he was too high. I kept going, though, higher and higher. Was it to show up Matty? To impress Mister Barnes, or win Pa's approval? Maybe it was to get Angelina's attention, something that had become more and more important to me of late. Or maybe it was just to climb, to rise above and escape from the world below.

Whatever it was that drove me, I made my way to the very top of the tree, steadied myself on the thin branches and peeked above the leaves. The world spread out below me like one of Ma's patchwork quilts. The land was a checkerboard of fields, rimmed by hedgerows and centered on the shade trees that provided a midday harbor for me and the field slaves as we worked the crops. In the distance, the great bend of the Arkansas winked lazily under the midsummer sun.

I looked down and could hardly make out the faces some fifty feet below. The tree limbs shook as I shifted my weight, and my foot slipped from the crook of the branch that supported me. I started to fall, but caught the branch in the pit of my arm. I gripped the limb with both hands and dangled there for a moment to catch my breath. When I looked down again, seven pairs of wide eyes gaped up at me. I forced a laugh, then waved down with one hand while I pedaled my feet like the velocipede rider I'd seen at the fair.

With a loud snap, the limb gave way and I plunged toward the ground. Branches raced past me. Leaves and twigs tore at my skin and snagged on my faded hickory-cloth trousers and burlap shirt. I mused briefly that Ma would soon have more scrap material for her quilts, then screamed as one of the thick lower limbs came straight toward my head. I awoke at Doc Aubry's with bandages wrapped around my head and a heavy plaster cast on my arm.

For weeks after, I'd been of no use to anyone as I suffered through a hot, sticky, itchy summer. Becca had sat by my bed and made up stories that I only half heard and now could not remember at all. Ma fussed over me and kept telling me to rest up so I could heal good and proper. Pa would look in from time to time — to see if I was still breathing, I guess — then just grunt, shake his head and turn away.

Guilt settled uneasily atop the pain of my injuries, at being unable to work while I recovered. Pa's leg was never quite right again after his accident. He had enough trouble just getting around our little homestead to split wood, let alone walking the mile to Barnes's and working the fields all day. When he wasn't in a stupor from the laudanum, he brought in some carpentry work, while Ma took in laundry and mending, and worked on quilts to sell to the peddler man who came by every couple of months.

As soon as I was old enough, I started working for Mister Barnes. At first I just hauled water and mucked out stalls. As I got bigger, I began working with the slaves in the fields, or in the woods gathering timber. The hard labor and Belle's lunches had worked together so that, now twelve, I was nearly as tall as Pa, and already starting to fill out.

"Ho there, Balaam."

The call interrupted my gloomy thoughts and I looked up, surprised to see Zeke drawing in the reins on his mule.

"How-do, Marse Jim, Miz Robbins," he said, raising his straw hat in greeting.

"How are you, Zeke?" Ma asked.

"Fine, ma'am, just fine," he said. "Marse Barnes told me to come fetch Marse Jade here, if he's up to it. We got to start clearing out the corn cribs to make room for the harvest."

"Fine by me," Pa answered for me. "About time he got back to work."

"And Miz Barnes sent these along, too," Zeke went on. "Belle's mulberry jam — best in the county." He leaned down from the mule and handed the jars to Becca, red and white checked toppers tied around the lids. "Don't go eating that all at once," he cautioned her, then playfully tapped her button nose.

"Thank you, Zeke," Ma said. "Give Belle my thanks, and tell Charlotte I hope to visit her soon."

"I'm sure she'd like that, ma'am. You ready, boy?" he asked me, and held a hand out to me.

"Sure," I replied.

I gripped his wrist, swung up onto the mule and wrapped my good arm around him. Balaam shuffled and brayed in protest as I settled in behind Zeke.

"Hush up," Zeke told him. "We won't keep him too late," he promised, then kicked the heels of his bare feet into the mule's ribs and steered him back up the road.

"Keep him as long as you need," Pa called out after us, and I could feel his glare on the back of my head.

"How's that arm doing?" Zeke asked over the clop of Balaam's hooves.

"Fine," I said.

"Hmph. That don't sound fine."

"Then I reckon it ain't my arm that's bothering me," I said.

"Your pappy's a good man," Zeke said, readily catching my meaning. "If he's hard on you, maybe it's just to get you ready for life."

"What's that supposed to mean?"

"It means life's hard, boy. Ain't no place for softies or lay-abouts. You wanna make something for yourself in this world, you got to be tough."

"I don't see how that's enough to help," I said. "Pa's maybe the strongest man I know

— even with his bum leg — and what's that gonna do for him? He ain't never gonna own his own land, won't ever be more'n a sharecropper, taking on other people's chores. Some things you're born to, and that's that. And some things are always gonna be out of your reach, no matter how hard you work or how strong you are."

"We talking 'bout your pappy, now, or someone else?" he said.

My cheeks grew hot, and I was thankful Zeke couldn't see my embarrassment.

"I don't know what you mean," I said.

"Aw, come on, Marse Jade. I seen how you look at Miz Angelina. Now don't get all in a flutter," he said as I tensed and tightened my grip on him. "I don't reckon no one's noticed but me. And even if they have, ain't no harm in that. She's a right pretty girl. They's nothing wrong with having your heart tug away at you in her direction."

Just the thought of Angelina made me forget my troubles for the moment, and brought a grin to my face. In my mind I could see her long, deep-auburn hair catching the sunlight, her cool, green eyes ablaze with life above a pert, freckled nose and full, crimson lips that wrapped daintily around a laughing smile. I thought of the willowy, graceful figure that had bloomed out of a gangling adolescence. The thin, boyish frame of a year earlier had transformed into that of a distinctly feminine mold, and the twin buds developing on her formerly flat chest stirred a strange yearning deep inside me.

"What's the point?" I asked, as reality overcame infatuation. "I ain't nothing but a hired hand, the son of a sharecropper. I just need to remember my place, not go trying to get above my station."

"Maybe," Zeke said. "But at least you free to try or not, free to make that choice for yourself. Your family may not have much, and maybe you got to work side by side with us niggers, but they's a world of difference 'tween being poor and free, and being a slave."

"Did you talk to Mister Barnes?" I asked sheepishly, shamed by my self-pity.

"Oh, I talked with him, all right," he said, his voice hard and cold. "Asked him for Ketty's hand, even offered to buy her off of him with what he let me keep from selling my carvings and such."

Zeke had made a name for himself — and a fair profit for Mister Barnes — with his unique carving and wood-working skills.

"Marse Jade, you should've seen the look on his face when I pulled out that money

— twenty-five dollars cash." Pride replaced some of the hurt and anger in his voice. "Why, I couldn't tell if he was gonna laugh at me or set to beating on me. Didn't make no difference, though. He just throwed the money back in my face, told me to mind my place, not go getting above my station." Those words from his mouth made my own complaint ring hollow in my ears.

"What're you gonna do, then?"

"Right now," he said, as he turned Balaam onto Barnes's clamshell drive, "I'm fixing to rake out a corn crib. I reckon I'll figure the rest out later."

"Your freedom's a precious gift, Marse Jade," Zeke said later, as we took a break from the work and lounged atop a bed of dried cobs and straw in the corn crib. "Ain't nothing you can't do, nothing you can't make of yourself if you's free."

The words hung on the still air as he took a puff from his briar pipe, then dissolved on the cloud of smoke he blew from his nostrils.

"I got it," Matty yelled as he rounded the corner of the crib. "Look, JD, I got it."

He proudly held up a pouch of tobacco and a carved-horn pipe with its cherrywood stem. I stretched out my right arm, which I'd left out of the sling most of the afternoon, and reached for the pipe.

"What is you boys up to now?" Zeke asked, the words punctuated by blue clouds.

"You're gonna teach us how to smoke," I said.

"Is that right?" he asked. "Now, Marse Matty, what your mammy gonna say 'bout that?"

"She won't say anything if she don't know about it," Matty said. "Oh, c'mon, Zeke, please? We'll even share some of our store-bought with you."

Zeke's eyes lit up at that. Mister Barnes held back some of the tobacco crop for the slaves to use, but he only used tobacco that he bought out of Virginia or the West Indies. The smoke all smelled the same to me, but I figured the store-bought tobacco must be something special if it came from so far away.

"Well," Zeke drawled, "I reckon you boys is just about men." He swept away corn and straw with one bare foot until he found the dirt floor of the crib, scraped out a shallow hole and dumped the smoking contents of his pipe into it before covering it back up. "Let's see that tobacco, then."

Matty handed the pouch to Zeke, then plopped down beside me. He was a good head shorter than I and still had his baby fat. He was ever trying to impress me, to win my approval — and I hated him.

I hated him for being rich, while my family barely managed to get by. I hated him for being tied to his mama's apron strings, while I worked his father's fields. Mostly, I hated him for being able to be close to Angelina, to see her every day, to be able — as he once admitted to me — to crawl into bed with her for comfort on stormy nights.

"First, you fill up your bowl like this," Zeke was saying. Matty obediently dipped the horn bowl into the pouch. "You got any Lucifers?"

Matty's victorious expression collapsed.

"Dadgummit," he said. "JD, you got any matches on you?"

"Now, why would I have matches on me?" I said. "I ain't the one pinched the pipe."

"Well, now," Zeke chided us, "if you boys is gonna become regular smoking gents, you got to carry Lucifers with you. Ain't fit for proper folk to go about begging for a light. But here," he said, and pulled a few red- and white-tipped sticks from his bib pocket. "You take some of mine, and just remember the time ol' Zeke done you a kindness."

I accepted the matches while Matty

reached out a trembling hand, then pulled it back.

"I ain't allowed," he said.

"Baby," I said. "Here, watch this. I seen Bull strike 'em this way."

I curled my fingers around the match stem and cocked my thumb so the nail rested on the match tip. I struck once with my thumbnail with no effect. The second try gave an encouraging pop, and the third brought the match to life in a hissing rush of flame.

I howled and flung the match away, then jammed my thumb into my mouth.

"Look who's a baby now," Matty said, and rolled laughing in the straw.

"Yep, the sulfur'll get up under your nail if you ain't real careful 'bout it," Zeke explained. "Best to let your nail grow out if you want to strike 'em that-a-way. Me," he added, choosing a match, "I just as soon use my boot heel if I'm wearing 'em. 'Course, a good board'll always do."

He leaned toward the back wall of the crib and struck a match, then curled the flame into the cup of his hand and set it to his pipe. He drew at the flame once, twice and again, then blew out the match with a puff of smoke. He spat in his palm and moistened the tip of the dead match before sticking it headfirst in the dirt.

"Go on, JD," Matty urged, handing me the pipe. "Try it again."

I mimicked Zeke and leaned toward the wall, then held my breath as I struck the match. It took on the first try, and I drew the flame to the pipe bowl. It seemed against nature to bring the fire so close to my face, but I held the match steady over the tobacco and sucked on the stem until the leaves glowed red and gold.

"Watch you don't burn yourself," Zeke said, a second too late.

I coughed out a scream and shook away the nearly-consumed match as the flame licked at my fingertips. I shook my hand to cool my fingers, and the not-quite-healed bones protested the abuse.

"C'mon, JD, let me," Matty whined.

I slapped his hands away as I puffed again and again. My eyes watered and I tried to stifle a cough, but it escaped through my nose with a snort and a stream of smoke.

"Here." I placed the pipe in eager hands, then fell into a fit of hoarse coughs.

"That's fine, now," Zeke observed as he leaned back against the wall. One hand fiddled with the carved wooden charm he wore about his neck, while the other lazily cupped his pipe. "You boys keep on a-practicing while I catch me a little shut-eye."

Between coughs, I managed to look at Matty, who held the pipe in a white-knuckled grip. He tucked his head between his knees and took in shallow, shuddering breaths. My gut ached as I coughed as deeply as I could, trying to rid the smoke from my lungs. I swallowed some air, and my coughs were soon interlaced with merciless hiccups.

Suddenly, my mouth filled with saliva and I worked feverishly to swallow in between coughs and hiccups. I looked around desperately, then scrambled to a corner of the crib as a wave of nausea overwhelmed me. I heard Matty rush to the opposite corner where he joined me in a duet of heaves and coughs and moans.

When the chorus was finished, I wiped my mouth on my sleeve and crawled back to the middle of the crib. I flopped down beside Matty, who was curled into a ball. As my eyelids drooped shut, a mischievous grin played across Zeke's lips and was the last image I had before slipping into a fitful sleep.

"Get up, boy."

Thick smoke played under my nostrils and

suffocating heat filled my lungs as I hacked and coughed.

"I said get up," Zeke repeated, and I was hoisted aloft by the rope cinched about my waist.

Zeke's eyes stared into mine, the whites showing all around the dark centers and strangely lit in a red-orange glow. I took a deep breath and was rewarded not with the pungent smoke of tobacco, but with the dry, sharp smoke of a bonfire.

My eyes widened as I looked around to find the straw and corn cobs being consumed by bright orange flames.

"Matty?" I managed to ask.

"I'll get him," Zeke assured me. "You run and fetch some water."

I pulled the neck of my shirt over my nose and mouth, shielded my face with an arm, then rushed through the shallow wall of flame that separated me from safety.

"I gotcha now, Marse Matty," I heard Zeke say over the crackle of the fire. "Don't you fret none."

I burst from the smoke and flames into clear daylight, and sank to my knees as I sucked in a few lungfuls of fresh air. I forced myself up and nearly tripped over my feet as I raced to the pump in the middle of the barnyard. A bucket was already slung under the mouth of the pump, and I began working the handle.

Half a minute's pumping brought nothing but a wheezing sound from the pipe, summer having drawn down the water table. I looked around and found a small can of water sitting beside the pump. I grabbed the can and poured the water into the small priming reservoir in the head of the pump before again working the handle. The resistance grew stronger and I was rewarded with two coughs from the pump, followed by a gush of water that streamed into the bucket.

By this time, Zeke had arrived with a groggy Matty in his arms. He eased the boy to the ground, grabbed the full bucket off the mouth of the pump and replaced it with an empty one.

"You keep pumping now, y'hear?" he said. "I'll come back for this here bucket, but you keep pumping till the trough's good and full, understand?"

I nodded and bit my lip against the ache already settling into my arms. Zeke turned and ran back toward the fire, the soft padding of his bare feet on the loose dirt blending with the rhythmic whistle of the piston and the steady stream of water filling the bucket.

A high-pitched squeal echoed across the barnyard and broke my rhythm as I turned to look. Angelina had stepped out from the kitchen and now stood riveted on the back porch, hands cupped over her mouth and eyes wide beneath auburn bangs. Within seconds, shouts erupted from all quarters. Slaves tumbled out of the bunkhouse and through the kitchen door. Angelina was nearly knocked into the small garden off the kitchen porch, but Bull caught her with an arm around the waist, hefted her back up onto the porch and handed her off to Belle.

"Buckets," he ordered the others as he ran toward me.

Belle was right behind him and she pulled Matty out of the way, stroked his head and fussed over him like a mother hen.

"I'll take the pump, boy," Bull said. "You run fetch some more buckets out of the shed."

I nodded and ran as fast as my feet would carry me. By the time I returned, two buckets carried awkwardly in each hand, the trough was almost full and the men — joined now by Mister Barnes and Hick Adkins, another sharecropper — had organized into an orderly fire brigade.

"You think you can keep up with us now?" Bull asked, his operation of the pump arm slowed to a pace just sufficient to keep the trough full.

"I think so," I said.

"All right, then." Bull nodded and picked up a bucket of his own. "You just holler if you need to change out." He filled his bucket and ran to join the battle.

I settled into the rhythm needed to keep pace with the men's efforts. Within a few minutes, Zeke dropped out of the queue and disappeared into the tool shed. He returned moments later with a collection of rakes, hoes and shovels. Each man returned to fill his bucket again, but their less urgent pace suggested that the worst was over.

"Come lend a hand, JD," Mister Barnes said.

"Yes, sir." I dropped the pump handle, flexed cramped fingers and massaged my aching right arm. I followed along to the corn crib, trailed closely by Matty and the women.

Smoke curled around the eaves and sides of the crib, and water streamed away in tiny rivulets. The slaves raked the fodder out of the lean-to and into the mud, while Mister Barnes and Adkins stood by the rows of buckets to guard against a flare-up.

"Looks like we got it in hand," Adkins said. He pitched an occasional shovelful of wet dirt on the mounds of charred straw and corncobs.

Mister Barnes grunted, a mixture of fear and anger playing across his face. He turned toward Matty and knelt in front of him, stroked a pudgy cheek and tousled the unruly hair.

"You all right, son?" he said.

Wide-eyed and with tear-streaked soot on his cheeks, Matty managed a nod between sobs.

"Can you tell me how this happened?" Mister Barnes looked first to Matty, then to me, and my gut seized in a knot of fear.

"We — we was —" Matty stuttered.

"We was learning from Zeke how to carve," I said, my eyes fixed on Matty's. "Zeke was having a pipe, and I guess we all just drifted off. When we woke up, the whole works was afire."

Matty stared at me in confusion, but I shot him my hardest look that meant *Keep your mouth shut.*

"Is that the way of it?" Mister Barnes asked Matty.

The crybaby looked at me, trembling, then gave the barest nod of his head.

"Bull," Mister Barnes said in a steely, calm voice, "go fetch me a rope and the bull-hide."

The older slave stood still for just a moment, then mumbled, "Yes, suh," and made for the tool shed.

"You," Barnes continued, pointing to the other slaves, "bring that rot along with you." Without another word, he turned and headed toward the front of the barn.

"Come on 'long now, children," Belle whispered to Angelina and Matty. "Ain't no call to be standing 'round here. You got to get cleaned up for supper." As she herded her charges toward the house, she turned to her daughter. Ketty stood rooted to the spot, one hand over her mouth, her wide eyes following Zeke.

"Ketty," Belle rasped, to no response. "Keturah," she said more sharply, finally getting the girl's attention. "You stop that gawking and come help me with supper."

The girl's almond eyes clouded over as her head shook and she gnawed at her fingertips. Belle came alongside her, gently pulled Ketty's hands from her mouth and whispered something in her ear. Ketty nodded. Belle squeezed her shoulders and steered her toward the kitchen. Along the way, Belle cooed a cheery "Come 'long now, children" to Matty and Angelina, and led her brood into the house.

I stood there for the longest time as my

conscience cursed me for a coward. I looked at the ruined corn crib, the smoking fodder, the muddy footprints. I expected to see a pair of heel tracks to show how Zeke had been dragged to his punishment, but there was none. He'd gone along willingly, and he hadn't said a word.

My spine stiffened in that moment and I was about to run after the men when I heard the first whistle and crack of the whip. A heart-rending wail filled the air as rawhide met flesh. My knees buckled and I crumpled to the ground as a second, then a third crack lashed out. My body shuddered and I pressed hands to my stomach and — from a very different cause than earlier — began to retch.

Supper was a gloomy affair.

The Barneses were from good people and hosted a fine supper table. The talk was usually of politics or history, music or philosophy, and Missus Barnes always made sure to ask my opinion on this or that. I'd had to give up my schooling when I went to work for Mister Barnes, but I thought the supper discussions more than made up for what I missed from books.

This night, though, there was no talk other than the Please-pass-the-salt kind. The dining room echoed of clinking forks and scraping knives, of slurped coffee and stifled belches. Matty thumped his heels against his chair legs, and Angelina had to shush him three times.

"Quit it, Matty," she said the fourth time, and laid her knife and fork noisily on her plate.

"I ain't doing nothing," he said amid the *thump-thump-thump* of his heels.

" 'I'm *not* doing *anything,*' " Angelina corrected him, "and you most certainly are."

"That's enough," Missus Barnes broke in. "Mister Adkins, JD — I apologize that we are not very good hosts this evening."

"No need t'apologize, ma'am," Adkins said through a full mouth, spewing bread crumbs as he spoke. "But, seeing as it's been a long day and all, I think I'd best be getting along."

"Me, too, ma'am." I wiped my mouth and leapt at the chance to escape from the memories of that night.

"Another good day of work," Mister Barnes offered without enthusiasm as he scraped his chair away from the table. "Belle, would you fix a plate and take it out to Zeke for me?"

"Yes, suh," she said, and hastily started clearing the table. Her eyes were red and puffy now, though she'd seemed fine before supper.

"Marse Barnes." Bull ducked his head at the doorway to the kitchen, hat in his hand.

"Yes, Bull, what is it?"

"The boy gone, suh."

It took a moment for the words to register.

"What do you mean, gone?" Mister Barnes said.

"Gone, suh," Bull repeated. "I laid him out in the barn after you — after you was through with him, so's Ketty could tend his back. He gone from there, and he ain't in the bunkhouse neither."

The pall that had clouded the room now choked the breath from it entirely. I chanced a look at Matty, whose eyes I'd avoided all evening, and saw a spark of satisfaction.

"Ketty gone, too, suh," Bull added, and heads jerked up all around the table.

"Saddle three horses for me, Bull," Mister Barnes ordered, "and ready the dogs. Boys," he added, looking at me and Adkins, "looks like your day's not over yet."

"Yes, sir," Adkins said, while I nodded dumbly.

"Give Bull a hand, JD. Hick, come with me."

I followed behind the big Negro while Adkins went with Mister Barnes. Belle settled

50

into a chair — her tears no longer held back — and Missus Barnes and Angelina fussed over her while Matty disappeared up the stairs.

"If you start with the horses, Marse Jade, I'll find some scent for the dogs," Bull said.

I nodded my agreement and hustled to the stable. I had two horses saddled by the time Bull joined me, a sweat-stained shirt and a yellow headscarf in his meaty hands. He set the cloths by the stable door and helped with the last horse.

"The dogs?" Mister Barnes asked as we led the horses into the barnyard.

I whistled and yelled, "Here, Argos. Hounds, come."

A pack of bluetick hounds tore from under the kitchen porch and raced toward the barn. The horses shied at the rush of panting, slavering dogs, but Bull hushed and steadied them. Argos, my own dog from the pack, came to my side, sat and pawed at my leg until I let him nuzzle and lick my hand.

Mister Barnes picked up the shirt and scarf and passed them around the hounds, who whined eagerly as they snuffled at the scent cloths.

"Seek, dogs," he ordered, and the six hounds raced across the barnyard as moonlight glinted off their sleek, dappled coats.

"Here you go, JD," Adkins said as I swung into the saddle. He handed me an under-hammer rifle and I laid the ungainly thing across the saddle in front of me.

"Wait for me."

The screen door slammed shut behind Matty as he jumped down from the kitchen porch. He hopped on one booted foot while he tugged at the bootstraps of the other. He made it a quarter of the way across the yard before his belly outpaced his foot and he went down in a red-headed, flannel-clad tangle. He squirmed on the ground until he forced the stubborn boot into place, then picked himself up and trotted the rest of the way to us.

"Get on back inside, son," Mister Barnes said.

"But I want to go with you," Matty insisted, his voice cracking.

"This is no business for a boy," Barnes said as he mounted his horse.

"But, what about him?"

Mister Barnes turned in his saddle to consider me for a moment.

"JD's a right good hand," he said. "He does a man's job even half busted up. Until you start pulling your own weight, son, take on a man's responsibilities instead of holding on to your ma's apron strings, you're

52

still a boy."

Matty's cheeks flashed red under the pale moonlight. He fixed me with his green eyes, made greener still by envy and spite. He opened his mouth to speak again, and I feared he was about to spill the truth of the fire until Mister Barnes said, "You get back on into the house, boy," and spurred his horse after the hounds. Adkins set off after him. I was about to follow when my eye was drawn to a slight motion at one of the upstairs windows. Angelina's window.

A white lace curtain was pulled back slightly with a set of elegant fingers curled around the edge. It seemed a bright pair of emeralds glowed out from the darkness behind the window panes. My horse nickered impatiently and reined in my thoughts. I gave a *Hey-yup* and squeezed my knees, and the horse raced after the other two. I stole a last glance before rounding the corner of the house, only to see the delicate lace falling back to rest.

I soon caught up with Barnes and Adkins. Though I had no stomach for the chase, the cool night air was invigorating, and I relished being part of a man's mission. We rode after the hounds for hours. Three times they lost the scent, and Mister Barnes had to dismount and pass the cloths under their muzzles. Each time the pack tore off in a new direction, only to begin wandering aimlessly a short time later.

"Maybe we should head into Van Buren and raise the sheriff," Adkins suggested when the coon dogs lost the trace yet again.

"Not a bad idea," Barnes said. "Hounds, get home," he called, and the dogs broke away from snuffling at the grass, looked at their master for confirmation, then turned and raced in the direction of the farm.

Argos looked at me quizzically, and I called, "C'mon, boy." He bounded after me as I followed the other men to the county seat.

I'd been to Van Buren twice before and had been amazed by street upon street lined with wooden and brick buildings, the sidewalks teeming with people. This night it seemed abandoned, and I had to bite my lip to keep from quivering at my own reflection in the darkened windows we passed.

"Wake the sheriff, Hick," Mister Barnes said. "JD and I'll check down by the river."

"Yes, sir," Adkins replied, and reined his horse toward the one building with a light still peeking out from behind closed shutters.

I followed Mister Barnes along the riverfront, and it struck me that this would be the way for Zeke to come. Across the Arkansas River lay Fort Smith and, beyond that, Indian Territory. Years earlier I'd seen the groups of Indians being herded westward by armed soldiers, seen the fear and anger on their faces as they were driven from their ancestral lands. They'd been cowed then, but the thought of facing those Indians out on the desolate plains — while chasing after my runaway friend — was not something I welcomed.

"Jacob?" I heard Mister Barnes say, and I pulled up my horse, surprised to see a wagon at the ferry landing.

The peddler, Jacob van der Meer, apparently hadn't heard us coming, and he almost toppled from his seat on the wagon as he spun around, his eyes wide under bushy, black eyebrows.

"Benjamin?" he said in his thick accent, pronouncing the name *Ben-ya-min.* "What brings you out this time of night?"

"Tracking down a pair of runaways."

"Really? Which ones?"

"Zeke and Ketty," Barnes replied as he eyed the merchant's wagon loaded with pots, tins and other sundries.

"*Oof-dah,* is that right?" the peddler said. "I shall miss his carvings very much."

"With luck, you'll be able to buy them

again," Barnes said. "Once I'm through with him, though, it may be a while before he's able to handle a whittling knife. What are you doing out so late?"

"Oh, I got some things for the boys at the post," van der Meer said. "Finally got a chance to deliver some supplies, so I got to be there bright and early to meet with the quartermaster before he gets too busy to see me."

Argos had been snuffling at the ground during the exchange and now began baying at the back of the wagon.

"Hush up," I told him, then, "No. Off," as he jumped up to put his front paws on the tailgate. "Sit."

"What do you have in there?" Barnes asked van der Meer as he sidled his horse toward the rear of the wagon.

"Oh, you know, just some things for the boys at the post. Supplies and dry goods and such." The peddler climbed down from his seat and wrung his hands as he stepped toward us.

"Mm-hmm," Barnes grunted. "That's far enough, Jacob." He shifted his rifle in his hands and added, "JD, take a look in the wagon."

I was stunned by the sudden change in atmosphere, but I nodded and slipped down from the saddle. With the underhammer still gripped in one hand, I eased over to the wagon. Argos sat by the tailgate, and I scratched him between his ears as he whined and pawed at the air. I pulled the pegs from their brackets, then held my breath as I eased the tailgate down.

Nothing seemed out of the ordinary as I bent to peer into the wagon — just small crates and bags of dry goods, neatly stacked at the mouth of the cargo area. I glanced back at Mister Barnes, and the nod of his chin suggested I dig deeper. I shoved aside crates and sacks to make a gap in the pile of supplies.

My heart leapt to my throat as two pairs of eyes stared back at me, their whites glowing brightly out of the darkness. Zeke and Ketty lay huddled together beneath the heavy tarpaulin cover of the wagon, within inches of my outstretched hand. Ketty gripped Zeke's arm that wrapped around her. In his other hand he clasped the small totem carving he normally wore around his neck, and he rubbed the dark wood with his thumb and forefinger.

"What is it, JD?" I heard Barnes ask, and his voice seemed so far away.

I swallowed hard as I looked at Ketty, her face twisted into a mask of fear. My gaze

57

shifted back to Zeke. The way he lay, I could just make out the lash marks across his back. The blood drained from my face, and I lowered my eyes. A touch on my hand made me look back. Pleading and forgiveness filled Zeke's eyes as he placed the small carving in my palm and closed my fist around it.

"Ain't nothing," I managed to squeak out. I cleared my throat and pulled myself out from the wagon. "Just some salted pork is all. I reckon Argos is a mite hungry after chasing halfway across the county tonight."

Barnes grinned and chuckled at that, and the tension evaporated as he eased his rifle down.

"If he is hungry," van der Meer said, "I got me a nice knuckle bone for him to chew on."

With that, the merchant dove into the back of the wagon and rearranged the goods I'd shifted in my search. He emerged with the promised treat, which he handed to Argos while he patted my shoulder. Silent gratitude sparkled in his eyes before he replaced his mercenary mask, turned and hitched up the tailgate.

My heart was still pounding away and my knees went wobbly. I sank to the ground, covering my weakness by fussing over Argos who happily gnawed on the bone.

"Sorry for the misunderstanding, Jacob," Mister Barnes offered. "We'll stop by the ferryman's shack and see if we can't get you on your way a bit sooner."

"Thank you, Benjamin," the peddler said. He stretched up a trembling hand, which Barnes leaned down to shake. "You all be safe, *ja*?"

"We will," Barnes assured him. "Don't be a stranger, hear? Charlotte's eager for more of those fashion books from back east. Ready, JD?"

"Yes, sir," I said.

I hefted myself back into the saddle while van der Meer climbed up to his seat on the wagon. I reined the horse to follow Mister Barnes, whistled for Argos and took a last glimpse at the wagon. It felt as though I was leaving a part of myself behind, that I would never again be the boy I'd been.

As I followed Barnes up from the river landing, I chanced a glimpse at the small carving in my hand. It was just two inches long, cylindrical, with a leather thong threaded through a hole in one end. The charm was carved all over with strange whorls and swirling patterns, but now seemed to possess none of the magic I'd always associated with it.

Maybe it just used it all up, I thought.

I looped the thong around my neck and tucked the figurine beneath my shirt. I squinted my eyes against the morning sun that was just beginning to cast its rays over the peaks of the Ozarks and felt the wonder of a new day dawning.

The totem on its thong is twisted so that it drapes across my back. I'm struck again by the strange patterns, the swirls now grotesquely repeated in the shredded cloth of my shirt and the torn flesh of my back. Belatedly, I realize that I'm staring at myself, watching from above as my body lies sprawled among the scrub brush.

A wave of vertigo rolls over me. I reel away and look about the familiar plain. A plume of black and grey dust rises from the shaved-off peak of Hundley's Pass, the cloud draping the sun with a mourning veil.

"Jim."

I turn toward the voice to find a group of men racing toward me. I wave to them, try to tell them I'm fine, but they ignore me, intent on the body that lies beneath me.

"Easy now," one of the men says. His dark face is familiar, but his name is lost to me. "Let's roll him in nice and gentle."

A quilt is shaken out next to my body, and strong hands grip me by the shoulders and ankles to ease me onto the makeshift stretcher. Despite their care, pain surges through the burned and torn flesh, but the feeling is simply a report of my senses: the earth is brown, my blood is red, every nerve of my body is afire.

My eyes flicker open and my awareness is constricted as I'm forced to see through the narrow slits.

"Zeke?" I say to the face that looms over me, my voice no more than a whisper.

"No, it's me — Seth. You just rest now, and we'll get you fixed up. Don't you worry none."

My eyes close, and I find myself once more floating above my battered shell. I watch as the men nod to each other and lift the corners of the quilt. My body is raised off the ground and, as it passes through the space where I'm floating, the pain is no longer an impersonal observation.

I feel the fire in my back, the seep of blood from ruptured organs, the grate of bone upon shattered bone. I try to scream, but I have no breath. My ears ring with the echoes of the explosion, all but drowning out the shriek of a steam whistle.

CHAPTER THREE

Van Buren, Arkansas — September 1854

The shrill sound cut through the thick morning air. I looked up to see a black plume of smoke and a thin white cloud of steam rising from behind the trees, where a steamboat waited at the Van Buren docks. As suddenly as it started, the whistle stopped and was replaced by the steady *clop-clip-clop* of horses' hooves beating out a tattoo against the hard-packed clay road. The rhythm was underscored by the swish of tails and by Argos's panting as he trotted alongside me. I rode on horseback, following the wagon where Ma and Pa sat behind Mister and Missus Barnes, along with Becca and Angelina. Beside me, Matty rode astride his own horse.

The dumpy little boy of just two years ago had been replaced by a lean, fit young man. The gentle disposition had also been replaced, but this change was not so attractive. The meek, timid boy had become arrogant and callous, and insecurity had grown into a vain cocksureness. He must have felt my stare, for he turned his head and bore his green eyes straight into me.

I held his glance for a sliver of time before lowering my eyes and staring at the space between my horse's ears. I could still feel his gaze, and the very air around me seemed to crackle with the cloud of his disapproval.

Don't you never, ever *say such a thing again.* The words still echoed in my head. *You ain't nothing but a hired hand — not fit to look at her, let alone talk about her or even think of her that way.*

That had been Matty's reaction when he found the initials I'd carved inside a heart on the big walnut tree in his yard, and I admitted to him that I thought Angelina was . . . well, pretty. *Lovely* would have been a truer description, or *heart-breaking, mind-numbingly beautiful.* Considering how that meager compliment had been received, I reckoned it was just as well I'd been sparing in my praise.

The tables had turned between us after Zeke and Ketty's escape. Mister Barnes had recounted his side of the tale, but Matty soon guessed the truth of the matter.

"Jews don't eat hog meat, dummy," he'd

told me privately. "They don't even touch the stuff. I'll be a long-eared jackrabbit if the back of that wagon was loaded with salt pork. Sweaty monkey's more like it."

He wasn't big enough to threaten me bodily, but his temper put fear into me.

"I'll tell Pa about Zeke. He might put up with your pa being a drunk, but I let on you helped Zeke run off, you and your family'll be kicked out faster'n you can say, 'Boo.' "

So went the oft-repeated threat. I'd never been much above a slave, but I might as well have clamped on an iron collar now.

I followed the wagon through the streets of Van Buren and down toward the dock, retracing the path of two years earlier. Matty cleared his throat and raised his eyebrows, in case I missed the irony. Then he spurred his horse ahead of the wagon.

"Ho, there, step aside," he shouted as he cleared a path through the crowded streets.

Slaves shuffled back and forth between the dock's warehouse and the *SS Ben Franklin,* backs bowed under the weight of baggage or cotton bales, and leg muscles taut beneath thin trousers.

I pressed on behind the wagon, mumbling my apologies to the men forced to wait for us to pass. Mister Barnes drew his team to a halt outside the shipping office. The brick façade opened directly onto First Street, while a floating rear staircase led down to the docks. I hopped down from my horse and tied the reins to the wagon as Pa limped up the stairs behind Mister Barnes.

"C'mon, Squirt," I said to Becca.

I reached up to the wagon for her outstretched hands. She squealed as I flung her over my shoulder like a sack of potatoes. Still shy of seven, she wasn't yet ladylike enough to mind being manhandled by her big brother. Ma, on the other hand, was plenty ladylike enough for the both of them. I spun Becca around twice before Ma's "James Douglas Robbins!" ended the horseplay and I lowered a dizzy bundle to the ground.

Becca swayed a little as she fixed me with an oh-so-serious look, planted one fist on her hip and waggled a forefinger at me.

"You should know better, young man," she scolded, nostrils flaring as she fought back the giggles.

"Yes, ma'am," I said, then grabbed the pointing finger and shook her hand in mine.

"That's enough, you two," Ma said from her seat atop the wagon. "Hand me down, Jimmy."

I gave Becca a playful smack on the cheek and dodged her return swat, then reached up to help Ma down. I steadied her as she stepped on the running board, then wrapped my hands around her waist and lowered her to the ground. She looked up at me for a moment with a mix of pride and sadness before she turned to fuss over Becca.

"My turn," came a soft, warm voice behind me.

I turned to see Angelina waiting atop the wagon, her hand held out to me in a gesture both commanding and inviting. I glanced at the other side of the wagon, where Matty stood ready to help his mother down. His pale-green eyes flashed daggers at me, but he said nothing.

"It's rude to keep a lady waiting," Angelina said.

She crooked a slender finger at me, beckoning me to come. Unable to resist the call, I forced my feet to carry me to the wagon, then stretched out a trembling hand to help her down.

Her touch sent a jolt through me, like the buildup in the air before a summer storm. Her hand was soft and supple, but its grip in mine was firm. Once on the running board, she put her hands on my shoulders, and a hint of lilac filled the air around me. She leaned deeply toward me and the loose tresses of her copper-red hair cascaded over one shoulder. I tried to avert my eyes, but they were drawn to the loose cut of her dress that revealed milky-white skin from an elegant throat to a shadow of cleavage, before delicate white lace drew a veil over any further treasures.

I swallowed my longing as I lowered her to the ground, and her lingering touch on my shoulders deepened the yearning. She held my gaze for countless seconds, her eyes level with mine and the bouquet of her presence sweetening the air. At last her eyes narrowed and a sly smile crimped the fullness of her lips.

"Why, thank you, sir," she said, then turned to join Ma in fussing over Becca.

I stepped to the rear of the wagon and began unloading valises and travel trunks — in part to be helpful, but mainly to work the fire out of my blood.

"Miss Barnes," a deep voice boomed in greeting.

I turned to see the unmistakable figure of Captain Braddock, a young army officer from Fort Smith. The man had spent a good deal of his free time during the past summer at the Barnes farm. Far more time than was to my liking.

"Simon," I heard Angelina say, despite my

attempts not to listen.

"I'm so pleased I was able to catch you before you boarded. Missus Barnes." The soldier greeted the older woman with a bow and flourish of his campaign hat.

"Captain," Missus Barnes said, her voice full of flowers and silk. "Were you able to arrange your leave?"

"Sadly, no," Braddock said. "The colonel was quite insistent that he wouldn't be able to do without me, not even for the time it would take to steam to Little Rock and back."

"Oh, surely there's nothing so important that he can't do without you for a few days," Missus Barnes insisted. "Suppose I had a little chat with him . . . ?"

"I'm afraid not, ma'am. Colonel Jeffreys is quite resolute. I doubt that even your charms could persuade him."

"Captain," Mister Barnes said gruffly as he led Pa back from the shipping office.

"Good morning, sir."

"Now, JD, there's porters to take care of that," Barnes said.

"Yes, sir," I replied, and set down an especially heavy trunk.

I couldn't imagine how one person could need enough clothes to fill a trunk but, between them, Matty and Angelina filled three trunks and two valises. Besides what I had on my back, my own belongings — two pairs of woolen socks, a change of drawers, a set of long handles, a Sunday shirt and a dog-eared Bible — barely made a lump in my burlap travel sack.

"Are you going along to Little Rock, too?" Braddock asked me.

"That's right," I blurted out, and Pa shot me a warning glare. "Uh, yes, sir."

"Well, that's fine," Braddock said. "Once you learn to read and write properly, the army can always use a few well-trained enlisted men."

"Thank you, sir," I said through gritted teeth.

Mister Barnes hailed a team of slaves, who hefted the trunks and carried them to the riverboat.

"May I have a word with you, JD?" he said, his voice oddly soft.

I nodded and followed him to a spot away from the others.

"Don't mind Braddock," he said. "He's a pompous ass."

"Yes, sir," I said.

"You have enough money for the trip?"

I blinked at him and managed to stammer, "Plenty, sir."

"Here, take this." He pulled a small roll of

bank notes from his shirt pocket.

"No, sir," I said. "Thank you, but I can't. You've been more than generous already."

And that was the truth. Angelina had spent the past few years with Missus Barnes's sister in Little Rock, just coming home for summer. This year Matty would go with her, and Mister Barnes had arranged for me to join them for schooling. He'd even set up an apprenticeship with a blacksmith called Rawls so I could earn my keep while learning a trade.

Barnes smiled at me and put the cash back in his pocket.

"I'm glad we're able to give you this chance, son," he said. "You listen close to what Rawls has to teach you, but don't forget to have fun. A young man, his first time away from home, in the big city. Enjoy yourself, now, but don't get too deep over your head, y'hear?"

"Yes, sir," I replied, though I wasn't sure exactly what he meant.

"There's one more thing," he said, and rubbed the back of his neck. "Matty's still a boy, about to enter a man's world. I know he thinks he's ready. Been champing at the bit for months now, years maybe. I've tried to make a man out of him, but . . ." A sigh. "Well, Missus Barnes coddled him for too long, and the man he's looking to become ain't what I had in mind for him. It's one thing to scratch and crow at slaves and the like" — the like being me, I gathered — "but the real world ain't so forgiving."

Barnes took a deep breath, looked me in the eye and finally came to his point.

"I'll look after your ma and Becca while you're gone."

I blushed at that. Pa's troubles just weren't something we talked about.

"At the same time," Barnes continued, "I'd like you to look after Matty, see he don't fall too far too fast. And, if you have to knock him down a time or two in the process, well . . ."

I started to protest, but he raised a hand to shush me.

"You two have been friends since before you could crawl. I know you've had a falling out here of late. I don't know why, and I don't need to know. But I'm asking you, in the name of the friendship you've had, in the name of your pa's and my friendship, keep an eye on my boy." He gave a helpless shrug. "Maybe you can succeed where I've failed, help turn him into the kind of man you're becoming."

I blinked a time or two and finally said, "Yes, sir. I'll do my best."

The boat's steam whistle tore through the morning air, and a gruff voice boomed out over the docks.

"All aboard for the steamboat *Ben Franklin*. All ashore who're going ashore."

Mister Barnes patted my shoulder and steered me back toward the wagon where tearful farewells were already being made. Ma placed her hands on my cheeks, pulled my head down for a kiss and gave me a hug.

"Don't you worry about us," she whispered in my ear.

Pa had quit the laudanum but taken to whiskey instead. In place of opium's stupor, his new medicine threw him into fits of rage, mixed with tearful rounds of sorrow and remorse. He'd never hit Ma or Becca, and I did my best to egg him on and get in his way when I saw a spell coming on, to make sure I was the one to take the brunt of his anger.

"How can I not worry?" I said.

"We'll be fine," Ma said. "I'm proud of you, Jimmy. Know there's nothing you can't do, if you set your mind to it. And know I love you."

I'd tried to keep my emotions in check, but my heart melted at that and I tightened my arms about her, lifting her slightly off the ground. After a moment's embrace I set her back down and stooped to kiss her on a cheek wet with tears. I turned away before tears could form in my own eyes, and knelt beside Becca.

"I don't want you to go," she said.

I stroked her dark curls and chucked her under the chin.

"Well, I don't really want to go," I said. "But I'll be back and picking on you before you even know I been gone. You be good, and help Ma out around the house. And if you ever feel scared, you just hightail it over to the Barneses', y'hear?"

She nodded slowly, and delicate lashes blinked away tears as I stood and turned to face Pa. He looked back at me through bleary, red-rimmed eyes.

"I reckon I'll be looking up at you next time I see you," he said as he handed me my bedroll, burlap sack and boat ticket.

I shrugged as I slung the travel things over my shoulder and accepted the ticket.

"Barnes has gone to a lot of trouble giving you this chance," he said. "Don't go pissing it away."

"No, sir," I mumbled, and Pa turned away with a sniff and a grunt.

I watched his back for a couple of seconds before I headed for the boat. A plaintive *bar-rar-roo* made me stop, and I knelt as Argos bounded up to me. He put his paws on my shoulders and looked at me through soulful brown eyes, his tail slowly tracing from side to side. I ruffled his fur and hugged on him.

"You can't come with me, boy," I said. "You have to stay here and take care of Becca."

The hound cocked his head and his tongue lolled out. He turned his head and looked back at Becca.

"That's right," I said, "go with Becca."

Argos gave me a sloppy lick and scratched my knee with his paw, then turned and padded up the landing to take his place at Becca's side. I wiped my face — now wet from more than the dog's slobber — on my shoulder, turned and headed again toward the boat.

"What was all that about?" Matty demanded as I caught up with him and Angelina.

"He just wanted to say good-bye," I said.

"Not your mutt, dummy," Matty said, and poked my chest. "I meant Pa. What'd he say to you?"

"Oh," I said. "He just wanted to wish me well. Told me to pay attention to Mister Rawls."

"Mm-hmm," Matty grunted, then pushed

his way through the crowd at the base of the loading ramp.

"You're a terrible liar," Angelina said as she bent to pick up her valise.

"What's that mean?" I asked, and felt a pleasant chill as I took the bag from her hand.

"Just that. There isn't a dishonest bone in your body," she said. "Never has been. Lies don't suit you."

I blushed at that, mainly because I knew it wasn't so.

"Your ticket, miss?" The steward took the yellow slip from Angelina's hand, and I chafed at the look he gave her. "Pleasant trip," he said with a dip of his hat, then turned to me. "Ticket."

I handed him the plain brown form Pa had given me.

"No, no," he said. "You can't board here."

"But this is my ticket." I stammered the protest. "I'm on this boat."

"This is a passage-only ticket," he explained, as to a three-year-old. "You board aft, with the niggers and the bums." His tone made it clear that he esteemed me about as much as those groups. "That way," he pointed, in case I misunderstood *aft*.

"Oh, JD, that's just awful," Angelina said, and her regret sounded genuine. "But maybe we'll see you during the trip." She held her hand out to me, and it took me a moment to realize I still had her bag.

"Let me get that for you," the steward offered as I handed up the bag.

"Why, thank you, Mister . . . ?"

"Crawley," he said, and his neck flushed above his collar.

"Thank you, Mister Crawley." Without a backward glance, Angelina took the sailor's arm and let him escort her up the gangway.

I clenched my teeth, and blood pounded in my ears in jealousy and humiliation. I headed toward the ass end of the boat and threw a scornful glance up the landing. Pa stood there with his hands in his hip pockets, hat pushed back on his head as he watched me.

As I took my rightful place on the rear deck of the boat, the lesson hit me square in the face. Ma had said there was nothing I couldn't do, if I set my mind to it. Pa was there to remind me, though, that there were some things I just shouldn't set my mind to.

I dangle from the tree branch and wave my free hand.

It's a familiar dream and, though I recognize it as such, I wait to see how it will unfold.

77

I look down to see Angelina — Gina, I can call her in my dream. Cherry-red lips frame her pearl teeth as she smiles up at me. Her sparkling eyes are the color of early spring. Her gaze sends a chill up my spine. Goose-bumps rise on my arms and chest. A heady warmth floods over me, and my neck and cheeks grow hot as my pulse pounds in my ears.

Suddenly, the tree limb evaporates and my hand grips nothing but air. A flutter of panic rises in my stomach before I realize that I don't fall. My eyes are still locked onto Gina's, and it seems her smile has given my heart wings. I drift on the breeze that whispers through the boughs. Leaves and twigs part of their own accord to allow my passage.

Encouraged, I will myself to chart my own course, tacking against the gentle breeze. With growing confidence, I begin to dart between the branches and around the tree. Gina's laugh and the approving clap of her hands spur me on to more daring feats.

After a while, my movements begin to grow sluggish and the air thickens around me. I try to kick and stroke, but my efforts only make things worse. I shoot a look at Gina, but her eyes are no longer on me. I follow her gaze to see a jet-black stallion strutting up the clam-shell drive on long, slender legs.

A uniformed rider sits astride him in a warrior's pose, feet square in the stirrups, legs taut, back ramrod straight. Like Matty's long-ago toy rider, one gauntleted hand holds the reins while the other rests on the hilt of a curved saber. A campaign hat casts most of the rider's face in shadow, but his jaw is square and firm as chiseled granite.

Gina sits entranced by the approaching figure, and the magic that held me aloft slips away. I plummet toward the ground. Branches race past me. Leaves and twigs tear at my skin and snag on my clothes. I scream Gina's name, and she throws me a mocking sneer as a thick lower limb rushes straight for my head.

I woke with a start, my ears echoing with a voice that sounded like my own. I looked around and found myself surrounded by grinning black faces.

"Must've been some dream."

"Wish I could see that Gina girl of his."

"Not too shabby for a white boy."

I looked down to see the dream's effect on me. I jerked myself upright and turned away to hide my shame.

One of the older slaves came up to me and clapped a callused hand on my shoulders.

79

"Ain't nothing to be ashamed of, boy," he said. "Why, half these fellas prob'ly wish they had half as good of dreams as that. Who that Gina girl, anyway?"

I glanced up toward the rail of the boat's observation deck and breathed a prayer of thanks that it was empty.

"Ah, I knows the one," the man said. "Pretty thing, hair full of fire. Gots plenty of beaus to take moonlight walks with."

I didn't say anything, but the fire in my cheeks told him he was right.

"Now, boy, why you want to go looking beyond your reach for?" he said. "She ain't never gonna go for some poor boy what gots to go about with niggers. She too fine to dirty her hands with the likes of you. Best mind your place, you ask old Moses."

I hadn't asked him, but I knew he was right all the same.

The *Franklin*'s arrival in Little Rock was like nothing I'd ever seen. A brass band played at the end of the pier, and the mob that gathered to welcome the boat seemed to outnumber the stars. Not sure where to go, I waited at the bottom of the aft gangway until I spied Matty and Angelina, then pushed through the crowd of passengers and slaves and stevedores. I ducked beneath cases and bundles that swung from their handlers' shoulders, and hopped over those that had already been set down.

"Oh, there you are," Angelina said as I met them at the bottom of the ramp. "I was afraid we'd lost you."

For days I'd watched Angelina flirt with sailors or soldiers or dandies as she strolled the boat's decks, and I despised her for it. All that melted away as she stood before me now.

"No chance of that," I said as evenly as I could. "May I?"

"Thank you," she said and gave me her valise, then steadied herself with a hand on my shoulder as she stood on tiptoes to look over the crowd. "There, up by the tobacco warehouse."

"I see 'em," Matty said. He picked up his bag and plunged into the ocean of bodies.

"I so hate crowds," Angelina said, her lips forming a delicate pout. "But there's nothing to be done about it. Stay with me."

She darted after Matty into the writhing crush. With no choice but to follow, I dove in behind her. I found I made better progress when I forgot any manners and just barreled broad-shouldered into the mob until I emerged near the warehouses. Though still crowded in comparison to anything Britton, or even Van Buren, could muster, the docks outside the warehouse seemed a desert compared with the lower landing.

I followed Matty and Angelina until they stopped beside a carriage. The driver was a slave of about forty, whose finery made my clothing look little better than rags.

The carriage's owner stood beside the rear wheel. He was of average height, about a half-inch taller than me. A thick mane of black hair, streaked with wiry, grey strands, was brushed back from his forehead and ended in a rolling curl just below his starched collar. A thick beard and moustache, the negative image of his hair, hid most of his tanned face but did little to disguise the firm cut of his jaw. His high forehead was free of creases, the only lines a set of good-humored crow's feet at the corner of each eye. The lines deepened when he laughed — which he did frequently — and accentuated the twinkle of his soft, brown eyes.

His wife stood beside him and, other than her height — which was nearly equal to her husband's — the pair was a study in contrasts. Where he was beefy and powerfully built, she was gaunt with a sharp, angular face etched with worry lines that her tightly pulled-back hair and severe bun did little to smooth. Thin eyebrows, the same colorless tint as her hair, were raised in perpetual arches above deep-set, black, brooding eyes. Blue veins showed beneath her translucent skin, and a beaked nose roosted over pursed, wrinkled lips that relaxed into a frown when not tightly drawn.

As we approached, one set of eyes brightened over a wide grin, while the other set narrowed and squinted, accompanied by a deeper pursing of the lips.

"Angelina, my dear," the man boomed, and wrapped his niece in a warm embrace while planting kisses on each cheek. "You're lovelier than ever. And, Matty," he turned to his nephew. "Or is it Matt, now? Why, you've grown into a man since I last saw you."

Matty shook the man's hand and gave the hint of a genuine smile as his back straightened a little. "Matt," he repeated, as though trying it on for size. "It's good to see you, sir."

"Where's Cassandra?" Angelina asked, referring to the cousin I'd heard her and Matty mention.

"She's resting, but you'll see her at dinner. Of course, you still eat too much," came a greeting from the skeletal half of the pair.

"And you," she said, and clamped a talon under Matty's — Matt's chin. "Your mother never could make more than a rat's nest out of your hair. We shall see what we can do about that."

"You must be James," the man greeted me, and extended a mighty paw in my direction.

"Yes, sir." I stretched my hand to wrap around his. "They call me JD or Jimmy."

"Pshaw. Jimmy's a boy's name, but I suppose JD will do. I'm Cyrus Warren," he said, still pumping my hand. "From what Ben tells me, you're practically a brother to these two, so you can call me Uncle Cy. This is my wife, Helen," he added as he released my hand.

I opened and closed my fist to restore the blood flow.

"Ma'am," I said, unsure how to greet the cadaverous woman. I didn't want to be rude, but I shuddered at the thought of touching those gnarled, bony hands. I settled on a slight bow.

"You may call me Missus Warren," she cawed. "And family or no, you are here to learn and to work."

"Yes'm."

The peaks of her eyebrows rose slightly, and I thought the strain of her furrowed brow must surely cleave her hair from her scalp.

"What was that, young man?" she said.

"Uh — yes'm?"

"In this place, we use proper grammar," she informed me. " 'Yes'm' is not a word. I defy you to find it in Mister Webster's lexicon. We will not even deign to consider such mumblings as 'uh' or 'um.' Since this is your first offense, we will not mete out any punishment. Judging from your appearance and your speech, it is clear that you have not had the advantages of proper learning, but we shall correct that failing directly, is that clear?"

I bristled at the scolding and the implied insult to Ma's teaching, but I choked back my pride.

"Yes, ma'am," I said.

"And you." The crow directed her attention to a sniggering Matt. "You have no excuse for crude behavior." She delivered a cuff to his ear, and he yelped in surprise.

"Well, now," Mister Warren said, "that's enough for now. We can get reacquainted back at the house."

With that, he handed his wife up into the carriage while the driver leapt nimbly down to put our bags in the boot. The carriage leaned dangerously on its axles as Mister

85

Warren climbed up behind his wife.

"I'm afraid we've only the room for four here," he said. "One of you boys will need to ride up front with Timothy."

"That's fine, sir," I said as Matt leapt to the step of the carriage and settled into a deeply cushioned seat.

I held the door open with one hand and steadied Angelina with the other as she stepped up to take her seat, then closed the door behind her.

"I'll get that, sir," Timothy said as I fumbled with the door's latch.

I turned away, embarrassed, and climbed up to the high bench of the driver's seat. Timothy climbed up beside me and gave me a friendly wink before settling in and taking up the reins.

We left the busy port behind us and set out on the main thoroughfare and across the Broadway Street Bridge. I marveled at the monstrous thing of iron that spanned more than a thousand feet to join the banks of the Arkansas River. As we moved into town, buildings towered five and six stories over my head, and I gaped at the four-columned portico of the statehouse.

At last, we passed through a wrought-iron gate between two large stone columns, wended up a tree-lined path and drew up under a lofty colonnade. I realized I'd been fingering the wooden totem around my neck, and fumbled to tuck it back under my shirt before anyone noticed. I glanced at Timothy, who gave me a curious look but said nothing.

"No need to dismount, Mister Robbins," Missus Warren said as the slave hopped down and the others climbed out of the carriage. "Timothy will take you to your quarters."

"Uh," I started to say, and a warning glance from the beady eyes froze the word in my throat. "Yes, ma'am. Thank you."

The forbidding brow relaxed slightly and the head nodded just a little, in the barest gesture of approval.

"You will bathe and change into proper clothing," she said. "Dinner will be served promptly at six."

"Yes, ma'am," I replied, but she had already turned and was screeching orders to the household staff even before crossing the marble threshold.

"How shall I call you, suh?" Timothy asked as he climbed back up beside me, his diction relaxed in the absence of his mistress.

"Folks back home call me JD," I said. "That's always worked well enough."

"JD," he repeated, and the word was almost a single syllable. "I wondered if it was you."

With a grin that raised more questions than it answered, he flicked the reins and directed the carriage toward the outbuildings behind the grand house.

"You'll bunk up there." Timothy pointed toward the upper window of a small clapboard workshop. "They's a bath drawed up for you, and fresh clothes set out. Best get yourself cleaned up right quick. Miz Warren don't abide with no tardiness."

"Now why doesn't that surprise me?" I said as I dropped down from the driver's seat and retrieved my bag.

Timothy chuckled at that, then headed the team toward the carriage house.

Inside the workshop I dropped my bag, latched the door, stripped and sank into the steaming water of the large metal tub. I drifted and soaked and dreamed, letting the images and thoughts of the past few days sort themselves out in my head.

The cooling water roused me, and I hurriedly soaped and scrubbed myself. I took care with my neck and behind my ears, as I guessed Missus Warren would be an even harsher critic of my cleanliness than Ma ever was. I dried myself with a towel that was thicker and softer than I imagined possible, then grabbed my things and climbed the narrow ladder to the loft.

The space was smaller than the loft back home, with room for little more than the necessities. Those necessities, however, included a writing desk topped by two shelves loaded with books. Homer, Plato, Hume, Smith, de Toqueville and a host of others lined the sagging boards. Other than Homer and Smith, I'd never heard such names, and I was eager to learn what they had to tell me. I reached hesitant fingers toward the bindings, and stroked the smooth leather and gilt embossing as I read each name and title.

I had to squint to make out the last one — *Essay on Man* by Alexander Pope — and realized my trouble seeing was due to the fading light outside. I rushed to the clothes stand at the foot of the bed and donned the new suit and boots laid out there. In my hurry I barely had time to notice the fineness of the materials and snugness of the fit, or even to wonder how the clothes happened to be there in the first place. I glanced in the mirror and ran a brush through my hair, then raced down the ladder.

The leather soles of the boots were smooth

and slick, and I slipped off the third rung and bounced past the other seven. I grabbed at the rough wood as I fell — more concerned about mussing my suit than breaking a leg — and managed to catch my fall at the expense of an ugly splinter in one finger. I plucked out the sliver of wood and jammed the finger in my mouth to stanch the trickle of blood while I hurried to dinner.

The large front door swung open as I approached. Missus Warren's bony figure was outlined by the bright lights inside.

"You were told that dinner is at six, were you not?" she said.

"Yes, ma'am."

"What time is it now?"

I looked for the sun to gauge the hour, but it was hidden behind the house.

"I don't know, ma'am."

"Hmph," she snorted, her only deviation from Mister Webster's lexicon. "Haven't you a timepiece?"

"No, ma'am."

"Come with me." She led me into a richly appointed sitting room with a beautiful pendulum clock resting on a carved mantel. "Can you read a clock?"

"Yes, ma'am."

"And what time does it tell?"

"Six o'clock and six minutes."

"Hold out your hands," she said.

"Ma'am?"

"I will not repeat myself," she informed me.

I didn't understand, but obediently held my hands out to her. She took my right hand — her fingers icy cold on my skin — and turned it over and back, inspecting between the fingers and under the nails.

"What's this?" she said.

"Just a sliver, ma'am. It's nothing."

"I will be the judge of that." She dragged me toward a table and held my hand under the stained glass shade of an oil lamp, where she twisted and probed the wound. "You'll live, but you missed some dirt under your thumbnail. Now, let me see the other hand."

"Yes, ma— Oww," I shouted as a wooden spoon appeared out of thin air and struck my knuckles.

"Did I instruct you to withdraw your hands?" the old biddy asked.

I glared at her for a moment, but managed to swallow my anger. "No, ma'am."

"You were six minutes late. You will receive one stroke for each minute."

"But it was only five," I objected, still rubbing my hand.

"I beg your pardon?"

"Well, ma'am," I said in as reasonable a tone as I could muster, "it was just six after when you had me read the time. I reckon at least a minute must've passed between the time I came to the door and then."

Her face screwed up as she considered the argument, then relaxed slightly.

"Very well," she said. "Five."

I held out my hands and clenched my teeth, more against the insult to my dignity than the pain. "Two — three — four — and five. And one more," she added with a final blow on my right hand. "For impertinence. Do not ever presume to correct me."

Without another word, she led me from the sitting room, across the entry hall and into the spacious dining room. Mister Warren sat at the head of the table, with Angelina on one side, and a younger girl on the other.

"Ah, here you are," Uncle Cy said. "JD, this is my flower, Cassandra."

"Pleased to meet you," I said.

The girl looked to be a year or two younger than Matt and me, her hair a dull orange-red compared to Angelina's copper. Her pale face was dotted with freckles and her sunken eyes were a limpid blue-green.

"Likewise," she mumbled as she looked shyly up at me, one hand over her mouth to hide her slightly bucked teeth.

"If you are going to speak, Cassandra, speak clearly," Missus Warren scolded her, and I felt badly for having greeted the girl in the first place. "Take your seat, Mister Robbins," the woman ordered, indicating the empty seat next to hers, across from Matt. "Would you say the grace, Mister Warren?" she asked.

Heads bowed around the table and I bowed my own and clasped my hands together in my most reverent posture. At the conclusion of the short prayer, the others repeated, "Amen," while I managed only a strangled "Am— Ow."

I jerked away from the serving fork whose tines had left their bite marks in my elbow.

"Proper gentlemen and ladies do not place their elbows on the dining table," Missus Warren said.

I heaved a sigh through my nose, but kept my temper in check and lowered my hands to my lap.

"Yes, ma'am," I said.

The meal passed with only three raps on my knuckles and one more skewering of my elbow. After dinner, Missus Warren walked me to the door.

"A servant will see that you are awakened on time," she said, "but you must learn to rise on time of your own accord. You may have your devotions and read briefly before retiring. However, you will receive only one candle each week so I suggest that you spend your evening hours wisely. Good night, Mister Robbins." Without another word, she closed the door on me.

I cursed myself as I entered the darkened shed, having failed to set out a candle. Tools and harnesses rattled to the floor as I searched for the ladder. I climbed up, felt my way to the desk and fumbled for the box of matches I'd seen earlier.

With the candle lit, I dressed for bed, careful to smooth and hang the new set of clothes. In the flickering light I again read the titles of the books, but finally settled on my own tattered Bible. I flipped through the pages and stopped somewhere in Proverbs.

Despise not the chastening of the Lord, neither be weary of his correction.

I laughed aloud and shook my head. Missus Warren seemed a strange choice of instrument for the Lord to carry out His work. I left the answer to that riddle for another time, and placed the Bible on the desk. I blew out the candle and cracked open the small windows to let in the cool evening breeze. Then I slid between the fine linen sheets, and drifted into dreams of this strange, new life.

CHAPTER FOUR

Little Rock, Arkansas — June 1856
I gripped the metal with a pair of tongs, and lifted it from the coals. The air shimmered around the glowing iron, and water seethed and roiled as I plunged it into the tempering bath. The foundry filled with clouds of steam, and the groan of shock-cooled iron joined with the sigh and hiss of the boiling water. I pulled the scrollwork from the tub, hung it on the cooling rack next to its twin that I had formed earlier and took a keen satisfaction from the near-perfect match.

"Not bad," came a gruff approval from over my shoulder.

I turned toward the voice and took a step back from my mentor, Rawls. His habit of standing closer to people than good manners allowed still caught me off-guard, even after nearly two years.

"The scrolls aren't quite even," I sug-

96

gested, quick to point out any flaws before his critique could begin.

"Oh, I didn't say they was anywhere near perfect." His words tempered my glowing pride before he stoked the flames again. "But I know men been smithing for twenty years couldn't do no better'n that. Nope," he decided as he stepped to the rack and took the two pieces in his hands. He seemed at once to weigh, gauge and take the pulse of the creations. "These ain't the work of no novice. You're like to be as good as me before too long — even better, if you keep at it."

I was dumbstruck by the generous words. Rawls was always quick to give praise when he felt it was deserved, but he despised hollow compliments.

"Thanks," I muttered, unsure of what more to say.

Rawls ran a hand over his stubbly scalp and scrunched up his pockmarked face, as though trying to remember something.

"Mister Warren's landed a commission for a new clock tower down to Arkadelphia," he said at last. "His carpenters and masons'll be doing most of the work, but it's for us to build the clock itself."

I stared at him for several moments as the words sank in.

"We're making a clock?" I finally said.

"Not just any clock. The face of the beast'll be half again as high as you. Gonna take brass, copper, maybe even gold, on top of all the iron, and that's just for the face. The gears are the tricky part. Got to be precise and even, take a skilled hand. I told Cy it was too much for just me, but with my chief assistant we ought to be able to handle her."

"Me?"

"I wouldn't have agreed to take the job if I didn't think you was ready," Rawls said. "I'm gonna trust you with the bulk of the large work. I'll handle most of the precision workings, but I reckon you'll be able to lend a hand there, too, before it's all said and done. Well?" he prompted me after a moment's pause.

I forced a couple of swallows, my throat gone dry at this unexpected opportunity. What took most apprentices seven years — sometimes as many as fourteen — was being handed to me in less than two. One, really, if you considered the fact that most of the first year had been spent solely in managing the bellows.

For ten months, my only instruction in the smithy's art had been "Too hot" or "Too cold." Though I'd balked at the monotony of working the bellows, when it came time to pick up the hammer and tongs I found that my arms had been strengthened so I could handle the heavy tools with little effort. Now, in just a fraction of the time it usually took, I had the chance to perform a journeyman's work.

"Yes," I finally managed to answer.

Rawls grinned broadly at that, his eyes all but disappearing among the bushy eyebrows and bushier beard that framed his gnome-like face. His teeth gleamed a brilliant white as he smiled, his one attractive feature.

"Good man," he said, then slapped me soundly on the back and pumped my hand in a massive paw. "We'll be working on-site most of the summer. They want to hold the ground-breaking to celebrate Independence Day, but we won't need to be there as early as that. Probably head down in a couple of weeks."

My excitement ebbed as it dawned on me that I wouldn't be going home this summer either. Last year's break had been spent advancing my apprenticeship, and the winter holiday had been too short to allow for much of a visit even if the money had been available to make the trip up-river — which it hadn't. It'd been nearly two years since I'd been home, and it looked like another year would pass before I'd have my next chance.

"I know you were looking forward to going home," Rawls said, seeming to read the expression on my face. "A chance like this don't come along very often, though. And we'll see how it goes. Maybe there'll be time at the end of the summer."

I nodded my thanks for this seed of hope, though I didn't really expect it to bear fruit.

"Yeah, maybe so," I said.

"Meantime, Miz Warren wanted me to scoot you on back to the house," Rawls said. "They's some kind of shindy tonight, and she wants you properly cleaned and turned out."

The news took me by surprise. Matt hadn't said a word about a party. But, then, he really hadn't said much about anything to me for quite some time. I shrugged and untied my heavy leather apron.

"You going?" I asked.

Rawls roared with laughter at that.

"No," he said. "I ain't exactly what you'd call the social type. I got better things to do with my time than listen to a bunch of dandies flapping their gums. Though I wouldn't mind catching me an eyeful of them spring flowers that's blooming here about."

The beginning of summer was just the next day, so I gathered he was talking about the young ladies who would be walking around the Warrens' gardens, rather than the blossoms that grew there. I grinned as I thought of the young ladies of Little Rock society. Few, if any, could compare favorably with Angelina. As she was spending this year in New Orleans, though, I figured a daisy in my garden was better than a rose in someone else's.

"I'll see you Monday, then," I said, and hung the apron on its peg.

I stripped off my sweaty shirt, plunged my head in the water trough and let the cool stream run down my back and chest. I gave Rawls a backward wave and ducked out the low doorway.

I squinted as I stepped into the bright sunlight, and shook loose the muscles of my arms and fingers. Eyes closed, I breathed deeply of the air tainted by laundry and livery, tannery and net. I braced my hands against my lower back and stretched back and forth, side to side to work the kinks out of muscles strained from bending over the anvil. My skin had been tempered by the heat of the forge, and the brilliant rays of the sun were but a gentle caress on my chest and shoulders. I ran a hand over my scalp

— I'd cropped the hair short like Rawls's, to avoid catching any sparks from the forge — then slung my shirt over a shoulder and started home.

Bare-chested, save for Zeke's totem around my neck, I walked up the narrow streets of the lower riverfront. I tried to keep my composure as the girls and younger women of the trades district turned to watch me pass. Smiles and nods, waves and whispers greeted me as I passed laundresses, fish mongers, rope weavers and the girls who waited at the entrances of alleys that led down to the piers. Rawls had cautioned me against venturing into those alleys, but I longed to discover the mysteries that lurked there.

Just sixteen, I had yet to kiss a girl. Not that I hadn't had the chance. Cassandra Warren had a crush on me that she'd tried to disguise since we first met. I was flattered by her awkward flirtations, but couldn't bring myself to take advantage of her feelings. For one, Missus Warren would never stand for it. And, I admitted to myself, plain though she might be, she was still above my station. If I was going to aim that far above myself, I may as well go all the way and hold out for Angelina.

Still, I longed to be with someone. The

young women I passed as I left the foundry were well within my reach, and I could imagine myself being with any one of them. Well, maybe not the ones waiting by the alleys. But pretty or plain, a hard-working woman would make a fine wife for an up-and-coming tradesman. And far more attainable for a sharecropper's son, I reminded myself, than the blossoms of Little Rock aristocracy.

I left the common folk — my folk — behind, and pulled my shirt on as I entered the commercial district. Out of habit, I walked out of my way to pass by the men's clothing shop that boasted all the eastern fashions. With the sun behind me, my reflection was cast in the storefront glass and I could almost see myself wearing one of the suits on display. I stood tall and cocked my chin, as Matt often did when he was trying to be impressive. The gesture felt silly and I left the little shop for the Warrens' fashionable neighborhood.

Through an alley to the servants' gate, I made my way up familiar paths, past the carriage house and stable to the little shed that had become my home. I paused outside the door as I heard the raspy twang of a metal file and the raspier treble of a voice that sang in time with the tool's strokes.

"Jordan's water is chilly and cold, it chill the body but not the soul. Wade in the water, children. God gonna trouble the water."

Sorry to interrupt the song, I loudly cleared my throat, then pushed open the door. Timothy smiled up at me from his seat at the tool bench, but his eyes glistened in the dim light of the shed.

"Marse Jade," he said. "What brings you home at this hour?"

"Mister Rawls let me go early," I said. "I suppose Missus Warren wanted me to have plenty of time to wash off the stench before the party tonight."

Timothy laughed, and set down the harness he'd been working on.

"I reckon that's the case," he said. "Miz Warren gots a delicate nose, like most the fine ladies be showing up tonight. Ain't nothing wrong with a little stink, though. That just the smell of hard work. All the same, I'll run and have Miriam fetch you some bath water."

"No hurry," I said, and motioned the man — I couldn't think of him as a slave — to his seat. "What're you working on?"

"Oh, just a harness got whacked up some, is all," he said. "The rings got spurs in them that'll dig into the horses, so I'm filing them down a bit."

I looked at the harness and recognized it as one of the first pieces I'd made on my own. I remembered my pride as I'd forged the rings and studs, then joined them with the leather to form the harness. "It'd take some doing to bung them up like that. What happened?"

"Marse Matthew," Timothy answered. "He tried breaking that new stud this morning."

"Pegasus?" I said.

I couldn't imagine even Matt would be brash enough to try such a stunt. Mister Warren had added the stallion to his stables just a week earlier. The name had come from Uncle Cy's beloved Greek mythology, and seemed quite fitting. Like the mythical winged horse, the black beast's feet never seemed to touch the ground as he bounded madly about the stable yard.

"I wouldn't have believed it if I hadn't seen it," Timothy went on. "Dang fool boy got close enough to try slipping the bridle over the monster's head before the thing put him backside-down in the dirt. Did that two or three times before he finally landed in a pile of manure."

"You're joking," I said, unable to keep from laughing at the thought.

"No, suh," he said. "Marse Jade, you should've seen the look on that boy's face. Why, I didn't know if he was gonna cry or spit, up to his middle in filth the way he was. Well, he up and takes that bridle, storms out of the pen and starts in to hammering everything in sight with it. Lucky for me and the others, we managed to stay out of his way. I'd say the fence post got the worst of it, but the bridle took a pretty good licking itself."

I picked up the harness and examined it. I'd decorated the leather straps of the brow band and cheek pieces with metal studs, many of which were now loose. The buckles and rings were scored and spurred from the beating.

"Well that's shot," I said, indicating the twisted snaffle bit.

"Yep," Timothy said. "I got most of the spurs ground down, but ain't no horse gonna take that bit. Now, if someone was to figure a way to harness a horse without shoving a bar halfway down his throat . . ."

He let the suggestion lie there for a moment before he picked up the file and examined the bridle again. He hummed as he ran his fingers deftly over the metal surfaces, smoothing down the remaining rough spots.

"Why have you always been so nice to me?" I asked, unsure where the words came from.

"Suh?" The question seemed to surprise him as much as it did me.

I tried to put words to the sudden stream of thoughts that flitted around in my head.

"You've treated me good from the first day I showed up here," I said. "You and Miriam and Izzy, you've made this place a second home to me, like I belonged. Even when I haven't deserved it, you've treated me like *somebody*." I threw up my hands, frustrated that I couldn't express myself any better. "I'm curious as to why."

Timothy was silent for a few moments, his eyes fixed on the table where the harness lay.

"It's that," he finally said, indicating the totem that hung around my neck. "Ezekiel's my boy."

It took me some time for the meaning of his words to register.

"Zeke?" I said at last.

Timothy nodded.

"I got word back through that old peddler man, told me what you done for my boy," he said.

"Does anyone else know?" I blurted out the question and was immediately shamed

107

by my cowardice.

"I ain't told no one else. Isaiah's a good boy," Timothy said of his son — his younger son, I reminded myself. "Good, but simple. I'd fear he'd let the cat out of the bag. And Miriam — poor thing almost fell to pieces when Marse Warren sold Ezekiel up to the Barneses. She'd just got over him going missing when word came from the peddler. Maybe it ain't right of me, but she done lost that boy twice. I couldn't stand to see her suffer if something was to happen and she was to lose him a third time."

Timothy looked me square in the eye, and I was unable to break away from his gaze.

"Now, I know I ain't got no call to ask nothing of you, Marse Jade," he said. "All the same, I'm begging you not to let slip word of what you done for Ezekiel. Not to Isaiah, not to Miriam, not no one."

"I promise," I replied immediately, and the older man's eyes brightened.

He nodded at me, then looked back at the harness.

"Well now, that ought to do, don't you think?" He ran his hands once more over the rings of the harness, then handed it to me.

I checked the rings and pulled out a couple more of the loose studs from the brow band.

"I think we can get rid of the bit," I suggested. "Ought to be some way of taking a horse to heel without shoving a bar halfway down his throat, don't you think?"

Timothy's eyes sparkled as he read my thoughts.

"I'll see what I can do about that," he said. "And I'll have Miriam fetch that hot water for you in, what, about a half hour?"

"Better make it an hour," I said. "This could take a while."

"I'll meet you at the stable," he promised, then disappeared out the door.

I climbed up to my room in the loft and changed into a pair of worn breeches and an old, oversized shirt, then stuffed the generous tails into the seat of the pants. I grabbed a pair of thick leather gloves and scuttled down the ladder, then over to the root cellar to collect a few pieces of fruit before I made my way to the stables.

The last evening of spring was about as pleasant as could be. A small storm had blown up in the late afternoon, lasting little more than an hour and leaving the air clean and fresh in its passing. As soon as the weather cleared, the servants set up pavilions on the sprawling front lawn and laid down a plank floor for dancing.

The challenge I'd set for myself had gone well. What I'd estimated to take an hour had lasted — not counting the time waiting out the rain — only fifty minutes. The longest, most bone-jarring fifty minutes I'd ever known. When the deed was done, I hobbled back to the shed, where I dumped several handfuls of Epsom salts into the steaming tub before falling into the scalding hot water.

"It's me, Marse Jade," came a familiar voice from outside the door.

"Come on in, Izzy," I called, unsure how long I'd been soaking.

The boy stepped into the shed, a big grin on his face as he tried to hide something behind his back.

"What are you about?" I asked, and he fell into a giggling fit.

"Just this," he managed to say, and produced a hanger with a new suit of clothes — the same suit I'd coveted at the tailor's shop. The three-button banker's coat was of cadet grey wool, with a collar trimmed in blue velvet. The suit had matching trousers and a notch-collared vest, and included a new cotton shirt and cravat.

"What's this?"

"Just a late birthday present, I reckon."

Izzy was almost doubled over with glee at the surprise.

"From who?"

The boy just shrugged, then climbed up the ladder and left the suit in the loft.

"You got about ten minutes before guests start showing up," he said as he climbed back down and headed for the door.

"Thanks," I said, too puzzled to say anything more.

I finished my bath and started dressing for the party, fumbling with the cuffs and collar of the starched shirt. Once dressed, I stole a glance in the mirror and felt a jolt of guilty pleasure as I noted the fit of the suit, cut to accentuate my broad shoulders and trim waist.

Not for the first time, I wished Angelina could see me. Not that anything could come of it — our difference in class made such a dream impossible. If I could just turn her head, though, what a feat that would be. With a sigh and a shake of my head, I turned away from my reflection before dismay could replace the look of confidence.

"Lord-lord, ain't you a sight," Izzy said as I stepped through the door of the shed.

"Let's just hope we did a good enough job this afternoon to keep it that way."

"Oh, I reckon you'll be a sight one way or

the other, Marse Jade." A mischievous glint in his eye, the boy reached out a hand to straighten my cravat.

"I suppose that's so," I said. "Why don't you run to the cellar and grab a few more pieces of fruit to ease things along?"

"Already done it," he said. "Got some nice apples and good, juicy peaches."

"I hope you saved some for the horse," I teased him, indicating his chin.

His eyes grew wide and his tongue jutted out as he licked at the dried juice still under his lower lip. I laughed away his guilt and turned toward the stable yard. Guests had already started arriving, and the fence around the pen was lined by several of the carriage drivers, their eyes fixed in admiration on the fiery black beast that tore around the enclosure.

I saw Izzy had already laid out halter and blanket and saddle, along with the pieces of fruit — bites taken out of two of them. I handed the boy my jacket, then stood with one boot on the bottom rail of the fence. It took several seconds before Pegasus noticed me and bolted straight toward the rail. His nostrils flared as he bore down on me. Several of the men flung themselves to the ground and covered their heads, but the charger turned away at the last second and trotted toward the opposite side of the corral.

The drivers picked themselves up and brushed the dust from their clothes, laughing and slapping me on the back. An ache in my chest reminded me that I was still holding my breath, which I let out as I loosened my white-knuckle grip on the fence rail.

"Wish me luck," I said to Izzy, then climbed into the corral.

The afternoon rain had settled the dust in the stable yard, rather than turning it into a morass.

"Well, that's one good thing," I said to myself. "At least my funeral suit won't be all muddy."

I breathed deeply to work up my courage, then picked up the bridle and reins, along with an apple, and stepped toward the middle of the pen.

Pegasus shied away from me and paced uneasily back and forth. He flicked his ears and tossed his head in defiance, his long mane flowing majestically. I stopped in the center of the stable yard, and his pacing also stopped. He turned to face me square on, lowered his head and snorted. His ears flattened against his head as one hoof scraped at the ground.

Like a lightning bolt, the charger leapt at me. In an instant he was at full gallop and quickly ate up the distance between us. I fought the urge to run and, instead, forced myself to stare straight into the maddened eyes. Mimicking a calm I didn't feel, I took a bite of apple, crossed my arms and turned my back on the beast.

The ground shook as Pegasus thundered past me, and the wind of his passing almost blew me off my feet. He began to pace around me, and I turned to keep my body side-on to him, all the while munching on the apple. Finally, rejection overcame the beast's fear and hostility, and his heavy, damp breath melted my starched collar.

"So you want to be friends again, huh?" I said.

I slowly turned to face the brute and raised my hand to brush his muzzle. He shied a little at my touch, but drew closer as I scratched his head and nose.

"Good boy," I said, and offered him the rest of the apple.

I kept speaking softly to him as I slipped the halter over his nose and fixed the head strap in place behind his ears. I clucked my tongue at him, then turned and led the horse toward the fence.

Pegasus rebelled a little as I burdened him

with the blanket and saddle, but with a little cajolery and bribery, I soon had him fitted for riding and climbed on his back.

"Let's try you out some," I said, and squeezed his middle with my feet.

First at a walk, then a trot and a canter, we took a few turns around the corral in each direction, followed by some figure-eights. Once we found our stride, it seemed I directed the horse more with my will than the reins. After several minutes of the workup, I brought him back to the fence where some twenty pairs of eyes gaped at us.

"I think he's ready," I said. "Hand me up my jacket, Izzy."

The boy climbed up the fence and handed over the coat.

"I'll run get the gate for you," he said.

"Don't bother." I stood in the stirrups and slipped into the jacket. Pegasus nickered and nodded his head in agreement. "Just meet me at the house to bring him back when we're through."

Without waiting for a response, I tugged at the reins and turned the horse toward the middle of the corral. Without a pause, I steered him toward the far end of the fence, eased him into a canter, then a full gallop. Less than a heartbeat away from the fence,

115

it struck me that it might have been wise to get Pegasus accustomed to jumping by himself before trying it with me on his back. The thought wasn't even fully formed before my stomach lurched and we were airborne, sailing in an arc of graceful power over the four-rail fence.

The landing was so smooth I could hardly tell when the jump was complete. Exhilarated, I rose in the stirrups and leaned over the horse's neck. His mane and tail streamed like battle pennons as I drove him toward the front of the house and our unsuspecting audience. With no fanfare other than the thundering of hooves, we raced along the hedgerow that bordered the formal lawn while I searched for the best point to make our entry.

Amid a confused buzz of voices and a few startled gasps, I steered us a couple of dozen paces away from the hedges. Satisfied I had the crowd's attention, I yanked back on the reins. Pegasus reared up on his hind legs and let loose a triumphant whinny. We bolted toward the lawn and, as before, the myth-born horse took wing as we soared over the five-foot hedge. We passed through the parted crowd and took two turns about the carriage round before I eased the stallion into a trot, then walked him to the central clump of onlookers where Uncle Cy and a red-faced Matt stood.

I hopped down from the saddle and held the reins out to Matt.

"I think you dropped these earlier," I said.

Red turned to crimson, then scarlet as I leaned toward Matt, sniffed and wrinkled my nose in disgust. Matt's green eyes opened wide and shot daggers at me before he turned and stomped toward the house. I felt a pang of guilt and avoided Missus Warren's gaze, which I knew would condemn my pride. Instead, I patted Pegasus's neck and handed the reins to Izzy, then accepted the cheers and backslaps of Uncle Cy and the other men standing nearby.

"That was wonderful," Cassandra gushed as she came up to me.

"Oh, um, thanks," I said.

The girl held up a lavishly decorated dance card and took a step nearer to me. "I was hoping maybe —"

"Why, hello, JD."

The voice came from behind me, and it took a few seconds to recognize the sweet, soft timbre. Even then, I could hardly believe my ears.

Or eyes.

I forgot all about Cassandra, forgot the girls by the foundry and every other girl in the world. I turned to face the speaker and was instantly cast adrift in the twin emerald seas that sparkled in the late-evening sun. Auburn brows arched playfully over those magnificent eyes and a delicate, pert nose perched above full, smiling lips. The enchantress's face was wreathed by a halo of auburn curls, the tresses pulled back and tied loosely at the top of her head, with twin ringlets hanging down on either side to frame high cheekbones.

Her dress was of vibrant lavender satin that shone almost violet in the evening sun. Ribbons held pink roses in the hem of her crinolette, at her shoulders and in the bodice. The short sleeves and low neckline revealed the enticing fair skin of elegant arms and a delicately sculpted bosom.

"Gina," I blurted, before correcting myself. "Angelina, I mean."

Her lips parted in a warm smile to reveal even rows of pearly teeth, the merest hint of an overbite adding an indefinable charm.

"I was afraid you'd forgotten me," she said, and extended a gloved hand to me.

I took her hand and, not knowing what else to do, bowed my head over her knuckles.

"Is that the best you can do?" she scolded with a heart-rending pout. "This is how you greet an old friend."

With that she tugged at my hand, drew me close and stood tiptoe to plant a kiss on my cheek. The warmth of her lips set my skin ablaze. My ears filled with the roar of a thousand fires, my eyes blinded by their light. By the time I regained my senses, Gina was steering me across the lawn, her arm drawn tightly in mine.

"— a glass of punch for an old friend?" she was saying. "But, my goodness, it was perfectly awful of you to do that to poor Matty, this being his big night and all."

"Big night?" I said.

"Don't tell me you didn't know."

The blank look in my eyes told her exactly that.

"Of course, not," she said. "JD, Matty's been accepted into the state militia, the cavalry. And you just showed him up on his own horse in front of the colonel of his new regiment."

"I didn't know," I stammered.

"I know," she assured me. "But, intentional or not, maybe this will teach my dear little brother a lesson. One way or another, he'll get over it. In the meantime, I'm not getting any less thirsty."

Gina steered me toward the refreshments, and my unease frittered away under the

119

spell of her voice. My spine straightened with each step as I noted the approving nods of the older men and the jealous glances of the younger folk of both sexes. The setting sun tinged the scattered clouds with a vibrant purple, and I inhaled deeply the last breaths of spring while I looked forward to this most splendid of Midsummer's Eves.

The sun dipped below the horizon around seven-thirty, but it was well past nine before darkness took hold on this shortest night of the year. The full moon wasn't due for several more hours, and the sky was a diamond-crusted crown, surmounted by the ruby of Mars's red glow. Too soon, Gina was taken from me to meet the obligations of her rapidly filling dance card. Out from under her protection, I was set upon by a bevy of well-meaning matrons who insisted I enroll myself in the queues of several other young ladies.

While Gina danced with army officers and the scions of Arkansas's well-bred, I was found to be a fit suitor for the less-promising young ladies of the upper crust. I somehow managed to dance with Cassandra and one other reasonably pleasant — if plain — partner. Otherwise, I was made to suffer through five sets of buckteeth, one pair of lazy eyes, three half-blind myopics and a twin set of sadly misshapen noses — the nostrils gaping straight out of the piggy faces — whose owners' laughter seemed more fitting to the sty than the drawing room.

By the time the orchestra was granted a respite, I'd had more than my fair share of inane twittering, nasal voices and overly done perfume. I stole away from the crowd and pulled off my jacket. I sniffed the collar and recoiled at the stench of lavender and verbena and a half-dozen other odors. I hung the jacket over a porch rail to air out, then slipped around the back of the house, away from the mind-numbing chatter of the crowd and the flaring torchlight that threatened to wash out the beauty of the night sky.

"You made it longer than I'd have thought," said the voice of another stellar beauty.

"One more dance would have done me in," I admitted.

Gina stepped from the shadows at the side of the house, my jacket in her hands. Starlight made her milky skin glow, while the twin stars of her eyes cast their own light upon the night sky.

"This may be ruined, too," she said with a sniff at my vest. "What a shame — the suit looked so good on you. Maybe Miriam can work her magic on these. Now, off you go," she ordered, and began to undo the buttons of my vest.

"I'll do it," I blurted, and hoped the darkness hid the flush of my cheeks and ears.

I undid the remaining five buttons, stripped off the vest and laid it on the rear porch where Gina had set my jacket. Having gone this far, I gave a little laugh and pulled off the cravat and collar that had been choking me all night.

"Better?" Gina asked, a lilt in her voice.

"Much." I enjoyed the moment, but was unsettled by her nearness. "Would you care to walk some?" I wasn't *that* unsettled.

"I'd love to."

She took my arm and let me set our course across the backyard of the house. We walked in silence for several minutes, content with the close company and the chaperonage of the stars. When the silence was broken, we spoke at once, paused to let the other speak, then both continued.

"You first," I said with a laugh.

"I was just going to ask what it was you called me before. Gina?"

"Yes," I admitted.

"I like it. Most men call me Angel for short, and I can't stand it. It's so unimaginative. And I'm no angel," she added with a mischievous grin. "But Gina — I like that very much."

I felt a curious stirring at that. I wasn't sure what it implied but was glad she approved of my secret name for her.

"I didn't expect to see you tonight," I said after a long pause. "I thought you'd be in New Orleans a while longer."

"The school year is over, so there really wasn't much more for me to learn," she said. "I suppose I could have stayed for the social season — which is the real reason Mother wanted me to go down there in the first place — but the thought of a hot, sticky summer on the bayou was just more than I could stand."

"So you chose a hot, sticky summer on the river?" I said.

She squeezed my arm and laughed.

"Yes, as a matter of fact. Cassandra wrote me about how handsome you were getting to be, so I just had to come back and see for myself."

I was dumbstruck by that and just walked on in silence. I willed my feet to keep moving, one in front of the other, lest I stumble and fall, a helpless wreck on the ground.

"Well," Gina prodded after several steps of awkward silence, "did you miss me even a little?"

I stopped at that, unable to trust my feet any further. I turned to face her, stared into those luminous emerald eyes and found myself adrift once more on the sea of her gaze.

"More than I can say," I admitted, my voice husky with fear. "I thought of you every day, every minute. I must've thought about writing to you a hundred times, but what would I have said? 'Dear Gina, there can never be anything between us, but I miss you — please come back'?"

"Why not?"

I snorted at the foolish question, then thought about the answer.

"It's true, I suppose," I said. "It's not as though there was anything to lose. Except my pride, of course, but what's that worth?" I stared up at the stars, found no inspiration there and lowered my gaze to meet Gina's. "I've loved you for years, since before I even really knew what it was. You've been a part of my every waking thought for as long as I can remember, but I —"

The words dashed against my teeth, the wave of emotion unable to carry them farther until Gina's grip on my hands and her look of encouragement gave me the strength to press on.

"I suppose Matt said it best, years ago. He reminded me that I'm nothing but the son of a hired hand. That I'm not fit to look at you, let alone think of you that way. Or touch you," I added, acutely aware of my damp palms against hers.

"Well, you're looking at me now," she said, her eyes fixed on mine. "And touching me." She squeezed my hands and stepped closer to me. "And thinking of me that way?" She whispered the question, her breath warm on my skin as she drew nearer still.

I could only nod as she pulled my arms around her and placed my hands on her waist. She moved her hands to the small of my back and tilted her chin toward me as her lips issued a siren call I couldn't resist.

If the earlier kiss on my cheek had called forth an inferno, this second kiss loosed the fire of a thousand volcanoes. My head buzzed and my heart pounded, my lungs uselessly inert. My stomach lurched as though I was falling, and my knees threatened just that. After what seemed an eternity of heavenly bliss, Gina broke the spell and eased away from me. She took my hand in hers and led me toward the stables and into the little workshop.

In the dark of the shop, I heard the swish of her skirts and the soft tread of her shoes on the ladder. I followed mutely up the rungs and crossed to where she stood by the window, bathed in starlight.

"Now, where were we?" she prompted, and drew me to her. Her hands massaged my back, then she loosened her embrace and explored the muscles of my chest, running her hands along my shoulders and easing off the braces of my suspenders.

"Gina, no," I protested weakly, the vestiges of Missus Warren's lectures on propriety ruining the moment.

She stepped back from me, a look of mischief and amusement on her face.

"Suit yourself," she said. "As for me, it's terribly stifling up here."

She pulled loose the clutch of roses that adorned the top of her bodice, tossed them at me and undid the clasp at the front of her dress. I stared open-mouthed as, with excruciating slowness, she worked her hands down the row of buttons, slipped the short sleeves off her shoulders and wriggled the material over her hips until it fell in a bundle at her feet.

We'd swum together as children, but it had been years since I'd seen her in this state of undress. And she was no longer a child. The naggings of good counsel fell silent as I unbuttoned my shirt and pulled it over my head. I drew Gina close and lost myself in the passion of her kiss.

By the time I managed to take another breath, the pile of clothes had deepened. The moon peeked through the trees, dappling Gina's alabaster skin in a soft glow. With only the ribbon in her hair to remove, she slowly pulled the knot loose, shook out the flowing tresses and pulled them over one shoulder.

She approached me slowly, like some goddess out of a dream. My heart raced ever faster as she pushed me back on the bed and — with the moon cresting over the treetops — initiated me into the mysteries of love.

CHAPTER FIVE

Franklin County, Arkansas — May 1858

"Dadgummit all to tarnation."

The almost-curse was followed by an equally vexed "Son of a —" The words were bitten off as their speaker struggled to find a substitute. "Sow."

I was jerked out of my midday nap, and lifted my hat up from my eyes to look over at Izzy. He, too, had been startled awake and blinked dazedly back at me. For nearly two weeks we'd been following the pike between Little Rock and Van Buren, and this was the first time our afternoon rest had been disturbed.

I crawled out from the shade of the sprawling elm tree and up to the side of the road to see what the fuss was about. A man of about Pa's age — though much more slender of build — was bent at the middle, legs straight, as he peered underneath his wagon. His thin hair revealed a bald spot that shone in the noonday sun. A quick glance at the wagon showed that the spate of cursing had been brought on by a broken axle.

I pushed myself to my feet and walked toward the man, who now squatted on his haunches, picking at an ear as he stared under the wagon.

"Looks like you could use a hand," I said.

The man jerked and tried to stand, but failed to clear his head from the edge of the wagon's bed. A dull *thunk* rolled across the road and was closely followed by a bellowed "Sh— shortcake."

"Sorry," I said as the man fell on his backside and rubbed his bald spot.

He skittered away like a crab and looked nervously about as I extended my hand to help him up.

"I didn't mean to startle you," I said. "Just looks like you could use a hand."

The crab blinked up at me through squinty eyes.

"Are you a traveling man?" he asked in a wheezing voice.

"I guess you could say that. I'm on my way to Britton, over in Crawford County."

He blinked at me a few more times, rubbed his head again, then smiled sheepishly as he reached out a hand.

"Thanks," he said as I pulled him to his

feet. His hand gripped mine strangely, and he looked expectantly at me.

"Happy to oblige," I said, puzzled by his odd behavior.

Izzy poked his head above the edge of the road, and I shook my head slightly, warning him to stay put until I had a handle on the situation. The man apparently noticed the gesture and spun around to see, but Izzy had already ducked back down behind the roadbed.

"I'm JD," I said. "JD Robbins."

"Harvey Walpole," he replied.

"Pleased to know you, Harvey. You mind if I take a look?" I nodded toward the nearly collapsed wagon.

"Um . . ." Walpole hedged, and looked from me to the wagon, then back again.

"I might be able to help," I said. "I'm a bit of a blacksmith by trade."

"Much good the last smith done me," he griped before chewing on one of his thumbnails. "But I don't suppose it'd hurt to have another set of eyes on the damn — er, dang thing."

His face reddened as the curse escaped his lips, and he grimaced as he pinched the inside of one arm.

"My missus don't much care for the rough language," he explained, seeing my curious look. "She says if I pinch myself every time I let loose with a foul word, before too long my body'll tell my mouth to watch itself."

He grinned good-naturedly at my skeptical look.

"Naw, I don't know how well it works," he said. "Reminds me to watch my tongue some, but mostly it just gives me a sore arm."

I laughed along with him, and his pleasant chuckle dispelled the air of suspicion that had clouded our meeting.

"If you could take a look at that axle," he said, "I'd be much obliged."

"Be happy to," I said, then dropped to my hands and knees to peer under the sagging wagon.

The rear axle was broken in two, the pieces buried in the ground where they'd gouged a rut before dragging the wagon to a halt. An iron sleeve was wrapped around one of the pieces and slid freely when I tried it.

"You had it fixed before?"

"Yep," he said. "A few days ago, out to Marshall. Feller there said he'd patched it up good as new, scheming son of a . . . . gun. Paid him three dollars for the job, and here's what I get for it."

"Well, it's not all that bad. He's drilled

through the strong part of the axle. The wood's still whole, except where the original break was. I reckon you just lost your pins somewhere on the way. If we can fix the sleeve back in place, it ought to get you where you're going, assuming it's not too far."

"Heading to Fort Smith," he offered, scratching his chin as he tried to figure the distance.

"About thirty miles," I offered. "Shouldn't be a problem if we can find something to hold the sleeve good and firm." I stood and brushed off my hands and knees. "This ought to do," I said, and reached for the hasp pins holding the tailgate closed.

"No." Walpole rushed at me and pushed me roughly away from the wagon, surprising me with his strength and speed.

"Hey, easy there."

"What you mean, fooling around with my rig like that?"

"I wasn't fooling with anything," I said. "If you want to move on, you need something to hold that collar in place. Those pins there are your best bet."

"What about the ones that come out of it to begin with?" he suggested, his voice calming slightly despite his beet-red face.

"If you want to backtrack this road on foot

looking for them, be my guest," I said. "I have better things to do than wait on you when there's a perfectly good fix right in front of us."

With that, I clamped my hat down on my head and crossed the road toward the ditch where Izzy still lay hidden.

"Wait," Walpole called out after me. "JD. JD, was it? Wait."

I checked my temper, paused and turned as the man chased after me.

"I apologize. It's just I got an important load to carry out Fort Smith way. Makes me a little leery of strangers. I'm obliged for any help you can give me." He stared at me with imploring eyes until I finally relented.

"If we're going to fix it," I said, "that load has to come off. It'll be hard enough lifting up the empty bed to set the axle right with just the two of us, let alone with a full load aboard. Once we're through, we can figure a way to keep the gate shut, but we need those pins for the axle."

He considered the solution so long I turned away again before he at last agreed.

"All right, we'll do that," he said. "Whatever you say."

I gave a frustrated sigh, then nodded and turned back toward the wagon.

"Go ahead and start unloading," Walpole

133

suggested, rather ungraciously I thought, "while I get some tools from the front."

I wasn't happy about doing all the work, but was eager to carry out my Good Samaritan's duties and have done with the odd little man. I moved to the rear of the wagon, pulled the pins from their hasps, threw back the tarpaulin cover and lifted the gate out of its place.

And met three sets of wide, brown eyes that stared at me out of frightened black faces.

The three huddled together beneath the tarpaulin — a man, woman and little girl. There was actually a fourth, an infant who was nearly hidden from view as its mother clutched it tightly to her breast. The little girl's eyes were a mix of fear and wonder, while her mother's were pure fright. The man's eyes bore a hint of anxiety, though their menacing gaze suggested he wasn't one to be backed into a corner. It took several moments of looking from eye to eye to eye before I recovered my wits enough to speak.

"I —"

"Marse Jade, look out," Izzy called from the roadside.

I heard the distinctive *clack* of a rifle hammer, followed immediately by a shot. I ducked for cover and saw a pair of legs running across the road from the direction of the ditch.

"Damn fool cracker," Izzy shouted. "What you think you're doing?"

Another shot rang out, and Izzy slumped to the ground, a bloody gash in his temple. I charged Walpole, hoping to catch him with his gun unloaded, but he jerked at the rifle's lever and aimed for my chest.

"Just take it nice and easy," he said calmly.

I'd heard of repeating Volcano rifles but I'd never seen one, and scarcely thought it possible that a gun could be reloaded with just the cycling of a lever. True or not, I froze in my tracks and held my hands out to my sides.

"Look, Mister Walpole," I said, fighting to keep my voice even, "there's no need for that. Just let me see to my friend and we'll be on our way."

"Elijah, y'all come on down from there, now," he said, ignoring my words.

I looked back to where the big black man hefted himself from the wagon bed. His eyes didn't leave me for an instant as he slid from the edge of the wagon to the ground.

"Come now, Hannah," he ordered the little girl. He swept her up in his arms and set her gently on the ground behind him.

"You help your mammy with the baby, hear?"

"Yes, Papa," she said, and took the infant from her mother's outstretched arms.

Once on the ground, the woman took the baby back from the girl and hustled the children to the far side of the wagon.

"You don't need that rifle, Mister Walpole," I repeated.

"I'll decide what's needful and what ain't. Elijah, this here young feller fancies himself a blacksmith of sorts. Reckons he can fix that bum axle. Now you help him out and do as he says, while I make sure he don't start no trouble."

"Yes, suh, Mister Harvey. What you be needing me to do?" Elijah asked me, the menace in his eyes ebbing slightly.

"What about Izzy?" I demanded of Walpole.

"You just see to the wagon," he said. "We'll take care of the boy in due time."

With no choice but to agree, I turned to the big man by my side.

"We need to lift up the wagon a bit so we can join the axle again. Once the sleeve's in place, it should be able to hold the load just fine."

Elijah nodded slowly then squatted to peer under the wagon. "How you thinking to go 'bout it?" He squinted his eyes against the sun as he looked up at me.

"Well, if you can hold up the bed, I can probably work the axle together."

He grunted.

"You got some other way?" I said.

"Well, that all right, if you trust me not to drop the thing down on your head." He looked me square in the eye before cracking into a slight grin.

"What'd you have in mind?" I asked, relaxing a little.

"That axle's none too flimsy itself," he said. "Might take a bit more doing than one man's got in him. Now you ain't no scrap of a boy, but I don't know that even I could pull them ends together on my own. If we was both to get in under there, why I'll bet we'd get her done."

"I suppose," I said. "But who's to hold up the wagon bed while we're underneath?"

"Well, now, the Good Lord didn't give us legs for nothing," he said.

"All right," I agreed, "let's do it."

I pulled off my hat and shirt, then took another look at Izzy before wriggling under the wagon. Elijah joined me a few seconds later, and I marveled that he was able to fit his massive chest into the tight confines.

"Ready?" he asked as he placed his palms

137

against the wagon bed.

"Say when."

Together we hand-walked our way under the wagon, braced the weight with our legs and forced the ends of the axle together. The ends butted together nicely, and I slipped the wrought iron sleeve over the ends, then secured it in place with the pins.

"Fine work," Elijah said after we'd set the wagon back onto its wheels and crawled out from underneath. "What'd you say your name was?"

"JD," I said, accepting his outstretched hand. "JD Robbins."

"Well, Mister JD," he said, carefully pronouncing each syllable, "that was a nice piece of work."

"Yes, very nice," Walpole agreed, and stepped toward me, his rifle still at the ready. "Now, if you'll just step over that way," he motioned with the rifle barrel. "Elijah, you get yourselves settled back in."

"What about them?" Elijah asked as he helped his wife back aboard the wagon.

"We can't very well have this one running to the next town and telling about a bunch of escaped slaves, now can we? We'll take the boy with us, though."

"The hell you will," I shouted and started toward the skinny man, but he leveled the rifle at my chest and froze me in my tracks.

My sight narrowed and the black hole of the barrel grew to fill my vision until my view was blocked by the expanse of Elijah's back.

"No," I heard him say in a deathly calm voice.

"Step aside, Elijah."

"No, Mister Harvey. You ain't gonna do this. Mister JD here ain't done nothing but help us. And he don't appear to want nothing more now than to help his friend. I won't stand for you repaying his Christian kindness with evil."

"If he rats on us, we'll all be repaid for our troubles at the end of a rope. Now step aside."

From where I stood, I could see no change in Elijah's demeanor, but the change in his voice made my blood run cold.

"If you harm this boy, I'll twist that little head of yours off that scrawny neck so's a rope won't matter."

Stillness settled over the road and the only sound was of the gentle breeze and a slight moan that passed Izzy's lips.

"Mister Harvey," Elijah continued, his voice softer now, "you doing the blessed Lord's work in helping me and mine to be free. Don't give the devil a share in it by

139

doing this evil thing. The boy ain't hurt no one and ain't gonna betray us." He didn't change his position, but said to me, "Mister JD, you go on, help your friend here and clear off the road, y'hear?"

Without a word, I grabbed my hat and shirt, looped Izzy's arm over my shoulder and hefted him off the road and into the brush. A whip cracked behind us, and the rumble and rattle of the wagon faded down the road as I helped Izzy to the shade tree. He slumped against the trunk, one side of his face wet with blood. His eyes were open but unfocused, with one pupil bigger than the other.

I pulled a clean shirt from my bag and soaked it with water from my canteen to clean the blood off Izzy's face. He winced and groaned as I scrubbed away the dirt and clotted blood from his wound, then I tore the shirt into strips and wrapped his head. I held the canteen to his lips and he sipped at the water, though more went down his chin than his gullet. Drifting eyes moved in my direction, and he squinted as he tried to keep me in focus.

"We there yet?"

A light mist rose from the meadow, and the dew on the tall grass stained our trouser legs as we waded through the field. Still fallow, the grass had grown high enough to tickle my palms as I brushed them over the seed stalks. The sun hid behind the morning haze, a muted ball of orange, and the world was silent except for the rustle of grass with each step homeward.

Home.

The word seemed alien to me. It'd been nearly four years since I'd seen the little cottage that lay just beyond the hill, even longer since I'd felt like I belonged there.

"Your pa's not a bad man," I remembered Ma's words from the night before I left home. "If he's hard on you, it's because the world's been hard on him. He just wants to make you strong so you can stand on your own."

Pa's happy all the time now, Becca wrote a few months later. *He even whistles some. Whatever made him sad for so long seems to be gone.*

And here I was, coming home again.

Well, it won't be for long, I told myself. *Just long enough to say hello, then I'll be on my way and he can go back to being happy.*

"Mmm-mm," Izzy hummed. "Somebody doing some cooking already."

I stopped and sniffed and, sure enough, the dusty tang of wood smoke floated on

141

the morning air. I imagined Ma at the stove — or maybe that was Becca's job now. I wondered if I'd recognize her — a young lady, not the little girl I'd left behind. A knot formed in my stomach and I struggled to keep my pace steady, to let Izzy keep up with me, but the breeze at my back seemed to push me along toward . . .

That's odd, I thought.

The wind was behind me, but I could already smell smoke. I sniffed again, and the smoke was definitely in the air, but without any of the usual cooking smells. I strained to see through the morning mist and could just make out the plumes from the hearth — only there seemed to be several columns of smoke, not just the one.

I left Izzy behind and raced to the top of the hill — and froze as I looked down on the scene.

House and barn and shed had been replaced by smoldering piles of ash. Even the outhouse had been reduced to a ring of black ash. The smoke made my eyes water as I raced down the hill and walked about the ruins.

"That don't look like no accident." Izzy caught up with me and spoke the very words I was thinking.

"Let's go over to Gina's folks," I said as

142

numbness settled over me. "They'll know what's happened."

Gina and Matt had taken the boat home from Little Rock, but I'd chosen to walk the hundred fifty miles. There was the cost of the boat ticket, of course — I needed to mind every penny if I were to save enough to make a home for Gina one day. Too, I didn't cotton to the idea of making Izzy sail at the back of the boat as I'd had to do. The only slaves permitted on the passenger decks were personal attendants, and — despite Missus Warren's best efforts — we seemed unlikely to pass for a gentleman and his valet.

Mostly, though, I'd just needed the time to think. Gina and I had kept our romance secret for two years. Well, Izzy knew, which meant that Timothy and Miriam were likely in the know. Uncle Cy's and Rawls's occasional conspiratorial winks, along with Matt's baleful glares and Cassandra's sad glances, suggested that they had all guessed the truth. Secret, then, would seem to be a relative term, meaning only that those who might stand in our way were kept out of it.

I hated the secret almost as much as the need for it. The nights when Gina came to me — after we'd made love and she left my straw mattress in the shed to return to her feather-stuffed one in the mansion — I'd lie awake until dawn and curse the rift that separated us. I cursed myself for being unable to cross over to her side, to take her hand in public. And I cursed her for fearing to come over to my side.

So I walked, to sort out my scattered emotions as much as to form a plan. To find a way to make a home for her, a home somewhere between the manor to which she'd been born and the little cottage that lay in a smoking ruin behind me.

A jangle of harnesses caught my attention, and I steered Izzy to the side of the road as the *clip-clop* of shod hooves came up behind us.

"Ho," the driver called to his team, and the hooves slowed as the carriage stopped beside us.

I turned and immediately recognized the livery and the signature black felt hat and morning coat, one sleeve banded with a strip of black crepe. The hair was greyer than I recalled, and the eyes lacked their normal brightness, but there was no mistaking the man behind them.

"Doc Aubry, sir."

"JD?" he said, his eyes gone wide in recognition. "My land, if you haven't grown, son. You're all of a man now." His mouth opened and closed as he tried to find words to continue.

"We just came from the place," I answered his unspoken question. "We were heading over to Barnes's to find out what's happened. I'm glad we found you, though. My, uh, my friend could stand to have you take a look at him."

Slave was the truth of it, but *friend* seemed closer to the mark. The Warrens had given Izzy to me when I left them, but I couldn't bring myself to think of him as property.

"Sure, sure," Doc replied as he set the brake and climbed down from the rig. "Sit here, boy," he offered, and propped Izzy on the sidestep.

"Matt rode out looking for you boys," he said as he removed Izzy's bandage and examined the wound. "Rode out clear to Dover before turning around. I don't mind saying, we were all a mite worried after you."

"We ran into a little trouble this side of Ozark," I said. "Decided it'd be best to keep off the roads. What's happened, sir?"

Doc Aubry ignored the question as he finished inspecting Izzy's wound, then put on a fresh bandage.

"Take a seat on the tailgate, boy," he said to Izzy before finally turning to face me.

"Put in your things. I'll take you to see your folks."

I made sure Izzy was settled in, put my bag in the flatbed, then climbed up beside Doc. He flicked the reins and pulled the team around to head back up the road.

"Aren't we going to the Barneses'?"

"I thought you wanted to see your folks."

"Yes, sir. I just figured they'd be at the farm."

"No, son, they . . ." His eyes clouded over and he looked away from me. "They're in town."

I nodded, not really understanding, and settled in for the ride. Questions — and now fears — mounted with each step of the team. Images flashed through my mind, of Ma, Pa and Becca so badly injured they had to stay with Doc Aubry. When we entered town and continued past his house, the images faded away as though a black veil were drawn across them.

Finally, he drew rein and brought the carriage to a stop in front of the little whitewashed church. He studiously set the handbrake and wrapped the reins around the handle, his eyes avoiding mine all the while. Without a word, he stepped down and walked around to the back of the building. I climbed down and helped Izzy to his feet.

He looked at me, his eyes full of pity. For the life of me, I couldn't fathom what was happening, and it angered me that everyone but me seemed to know.

I followed Doc to the back of the church, my hand gliding along the weather-beaten boards of the siding. We came to the low wrought-iron fence that enclosed a small yard behind the church. Doc removed his hat, opened the gate and stepped in. He held the gate open and beckoned for me to follow. A cold hand gripped my heart as I passed through the gate, and light began to shine around the edges of the veil in my mind.

Markers of wood and stone stood in neat rows among the closely cropped grass of the yard. Toward one corner, a lone figure lay next to a wide mound of freshly turned earth. The head rose and brown eyes looked at me across a white muzzle and black nose.

"Argos?" I said.

I sank to my knees and the hound struggled to his feet, then slowly came over to me and laid his head in my lap. I scratched his ears and rubbed his flanks, startled at the ribs that poked out from beneath his flecked coat.

"Has no one been feeding you, boy?" Anger mixed with my uncertainty.

"I tried to bring him home with me," Doc said, "but he wouldn't come with me. Even brought him food, but he wouldn't eat or drink. Just wanted to lie there by her."

"By who?" I said.

The edges of the veil pulled away a bit more, and I began to fear what lay on the other side. With a whine, Argos rose on stiff legs and paced between me and the mound of earth. When I failed to follow, he let out a mournful bark and pawed at the air in my direction.

I stumbled forward, my feet cased in lead. With each step, the mental veil drew back farther and farther until my eyes burned with the light of realization. I reached Argos and patted his head, his eyes fixed on the freshly painted marker board. I followed his gaze to read the dreaded word: *Robbins*.

In the next instant, my eyes blinked open and I jerked my head back from an acrid stench beneath my nose.

"Easy, son," Doc said as he braced one hand against my shoulder and waved a small vial under my nostrils. "Just a couple more whiffs should do you."

I found myself lying on the dew-moistened ground, my knees propped up. Izzy knelt to one side with Argos on the other, his chin propped on my arm. I eased into a sitting position, and the world spun around me.

"Take your time," Doc cautioned, then helped me to stand when I felt ready. I waved off his hands and turned back toward the grave marker.

ROBBINS		
James	Sarah	Rebecca
Douglas, Sr.	McKenzie	Noelle
June 14,	November 28,	December 24,
1816–	1820–	1847–
	May 24th,	
	1858	
	Joined in Life,	
	Unseparated	
	in Death	

"It was the typhus," Doc explained as we sipped bitter, steaming coffee around his kitchen table. "I reckon Becca picked it up playing with a rat or somesuch. Your Ma would have caught it right quick, and Jim sat with them till the end."

"Why do you say that?" I asked. I thought of Pa's brusque demeanor and found it hard to imagine him playing nursemaid.

"When I found them, Becca and Sarah were tucked in bed together," Doc said. "Your pa was sitting beside the bed, tending to them until he succumbed. Near as I can tell, he spent his last bit of laudanum on them to help ease their way."

"So he was back on the hop," I said, my voice dripping with disgust.

Doc Aubry set his cup down and fixed me with a solemn glare.

"Boy," he told me, and I'd never heard his voice so stern, "there are some things you need to get straight in your head."

I was surprised at the chastisement, but said nothing.

"First thing," he said, "Jim was in pain every minute of every day after his accident. A man suffers an injury like that, gets his leg smashed and shattered — well, even with the best doctor, it doesn't ever heal quite right, and your pa had to make do with me. Add to that the shame of having to send you to work to care for the family, plus the guilt of Sarah's losing the baby . . ."

I looked up at that.

"I always blamed myself for that," I said.

Doc gave a mirthless laugh.

"Then that's one more thing you have in common with him," he said. "I told Jim, and I'll tell you. It wasn't anyone's fault. For whatever reason, that baby just was not ready to come into the world." He sipped thoughtfully at his coffee and gave a shrug. "And, if not for losing that little one, your sister might never have come along. I tell you what, boy, it's that little girl who saved your pa."

"How's that?"

"I've seen more than my share of broken men in my day," Doc said. "Especially after the Mexican War. Men broken in body and spirit, where all they have is a bottle to drown their pain. Your pa might easily have gone down that road, but little Becca kept him on the right path. He quit the whiskey for fear of his temper, and asked me for just enough laudanum to take the edge off. Said he wanted to keep his mind clear enough to watch that little girl dance and play and grow. For all his faults — and don't get me wrong, he had plenty — your pa became a good man when your sister came along, and he became damn near a saint as she and your ma passed."

I crossed my arms and pushed back my chair. Argos grunted as the scraping chair legs disturbed his nap.

"What was the second thing?" I said.

Doc mimicked my posture and tipped his chair back on its rear legs.

"Oh, it's a small thing," he said with a drawl. "Hardly worth mentioning."

I fixed him with a tired stare, but uncrossed my arms and leaned forward on the table.

"The second thing is," he continued, "your father was proud of you."

"Proud?" I scoffed. "He didn't even know me."

"He knew you well enough. I should say, he knew himself well enough, and the fruit don't fall far from the tree."

"What's that supposed to mean?" I said.

"It means you're a lot like your pa. If he was hard on you, it was only to make you stronger than he was. If he pushed you, it was to help you go farther than he could."

"And if he sent me away?" I said. "Kicked me out of my home?"

Doc fixed his eyes on mine and sighed deeply.

"Then I'd say it was to help you find a home of your own."

For as long as I can remember, home *has* had canvas walls and folding furniture. Anything of a more permanent nature has simply been the place I happened to live. As I watch the men clustered about the cot in my home of the past few years, a murmur ripples through them, hats come off their heads as they step away from the tent flap . . .

And home *walks in.*

Her clothes are dusty and her hair windblown from the train ride. Time has added a dozen creases to her once flawless face, and the fiery curls have been tamed by strands of ash-grey. Life has sapped a bit of the glow from the emerald eyes, but they sparkle with tears in the dim light of the tent.

She moves to the cot and raises a trembling hand to her mouth as she looks down on me. The quilt is wrapped around me so only my head shows, face scraped raw from the fall and hair matted with blood. The woman

153

kneels beside the cot and places a soft hand on my forehead. I feel the cool touch in the corner of the tent where I'm hovering.

"Is there anything we can do for him?" she asks.

"Best to patch him up here as best we can," one of the men answers. "Once he comes around some, we can think about moving him."

As I watch the sorry scene, a haze slowly fills the tent. The figures huddled around the cot begin to fade while, out of the gloom, others emerge. The newcomers stand in a perfect circle around the cot, heedless of any obstacles. Three of them are half in and half out of the tent, one stands in the middle of the camp stove, and another actually shares the same space as one of the men. Through the fog I see the big black man shudder and step away from the intruding wraith. As one, and without a sound, the figures join hands and begin a slow funereal dance around the cot, circling like a great cloud of witnesses.

Or vultures.

Silence looms, with no one willing to speak — or maybe with nothing to say. The sound of dripping water breaks the spell, and a pair of hands reaches out from the pall with a handkerchief, to soothe and clean my face.

The woman leans toward my body and from across the tent I hear her whisper, "I'm so

154

sorry I was late."

A tear falls from her cheek to mine, followed by the warm softness of her lips.

CHAPTER SIX

Van Buren, Arkansas — February 1861
Gina's lips were soft and inviting, and returned my kiss with an ardor equal to my own. Her body pressed hard against me and her mouth was full on mine as we shared a hunger that the passion of the past hour had done little to satisfy. Indeed, the desire seemed all the greater for the separation that had preceded our reunion, and the one that would shortly follow.

"Stay," she whispered softly, and my heart leapt, willing to obey her every command.

I pulled her closer still, as though I could imprint the image of her body upon my heart, and so carry her with me on my journey.

"You know I can't," I heard myself say as I loosened my arms about her waist and rested my chin atop her head.

"How long will it be this time?" Longing was replaced by resignation as she pressed her cheek against my chest.

"Hard to say."

On my return from Little Rock, I'd taken a job as surveyor's assistant for John Butterfield, who believed his Overland Mail route would lay the foundation for the proposed Transcontinental Railroad. While Congress squabbled over the choice of a northern or southern route, Butterfield formed survey crews to chart the best path along his own road.

Particularly troublesome was the stretch through the Boston Mountains north of Van Buren. That short span was among the steepest and most jagged of the entire 2,800-mile road. It would never meet the grade and bend specifications Congress had set for the railroad, so Butterfield tasked us with finding a better way along that spine of the Ozarks.

"Maybe they'll finally declare war, and you can come back to me."

"Gina, don't even think such a thing," I said, though I'd had the same thought many times.

Seven states had already seceded from the Union and formed a loose confederation. Arkansas shared borders with three of those states, and the papers were full of bitter arguments both for and against secession.

I feared war, but part of me hoped Arkansas would secede. If Missouri and Tennessee followed suit, any fighting would be along far-distant borders, and Gina and I could be together in peace. As far as I cared, the devil could take the politicians, soldiers, abolitionists. All that mattered was the woman in my arms and the days between now and when I could again hold her.

Gina raised her gaze to mine and rested her chin against my breastbone.

"Well, then," she said, "I'll just have to promise to make it worth your while to hurry home."

I smiled at that, both for the promised welcome and for the possibility that we might, indeed, make a home together. I lowered my head and met her lips in a kiss that was not so much one of hunger as of assurance — that I would soon return, that she would wait for me, that what we shared would bind our hearts together despite the many miles and weeks that might separate us. I softly stroked her cheek and drew back, cupping her chin in my hand while I studied her face and eyes, etching every contour and line on my memory.

"Keep looking at me like that, and you'll never get out of here," she warned me.

"Yes, ma'am," I said.

Gina picked my hat off the small dining table and set it squarely on my head, then held open my duster while I shrugged into it. I turned to face her again and she tugged at my collars to straighten them. "That should do," she allowed.

I threw her a crooked grin, then swooped in for one last, quick kiss.

"I won't be long," I whispered, then picked up my saddlebags and stepped out the door. I didn't dare look back, for fear I'd never leave.

The morning air was cool and laced with fog, but the chill bite of winter was gone. I pulled the duster tight about me as I made my way through the early morning gloom. To avoid prying eyes, I went by the narrow alleyways behind Gina's cottage at the Wallace Institute, where she was now a teacher. I hoped the need to slink through the back alleys would be gone by the time I returned.

Mister Barnes had delivered a sizable legacy to me when I came back from Little Rock — several hundred dollars that Pa and I had worked off against the mortgage on our land. I hadn't even known of the arrangement, but Barnes insisted I take the money, unless I wanted to rebuild and continue working for him. The choice had been an easy one.

I combined that windfall with the money I'd earned from Rawls, keeping just enough of the funds to buy horses for Izzy and me, along with a good set of surveyor's instruments, and entrusted the rest to Uncle Cy for safekeeping.

After nearly three years of hard work and simple living, the little nest egg had grown quite nicely — nine hundred thirty-three dollars and fifty-eight cents, by the last reckoning. The number was beyond anything I'd ever imagined, but wasn't quite enough. One thousand dollars was the goal I'd set for myself before I would approach Mister Barnes to ask for Gina's hand. A nice, round number, but also evidence that I'd be able to provide for his daughter in a fitting, if not luxurious, manner. The sum made this survey trip all the more important, as my earnings from the next few weeks should put me past my goal.

"I thought I told you to leave her alone," a voice called out behind me, the words slurred.

My heart lurched into my throat at the unexpected challenge. I spun around and lowered myself toward the ground to prepare for an attack. Silent seconds passed as I stared blindly into the blackness of a doorway off the alley, before the voice registered as one I knew.

"I seem to recall something along those lines," I answered, "back when we were kids. But we're all adults now. Why don't you leave it to Gina to decide who she ought and ought not see?"

"Her name is Angelina," Matt spat back at me as he stepped into the alley. "Given the company she's keeping, it's pretty damned clear she ain't in a position to make any sound judgments."

"Look, Matty," I said, deliberately taunting him with the diminutive, "she's a grown woman now —"

I got no farther than that before his hand flashed out from behind his back. A menacing blur trailed behind it and hurtled toward me. I jerked back, but was too slow to avoid the attack. The leather sack connected with my nose and drove across my face in a vicious blow. Blood gushed from my shattered nose as I fell to the ground.

I pushed myself to my feet and raised an arm to protect myself as I caught a hint of movement through blood- and tear-blurred eyes. Matty rushed me again, but I managed to avoid the blow. He sailed past me off balance, and I snaked an arm through his and planted my hand against the back

161

of his neck. Our combined momentum brought us to the ground, and a sickening *Pop* echoed off the alley walls as I fell on top of him.

Matt let out a scream of pain and anger. I let loose of him and grabbed up the small leather bag. My eyes were starting to swell shut as I stepped toward where he lay moaning and clutching his wracked shoulder. I hooked my boot under his armpit and rolled him onto his back. He screamed again, then stared up at me through eyes blinded by hatred and pain and fear. He let go of his shoulder and crab-walked away from me.

I stalked after him, slapping the heavy leather bag against my thigh as I went. He backed into a wall and his eyes darted from side to side like a cornered fox. A sly grin twisted at his mouth as he fumbled at the top of one boot. He pulled a Bowie knife from his boot sheath, but I pinned his knife hand under my boot. He gasped as I brought my full weight to bear, and dropped the knife.

I picked up the blade and released his arm, then set my heel into his stomach. I slowly pressed down, and he beat at my leg as the air wheezed from his lungs. A sharp smell cut through the still air and I was surprised — and not a little gratified — to see a damp stain growing between his trouser legs.

Through swollen eyes I saw the humiliation that colored Matt's face. I knelt with one knee on his chest and waved the Bowie under his nose while I swung the bludgeon in my other hand. Matt's eyes opened wide as I stabbed the knife into supple, tanned skin. I drove the blade deeper, surprised at how easily it penetrated. With a savage ripping motion, I tore the knife out through the skin and the contents spilled out on Matt's chest. Lead pellets poured from the torn bludgeon onto Matt's shirt with a dull clicking sound.

When the leather bag was empty, I flicked it harmlessly at Matt's face, then stood and slipped the knife through my belt. Without a word, I turned and started up the alley toward the livery stable.

"Coward," Matt yelled after me. "Can't even finish a fight. You stay away from her, you hear me? You don't deserve her. You're nothing. Nothing but a nigger in white skin — a worthless, white nigger piece of filth."

I straightened my shoulders as I walked. It was enough effort just to stay on my feet, without turning back to renew the fight. I turned a corner and slumped against the wall, but kept moving toward the livery, while Matt's insults echoed behind me.

"What the hell happened to you?" I recognized Tom Halsey's voice as I neared the stables. He rushed toward me, and I took the blurs behind him for Izzy and Argos.

"Just a little run-in," I said as strong hands eased me to the ground.

"With what, a brick wall? Izzy, run fetch some water for me," Tom ordered, and I heard feet run off while Argos licked my hand. "Ol' Tom's here, now," he assured me.

The survey crew's rodman was short, but built like a hogshead. With him nearby, I needn't worry over another attack.

I heard Izzy return and set down a bucket, then screamed in pain as Tom began cleaning my face.

"Easy now, Jim. I'll be as gentle as I can, but I got to get this blood washed off. Might hurt a bit," he added needlessly. "Help hold him still now, Izzy."

Strong but gentle hands gripped my shoulders while Tom resumed his care of my battered face.

"There, now, that wasn't so bad." Tom's voice came as through a thick blanket, my mind having dulled all my senses against the pain. "Had my own nose broke three times, but you'd never know it."

I peered through slit eyes at the bent and twisted nose.

"Only three?" I said.

"Aye, well, I didn't have good ol' Tom to see to myself, now did I? Here," he said, and placed a small flask in my hand. "Take a few sips of this — it'll help with the pain."

"What is it?" I held the flask close, but could smell nothing through my ruined nose.

"Just a little home-brewed medicine."

I took a pull from the flask, gagged and spat out a mouthful of alcohol and blood.

"Don't waste it all now," Tom said. "Just sip at it. Trust me, it'll help."

Warily, I raised the flask again, drank and fought to swallow the harsh liquor. Almost immediately, I felt the blanket over my senses draw more snugly about me.

"That's the way." Tom's voice was muted even more, and I barely heard the words, "Hold him steady, now."

With a violent jerk, Tom reset my nose and all my senses were restored with a vengeance. Pain shot through my entire body, and Argos yelped and skittered away as I fought against the hands holding me down.

"Steady, boy," Tom said quietly. "Sorry about that, but I had to set it before the swelling got any worse. With luck, you won't have much more than a little bump. You're lucky, y'know? Whatever it was hit you, a half inch off and you'd be minus a few teeth."

"Here you go, Jade." Izzy had torn strips from his shirt and offered me the rolls of cloth. "For the bleeding," he explained.

I nodded, then squeezed the swabs into my nostrils.

"That's the way," Tom said. He picked up his flask from where I'd tossed it in my struggle, wiped off the mouth and took a quick pull before handing it back to me. "A couple more snorts, and you'll be right as rain."

My ears popped as I swallowed against my plugged nose, but the liquor seemed to go down more smoothly this time. Izzy helped me to my feet and led me into the stable, where the rest of the crew had begun gathering.

"What — ?" a startled voice asked, but Tom cleared his throat roughly and cut off any further questions. In a few minutes, eight riders and three packhorses left the livery and set out north along the Fayette-ville Road.

"It is the natural yearning of man to be free."

The fire crackled as we huddled around the glowing warmth that kept the evening chill at bay. A pleasant mid-February had turned into a miserable and bitter March. Foul weather had hampered our progress, and I feared it might be months, rather than weeks, until I could again hold Gina in my arms.

"But what is the value of that yearning, if a people lack the facility to maintain and treasure their freedom?"

Days were spent tramping about the Boston Mountains, tracking down old survey markers — some dating back to the Louisiana Purchase survey of 1816 — and spiking new ones. Evenings were spent around the campfire or — if, like tonight, we were close enough — around the big fireplace of the Elkhorn Tavern, engaged in lively, usually friendly, debate.

"If a man has the desire," Evan Bornholm, the company's lead surveyor, insisted, "he must have the capacity to seek its fulfillment."

"But are all people equally endowed with

that desire?" Silas Ramsey pressed his point. The tracker was as dogged in his pursuit of an argument as he was in chasing down game. He took a bite of venison, and his brother Paul took up the point.

"Where would the Negro be without slavery? Still stalking about the African jungle, chanting to his gods, painting his face and hurling spears at his neighbors."

Mike Adams plunked away at a Jew's harp while Tom Halsey strummed his Kentucky banjo and shook his head — whether in time to the music or in dismay at the endless argument, I couldn't tell.

"Who's to say what is the right course and the natural growth of a people?" Nathanael Reiss chimed in, the artist's New England accent a stark contrast to the Ramseys' Carolina drawl.

"God is," Silas replied around a mouthful of cornbread. " 'And the son of Ham shall be a slave unto his brethren.' "

"That is a fable written three thousand years ago," Reiss objected.

"Are you saying God's word loses value with time?" Silas said.

"No," Reiss said with a shake of his head. "I'm saying the scriptures must be taken in the context of the times when they were written."

" 'The Lord hath sent me to preach deliverance to the captives,' " Bornholm joined in. "No context needed for that."

"Look," Paul Ramsey said, his hand raised to still further preaching, "I don't say that slavery is good or needful — our peculiar institution is just about dead, as it is. But I do say that sometimes good can come out of what some see as evil. Take Izzy, here." He gestured toward our end of the hearth circle.

"If it wasn't for generations of slaves, where would the boy be today? Probably traipsing around some infernal jungle, or dead with a spear in his gut."

Izzy looked up wide-eyed at that.

"I'm just saying, is all," Paul went on. "A good many Negroes are alive today that might otherwise not be. Maybe someday, once this country straightens herself out, they or their children can breathe free, have a chance to make something for themselves. And, good or bad, it's slavery will have made it possible for them."

Reiss opened his mouth to speak, but Tom struck a harsh note on his banjo and spoke up.

"I don't reckon we'll solve the world's troubles just tonight." With that, he stood, set his banjo in a corner and turned to Silas

Ramsey. "Brother Junior Warden, call the brethren from refreshment to labor."

Izzy and I looked at each other, then stood to follow the others as they headed for the tavern's stairs. Argos — who seemed to know better — merely looked up before resting his head on his paws again.

"Y'all stay put," Tom said, not unkindly. "We'll be back down in a while."

With that, he led the other men up the stairs, followed by Jesse Cox, the tavern keeper. A few men from other tables stood and followed up the stairs.

"Don't you boys mind them," Lucy Cox, Jesse's daughter-in-law, said to us as she picked up the plates and cups abandoned by the men. "They all got to go play at spooks or some such moonshine. You boys have some more cider." Lucy couldn't have been more than sixteen but she had a matronly air about her that belied her youth.

"Thank you, ma'am," I said as she refilled my mug.

"Thank you, ma'am," Izzy repeated, with much more depth of feeling.

It was rare enough for a slave to be allowed in a tavern, let alone be waited on, but the Coxes cared little about convention. Lucy refilled Izzy's cup and went back to cleaning up the place while Izzy and I settled on the floor in front of the hearth.

"What you think she meant about them playing at spooks?" Izzy wondered aloud.

"I don't know," I admitted.

Through the rough wooden planks, I could hear footsteps slowly pace about the floor above, first one way around, then the other. Voices rumbled through the floorboards, alone or in unison, but I couldn't make out the words. Every once in a while, Jesse would pace across the upstairs landing, a white apron tied around his waist and an old sword in his hands.

"What you think they doing?" Izzy persisted.

"I don't know," I repeated, then drained my cider, rolled out my bedroll and lay down. I ignored Izzy's whispered questions and pretended to sleep, while I strained my ears to make some sense of the noises above.

I'd drifted off by the time the men came back down the stairs, but their muted conversation and good-natured laughter — even between the cantankerous Yankee and the stubborn Ramseys — roused me. Men traded handshakes and arm clasps before going their separate ways — some out the door for home, others to their own bedrolls scattered about the tavern floor.

"Got a minute, Tom?"

"Sure," he said. "Pull up a rock."

Our crew was surveying the course of Logan Creek a few miles south of Osage Springs. I sat on a small boulder next to the rodman and stayed quiet for a spell, just listening to the babble of the creek, fat with snowmelt.

"I don't mean to be a snoop," I finally said, "but what is it y'all do upstairs at the tavern?"

"Oh, we're just seeing to the work," he said, and tossed a pebble into a pool at the side of the bank. The ripples spread out until they were caught in the flow of the creek and whisked downstream.

"Well, shouldn't I be a part of it?" I asked. "I mean, I'm a member of the crew, and all. Mister Bornholm says I'll be ready to lead a crew of my own after this job. Just seems to me that if there's work to be done, I ought to be part of it."

Tom wrinkled his crooked nose and grinned a little. "It's a different kind of work we're doing, Jim."

"Work other than surveying?"

"Oh, for certain. You might say we're

building something," he offered, as though that would clear up the matter.

"Building what?"

Tom didn't answer right away. Instead, he tossed another pebble into the creek, then another.

"A better place," he said after the third pebble went in the drink.

"A better place? You mean you're fixing up the Coxes'?"

He laughed at that.

"No. I mean a better world." I stared at him blankly, and he went on. "The work we do is on ourselves, trying to improve ourselves, make us better men. This country's getting itself into a pickle, for as good as we started out. And, if things is gonna improve any, it's men like us — you and me and the rest of these fellas — that's gonna make it happen. Oh, I ain't fool enough to think a little survey crew out in the middle of nowhere is enough to make much difference. But every man who can better himself, well . . . It's like those ripples there."

He tossed in another pebble.

"Everything we do sets up a ripple around us," he said. "Those ripples spread out and out, until they're caught up in the big stream of life. Now, it might look like the ripples disappear once they're out there in

173

the stream, but who knows but it don't change the whole creek somehow?"

I nodded at that. I wasn't exactly sure what he was talking about, but I nodded all the same.

"There's truths that wise men have known about since the beginning of time," he went on. "How to act toward one another, how to deal with your neighbor. Most folks would agree things like the Golden Rule are good and worthy things. In the day-to-day, though, it's awful easy to ignore truths like that, to just do what seems good for yourself, and hang the other fella. When we do our work, we try to remind ourselves there's more to this world than what's in it for ourselves, that we have a duty to each other and to God to do what little bit we can to make it a better place."

I sat quietly and thought about that for a spell.

"Sounds reasonable enough," I allowed, then tossed a pebble of my own into the pool. "Is there some way I can help out with that? Be part of the work, I mean."

Tom smiled, but said nothing. Instead, he just pushed himself to his feet, patted me three times on the shoulder and wandered back up the creek toward camp.

The next few weeks had me on pins and needles. Tom never mentioned the work to me again, and I feared to ask him about it, lest I jinx my chances of being part of it. One evening, while I helped Paul Ramsey dress a deer he'd brought down, I raised the subject. He just grinned, patted me a couple of times on the shoulder and hauled the take back to camp.

A few days later, I tracked down Nathanael Reiss while he drew with chalk in his thick sketchbook. His eyes never left the scene — a family of beaver repairing their lodge in the flood waters. He just nodded and grunted while I spoke. When I asked if he'd speak on my behalf about joining in the work, he finally looked at me, folded up his sketchbook, clapped me on the shoulder and walked away.

"I don't understand it, Izzy," I complained one night, after the others had left us to go to the tavern. "Tom seemed like he was inviting me to join them when he described the work to me. Since then, he hasn't mentioned it once. None of them has."

Argos grunted and tucked his head under my hand, as though to remind me of the more important things in life.

"Well," Izzy said as he chewed on a thick blade of grass, "maybe they just trying to see how bad you want it."

Weather forced us back to the Elkhorn Tavern a few days later. By now, all the talk was of the new president, Lincoln, up in Washington, and Jeff Davis, who'd been named president of the Confederacy until elections could be held. Again, Tom and Mike played their instruments, and again the argument between North and South grew heated.

As the debate reached a fever pitch, Tom strummed his sour note and directed Silas to call the men to labor. The crew trundled up the stairs, followed by a leavening of others, and Izzy and I settled onto the floor with fresh cups of cider.

"Jim."

I looked up to where Tom stood at the top of the stairs.

"You coming or not?"

The days that followed were like a rebirth for me. My initiation as a Free and Accepted Mason gave me a new outlook and perspective on things. The world was still the same, the political troubles unchanged, yet this Work — which had for generations been a beacon of goodness — offered a glimmer of hope for a better world, a renewal of humanity. On a more personal level, whereas I'd been without a family before, I now had a whole host of men that I could call brothers.

The only cloud over it all was the fact that Izzy couldn't be part of it. Among the requirements for initiation was being free-born and, while I'd long since given Izzy his freedom, it came about sixteen years too late.

"Don't you worry none about that, Jade," he told me, when I explained things to him. "I done already got me family enough. Don't see no need for a passel more."

In the days after my initiation, each man of the crew spent time to help me absorb the lessons I'd been given. By the end of March, we were back at the tavern, where I was passed to the next degree. Two weeks later, I was ready to receive the third degree.

It was a miserable Friday evening when we set out again for Elkhorn Tavern. A storm blew up just as we were ready to leave camp, and Izzy insisted on staying behind to keep an eye on things, despite the weather. Leaving him and Argos in the company tent, the rest of us set out on Telegraph Road toward the tavern.

By the time we arrived, the other men were already milling about upstairs. Tom and the rest of the crew hustled to open the Masonic lodge, while Reiss led me up the outer stairs to a small changing room to prepare. As in the previous two ceremonies, all my possessions were taken from me, my clothes arrayed just so, a blindfold placed over my eyes and a thick rope tied about me. At the proper time, a knock sounded on the door, words were exchanged and I was led into the lodge room.

The ceremony itself followed the same form as the previous two, and after I took the obligation, I was asked what I most desired.

"Further light in Masonry," I repeated Reiss's prompting.

The blindfold was removed. I blinked as my eyes adjusted to the bright candlelight, then gaped as I saw the faces gathered around me.

Standing among the crew and the other regulars were Doc Aubry, Uncle Cy, Sam Rawls and Mister Barnes. The blood rushed to my face as I realized the import of my oath, *I will not have illegal carnal intercourse with a master mason's daughter . . .*

If Barnes noticed my discomfort, he didn't show it. He just smiled broadly and gave me a friendly wink. After a moment, Tom — acting as worshipful master — presented me with the passwords, signs and implements of a master mason. Lastly, he gave me a white lambskin apron, similar to the ones worn by all the others.

The ceremony continued, and the origins of the Craft were presented to me in frightening drama. Finally, Mister Barnes took the master's chair to deliver the historical lecture — and the true horror began.

Shouts rose from the tavern room below, and a knock sounded at the door. Men looked at one another in confusion, but I couldn't tell if the reactions were genuine or a continuation of the ceremony.

"An alarm at the door," Paul Ramsey stammered.

Mister Barnes nodded hesitantly, and I gathered this was not part of the program.

"Brother Junior Deacon, see to the alarm," Barnes said.

Paul moved to the door and opened it, exchanged a few words with Jesse Cox, then closed the door and approached the master's chair. The blood drained from Mister Barnes's face as Paul relayed the message to him.

"Brethren," Barnes started, and his voice cracked. "We must close this lodge, trusting the complete instruction of our newest brother until a later time."

"Worshipful," Tom Halsey said, making his sign of respect as he rose to his feet. "What is it?"

Barnes looked slowly around the room. He paused as he met each pair of eyes, and his pained expression deepened all the more as he looked at the younger men.

"War."

"C'mon, Orion," I shouted, and slapped the horse's flanks.

We tore along the muddy Telegraph Road toward camp. Word had quickly spread of the Confederate attack on Union-held Fort Sumter. Already, rumors were flying. Jeff Davis and Abe Lincoln had both been assassinated. Little Rock was in Federal hands. Unionists were burning out the border farms.

I'd said a quick good-bye to Rawls and Uncle Cy, and promised to catch up to Mister Barnes. But, first, I had to get back to Izzy and Argos, gather our things, and take leave of the survey crew.

The rain had turned to sleet, and lashed at my face as Orion raced along. At last, we reached the camp and I swung down from the saddle before the horse came to a halt.

"Izzy? Argos?" I whistled, but there was no response.

Hooves pounded behind me. I yanked my rifle from the saddle holster and spun toward the newcomers.

"Easy, Jim." I recognized Tom's voice and lowered the rifle. "You see anything?"

"No," I answered, and continued to look around.

The rain had drowned the fire, and the heavy clouds threw a cloak over the night sky. I called out again and felt my way around the camp. I tripped over something and sprawled headlong into the mud.

"Jim?" Tom had managed to light a pair of lanterns and came toward me.

In the dim glow I saw a heap of fur, white with blue-black flecks. I scrambled to my knees and groped my way toward the pile. Argos lay in the deepening mud, his eyes open and teeth bared. I reached out a trembling hand to stroke the matted fur, and found his body stiff and cold. The white flash on his chest was marred by an ugly black wound.

"Come away, Jim," Tom said softly.

I clutched at Argos's fur and buried my face in his neck, but Tom tugged gently at my shoulders and pulled me away.

"Let him be, boy," he said.

I let Tom help me to my feet, and wiped my face on my sleeve.

"Izzy?" I asked.

Tom shook his head. "Nothing."

He handed me a lantern, and we searched the camp as the other crew members showed up. More lanterns were gathered, and the scene slowly came to light.

Hoof prints — more than our crew could have made — littered the area around the camp. Several tents were collapsed and trampled into the mud, and supplies and tools were scattered about the site.

"Over here," Silas called to us from a small stand of trees at one end of the camp.

A knife stuck out from one of the slender trunks, stabbed through what, at first, appeared to be a swath of flesh. On closer inspection, it turned out to be just a piece of butcher's paper.

"Abolitionists," Reiss observed.

In the lantern glow, the outline of a kneeling slave could be seen, his broken shackles scattered around him.

"I thought abolitionists acted out of principle," I said stoically.

"They do," Bornholm replied. "Most of them, anyway."

"Then tell me," I said, "where's the principle in killing a man's dog, in kidnapping his friend?"

"We don't know Izzy's been kidnapped," Bornholm replied.

"Murdered, then," I shouted. "I tell you now, there is no way in hell Izzy would have let this happen. He's either dead or taken, and I'll see that those who did this are made to pay."

"Jim, you can't —"

"Can't what?" I demanded. "Can't find the ones who did this? Can't bring Izzy back? Bring Argos back?" I looked around at the gathered crew, their faces spectral in the lanterns' glow. "Maybe not. But I'll return in blood what they've done here. This war's not about principle. It ain't about what's right or wrong. It's about men using force to get their way, consequences be damned. And, if that's all it is, then I'll help myself to it."

I knelt by Argos, closed his eyes and ruffled his fur.

"I got no truck for slavers or abolitionists," I said, as though I might make him understand. "I'd have been just as happy to let it all alone, let them that cared duke it out, so long as I could live in peace. But they've come to me, now. They've made this a war and, so help me God, I will take the war back to them."

I rose and slogged through the mud to where Orion stood impatiently stamping at the ground. I grabbed the saddle horn and was about to heft myself up when Tom called out, "Almighty God, Supreme Architect of the Universe."

I stopped, turned and lowered my head.

"You know the heart and mind of each man here," Tom prayed. "May your blessing be upon each one, taking him safely upon whatever path he may choose. Let the days of this conflict be short, oh God, and the losses few. May the blessings of freedom and liberty be granted to all men, and may peace and harmony prevail."

He set his hat back on his head, his eyes glistening in the scattered lantern light.

"And, now, brethren," he said, "be ye all of one mind, live in peace . . ."

His voice broke, and he seemed unable to continue. I stepped over to the burly man and placed my hand on his shoulder. He looked me in the eye, gripped me by the back of the neck, and pulled my forehead to his. I sniffed and cleared my throat so as to finish the benediction.

"And may the God of love and peace delight to dwell with and bless you."

And God help whoever stands in the way of me and mine, I didn't add.

■ ■ ■ ■

I rode back to the Elkhorn Tavern after burying Argos and saying good-bye to the crew. Mister Barnes had waited for me, and we rode back toward Britton together. For three days we traveled the road that had become so familiar to me during the survey, but it seemed alien now, as though the entire landscape had changed under the shadow of war.

Twice we had to lead the horses into the thick brush at the side of the road. Bands of riders — perhaps the same ones who had raided the survey camp — patrolled the Telegraph Road. Their exposed rifles and masked faces were warning enough for us to stay out of their way.

On the third morning, we forded Frog Bayou. We had talked easily enough during the ride, but the words of my oath weighed heavily on me, and I had tried to keep the conversation directed away from anything to do with Gina. Now, just a few miles from the farm, where I expected Gina would be waiting for us, I could avoid the subject no longer.

"Mister Barnes," I began, after clearing my throat.

"You have my blessing, JD," he said before I could continue.

"Sir?"

"You have my blessing. Angelina's a lovely young woman, and a father couldn't ask for a better man for his daughter than you." He threw me a crooked smile. "But I expect you to make an honest woman of her, Brother."

My ears buzzed as the blood rushed to my head. I could hardly believe what I'd just heard. Gina could be mine. We could be together, for all the world to see.

"Thank you, sir," was all I could manage.

Barnes laughed and kicked his horse into a trot. I followed suit, more eager than ever to see Gina, to hold her, to come home.

It wasn't long before we left the rolling foothills and crossed May's Branch, Barnes's northern property line. As we emerged from the trees that bordered the stream, we could see grey pillars rising through the morning haze. The columns of smoke were more than could come from the kitchen or forge.

"God, no," I whispered, then spurred Orion into a gallop.

The poor beast dug his hooves into the sod and tore across the fields. I clung to the saddle and whipped his flanks with my reins, heedless of the sprouts of wheat and corn laid to ruin in our wake.

We broke out of the fields and into the barnyard. I steered Orion around the remains of the barn, where the rebuilt corn-crib was again a smoking heap and half the barn was caved in on itself. The house seemed untouched, but the forge, tool shed and slaves' bunkhouse were blackened, skeletal ruins.

A rifle shot split the thick morning air and an explosion of dirt erupted a yard or two in front of Orion's charging hooves. He reared and threw me, then ran up the clamshell drive, away from the destruction. I landed facedown, and raised myself up as I tried to get my breath back. I looked around to find cover, and only then noticed the bodies scattered about the yard.

Two men lay not far from me, one with a bandana still fastened over his nose and mouth. A torch lay just beyond his reach, while the other man's cold, dead hands clutched a shotgun. Their faces were turned toward each other, and they exchanged shocked expressions through sightless eyes.

As I rose to my knees, I could see other bodies. Bull's unmistakable bulk lay crumpled at the doorway of the burned-out bunkhouse, his arms scorched and raw where they had landed in the fire. Across the threshold, three pairs of grisly arms reached out from the ashes for a salvation that could not come.

"Jim."

The voice cried out from the direction of the house, and I heard the screech and slam of the kitchen door and the muffled tramp of hurried footsteps. I just got to my feet before Gina threw herself into my arms. I managed to keep my balance, then squeezed her tightly and covered her face with kisses.

"Guess it's a good thing I missed," another voice said.

Matt strode toward us, a rifle tucked under his left arm, his right still in a sling. I released Gina and turned to Matt. Mindful of the wracked shoulder, I threw my arms around him.

"I'm glad to see you," I said.

He stood rigid for a moment before I felt the tension and years of resentment slip away. He let the rifle slip to the ground, wrapped his good arm around me and returned the embrace.

"Good to see you, too," he said. "How's the nose?"

Before I could answer, Mister Barnes rode into the yard, and Missus Barnes and Belle came out from the kitchen. After Gina embraced her father, I moved to her side, took her hand and wrapped an arm around her waist.

The family gathered around Belle, and we loved on her and whispered words of comfort. I didn't know what help words would be to this woman whose world had been shattered. But the world had changed for all of us. As I held Gina's hand and embraced her family — our family now — I couldn't help but think, somehow, the change was for the better.

CHAPTER SEVEN

Benton County, Arkansas — March 1862

I stood by the fire with my men, our hands held over the flames in a vain attempt to warm ourselves. The fire was one of many that stretched for a mile around Camp Stephens on the south bank of Little Sugar Creek.

For days the Army of the West had been on the march from Van Buren, battling snow and cold and exhaustion. The rugged slopes and shoddy roads of the Boston Mountains seemed to have allied with the Union snipers and skirmishers who harassed us at every turn. After thirty hours of forced march out of Bentonville, the army was now drawn up across from the Federals, whose fires could be seen along the wooded slopes across the creek.

The three-day rations passed out at Van Buren had mostly run out before leaving Bentonville, and the men of my battery were hungry and tired. I gave them a few moments at the fire to feel human again before ordering them to unhitch the horses from the caissons and wagons. I then had them see what food they could scrounge together while I took a pot down to the creek to fetch some water.

"Careful you don't fall in," a familiar voice said from behind. "You're not like to thaw out till high summer."

"I figured you'd be coming around to finally admit I'm the better rider," I said as I rose and turned. "What with hell about to freeze over and all."

"It ain't quite cold enough for that just yet." Matt swung a leg over Pegasus's back and dropped to the ground, came over and pulled me into a warm hug.

"You don't look too much the worse for wear," I judged as I held him at arm's length and examined his grey, wool uniform.

The cavalry troops at the front and rear of the army had taken the worst of the skirmishing on the march, and I'd lost count of the fallen horses by the roadside.

"Not too bad, I suppose," Matt allowed, "but I almost prefer the open field to what we've had to deal with today. It's a damn sight easier on the nerves when you know where the shooting's coming from. We almost had them at Elk Springs this morning, but the Yankees are better at running than we are at chasing, I guess."

I took Pegasus's reins and rubbed his black muzzle, then led him and Matt up the slope. I set the water over the fire and my men added what scraps of root, twigs and leaves they'd been able to find.

"Shouldn't you be with your troop, ravaging poor young maidens?" I asked Matt. "That is what you rough riders do, isn't it?"

He grinned and tilted his hat roguishly.

"Only on Wednesdays and Saturdays," he said. "Today, I had more important things to do, like keeping you out of trouble. Or getting you into it, maybe," he added, and reached into his jacket.

"What's this," I asked when he handed me a folded, sealed parchment.

"Your new orders."

I broke open the seal, tossed the small bit of wax and string into the fire, then opened the message.

Be it known by these presents that James D. Robbins, formerly of Rivers' Battery, Light Artillery, of the Arkansas State Guard, is Hereby relieved of Duty Therewith, and is assigned to the 1st Battery, Missouri Light Artillery, Army of the West, and is Granted the Commission of 1st Lieutenant, CSA, with all the Duties and Privileges appertaining Thereto. Given under my hand this 6th day of March, Eighteen hundred and Sixty-two. [signed] Earl van Dorn, Maj-General, Commanding.

"What is this?" I said as I looked up at Matt.

"Just what it says. Word came down that they were looking for some men who know the land around here. I told Rock I just happened to be acquainted with an artillery gunner who knows every square inch of this county."

"Rock?" I asked.

"Captain Champion, my company commander," Matt said. "Hell of a horseman — maybe even better than me, and with stones like you wouldn't believe."

I grinned at that. Since he'd left the Arkansas Militia to join the Missouri State Guard, Matt had learned to swear like a real soldier.

"I look forward to meeting him sometime," I said.

"Well, that'd be right soon," Matt said. "You're to make your arrangements and come with me."

"What, now?"

"Now."

"But I'm only just starting to thaw out," I said.

"Well, get ready to freeze up again, then, because you're to come back with me right now. Besides," he added in a low voice, "you'd only have another hour or so of warmth anyway."

"How's that? I thought we were camped for the night."

"That's what they think, too," he said, nodding his head toward the fires on the north side of the creek.

I opened my mouth to protest again, but thought better of it. I shook the hands of my confused men and collected my kit.

"I'll saddle Orion for you," Matt offered as I walked over to the fire where Captain Rivers huddled with his gun crew.

"Orders, sir," I greeted him, and gave him the parchment.

"How in God's name do they expect me to field my guns without any lieutenants?" he asked the night sky when he finished reading. "Sorry, Jim. I should be offering you congratulations. It's a fine opportunity for you. Good luck," he said, and offered his hand. "Shea," he shouted for his sergeant, then set about reorganizing his battery.

Matt rode up to me with Orion in tow, and I swung into the saddle and fell in behind. We threaded our way past flickering fires and shivering men who huddled in grey frozenness. At last we reached the headquarters tents, where I met Captain Henry Guibor of the Missouri First Artillery, whose battery I'd be joining.

"By the way, how's your gunnery, Lieutenant?" he asked after the pleasantries had been exchanged.

"Fair enough, I reckon," I said.

"Fair, hmm? Jim Stewart swears you're the best gunner he's ever seen — says you can just about will the shot on target."

"Captain Stewart's very kind, sir. I had the fortune of a good instructor. And I daresay the real thing's bound to be different than the range."

"You've not seen combat yet, then?" he said.

"No, sir," I admitted.

"Well, by this time tomorrow, I'd wager that will have changed."

"Yes, sir."

Guibor led me to where his battery was camped, toward the rear of the army, near a ford across the creek. He introduced me to the other officers and senior enlisted men, then gave the order to break camp and make ready to move out. There were a few grumbled protests, but the men set smartly about their orders. With orchestrated precision, horses were harnessed, guns limbered and the battery made ready to set out.

"Stay that shovel, Private," Guibor ordered as one of his men was about to douse his fire with a load of snow.

"Sir?"

"We wouldn't want our friends thinking we've skipped out on them, now would we?"

The young soldier's eyes slowly registered understanding. He lowered his shovel and, with a decidedly unwarriorlike giggle, ran off to join his comrades.

"Too clever by half," Guibor muttered.

"How's that, sir?" I asked.

"Call me Hank. And it's this plan of McCulloch's," he said of Brigadier General Benjamin McCulloch, one of the army's division commanders. "It's not at all a bad idea to try flanking the Federals, come up behind them while they're watching for us to charge across the creek. But it'll take more than a string of empty fires to make Billy Yank think we're sitting tight."

I thought about that as I scanned the fires on our side of the Little Sugar Creek. I looked across the water, and the flicker of Union campfires appeared to be mere candle flames against the dark canopy of night.

"More light." I hadn't meant to say the words aloud.

"What's that?" Hank asked.

I blinked away the fire glare from my eyes, then turned to the captain.

"I have an idea, sir."

I stood in the front of the rowboat, and wondered what I'd gotten myself into. In spite of the bitter coldness of the night, a trickle of sweat ran down my spine. Three other men had joined me — two captains rowed while a major steered the boat against the current as we crossed to the northern shore. I braced myself against the prow of the boat, a white flag gripped in my hand. Whether the position of honor was mine because the crossing had been my idea, or because I was the most expendable, I couldn't be sure.

A shout came from the shore as we neared, followed soon by the *clack* of rifles being cocked.

"Who goes there?" a voice called out.

My throat went suddenly dry, but I managed to answer, "Four widows' sons."

197

There was a confused pause, followed by a barked order and a scramble in the underbrush.

"Show me your hands," the voice shouted to us, and I quickly obeyed. "Keep 'em up," he demanded as I brought my hands down to my sides, and I raised them once more.

"I said, keep 'em up," the voice repeated as I made the gesture a second time. I could almost feel the poke of the barrel aimed at my chest and the pressure on the trigger that could any moment send a lead ball into my heart. Nevertheless, I raised and lowered my hands a third time. "God damn you, Reb', I told you to —"

"Stand down, Sergeant," a second voice called, then, "Come ashore."

"Steady on, men," Major Chilton ordered, and the captains pulled again at their oars. A few strokes later, we ground ashore and I leapt over the side to steady the boat while the others climbed out.

In moments, we were surrounded by blue-jacketed riflemen who glared menacingly at us.

"You men lost?" one man asked as he squeezed through the ring of soldiers. His shoulder markings identified him as an infantry captain.

"Must be," Major Chilton answered for

198

us. "We were traveling from west to east."

The captain stepped toward us and, one by one, clasped our hands and gave each of us a brotherly hug. When he reached me, we shared an embrace and, cheek to cheek, exchanged the Masonic word of recognition.

"Sergeant Coombs," the captain said after he had greeted us, "assign a detachment to secure this boat, then resume your post."

"Yes, sir," the burly man grunted. "And what about them, sir?"

"These men are under my charge," the captain said. "I'll see to their disposition."

"Yes, sir," Coombs replied, and turned to bark orders at his men.

"Gentlemen," the captain gave a slight bow, then gestured for us to follow him. He led us up the bank and, once we were out of earshot of the troops, said, "I suppose you brethren have a good reason for stirring up my men."

"It's my doing, Captain . . . ?"

"Holmon," he answered me. "Jesse Holmon, S Company, Eighteenth Indiana."

"Pleasure to know you, Captain," I said. "I was raised up at the Elkhorn Tavern just last year. Haven't been back this way since — well, since the troubles started. It struck me, though, that this being a Thursday there might be some brethren gathered there tonight." I took on a sheepish expression, and it wasn't just playacting. "I reckon I'll see my first combat come daylight. If this is to be my last night, I wanted to spend it among the brethren."

The words sounded contrived as they came out of my mouth, but Holmon looked at me grimly and nodded. Even Chilton and the two captains — combat veterans all — looked solemn, as though I'd struck on some deep truth.

"I don't suppose you're alone in that," Holmon assured me. "As a matter of fact, I was just getting ready to head up to the tavern myself. We'll have missed the master's table, but you'll be more than welcome for lodge."

We followed Captain Holmon up the road, past the curious looks of Union soldiers and officers. Aside from the blue uniforms, the enemy looked much like my own men, albeit better fed. The younger ones, in particular, shared the same look of innocence, bravado and fear I'd seen on countless faces during the march from Van Buren.

At length, we reached the tavern that had been a second home to me only a year before. The place where I'd learned of peace and brotherly love was now wrapped in a martial shroud. The building itself was little changed, but the big yard surrounding it was filled with campaign tents, supply wagons and pickets of horses. Men huddled in cloaks and blankets around blazing fires, and stamped their feet against the cold. I sank deeper into my woolen tunic and thought of my freezing men, two to a blanket, who by now had left their fires and should be fording the creek farther upstream.

"Jim?"

I heard the voice as we crossed the threshold of the tavern, and Lucy Cox ran to me and threw her arms around my neck, her pregnant belly pressed hard against me.

"I'll be damned," her husband, Joseph, swore as he crossed to me and held out his hand.

"How you doing, boy?" I asked as I took his hand and pulled him into an embrace.

"Well enough, I suppose. Pap's been stuck in Kansas since the war started, but Lucy and me, Ma and the little ones is doing fine." Joseph looked at me curiously, and for the first time seemed to notice the opposing uniforms in the room. "Jim, is everything all right?"

"Everything's fine," I assured him, then

put an arm around his shoulder and led him toward the fireplace at one end of the tavern. "Now you listen up, boy," I whispered. "Fighting's likely to start around daybreak. After we leave tonight, I want you to take Lucy and your Ma, Eli and Frank down to the cellar, and you stay there till the shooting stops tomorrow. Understand?"

The young man nodded and I clapped his shoulder, then followed the other officers up the narrow stairs.

A Union lieutenant stood as Tyler, guardian of the inner door of the lodge, and gaped at me and the others as we reached the upper landing.

"I vouch for these men, Brother Tyler," Holmon assured him.

The young officer nodded and indicated a table adjacent to the door. No weapons were permitted in the lodge, so I unstrapped my belt and laid my pistol and short artilleryman's sword on the table, alongside Union sabers and revolvers. A long rifle leaned against one wall, and I took a moment to admire the decorations on the barrel and the intricate carving on the stock before putting on my apron and following the others into the lodge room.

The room was arranged just as I had last seen it, but the aprons worn by the men couldn't disguise the uniforms underneath. More startled looks greeted Chilton and the captains and me, but the man wearing the master's jewel — a stylized set square hung from a thick collar about his neck — came over to greet us.

"Welcome, brethren," he offered as he extended his hand to Chilton and the rest of us.

The man was thickset and solid, his square jaw masked by a heavy, dark beard. His eyes glittered with confidence and good humor, but there was a steeliness there that spoke of cunning and strength. The eagle on his shoulder boards suggested he used all of those traits to good effect.

"Grenville Dodge," he introduced himself as he shook my hand.

"Worshipful," I greeted him, military rank and protocol replaced by the customs of the Craft.

"JB Hickok," another man introduced himself.

He wore a level on his collar and had long, blond hair that framed an elegant, almost feminine, face. The lone man out of uniform, his fur-trimmed deerskin identified him as a tracker and scout.

"Best mind our senior warden," Colonel Dodge advised. "He's a wild one."

"Yes, sir," I acknowledged as I shook a strong, calloused hand.

After a handful of other introductions, Dodge set a top hat on his head — a strange finish to his uniform — then picked up his gavel and said, "Brethren will be properly clothed and in order. Officers repair to their stations for the purpose of opening."

The officers took their places, while the remaining brothers found seats around the perimeter of the lodge room. Flickering candles and familiar words almost made me forget that the men seated around me were enemies, that on the morrow we might well face one another across a smoke-covered field. I settled into the comfortable ritual of the lodge, gave the signs and words of a Mason, listened to the invocation of the Supreme Architect of the Universe and the master's words of wisdom.

"May the blessing of heaven rest upon us and all regular Masons," Dodge prayed as he brought the meeting to a close. "May brotherly love prevail, and every moral and social virtue cement us." At the close of the prayer, he set his hat back on his head and looked solemnly around the assembled men. "You are now about to quit this sacred retreat of friendship and virtue, to mix again with the world."

The words of peace and love stood in stark contrast to the martial uniforms of blue and grey. Hickok's sharp eyes glistened in the candle light, and the emotion there was a reflection of my own as the worshipful master — soon to be an enemy colonel again — informed him, "Brother Senior Warden, I now declare this lodge duly closed."

No one moved for several seconds. Officers — Union and Confederate — looked from one to another with eyes that spoke of sadness and regret. Finally, Colonel Dodge removed his hat and extended his hand to Major Chilton.

"Godspeed, Major," he said. "Gentlemen."

He shook each of our hands, and we filed past the other men, then followed Captain Holmon down the stairs.

"Mind what I told you," I said to Joseph Cox in parting, then joined the others for the walk back to the banks of Little Sugar Creek.

The rowboat was where we'd left it, and the Confederate fires burned brightly on the opposite shore. "Many thanks, Captain," Major Chilton said as the Union soldiers pushed the boat back into the current.

"My pleasure, sir," he said. "You gentlemen watch yourselves now, y'hear?"

We waved and began rowing back toward the southern bank. I heard one of Holmon's men mutter, "We'll see you boys in the morning," followed by a chorus of muffled laughter.

In that moment, I transformed from brother Mason back to Confederate artilleryman.

"Maybe so," I said under my breath, "but not where you think."

The next day dawned grey and cloudy as the sun struggled vainly to brighten a heavy winter sky. It had taken hours to reach my battery after crossing Little Sugar Creek. Even on horseback, my progress was hampered by the slow-moving stream of infantry, engineers, supply wagons, artillery and cavalry. Sixteen thousand men filled the Bentonville Detour, which was little more than a game track tucked between the steep slopes of Elkhorn Mountain and Gann Ridge.

If the press of bodies wasn't enough, the Federals had made matters worse for us by felling several dozen trees across the road. These had to be cleared before artillery and wagons could pass, and what had been planned as an eight-hour march was now pushing twelve.

The one bit of good news was that the Union troops were still facing south toward Little Sugar Creek, our unmanned campfires having held their interest through the cold night. Scouts reported a small reserve at Elkhorn Tavern, with a rearward picket posted near the tanner's yard at the Cassville Road. This force reportedly had six artillery pieces, but they were all pointed south, away from our advance.

As we watched now, a small detachment of infantrymen silently scaled the ridge.

"I hope they hurry," Lieutenant Willis — the oldest and fattest man in the battery — said as he puffed out his bright red cheeks. "I'm freezing my ass off."

"I'm sure they'll do their best to accommodate you, Lieutenant," Captain Guibor said evenly. "Ah, and there they've done it," he added as, without a shot having been fired, the all-clear signal was given. "Onward and upward, boys," he ordered, then urged his horse up the steep shoulder of the ridge.

Horses strained and leather harnesses creaked against the weight of cannon and wagons. Iron-banded wheels crunched through the snow, which clung to the rims and further hampered our progress. Men whipped at the horses and beat the snow from the wheels until we finally reached the empty summit, one hundred fifty feet above the road.

"Something's not right here," I muttered as I surveyed the ridge. "Captain?"

Hank nodded as he directed the setting of his guns.

"I noticed. There, and there," he indicated, pointing out the deep scars in the snow that told of the retreat of the enemy guns. "Lieutenant Willis."

The older man heaved his way through the snow, his nose and cheeks bright red with cold and exertion. Sweat ran down his face in spite of the freezing temperatures.

"Yes, sir?" he managed between huffs.

"Locate Captain Galloway and find out how it is that the enemy's guns are no longer here."

Willis looked blindly about.

"Guns, sir?"

"I was told our Northern friends had a half-dozen guns on this ridge," Guibor said, a crisp edge in his voice. "I want to know where they are."

"Yes, sir," Willis replied with a salute, even as the captain's question was answered.

Before Willis's hand could reach the brim of his kepi, head and cap disappeared in a puff of red. The gauntleted hand continued its upward motion and turned crimson in the fountain of blood that erupted from between gold-fringed epaulets. The portly body collapsed in an unceremonious heap, the dull *thump* of its falling masked by a thunderous boom that trailed behind the shot.

I stared in horror at the grisly scene, but only for a moment. A high-pitched whistle screamed past my face and the shockwave of another passing round threw me off my feet. I found myself staring up at low, grey clouds as a dull ache radiated from the base of my skull and a thousand bells pealed in my ears. I felt the roar of the cannon pulse through my body, but could hear nothing over the ringing in my head.

Sergeant Parks, my lead gunner, appeared over me, his mouth moving insensibly as he helped me up. I regained my feet, shook him off and gestured clumsily toward our guns. He nodded and turned back to the battery while I reeled and tried to regain my balance. I managed only a couple of steps toward the guns before the ground pitched sideways and I found myself once more in the damp snow.

Half my face lay buried in the snow, and I watched with one lazy eye as the men of my battery danced a deadly ballet about the guns, their motions drawn out in dream-like exaggeration. A corporal straddled the stock of his gun and squatted behind it as two men tugged it into alignment with the target. Two others fused a shell and rammed it into the mouth of the cannon. The corporal spun the elevating screw to dial in the trajectory of the shot, while another man jammed the primer into the breech of the gun and pulled the firing lanyard tight.

At the corporal's signal, the last man yanked on the lanyard. The gun lurched back on its carriage as smoke belched from the mouth of the cannon behind a tongue of fire. The sound was little more than a muted rumble, but the concussion pounded my body like a hammer and shook the branches of the tree above me. Clumps of snow fluttered to the ground around me like hundreds of fallen angels.

I pushed myself to my feet and staggered toward the caisson while the crew readied the next shot. I shook my head and the ringing in my ears faded little by little until — like emerging from a deep pool of water — my head instantly cleared, the ringing replaced by the sounds of battle. As I reached the ammunition wagon, though, my head was again filled with a high-pitched scream. I clapped my hands over my ears and shook my head to clear the noise, when hands grabbed my shoulders and pulled me roughly to the ground.

A shell exploded not ten yards away, obliterating my second gun crew and throwing up a cascade of shrapnel and dirt and gore.

"The lieutenant would do well to learn to duck when shells start whistling in," Parks suggested as he lifted his body off mine.

He slapped his kepi against his thigh and brushed bits of soldier and grit off his shoulder, then stretched out a hand to help me to my feet.

"Thank you, Sergeant," I said as I balanced myself on wobbly knees.

Rage and horror welled up inside me as I stared at the wreckage of the gun, where my men — or what remained of them — lay sprawled about and atop the artillery piece. I managed to swallow the horror, but gave in to the rage.

"Where in hell are those guns, Sergeant?"

"That a-way, I reckon," he said without irony, and spat a stream of tobacco juice from between the thick handlebars of his mustache.

"Well, then, find a glass or peel your eyes," I ordered. "Just find me something to shoot at. Corporal Davis," I yelled, and turned toward the young man at the breech of the cannon. "Davis," I shouted again when he didn't answer. I grabbed his shoulder and spun him around — then jumped back as his face turned toward me.

Half the young man's handsome features had been torn away by shell fragments. He staggered toward me, his good eye fixed on mine while the other threatened to fall from a fleshless socket. Fighting the urge to run, I wrapped my arms around the boy and eased him to the ground. I packed snow into the yawning wound — the pristine whiteness rapidly changing to a sickly red — then turned back to the gun.

"Got them, sir," Parks said as he ran back toward me from the lip of the ridge. "Down on the road, not three hundred yards out. They must be elevated," he suggested, meaning that the muzzles of the guns were angled above forty-five degrees. "Gonna take them longer to reload. If we shoot now, we might be able to catch them between rounds."

"Let's hop to it, then," I said. "Show me."

Following Parks's lead, two privates swiveled the gun carriage in the proper direction and planted the stock on the ground. I squatted behind the gun and aimed along the barrel. The sounds and horror of the battle faded away, replaced only by what I could see through the bore sight of the cannon. Equations of speed, arc and distance flashed through my head as the blood and fire were reduced to cold, rational mathematics. "Case shot," I ordered. "Three-quarter second fuse, load."

The men rammed powder and shell into the barrel and I spun the elevation screw until the gun was aimed below the horizon in a depressed-angle shot.

"Ready," I shouted when I was satisfied, then, "Fire," and the cannon lurched in its carriage, rolling back two feet behind the force of the explosion.

Less than a second later, a ball of fire and smoke erupted as the short fuse ignited the charge within the case shot. Secondary explosions plumed up from the target area, and the men cheered my first murder as they rolled the gun back into place. A second set of explosions thundered across the distance as another round — from one of Hank's guns — took out another cannon.

"Target," I ordered, and my voice sounded strangely muffled in my unprotected ears.

As though in answer, a puff of smoke blossomed from the tree line along the road, fifty yards beyond the pair of guns we'd just taken out. The target was hidden a second later when a geyser of dirt erupted harmlessly in front of us.

"Shell shot, one second fuse," I shouted. "Load — Fire."

We traded shots with the Union battery for an hour until, one by one, their guns fell silent. As the last echoes drifted down the slopes of the ridge, a different sound arose — that of scores of riders and hundreds of infantry cheering and charging up the opposite hill toward the Union position. Gouts of smoke rose from the trees and brush as the embedded infantry fired on our advancing cavalry.

"Limber up," Hank ordered as the report of a thousand rifles rolled over us. "Double team, on the quick. Canister, and lots of it."

The captain's men attached the gun to its caisson and hitched up two teams of horses. The rest of his crew collected what ammunition they could from their other gun while Hank mounted his horse.

"You heard the man," I told my surviving crew. "Let's get this smoke wagon rolling."

The men quickly had the gun ready to move. We salvaged the remaining ammunition from the disabled gun and piled it atop the caisson. I pulled myself into Orion's saddle as Sergeant Parks whipped his twelve horses into motion, and the other men scrambled to catch up with the perverse flaming chariot that carried them into the pit of hell.

We followed Hank's crew, on the heels of the infantry that scrambled behind the cavalry charge, down the steep grade and into the narrow hollow toward the road that led to the Elkhorn Tavern. We passed craters and the smoking ruins of men and guns. Heedless of the stench of war and death, we drove on, thirsty for blood and hungry for victory.

During the mad dash, Guibor lost three of his horses to enemy fire. One of my own was struck, and another broke a leg when it stepped in a hole. I slashed at the harnesses with my sword to release them before they could foul the whole team. Parks tried to steer the rig around the fallen beasts of both teams, but wasn't able to avoid them all. Men, crates and ammunition lurched skyward as the rear wheel of the caisson rolled over the haunch of a fallen horse.

The beast screamed in agony and craned its neck to bite at the wagon wheel. Parks whipped on the remaining horses while men scrambled to collect what canisters and shells they could, then chased after the limber. I drew in Orion's reins as I reached the crippled horse, its mouth foaming and eyes rolled back in its head. The animal dug at the ground with its forelegs as it tried to stand, but the shattered hip refused to co-operate. Orion nickered in sympathy as I drew my pistol and fired a single round into the other horse's brain.

I raced after the crews and reached them where the road widened by the tavern. We followed Hank off the road, through the lines of our infantry and into position in the field at the front of the clearing. As my men raced to set up the twelve-pounder, I scanned the snow-covered field. The fleeing Union troops had not run as far as I would have liked — scarcely to the other side of the Huntsville Road — before their officers rallied them and drew up the line of battle. Less than a hundred yards separated the two guns of our battery from the hundreds of enemy rifles.

"Grape shot," I heard Guibor yell, even as I ordered canister for my own gun.

Despite the exposed position and the nearness of the enemy, the men ran the drill with precision and speed. Within seconds of the order, Hank's gun spat out its deadly barrage, followed closely by mine.

The effects of the short-range battery fire were at once horrible and fascinating. The canister fire spent most of its energy on the front ranks of the infantry, peppering wide swaths of men with lead pellets, as from a giant shotgun. The grape shot, on the other hand, was more concentrated, but each of the twenty-seven iron balls carried enough momentum to punch through whatever it struck, felling columns of men two and three deep.

We continued to peck away at the infantry with our guns, driving them farther and farther back toward the tree line. It wasn't long, though, before the Union batteries managed to reorganize. With an unearthly roar, twenty guns unleashed their fire and a deadly hail of shot and shell rained down on us and our advancing infantry.

"Never mind their infantry," Hank shouted. "We've got to take out those guns."

"Sergeant Parks!" I shouted for the man to replace one of my fallen corporals and to help in turning the gun toward the tree line that sheltered the Union batteries.

I could only aim at the bursts of light that flashed out from the darkened trees. As the men settled into the drill, we managed a shot every ten seconds between the two guns, but these were answered every one or two seconds from the other side.

While we exchanged fire with the Federals, our infantry and cavalry secured the area around the tavern and continued to push back the Union forces. A troop of horse regrouped from a charge and found shelter behind a blacksmith's shop.

I caught a glimpse of Matt, his head held high and a feral grin on his face. The grin turned to something else. He mouthed something at me, but I couldn't hear him over the cannon fire. Captain Champion rode over to Matt, looked to where he pointed, then cupped his hands around his mouth.

"Guibor," he shouted, "they're flanking you."

"I know it — Fire," came Hank's reply, as he continued the assault without pause. "But I can't spare a gun to turn on them."

I ordered my men to fire again, then looked to see what was happening. A picket of bayonets — hundreds upon hundreds — poked and waved through the brush on our flank as the enemy infantry tried to encircle our position. Our troops were halfway across the field and pinned down by the Union cannon fire. We had to support them, but doing so was sure to be our undoing.

"I'll charge them," Champion said, his voice booming across the tavern yard. He wheeled his horse around to rally his men.

"Battalion, forward trot — march."

The horsemen emerged from behind the smithy, and my heart sank. Fewer than two dozen cavalrymen rode out against several hundred infantry. "Gallop — march," Champion ordered his men, not seeming to mind the odds. He drew his saber — the blade gleaming in the sunlight that finally broke through the clouds — and shouted in a lusty baritone, "Charge!"

Twenty riders drove in behind their leader's suicidal rush against an army some forty times larger. The horseman immediately behind Champion lost his hat, exposing an unruly mane of fiery red hair that could only belong to Matt. While Guibor and I continued to nibble away at the enemy batteries with our guns, the surging lines of Union infantry met and swallowed up Champion's riders, including one corporal who ran on foot after his horse was shot out from under him.

The rough riders' progress was measured by the glint of sabers, puffs of pistol fire and an occasional flash of red hair against a blue and grey backdrop. Oddly, there was little return rifle fire. The foot soldiers seemed too stunned by the bold charge. Sheer numbers, though, must soon outweigh the surprise.

"Sir?" I shouted at Hank.

"Do it," Guibor said.

"Sergeant Parks," I said, "wheel left. Double canister shot, load."

While the gun turned toward the rushing infantry, two loads of canister were rammed into the bore and I lowered the muzzle of the gun for the short-range shot.

"Fire! Reload."

With no more than fifty yards between us and the advancing enemy, the double-shot load had a horrible, lethal effect.

It might seem like a waste of ammunition, I remembered my artillery instructor's words about the tactic, *but if you're the one on the receiving end of it, it'll ruin your whole damn day.*

In proof of those words, thirty men fell instantly as a swarm of lead pellets tore a line of smoking black pockmarks in faces and uniforms. The blue wave continued to press forward, but the second round of fire heaped another rank of wounded in front of their lines.

By now, the whole enemy line was flagging — the right from the hell-spawned charge of Champion's riders, the left from the supporting fire of my gun. As I loosed a third round into the infantry, the Union colors fell. The fight drained out of the Yankees then and, as one, they turned and fled back to the sheltering woods.

Champion gave a short chase to speed them on their way, but quickly recalled his troopers. Matt wheeled around and raced back toward the tavern yard. He reined in Pegasus when he reached the Union colors and leapt down to pick up the banner, then raised it in his fist in a triumphant gesture.

Matt's body stiffened, and triumph turned to confusion. Across the body-littered field, he looked at me, then lowered his eyes to his chest. Still clutching the Union colors, he pulled open his tunic to expose the growing red stain in the center of his white muslin shirt.

"Sergeant, take the battery," I ordered, then rushed across the field before anyone could object.

Matt fell to his knees, and I reached him just as he was about to pitch forward into the trampled snow. I wrapped my arms around him and eased him to the ground.

Blood trickled from the corner of his mouth and a gurgling sound rose with each breath.

"See my watch gets home," he told me, then his eyes fixed on mine. "JD, I'm sorry I didn't tell you."

"What, that I'm the better rider?"

He laughed at that — or tried to, but managed only a wet cough, then curled up in pain. I cradled his head to my chest and pressed my hand uselessly against the wound.

"Whatever it was," I said, "you can tell me later, once we get you patched up."

He nodded, then shuddered in my arms. The color drained from his face and his eyes went wide as he stared up at me.

"When you find your dream, don't look back," he said in a dreamlike voice. "You just follow right after her, and damn the rest."

Before I could question the words, Matt took a deep, heaving breath. A sigh rattled from his throat, and his eyes fixed on a passing cloud as his body went slack in my arms.

CHAPTER EIGHT

Williamson County, Tennessee — December 1864

"Gentlemen, I give you *progress.*"

"Progress," the toast was answered, along with a few *Hear-hears*. Sherry glasses were raised amid the rustle of wool and the creak of stiff leather, but the replies were muted and there was no clinking of glasses. The horrors of the past few days gave little cause for celebration, save for the fact that the men gathered in the command tent were still among the living.

For the past month, the Army of Tennessee had been burrowing into that state — through snow and freezing rain — in a march toward Nashville and an effort to reclaim it for the Confederacy. Skirmishes had punctuated the march through winding passes, across bone-chilling streams, and through towns and burgs abandoned by the retreating Union Army. At last, the Federal troops had dug in at Franklin and formed an impenetrable bulwark around that city.

The last day of November had seen our troops throw themselves up against the Union defenses in a wasted effort. By nightfall, some six thousand troops — more than a fifth of our entire army — lay dead or wounded. As December dawned, we watched impotently from outside the city's defenses as the Union troops pulled back across the Harpeth River and up the Nashville Pike. We carried the wounded to makeshift hospitals in nearby homes, and buried the dead beneath the field of battle. Then the remnants of the Army of Tennessee regrouped and began our own crossing of the river.

The sole bright spot of the engagement had been the capture of a small supply train. Most of the wagons had been burned by the retreating Federals, but three cars were salvaged. These provided a fresh supply of rations for the troops, along with a few bottles of sherry, which were now being consumed by the officer corps. The toast was both a remembrance of those fallen and a charge for the battle yet to come.

"Nashville is the linchpin upon which the southwest theater hinges, gentlemen," Brigadier General James Smith solemnly declared after the toast. The new commander of Cleburne's Division looked drawn and haggard. Fighting near the center of the pitched battle, Cleburne's men had witnessed some of the fiercest combat. Of the six generals killed at Franklin, two — Brigadier General Hiram Granbury and Major General Patrick Cleburne himself — had come from our division.

"Our dead urge us forward," Smith continued, his voice wavering, "to victory and to vengeance. With the names of Cleburne and Granbury on our lips, our victory at Nashville shall be theirs, and their sacrifice in the cause of liberty shall not have been in vain."

Smith nodded to his adjutant, who dismissed the junior officers while the brigade and battalion commanders remained for further discussions. I ducked out through the tent flap, replaced my cap and hugged my collar close to my throat.

"Sergeant Newton." I summoned the man from among the cluster of aides huddled about a small fire. "Let's make ready."

"Yes, sir," he replied, then shook hands with his comrades and came to join me.

My belly was still warm from the wine, but the chill air quickly overcame the small measure of sherry. Newton and I rode back to where our battery was camped, past clusters of frozen, battle-weary men. I set my mind to the task of mobilizing my men for the coming march. The prospect of trudging another fifteen miles in freezing weather was not a welcome one, but it was far less disturbing than the ravages of the previous day.

We rejoined our men and set them to limbering the guns and harnessing the wagon teams. Two thirds of the army had crossed the river the day before, and we worked our way into the 8,000-man queue of Cheatham's Corps, across the Harpeth River on a pontoon bridge, then onto the Nashville Pike.

Despite the freezing cold — or maybe because of it — the march went at a brisk pace. The road was soon thawed by the traffic, the snow and dirt churned into an ugly slurry. Fresh footprints appeared every so often in the pristine snow at the side of the road, the tracks reddened by the bleeding feet of shoeless soldiers. But the men with raw, frostbitten feet were among the lucky ones — the less fortunate lay by the side of the road, abandoned by their comrades where they'd fallen.

As a boy, I'd read accounts of wars in the Bible and the Iliad, and in the histories of

Josephus and Caesar. I'd always envisioned the sprawling armies, their lines drawn up across vast, open expanses. In my naivete, the warriors always appeared magically on the field of battle or — if conventional travel couldn't be avoided — they crossed barren wildernesses or vast oceans far beyond the normal haunts of men. Even when cities were clearly involved, my mind pictured only high stone walls, never the people within. The carnage of war, I'd thought, was something always held at a distance from civilization.

Not so, this.

This war raged in the fields and yards — and sometimes on the porches — of the men who fought in it. That fact was driven home as a door burst open and a woman rushed out to wave at the passing ranks. The home was a ramshackle cottage that looked as if the slightest breeze could bring it crashing down. Its walls and roof seemed held up by nothing more than hope. The woman — little more than a girl, really — looked as thin as the weathered siding and stood barefoot in the snow with one babe in arms and a towheaded, gunny-sacked toddler by the hand. The young mother pointed out her man to the children, and the baby squalled while the toddler buried his face in his mother's skirts.

The shack was tucked up among the trees, and came in and out of sight as I passed by. An old walnut tree blocked my view for a bit and, when the family reappeared, my heart froze as a ghoulish trio of specters stood in their place.

The girl now stood in filthy rags that failed to hide her nakedness. Her delicate features and straw-colored hair were now replaced by those of a sunken-cheeked horror, with wispy strands of parched hair tangled about a withered face. The infant clung to her bosom, its skeletal form wriggling madly as it suckled at a shrunken, empty breast. The toddler stood naked with browned parchment-like skin stretched tight over a bony frame and distended belly. The death-masked child stretched a blackened, bony finger straight at me as it fixed me with its hollow eyes.

I gasped and yanked hard at Orion's reins.

"Captain?" Newton said, an edge in his voice as he reached for his sidearm.

"Do you see that?" I rasped, pointing at the hellish trio who were again hidden by the trees.

"That I do," he replied. "A pretty little family."

I blinked hard as the young mother and

little ones reappeared from behind the trees, restored to human form. The toddler now dared to peek out and waved a chubby hand at his father.

My heart started beating again and I chanced a shuddering breath. The cool air jarred me back to full wakefulness and I ran a gloved hand over my face, adjusted myself in the saddle and tried to ignore Newton's curious stare.

"Mm-hmm," I grunted, then kicked at Orion's ribs to spur him beyond the horror, not knowing that more lay ahead.

The Army of Tennessee camped outside the gates of Nashville for nearly two weeks. The bitter cold and a heavy ice storm combined to keep both sides hunkered down. Cheatham's Corps was embedded on the extreme right, less than a mile from the Union stronghold at Fort Negley. Twice during that time, the entrenched Federals ventured out from their fortifications to drive back our right flank. Twice, our guns and infantry sent them scurrying back for cover.

My battery was positioned near the center of Cheatham's Corps, on the rise of Ridley's Hill near the Nolensville Road. The elevation gave a clear view and a broad sweep for artillery fire. It was from this height on the morning of the fifteenth that I scanned the enemy lines through my field glass.

"Lieutenant Hopwood," I said softly, my eye still on the glass.

"Sir?"

"Send word to Colonel Hotchkiss, please."

"Word about what, sir?" The last syllable stuck in his throat as he looked toward the Federal position. Even through the light morning fog, and without the aid of a field glass, the expanding blue lines of the enemy formations were clearly visible from two miles away. "S-sir, is that . . . ?"

"Looks like it." I sighed, and the cloud of my breath fogged the lens of the field glass. "Tell them our friends are forming lines of division strength or greater. Sergeant Newton," I called as I lowered the glass.

I glanced to my left, where the young lieutenant remained gazing out across the field. "You've seen combat before, Will," I said quietly. "Pass the word: division strength or greater."

"Yes, sir," Hopwood replied tentatively, then tore his gaze from the unfolding scene across the field. His eyes met mine, and resolve quickly replaced fear. "Yes, sir," he repeated with more confidence.

"Go." I turned him by the shoulders and

pushed him in the direction of the command tent.

"Sir?" Newton said as he joined me on the crest of the hill.

"Looks like we'll have some company this morning," I said, and handed him the glass.

"Billy Yank's finally grown a pair. Looks like he's coming out to play for real," he said as he panned the lens across the opposing lines. He surveyed the field, then swung the glass back a few degrees. "I'll be damned. Are those — ?"

I took the glass back and pointed it across the field.

"Well, how about that?" I said.

"What do you suppose it means?"

"Means we'll have a lot of blue targets to point at, same as always."

"Yes, sir," Newton said. "I reckon that's the fact."

"Looks like they'll be forming from the east," I said as I followed the assembling lines. "We'll have to shoot over the heads of our men. Let's set Lieutenant Marshall's guns for elevated firing." Marshall was my youngest second lieutenant, and greener than a spring meadow. "Wouldn't do to have any miscalculations."

"No argument here, sir." Newton's dislike of the young man was no secret, but he was careful to respect the distinctions of rank.

"God, I'm tired of this," I muttered, more to myself than anyone else.

"I know, Jim," came the reply, surprising both of us with the familiarity. "Excuse me, sir."

"It's all right, Liam."

"Thank you, sir. What I mean to say is, I'm tired, too. Hell, we all are — just look at 'em." He nodded his chin toward the crews milling about their guns, and the thousands of troops dug in below the summit of the hill. "Freezing, starving, half-naked. But this is our home. Those bastards have invaded our country. If we throw them back here, we may not have to fight too much longer. Begging your pardon, sir."

"I can't argue with you there, Sergeant. It's just a damned ugly business. I'll be happy to see it finished either way."

Newton raised his brow at that, but made no other reply.

"Regardless," I said, "they don't pay us to argue politics. Let's set to it, shall we?"

"Yes, sir." He turned away without a salute, lest he provide a target for any sharpshooter that might be in range.

I watched the distant blue line as it drew up a formation. A few hours earlier and the morning fog might have hidden their movements and given the enemy an element of surprise. Already, though, the morning sun was burning off the mist, exposing the Union movements to full view. When the Federals stopped moving, I held my breath in anticipation of what would come next.

I didn't have long to wait.

The guns at Fort Negley unleashed their rounds and signaled the advance. In reply, the distant thunder of field guns and the muffled cries of thousands of voices announced the fighting on our distant left flank. Closer by, under the cover of the barrage from the fort, the Union's left wing began its advance.

Slowly, stately at first, rank upon rank of blue-jacketed infantrymen began crossing the field toward our entrenchments. The advance itself was nothing of note, little different than the dozens I'd faced during the course of the war. Rather, what captured my attention — and that of every other man with a field glass — was the fact that no fewer than ten regimental banners flew over colored troops.

The Confederacy was no stranger to Negroes on the battlefield. While the government in Richmond frowned upon it, the state militias had enlisted more than fifty thousand blacks, free and slave, to fight against the Union. These men were scattered within the ranks and, I supposed, from across the field of battle were as nameless and faceless as their white comrades.

General Cleburne, God rest him, had proposed a further step. He'd proposed to free the slaves and enroll them in colored regiments. Doing so would swell our dwindling ranks and, more importantly, rob the North of any moral advantage. For a random Negro to be felled by a Union bullet was one thing. For the Union to fire against even a single company of free colored soldiers would prove the Federals as aggressive occupiers, not the liberators they claimed to be.

For his unorthodox vision, General Cleburne had been rewarded by having his command shot out from under him. While he had once been favorably compared to Stonewall Jackson, after his proposal he was made subordinate to far lesser men. The horror at Franklin bore testimony to the effect of politics on military strategy.

The Union Army, however, apparently had far less political generals — or far smarter politicians. Northern propaganda painted the Confederacy as enemy to an entire race, and now thousands of tan and brown and black faces marched in blue uniforms toward our lines.

In orderly ranks they came, like recruits on dress review. The covering fire from Fort Negley tapered off as the ranks drew nearer to our position. On the Confederate lines, men clambered up the earthworks for a peek at the advancing troops. As the enemy drew nearer, officers and sergeants started yanking men off the walls and readying them for battle.

My battery was farthest from the line of battle and would be the first to fire, followed by Turner's Battery, which was positioned on the front. I'd seen more than enough canister and grape shot since that first morning at Elkhorn Tavern, and I was content to fire explosive shell and case shot from the rear where smoke and dust would hide most of the carnage. I measured the enemy advance through my field glass and readied the crews, timing my command to deliver maximum effect.

"Fire," I ordered the battery when I reckoned the moment was right.

The entire hill shook as all eight guns discharged at once. The cannon spat their lethal venom over the tops of our own men's heads to rain death upon the enemy almost a mile away.

"Case shot, reload," I ordered my crews,

trusting my lieutenants to issue similar commands for their guns.

We would have time for only one more shot before the lines met and any further fire would be as dangerous to our own men as to the Blue Jackets.

"Fire." I repeated the order in little more than a whisper.

Again the ground shook as the guns loosed their murderous volleys. I ordered the crews to stand by, then raised my glass to survey the field. By this time, our entrenched infantry had mounted the tops of the works and was delivering its own deadly fire to the enemy. While the parade array of the advancing troops made for an impressive display, it also gave our riflemen and gunners far easier targets.

As I focused on the field, our second volley was just landing among what remained of the lines. Turner's guns were unleashing what must have been their second or third rounds while our infantry added to the destruction. What had been an orderly advance of Union soldiers turned quickly into a rout. Even as I watched, the white Union officers raced from the field, closely trailed by their men. A few Negro standard bearers tried to rally the soldiers around them but, when these fell to our sharpshooters, all heart was lost.

The lines that had come closest to the entrenchment had their retreat cut off by our artillery. Unable to escape, the Federal troops sought shelter in the ditches at the base of our earthworks. For them, destruction was swift and heartless, as their shelter became a mass grave.

Then, as one man, the Confederate infantry poured over the embankments. The few Union troops that remained on the field quickly threw down their arms and hurried to join their fleeing comrades. The wind cleared the smoke and dust from the field to reveal the brutal aftermath of the battle.

Southern troops stalked across the body-littered field and picked through the remains, collecting weapons and ammunition, supplies and souvenirs. I watched through my glass as a young soldier compared his bared feet against the soles of one of the fallen. Finding a good fit, he began to pry off the boots.

The body stirred and hands beat at the would-be robber. A lump rose in my throat as I saw through the blood- and dust-streaked mask to recognize Izzy. Even across a mile of distance and through a cloudy lens, I knew it was him. I shouted, though I knew it was useless — the Confederate soldier couldn't know and likely wouldn't care that the boots he wanted belonged to my friend. He stilled Izzy's struggle with a bayonet through the chest and went about his business.

I watched helplessly as the boy left his rifle upended, pinning Izzy's body to the ground while he stripped off the boots. He plopped onto the frozen earth beside my dying friend, even talked with him as he pulled the boots onto his own feet.

"Shot load," I heard myself say, and the men moved automatically to obey.

"Our men have the field, Captain," Sergeant Newton reminded me as I ordered the gun turned toward Izzy's murderer. "Captain?"

I judged the distance and spun the elevation screw for the proper angle. Newton laid a hand on my shoulder, and I spun around, drew my revolver and pulled back the hammer.

"Step back, Sergeant," I said.

"I don't know what you're fixing to shoot at, Captain," Newton said calmly, not seeming to mind the .36-caliber barrel just inches from his forehead, "but today's fighting is over."

"Not yet it's not. Primer," I ordered the private at the breech of the gun, and I could feel his and the other men's wide-eyed stares. "Now."

I heard the metallic rasp of the handspike as it ran through the breech vent, the crunch of gunpowder as the charge bag was pierced. The young private set the primer in place and pulled the lanyard taut.

"Ready, sir," he said in a faltering voice.

Newton sniffed and spat a dark stream of tobacco juice.

"You want to commit murder today, Captain?" he said, his tone dispassionate. "That's fine. I suppose you have your reasons. But don't make this boy a part of it."

His reasoning broke through my rage. I nodded slowly, thumbed down the hammer on my revolver and cleared the trigger.

"Thank you, Private," I said to the boy as I holstered the sidearm and took the lanyard from his shaking hands. "My apologies, Sergeant," I offered, then bent over the breech of the gun to verify the aim and tugged on the lanyard.

I felt the scratch of the friction powder, heard the hiss of the ignition as fire filled the breech of the gun. Two and a half pounds of mortar powder erupted, and the expanding gases welled up like the rage and grief in my own chest. In a great release, the twelve-pound iron ball burst from the barrel, taking with it my hatred and fury.

It took four seconds for vengeance to be carried out, five beats of my heart before I stilled that of another. When the shot found its target, it did so with deadly precision. The young soldier leaned back on his elbows, one leg crossed over the other as he studied his new boots. If he sensed Death coming, he never showed it. The ball arced toward the boy — he was probably about Izzy's age, I guessed — and tore through his gut before burying itself in the earth.

By now, Confederate officers were beginning to corral their troops and herd them back behind the lines. The guns at Fort Negley resumed their deadly hail and our men raced from the field, deaf and blind to the pleas of the wounded, their arms filled with bloody loot. When they reached the safety of the earthworks, they left behind a sea of crimson-stained blue, spotted only occasionally by flecks of grey and butternut.

"Captain Robbins," a voice called, and I turned to see a young lieutenant on horseback. "New orders, sir. You're to cover the withdrawal."

"Withdrawal?" I said.

"Yes, sir. I'm afraid General Stewart's men didn't fare as well as y'all did today." He handed me the orders, saluted and reined his horse away before I had time to respond.

I scanned the papers, shoved them into my jacket and reverted from murderer to warrior.

"Shell load, seven-second fuse," I ordered the men. "Let's give our boys some cover."

A cold night had fallen by the time my battery reached our new position, some two miles back and on the extreme left of the Confederate line. This end of the line had been flanked by the Union troops during the morning's fighting, with Yankee bullets tearing into our men from behind before reserve troops could shore up the breech. With the retreat of that line, several guns had been lost, which I fully expected would be turned on us come morning.

With my battery securely in place, I ordered our wagons turned toward the road south, should we need to make a hasty retreat. The easy victory of Cheatham's Corps had been overcome by Stewart's rout, and my men's confidence was shaken as we prepared to face an emboldened enemy.

I had the men build their fires in the lee of a hill so as not to backlight our emplacement and direct the Union gunners to their first targets of the new day. After a quick meal of hardtack and dried meat, I crept into the frozen darkness between the lines to get a feel for the terrain.

From the middle of the field, I traced the stretch of Cleburne's Division and took note of any weakness in our defenses, places where the enemy would have an easy target. I then stole closer to the Federal line — in some places only a couple hundred yards from our own — to see what we'd face come dawn. The waxing moon was low in the sky, and gave enough light to survey the emplacements while casting the hollow between the lines into deep shadow.

A shot rang out and I dropped to the ground. The gunfire came from the Southern side, and the shouts and scrambling among the nearby Yankees told me that our sharpshooters were doing their part to weaken the Union line. Keeping close to the ground, I crept farther westward until the field between the armies widened out to about a half mile. A narrow stream cut through the no-man's-land, and I followed the creek bed while I picked out more targets.

A splash in the creek stopped me in my tracks, and I quietly lowered myself to the frozen ground. I peered into the darkness, but could make out nothing more than the reflection of pale moonlight on the ripples in the water. Then I saw the pattern of the ripples change, moving from one side of the stream to the other. I traced the tiny waves upstream until I could barely distinguish a figure darker than the night itself. The shadow edged across the creek with movements so subtle I could only see them from the corner of my eye.

The coming battle looked to be hard enough without a Union scout carrying back information on our position. As quietly as possible, I gathered some pebbles from the edge of the creek and eased myself into a kneeling position. I tossed the stones over the shadow's head. They clattered to the ground a few yards beyond him. The man froze and melded into the rolling landscape. I held my breath until he started moving again, this time in my direction.

With agonizing slowness, the scout drew closer and finally passed between me and the Confederate lines. I eased my short sword from its scabbard and — when the shadow was only five yards away — hurled myself at the enemy.

I clamped one hand over his mouth and pressed my blade to his throat with the other, then pulled him to the ground and dropped my full weight on him. Wide eyes shone in the moonlight, the fear and surprise gleaming brightly. His face was smeared with soot but, up close, could not hide the humanity behind the mask.

The smart thing would be to draw my sword through the man's throat, to make one less soldier that might try to kill me in the morning. But, as I looked into those human eyes, saw myself reflected in them, I knew I'd had enough killing.

"Not a sound," I warned him, then lifted my hand from his mouth, the blade still at his throat.

"Have mercy on a poor widow's son," he whispered.

My eyes opened wide at the words, and I pulled my sword away and rolled off the man.

"What's your name?" I said.

The scout seemed as shocked as I was that the plea had worked, and he stammered, "Dave. Dave Perkins."

"Well, Brother Perkins," I said, recovering some of my wits, "it would appear you've lost your way this night. I believe your camp is over yonder." I jerked my head toward the Northern lines.

"True, but my job is over here."

"Not any more, it's not." I tapped his

chest with the tip of my sword to drive home the point.

"I ain't gonna beg," he said, resignation taking the place of fear. "Just have done with it."

I looked back at him, heaved a sigh and muttered, "Aw, hell."

I rose and sheathed my sword, then jerked the other man to his feet and spun him in the direction of the creek.

"Get out of here," I commanded, and pushed him toward the water's edge.

He staggered a couple of feet before he regained his balance, then turned to look at me.

"I won't forget this," he said in a low voice.

"You heard me," I said, and stepped menacingly toward him. "Get."

The man turned, and I planted my boot against his backside to speed him on his way. I heard him splash through the water and scramble up the opposite bank.

"God speed," I whispered after him, then headed back toward my battery for what I hoped would be a dreamless sleep.

CHAPTER NINE

Davidson County, Tennessee — December 16, 1864

"Incoming!" I shouted to my crew. "Take cover."

The still morning air was rent by the shrill scream of the approaching missile. I dove toward the inner wall of the revetment where my men already huddled together, bodies tucked into tight balls and arms wrapped over their heads. The enemy shell landed short of our position, its lethal shrapnel tearing harmlessly into the side of the hill between the battery placement and the entrenched troops below.

"Shell shot, percussion fuse," I ordered as my men raced back to their guns.

I peeked over the edge of the low dirt wall, willing the cloud of smoke and dust to clear. As the field emerged into view, I gauged the point of impact and the pattern of debris to work backward toward the source of the attack.

"Three-quarters degree elevation," I shouted as the crew wrestled the gun into alignment with my outstretched arm. The engineer in me balked at firing blindly into the morning fog, but the warrior insisted that the Federals would eventually sniff out our position if we didn't find theirs first. "Fire."

The gun roared and I cocked a ringing ear in the direction of the shot. A second and a half later the shell's journey came to an explosive end with a flash of light, followed by a rumbling echo that rolled back across the field of battle. Behind the concussion rose the muted cries of pain and anger from the enemy soldiers caught within the blast. There were no metallic sounds, meaning I'd found the Union troops in their entrenchments, not the guns that would be farther up the opposite hill.

"Reload same," I ordered, and twisted the elevation screw to raise the gun barrel. "Fire."

For the second time in a minute the gun gave its belligerent roar, answered moments later by the explosion of the shell. This time, the blast was followed a half second later by a huge eruption as an enemy ammunition wagon was ensnared in the carnage.

"Target," I shouted over the cheers of my men, then passed the coordinates to the other gun crews. "Case shot, second-and-a-quarter fuse — load."

Followed by the other guns, we rained fire and brimstone on the heads of the Yankees. The sulfur and coal-tar filling of the case shot arced out in fiery tendrils clearly visible through the thinning fog. At only a quarter-mile's distance, the cries of the men under the barrage were just as clear.

We pounded the enemy for nearly twenty minutes. The Federals shot back, but each muzzle flash only gave my guns a fresh target. When we ran out of targets I ordered the barrel swabbed, and the bronze tube guttered and fumed as the water-soaked sponge slaked the hot metal. Through the hissing steam and thinning fog I scanned the Union lines with my field glass.

With satisfaction, I noted the wreckage of several guns and caissons, willing myself blind to the burned and mutilated bodies that lay around and upon the mechanical carnage. Less satisfying was the fact that several of the guns bore Confederate markings, having been captured from Stewart's Corps the day before. We'd miss the service of those guns before the day was out, I thought, but at least they could no longer be used against us.

"Fine shooting, Captain," a voice said behind me.

"Thank you," I replied automatically, then lowered my glass and turned to see who had spoken. "Thank you, sir," I corrected myself as I recognized General Govan, the brigade commander. I resisted the urge to salute, given our exposed position on the hilltop. "I'm afraid that won't be the last of them, though."

"No, I don't believe it will," agreed Colonel Green, the senior regimental commander under Govan. "I suspect they'll be bringing their own guns into battery soon, seeing as they've wasted ours now."

"Colonel." A winded lieutenant rushed up the hill to join the commanding officers. "Major Hamiter's regards, sir," he blurted, forgetting himself as he raised his hand in salute. "Scouts report a picket on foot, approaching from the south, Colonel."

At that instant, a puff of red erupted from the back of the colonel's uniform, spattering my tunic and face with blood. Green tottered, a look of irritation on his face as he studied the red stain on his chest. A second later, the report of the shot caught up with the high-velocity round.

"Cover," I shouted to the men on the

guns, then helped the wounded man to the ground.

The young lieutenant was ashen-faced with the realization that his salute might have given the unseen Yankee sharpshooter his target.

"Sir, I-I —"

"Little time for that now, son," General Govan said, not unkindly. "How far out were those pickets? Lieutenant," he barked when the young man failed to answer.

"Just inside the edge of the woods, sir," he finally managed, and indicated the line of trees that bordered the southern edge of the hills.

"Very well. Tell the major to extend his position left around the flank and hold as best he can. Do not let them inside our lines," he ordered.

"Yes, sir," the young man replied, remembering not to salute as he turned to crawl back down the hill toward his post.

"We could use some cover in that direction, Captain," Govan suggested.

"Yes, sir," I said. "Sergeant Newton."

"Captain?" Newton answered as he scrambled over from his gun's position.

"Have our left-most guns slew toward the south. We have reports of enemy infantry coming about the flank. Shell and grape shot, I should think."

"Agreed. Sir?" the man spoke with uncharacteristic hesitancy. "Our left guns are Lieutenant Marshall's."

"Take over the gunnery," I said without a moment's thought. "If he has a problem with that, tell him I need his assistance here."

"Yes, sir," Newton said, then hurried to the farther gun emplacements.

General Govan looked at me for a moment through narrowed eyes, then cracked a slight grin and gave me an approving nod.

"Keep up the good work, Captain," he said.

"Yes, sir." I took that as my dismissal and turned to rejoin my crews.

I raised my glass to survey the changing enemy lines just as the opposite ridge erupted with multiple blooms of smoke, their deadly seeds sprouting ugly blossoms of dirt and debris as the shells were planted in the hill beneath my position. At the same instant, a cry arose to the left as scores of riflemen poured from the bordering tree line to charge our left flank.

So sudden was the assault, so well timed, that our dug-in infantry could offer but little resistance. I watched in horrified fascination as the charge developed. The enemy loosed a devastating round of rifle fire, then rushed our lines with their bayonets. As our flank was gouged by the surprise attack, the main line of Federal troops rushed across the field in a frontal assault.

"Maintain your fire on the field," I shouted to my rightward crews. "Case and canister. Traverse left," I ordered my own gunners to bring our weapon in line to support Newton.

I assumed the flanking maneuver to have been just wide enough to sweep around the end of our position, but was appalled to see the blue line extend half a mile farther beyond.

"Case shot, one second fuse, load," I ordered when the gun aligned with the extreme third of the enemy advance. "Fire."

Even as the gun belched out its deadly load, the approaching riflemen swept over the farther hill where Newton and Marshall were. I watched as their cannon cut through the charge with a deadly hail of canister shot. Dozens upon dozens of lead balls tore through the enemy, but the sheer number of Union troops overwhelmed the opposition of the two guns.

"Canister," I murmured, my breath taken away by the spectacle.

"Sir?" a corporal asked.

"Canister," I repeated more forcefully. "Zero elevation. Fire."

The hail of death shot out from the Napoleon gun and slashed into the handful of advancing soldiers. The main body of the skirmishers had stopped at Newton's emplacement, tipping over wagons and caissons and positioning the guns as a bulwark against the rest of our artillery. Thus sheltered, they fired into the unprotected backs of the infantry dug in below the hill.

"Shot load," I demanded, enraged at the brutality of the engagement and the foolishness that had, again, allowed us to be flanked. "Fire, reload same."

The cannon balls tore into the makeshift barricade and I nodded with grim satisfaction as, little by little, the protective barrier was broken down. The Yankees turned their attention from slaughtering our troops to strengthening their position.

My single gun continued to tear into the occupied hill while the rest of the battery fired on the field to drive back the frontal assault. Before long, help arrived in the form of reinforcements, who drove the Union troops off the captured hill.

Our flank was secure, but the reinforcements were fewer in number than the men who had originally lost the position. Nonetheless, with their advance troops driven back, the main body of the Federals retreated to the safety of their earthworks. To my relief, a second brigade of reinforcements soon arrived to further shore up our flagging left.

I ordered my gun back around to face front, then polled the other crews on their ammunition stores. Enough remained, I calculated, to repel one more assault. If we failed in driving the Yankees back with that, our guns would be useless without resupply. I dispatched a corporal to corps headquarters with that message, then focused on the shifting Union lines. Without fresh orders, it fell to me to try to read the enemy's mind, and I positioned my guns as best I could to counter the next move.

The sun was well past noon and I hoped that the next assault would be delayed long enough to waste the few remaining hours of daylight. Given time to strengthen our lines and resupply the troops and batteries, the next day might bring us the victory we so desperately needed. That hope was stillborn, though, as I scanned a nearby ridge where the unmistakable activity of the gun crews foretold the coming engagement.

"Sergeant Newton."

I called the name out of habit before I

remembered his body now lay broken on the adjacent hill. I cursed to myself and spat. There would be time for mourning later, but mistakes like that would only make more of my men dead.

"Sergeant Johnson," I corrected myself, and the new first sergeant came promptly to my side, his drooping, blond mustache giving his face a melancholy cast.

"Sir?"

"Direct fire on that hill," I said.

Johnson looked to where I pointed, but the target disappeared behind a cloud of smoke as the massed guns opened fire. The enemy manned their own guns far more effectively than they did ours, and our lines quickly ruptured. Howitzers lobbed shells onto the heads of the entrenched infantry while the rifled guns began the systematic demolition of the hill beneath our feet.

"Take out those guns," I ordered. "Shot load, half-degree elevation."

Even as my command was carried out, I caught the flash of one of the distant guns. A three-inch cast iron bolt spun from the rifled bore in a shallow arc. We held a superior elevation to the Union emplacement, though, and few of their rounds managed to reach the top of our hill. This round would be no exception. Even as it approached, I calculated it would fall short of my position.

I was mostly right.

Part of my mind rebelled at being able to track the round, even as I watched the bolt smash into the hill several yards from where I stood. The earth furrowed into a massive mole's trail and my heart sank as the round emerged from its tunnel and continued toward me.

The bolt smashed into my leg and sent me spinning through the air. The concussion of the shot rumbled through my chest. I felt the beginnings of a rush of pain as I crashed into the earth and slipped beneath the waves of consciousness.

"Jade?"

The voice called out as from a great distance, seeming to come from all directions.

Again, "Jade." This time more insistently.

I opened my eyes and shook off the echoes of cannon fire that still filled my head, propped myself up on my elbows and looked around. The field was covered by a thick layer of fog and smoke, and I could barely see the tips of my outstretched fingers. Occasional flashes of light appeared here and there, but these were quickly swallowed up in the cloudy gloom.

I flinched as a hand gripped my shoulder and I spun my head around as the voice said, "What you doing here, boy?"

"Izzy?"

The smiling face appeared in the mist, still streaked with blood and dust, and backlit by a strange blue-violet glow.

"Give me your hand," he said.

I accepted his offer and he pulled me easily to my feet and clapped his hands to my shoulders.

"Damn, but it's good to see you, Jade," he said.

"You, too," I said, still puzzled by his strange appearance.

The fog seemed to lessen as I stood, and I looked about the field for some sign of what was happening. Through the mist, hundreds upon hundreds of soldiers marched westward toward the lowering sun. The tide of blue and grey swept past me, the men giving me not so much as a glance. Despite wounds to their heads and chests and bellies, heedless of limbs that were twisted and bent at impossible angles, the soldiers pushed on.

"What is this?" I asked, turning back to Izzy.

It was then I noticed the ugly circle of

blood on his chest. I spun him around and found a larger twin to the stain, centered on a slender gash in the back of his jacket.

"What you think it is, boy?" he said good-naturedly.

"I saw you die," I protested.

Izzy tapped a finger against my forehead. "Now you starting to see."

"But I killed the one who did it to you."

"Don't I know it," Izzy said with a disgusted snort. "Bad enough I get me killed in some damn fool charge. Now I got this sorry thing to keep me company."

He nodded over his shoulder with his chin. There, standing still against the tide of soldiers, was the boy I'd shot. He held his grey forage cap in his hands and looked sheepishly toward Izzy. Up close, I could see that he was even younger than I'd thought, maybe only fifteen or sixteen. More shocking than his youth was the five-inch hole torn clean through his belly by my cannonball.

"Couldn't just let me go in peace," Izzy was saying. "Oh, no, you got to send this one along after me to keep me company till we get wherever it is we going. Got to listen to his sorry ass complaining the whole way. 'Oh, Mister Izzy, I'm sorry I stabbed you,' " he mocked the boy, " 'but my feet was so awful cold, and it didn't look like you was gonna need them boots no more. Then they shot my stomach clean out of me, so's neither of us gonna get no use out of them.'"

Izzy shook his head at me. "All I can say is, it better be a short trip to the Other Side, or I'll come back and haunt you like no spook ain't never done before."

"I don't understand," I said.

Izzy shrugged his shoulders and pointed downward with his eyes.

A bright, silvery thread shimmered and danced at my feet, its length disappearing into the smoke and fog. I bent down and took the strange thing in my hand and was surprised to find that one end of the thread was connected to me. It was then I noticed a faint glow about my hands and arms — indeed, about my entire body. The ruddy, purple glow was dimmer than the one around Izzy and seemed to fade before my eyes. I studied the thread in my hands and started to tug it loose.

"No!" Izzy shouted.

I stopped and looked back to Izzy. In spite of his earlier tirade, his deep-brown eyes burned with compassion. Puzzled, I turned my attention back to the thread. Hand over hand, I followed it into the thickening blanket of smoke.

At its far end, the thread was attached to the center of the chest of a figure that lay sprawled on the ground. The soldier was on his back, arms flung out and his left leg bent at the knee in a horrid angle. Beneath a tattered, grey trouser leg — torn and still smoking from the passage of an artillery round — the meat of his lower leg was exposed and pierced by a sharp, jagged point of bone. Blood oozed from the wound, already soaking the uniform fabric and the ground beneath.

I traced my eyes along the fallen man's body. His tunic and face were covered with blood, but showed no other sign of injury. I knelt beside the man and turned his head to get a better look at him. I fell back and skittered away. The thread between us grew tight and glowed brightly as I stared into my own eyes.

"Steady, Jade," Izzy said as he knelt beside me. "That there thread is what ties you — the real you, the forever you — to your body. As long as it ain't broke, you can get back inside yourself whenever you're ready."

"So this is just a dream?" I said.

"No," he said thoughtfully. "No, this is about as real as it gets. 'Course, if you remember any of this when you go back, it'll probably seem like it was all a dream."

"But why?" I said. "If I won't remember this, why are we even sitting here?"

"Why water run downhill, boy?" Izzy said. "Why the stars shine? The *why* don't matter, just that it is. Don't matter why we having this talk. We *are.*" He sat beside me, and Belly Wound crouched down next to him. "What does matter," Izzy went on, "is that you done put yourself in a pickle."

"What do you mean?"

"You took a life," he said.

"I've taken lots of lives. It's called war."

"That's so, but the taking of this one," he nodded toward the boy, "weren't needful."

"But he killed you," I said. "Killed you for your boots. You mean to say that was needful?"

"I ain't saying that. He made his own mess and he got to deal with that hisself. Ain't that right?" he asked his fellow corpse.

The boy nodded, eyes downcast as he picked at the edge of his wound.

"A man makes his own fate," Izzy continued, "and it ain't no one else's place to decide that."

"But to put down a murderer can't be wrong," I protested.

"Mostly," Izzy agreed, "when it's a bad man you putting down. You save a life in

261

the doing, stop a body from killing again, that ain't a bad thing at all. But this boy? Was you ever gonna kill again?"

The boy looked up and shook his head. "Oh, no, Mister Izzy. I didn't even mean to kill you. It's just that my feet was so awful cold. I thought you was dead already, and when you come to, it just startled me is all."

Izzy waved a hand to cut the boy off. "He killed because he was cold and scared. He didn't have a chance to think about it. Did you have time to think?" he asked me.

I looked away and nodded.

"Now I ain't trying to be hard on you, Jade," he said, his tone softer. "I appreciate what you done, that you cared enough to avenge me. I'm just saying that you've made a hard road for yourself."

"How do you mean?"

"Folks do good in their lives and they do bad. Most ways they balance out. You done plenty of good, Jade — helping Zeke and Ketty, helping out that little family back when. But this harm you done — not just to this boy, whether he deserved it or not. He got him a pair of little ones that ain't never gonna know their pappy now, a wife that got no one to put food on the table. You brung suffering and loss, and you got to account for that."

I started to protest, but he cut me off.

"It ain't punishment, mind you," he said. "Got nothing to do with sin or mercy or forgiveness. You throw a ball up in the air, it got to land somewhere. You toss a stone in a pond, it gonna make ripples. Nothing good or bad or right or wrong about it — that's just how it is."

I sat still for a time to let the words sink in.

"What can I do?" I asked at length.

"Ain't nothing you can do, boy," Izzy said, "except just be. You done throwed them rocks in the pond, and you got to man up and take what comes, whether it's ripples coming back at you or a hurricane."

I fingered the silver thread, strummed at it like a fiddle string.

"What if I just pluck this and have done with it?" I said.

"That what you really want?" Izzy asked.

I thought of all I'd already lost. Thought of Ma and Pa and Becca, of Matt and — soon enough — Izzy himself. Then my thoughts turned toward Gina. I couldn't know what future I'd created for myself, but I knew that — with Gina by my side — there was nothing I couldn't face. I dropped the thread and shook my head.

"Good," Izzy said as he patted my shoulder. "Quitting may seem like the easy choice sometimes, but you still got to face the lessons of what you done. Hurrying things along only makes it harder."

"Mister Izzy?" the boy interrupted with a tug on Izzy's sleeve.

Izzy looked at him, nodded and pushed himself to his feet.

"We got to get moving, Jade," he said. "Got to start heading west by sunset, and I promised we'd check in on his family before we go."

I stood and took Izzy's hand.

"Will I see you again?" I asked.

"Oh, I imagine one day," he said. "Meantime, you just keep your eyes on the road." He pointed toward the bright light of the sun. "We all gonna get there eventually, but it's what we see and do along the way that defines the journey."

Izzy led me toward where my body lay. The silver thread grew brighter and the fog began to clear. I could see movement on the field — the movement of the living — as the dead began to fade away.

A soldier in Union blue twill knelt beside my body and checked for signs of life before rummaging through my uniform. He found Matt's watch in the pocket where I kept it wrapped in a handkerchief, then turned his attention to Zeke's talisman that still hung about my neck.

"Son of a bitch," I shouted at the thief, to no avail.

"Son of a bitch," came another shout, and this one got the soldier's attention. He started to run, but a rifle butt caught him in the back of the head and he went sprawling along the ground. The newcomer retrieved the watch and brought it back to me. I recognized him as the scout from the night before. He put the watch back in my pocket and started checking my wounds.

"You go on now, Jade," Izzy said in farewell. "We'll see you back home along about supper time."

With that, he and the boy headed south toward the Franklin Pike and disappeared among the shimmering trees.

The scout — Dave, I recalled his name — slung his rifle over his shoulder and slid his arms under me. I let the silver thread reel me in and closed my eyes as I merged with my body.

In a blinding flash of light, pain shot through my senses. Like a foot fallen asleep, my body was pricked with thousands, millions of needles. Every fiber of my body cried out as fiery darts stabbed into them, securing the two halves of myself together once more.

My eyes shot open and I sucked in a sharp breath. The stench of battle filled my nostrils and the bitter taste of blood wet my lips.

"Hold steady, now," Dave said gently. "I'll get you out of here."

I clenched my teeth as he lifted me and the pain of my shattered leg washed over me.

"Told you I wouldn't forget," he said, and carried me from the field.

The walls of the tent and the people within them fade like a distant memory, while the strange visitors become more substantial. Where my cot and body had been, a tree now grows, a great walnut an arm's-breadth across at the base. I know it well from countless dreams. As I move closer I hear the wind rustling through the leaves and the sound of wind chimes.

I reach the ring of dancers. The nearest pair break their grip to allow me inside their midst before again closing the circle. They seem as real and as solid as I am, but all are draped in robes and veils that hide their figures and faces. I speak to them, but they continue their dance uninterrupted. I turn back to the tree.

With my hand on the rough bark, I pace around the great trunk, stepping over burled and knotted roots. I stop as I reach the lowest branch, and look up to see a carved JR+AB enclosed in a crude heart. The lines are in a shaky hand, and rough gashes cut through them, almost obliterating the initials.

"Sorry about that."

I turn to see a robed figure approach and remove the veil to uncover a head of thin, brown hair. My surprise lasts only an instant before it's replaced by a calm acceptance.

"Maybe I should've listened to you," I say.

"Horse shit," he retorts. "You were the best thing ever happened to her. She'd have been lost without you."

I bite off my argument and turn to lean against the tree. The bark scratches at my back.

"What is all this?" I ask, waving at the circle of dancers.

"Your life," the figure says. "A last chance to take it all in before you move on."

"Move on to what?"

A shrug. "Whatever you choose. It ain't like the church sermons. There's no judge all in white and seated on a throne. You're the judge, and where you go from here is up to you."

"That should make things easy," I say with an irreverent grin.

"Not as easy as you think," he says. "There's no excuses, no justification. Everything is what it is — or was — and you're stuck with that. No changing things, no going back to make things right. You get the cold, hard truth, and you make your judgment on that."

I'm sobered by the words, knowing that there's plenty I'd change if I could. But I nod my acceptance.

"All right," I say. "What do I do?"

"Just get on with it."

CHAPTER TEN

Nashville, Tennessee — April 1865

The thunder of cannon and the pop of small arms fire wrenched me awake.

"Double canister, load," I shouted reflexively, before I understood what was happening.

The weapons continued to fire amid the shouts of men. As I looked around, I saw no puffs of smoke, no clouds of debris or piles of wounded. Only the sterile white of starched sheets and lime-washed walls, and eleven pairs of wide eyes staring at me.

I felt my cheeks flush at the realization that my dream — nightmare — had spilled over into the waking world. But the eyes that looked back at me all bore the sympathy of shared experience. And something more.

For the first time in months, there was hope in those eyes. As the gunplay continued outside the hospital walls, a realization dawned on me. Hope began to brighten my soul. A conflicted hope, to be sure, but hope nonetheless.

On the one hand, the cannon fire could represent a renewed Confederate siege of the city, one that might finally reclaim Nashville for the South and signal the beginning of the end of the war. There had been little in the papers, though, to support that possibility.

More likely — and no less welcome to the men in the ward, it appeared — was not impending Confederate victory, but quite its opposite. Cheers erupted outside, which told us this was the case. An orderly burst open the doors of the ward room to confirm our guesses.

"Lee's surrendered in Virginia," he said. "Bless God, it's over."

The young man's excitement was tempered when he noted the downcast eyes of the men in the room, whose very presence here was owing to their sacrifice in service to the lost Cause.

"Amen, son," the senior patient, a lieutenant colonel from Mississippi, finally said. "Gentlemen, let us give thanks."

The tone of the invitation was only a few degrees shy of being an order. The colonel — son of a Methodist minister, I'd learned — invoked the blessings of heaven no less forcefully than he might have commanded his troops in the field. If the Almighty were subject to the dictates of military discipline, I thought, the healing of the nation and a just and equitable peace would not be long in coming.

As *amen*s echoed around the room, the dozen men began our daily routine on this most non-routine of days. I swung my legs — one bare, the other wrapped in a heavy plaster cast — over the side of the bed. I leaned on my crutches as I made my way to the corner privy and wash basin, then down the hall to the dining room. With practiced clumsiness, I balanced my food tray and hobbled through the serving line.

Between bites of runny egg, lumpy grits and gristly ham I studied the faces around the room. All the patients wore plain white robes, but it was easy to see who had formerly worn blue and who, grey. The Union veterans were almost giddy, and their gazes flitted about the room as they looked for others to share their joy. The Confederates, for the most part, kept their eyes on their food, each man sinking into himself to cope with defeat.

Those hardest hit seemed to be the higher-ranking Southern officers. These were the men who had issued the orders that sent hundreds, thousands to their deaths — deaths that, now, it would seem, were entirely in vain. A few of the men sipped their coffee or gnawed on stale crusts of bread, but all seemed to stare through their trays to distant horrors no one else could see.

I felt a twinge of guilt as I wolfed down my meal. To be sure, I felt some sense of loss, but it was more for the wasted years, years that could have been spent making a home with Gina. My war had been to protect that home, or the hope of it, and to avenge Bull and Izzy and the others killed by men that prized ideals above human life.

I'd not heard from Gina since Matt and I left Britton to join up, but most men had to endure through the war without word from home. I tempered my concern with the fact that the war had long been settled in northwest Arkansas. Now, with Lee's surrender, I looked forward to crossing the five hundred miles that separated me from my future.

I finished breakfast, returned my tray and limped to the courtyard of the hospital. Not wanting to offend the other prisoner-patients' grieving with my hopeful anticipation, I avoided their eyes. I breathed deeply to purge the staleness of the ward from my lungs, and the fresh spring air had a taste of freedom mixed with it.

"Mind if I join you, Captain?" The now familiar voice came from behind as I started my daily hobble around the courtyard.

"Feel free, Corporal," I said without turning. "But it's not *Captain* anymore. At least, I don't suspect it will be for much longer."

"True enough," Dave allowed as he came alongside me and matched his healthy gait to my hobbled one. "Any word when you'll be released?"

"Too soon for that, I imagine," I said. "Must be a passel of details yet to work out. Hell, it may not even really be over. Lee's was the largest army we had left, but there's no word of a formal peace yet."

"Let's not even look down that road," Dave said. "Oh, and it's not *Corporal* anymore, either. Leastways, not after tomorrow. Our company's being mustered out in the morning — just in time, looks like. From now on, it's just plain old *Mister* Perkins."

"Congratulations," I said. "So you'll be heading back to Ohio?"

"Indiana," he corrected me with a scowl. "And, no, I thought I might stay down in these parts for a while longer. Much nicer company than the girls back home."

"Well, you just mind yourself," I warned

274

him in the tone of an older brother. "On corporal's pay — *ex*-corporal's pay, at that — you won't be able to afford too much companionship."

During the course of the war, Nashville had been garrisoned by thousands of permanent troops, with thousands more passing through from the Northern states to the southwest theater. The swelling male population had been matched by a similar increase in the number of prostitutes and bawdy houses. An epidemic of syphilis among both soldiers and civilians had forced the city's military governor to take action.

His first attempt had been to round up and export the enterprising women. The effort was in vain as the exiles slowly returned, or others rose up — or lay down, as it were — to take their places. After the failure of that policy, Governor Johnson took the opposite measure of legalizing the trade, requiring licenses and routine physical exams. Like many other wide-eyed country boys, Dave had become a frequent and eager patron of the industry.

"Oh, it ain't like that," he said with a boyish grin. "Well, not all like that, anyway. And the Higgins sisters always cut a fair deal for us boys in blue, especially since I kept them in venison most of the winter."

I couldn't help but grin at that. Even in the confines of the hospital, tales of the largest brothel in Nashville were the stuff of legend. With nearly thirty mouths to feed — including more than a half-dozen children — I could see how Dave's hunting skills would turn a fair barter.

"I got nothing waiting for me back home, anyway," he went on. "Hell, it ain't even home, really — just the place I'm from. No, I figure I'm brought to this place for a reason and I might as well stick with the ride, see where it takes me."

We paced around the yard a few more turns before a warder caught my attention and waved me back inside.

"Looks like that's it for me," I said, and extended my hand to Dave. "You take care of yourself."

"I'll see you around," he promised, shook my hand firmly, then headed for the outer gate while I hobbled back to the prisoners' ward.

I was two pages into a new letter to Gina when a young major stepped in and cleared his throat.

"Inasmuch as the Army of Northern Virginia has capitulated to the United States' Army of the Potomac," he read from an official document, "all convalescent prisoners of war under the jurisdiction of the provost-marshall of the City of Nashville, and below the rank of colonel, shall be paroled on their honor, upon their release by competent medical authority and pursuant to their taking an oath of non-belligerence to the United States."

He handed the document to Lieutenant Colonel Randolph for his inspection.

"Colonel Hodges will be by this afternoon," the major added, referring to the provost's adjutant. "Godspeed, gentlemen."

He came smartly to attention, turned and left the room.

" 'Except the Lord build the house, they labor in vain that build it,' " Randolph quoted from Psalms before handing the document to the major in the adjacent bed. "Our labor is ended, gentlemen."

Two days later, the doctor cut away my cast and pronounced me fit for release. I dressed in my uniform — now patched and cleaner than I could remember its ever having been before — and gathered up my few personal effects. I hobbled around the ward on a single crutch to bid farewell to the other men, then followed a corporal, who ushered me to a small office.

"Have a seat, Captain. Robbins, is it? I'm Major Arthur," the officer greeted me, and pointed me to a chair.

"Yes, sir. Thank you," I replied, and lowered myself awkwardly into the chair.

"How's the leg?"

"It's still there," I said as I rubbed the aching knee. "I'm glad enough for that."

"Indeed. Here's the drill, then," he said as he placed a document in front of me. "Your parole states that you will not take up arms nor serve in any capacity against the United States of America, nor render aid to the enemies of the same, until such a time as you shall have been duly and properly exchanged."

I gathered he'd recited those words more than a few times in the past couple of days.

"Or . . ." He placed another form atop the parole.

"Or?"

"Given the state of things," he said, "it's only a matter of time until it's all over for good. Lee's done, Sherman's cut off any possibility of resupply for the remaining troops. Within a couple of weeks — a month at the outside — it'll all be finished. The president wants reunification to be as quick and painless as possible. Have you read his inaugural address?"

"I did." Several times, in fact. " 'With malice toward none, with charity for all . . .' "

"Exactly," Arthur said with a nod. "Chances are there'll be a general amnesty — certainly for the junior officers and enlisted men, at any rate. When that comes, you'll most likely be required to trade this," he indicated the parole form, "for this." He tapped the second form, which had *Oath of Allegiance* printed boldly at the top. "Sign this now, and you walk out the door free and clear."

"That's it?" I asked, skeptical it could be over so easily.

"Not quite," the major acknowledged. His chair creaked as he leaned back and steepled his fingers under his chin. "In consequence of your oath of allegiance, you will be provided with a pass for free conduct back home, along with two months of pay in grade. Let's see," he figured, leaning forward to review the documents. "As a captain, that would come to two hundred thirty-one dollars."

I sat dumbfounded as I searched the other man's face for some sign of a joke. There was none.

"You're serious?"

He nodded.

"I made one-thirty a month, though," I said, chancing a grin.

"Different army, different pay," he allowed. "But I think you'll find greenbacks a bit more valuable than Confederate scrip."

"True enough," I agreed, figuring I could do without the extra twenty-nine dollars. "Where do I sign?"

"How's it feel?"

Dave Perkins leaned against the heavy marble baluster at the base of the hospital's stairs. I smiled at the familiar greeting in a world suddenly foreign to me.

"Good," I said. "Strange, but good."

"I know what you mean. It's nice to be out of that itchy wool," he said, and theatrically shook out his arms and smoothed the collar of a new jacket.

"Nice suit."

"Brand new, right off the rack," he boasted. "Got four months' back pay when they mustered me out. More'n fifty dollars," he added in a low voice, after looking about to make sure no one else was in earshot.

I gave a whistle. "Impressive. Uncle Sam must've been mighty pleased with your soldiering."

Dave grinned and bobbed his head humbly. "Well enough, I suppose. How about you? Any bounty for the Godless Rebel heathen brought back into the fold?"

"A bit," I allowed with a grin. "Main thing is, I'm out, free and clear. Plus passage home." I patted my breast pocket where the pass lay.

"That's right good news, Cap'n."

"Jim," I corrected him. "My army — hell, my country — doesn't exist anymore, except on paper. Nope, now I'm just a lowly civilian like yourself."

"Well then, Jim," he said, emphasizing my name for effect, "what are your plans?"

"Beg, borrow or steal a way to get home."

"That safe-conduct ought to make things a mite easier." He scratched the peach fuzz on his chin for moment. "Alabama, right?"

"Arkansas," I growled.

"Right, right. That's somewhere west of here, yeah?"

"About five hundred miles that way," I confirmed, pointing homeward.

"Riverboat's probably your best bet, then." He picked up his rucksack and rifle. "Come on. I'll show you the way to the landing. There's one stop I'd like to make on the way, though," he said, a twinkle in his eye.

The stop was a surprisingly brief one as he led me to a large house on Front Street, facing the bank of the Cumberland River. I waited awkwardly in the parlor as Eliza and Rebecca Higgins, mistresses of the house, tried to make me at home.

"Call me Becca," the elder sister offered.

My mind reeled back to the too few and far distant memories of my own Becca. I sipped at my tea as images of loved ones lost paraded through my mind. I clung to the hope of the one, grand love that remained, and stepped back from the edge of despair.

"Thank you, ma'am," I said, and did my best to play the part of gracious guest.

Dave adjusted his jacket as he swaggered down the stairs. He paid his respects — along with his fee — to the ladies, then led me to the riverboat landing. I studied the map nailed to the agent's booth and traced the meander of the Cumberland as far as Clarksville, where the Louisville & Nashville Railroad intersected the river for a nearly straight shot to Memphis. The Little Rock & Memphis line would carry me from there, and it'd be a simple matter to board a riverboat up the Arkansas to Van Buren. To home.

"We'd best hop to it," Dave advised. "Looks like the *Baldwin* leaves in about an hour. Best stock up here — I know a good outfitter just down the way."

"Hold on a second," I said as he started up the street. "We?"

"Well, sure," he replied with a shrug. "I figure I've seen enough of this burg. I get a mite itchy if I set in one place too long. I got nothing particular in mind, so I thought I'd tag along with you, if that's all right. Besides, with that bum leg of yours, you could probably use a little looking out for. 'On foot and out of my way to assist and serve a worthy brother,' and all that."

I stared blankly at him for several seconds, then finally gave a shrug.

"Suit yourself," I said. "Lead on, Corporal."

Within a half hour we'd bought ten days' worth of food and supplies — more than enough to see us to Van Buren, I figured. I planned to stop in on the Warrens at Little Rock, so we'd have a chance to resupply there if need be. My pass got us aboard the *Baldwin* without any fuss, and by noon the dank, musky air of the river was gently blowing in my face.

Nothing much happened on the downriver trip, other than the ugly stares from men in blue uniforms. I quickly decided it'd be best to strip the rank and insignia off my uniform. There was no helping the grey of the woolen jacket or the red felt of my artilleryman's cap. The less I could make myself look like an officer of gunnery, though, the better.

Word of President Lincoln's assassination reached us while we waited on the train at Clarksville. A few diehard Rebels — older men and younger boys who, I figured, had never been witness to combat or violent death — cheered the news, only to be shouted down by Unionists. Even more arguments erupted over the nature of Andrew Johnson, Lincoln's successor and the man — traitor, the Rebels insisted — who'd been the military governor of Tennessee during most of the war.

By day's end, we'd witnessed a half dozen fights ranging from little scuffles to an all-out gun battle. With such violent reactions to the war's end in this little river town in a border state, I feared the reunification and healing of the nation as a whole would be neither quick nor painless.

A week after leaving Nashville, we reached the gate on the walk that led to the Warrens' door. The cast iron was blotched with rust spots where the black paint had peeled away. The hinges made a mournful racket as I forced the gate open. The lawn, always so well kept, was patchy and knee-high with weeds. Crabgrass sprouted from the flagstone walk and the pavers heaved and wobbled where roots forced them from their bed.

Several of the majestic walnut and oak trees that once anchored the lawn were gone now, only their ragged, blackened stumps remaining. As we neared the veranda, we could see the paint here, too, was flaking off. The porch rail was loose, and the warped steps and floorboards creaked as I hobbled clumsily up to the porch. One screen door hung drunkenly on a single hinge while the other leaned against the wall beside the door frame. The ornate lead glass of the main door was gone, replaced by knotty boards that had been scavenged from the far end of the porch.

I knocked on the door and it swung open behind my knuckles.

"Hello?" I called out as I stepped tentatively across the threshold.

My voice echoed strangely in the high-ceilinged space, and I realized it was due to the lack of any furniture in the foyer that had once been so richly decorated. Cobwebs hung where drapery and tapestries had once been, and the carpeting had been replaced by a thick layer of dust.

Trails in the dust led from the sitting room to the stairs and from the stairs to the kitchen, suggesting the house hadn't been abandoned all that long ago.

"Hello," I tried again, and led Dave into the sitting room.

The half-light through the shuttered windows revealed scattered stacks of books piled carelessly around the floor, the bookcases stripped of their shelves and trim. Even the mantel that once held the beautiful pendulum clock was missing, and the fireplace looked like it hadn't housed a flame in years.

I was about to turn and explore the rest of the house when the ominous *clack* of a gun's hammer froze me in my tracks.

"Hands out to the side," a gruff voice ordered, "and turn slowly around."

Dave and I both put our hands out, and I squeezed the crutch in my armpit as I hopped around on my good foot. The double-barrel shotgun had seen better days, but the business end still looked plenty serious as it traced from me to Dave and back again. The man who held it had a long, trim frame. His loose-fleshed face was clean-shaven and framed by a thick shock of white hair. The deep creases in his forehead were strangers to me, but the intelligent gleam of

286

the soft brown eyes was unmistakable.

"Uncle Cy?" I said.

The man stiffened. His expressive eyes narrowed at the familiar greeting. He craned his head to examine me in the failing light, then pulled the shotgun tighter to his shoulder.

"You're not Matt," he growled. "The poor boy's long dead."

"I know, Uncle Cy," I said softly. "I was there when it happened. It's Jim — JD."

"JD?" he repeated.

He appraised me with another long gaze before the lined face cracked into a grin and revealed the familiar creases around his laughing eyes. He lowered the gun and stepped toward me, clapped his free hand behind my neck to study my face more closely, then pulled me into a tight bear hug.

"Welcome back, boy," he said as he pounded my back. "Thank God you've come through safe."

"Thank you, sir," I wheezed from crushed lungs. "It's good to see you, too. This is Dave Perkins," I said when I'd recovered my breath from the rib-cracking welcome.

"Pleased to know you," Cy told Dave, who winced as he shook the big man's hand. "Helen will be so glad to see you. Come, come."

"I'm anxious to see her, too," I said, then pointed to his shotgun. "You planning to uncock that thing?"

"What, this?" Cy chuckled as he let down the twin hammers. "Damned thing hasn't seen a shell in nigh on a year. Come on along now."

We followed him along squeaking floors, past the shambling stairs, to the kitchen where Cassandra and Missus Warren sat with Miriam, a pile of snap peas on the table between them. Miriam and Cassandra hummed a duet — a practice Missus Warren had never tolerated, as I could recall — to keep cadence as they broke off the stems, snapped the pods in two and tossed them into a half-full pot.

"Did you frighten off those hooligans with your empty gun, Cyrus?" Missus Warren asked without glancing up.

Her scratchy voice had grown even harsher with time, but I couldn't help smiling at the familiar, no-nonsense demeanor.

"No, dear," Cy said. "I'm afraid they've taken us captive."

Miriam and Cassandra stopped humming at that, and looked up with wide eyes. Missus Warren's look was more curious than alarmed as she craned her long neck back to peer through her glasses — perched, as usual, at the end of the beak-like nose. Her steely eyes squinted in the dim light as she peered at me, then softened as she saw through the years.

"Well, my goodness," she said softly, then wiped her hands on her apron, rose and stepped toward me. "Praise the good Lord for carrying you safely through."

Emotion betrayed her voice as she placed her cold, bony hands on my cheeks and gave me a quick embrace.

"JD?" Cassandra said as she rose and came toward me.

Her hair was darker now, like burnished copper, and the years had melted away the baby fat that plagued the girl I'd known. In her place stood a slender, elegant young woman with keen, good-humored eyes that the war seemed to have passed by. She wrapped her arms around my waist, and I felt a guilty pleasure as her soft, warm body pressed against me. Not counting Missus Warren, it was the first time in four years I'd touched a woman, and the memory of that and other sensations quickly rose to the surface.

"Mind your manners, James, and introduce your friend," Missus Warren ordered.

I cleared my throat and introduced Dave to the women. They exchanged handshakes and greetings, and I noticed Dave's lingering stare on Cassandra.

"At least the good Lord saw fit to bring one of my boys home," Missus Warren said in little more than a whisper. She pulled off her glasses and pressed one hand to her eyes. "Oh, fiddle-faddle." Apparently, Mister Webster's lexicon had expanded during my absence. "The light's gone so far as a body can't see her hand in front of her eyes. I'd best go fetch a candle."

"They's one right on the counter, Miz Warren," Miriam offered.

The older woman waved off the help with a flailing hand before pushing through the side door of the kitchen. Uncle Cy laughed.

"Haven't seen her so fallen out in twenty years or more," he said. "You boys able to stay for a while?"

"Just a spell, if it's no trouble," I said. "I'm eager to get back to Britton, but I wanted to stop in to see you on the way."

"Well, we don't have as much to offer you as we once did," Cy admitted with his signature good cheer. "A warm meal with family, a soft bed and a dry roof are about the best we can do."

"The meal'd be a mite nicer if we could keep those dad-blamed rabbits out of my garden," Miriam said.

"Oh, hush," Cassandra said to the older woman. "They only pester you because you've the finest garden in all of Little Rock."

"Be that as it may," Uncle Cy went on, "I believe we'll make do. Fetch me one of those candles, would you, Miriam? Let's get these boys settled in."

"If you don't mind, sir," Dave spoke up, handing his bag to me and pulling his rifle from its sheath, "I might take a peek at that garden and see if I can't get us a little something extra for the supper table."

"Suit yourself, Mister Perkins," Cy said. "These Arkansas rabbits are cagey little buggers, though. Cassandra dear, show Mister Perkins the garden, would you? Can you manage the stairs, JD?"

"Yes, sir, I'll be fine," I said as Dave and Cassandra went out the back door.

Mister Warren lit his candle and led me from the kitchen to the stairway. Before we'd managed to climb halfway up the creaking steps, a shot rang out, followed less than two seconds later by another.

"If nothing else," Cy said, "he'll frighten those rabbits out of Miriam's cabbage."

By the time we returned to the kitchen, Miriam had a fire in the oven and a pot of water set to boil.

"I hope everyone's in the mood for some stew."

". . . and, Lord, we thank you for delivering JD and Mister Perkins safely to us," Uncle Cy prayed, concluding the grace. "May we ever be mindful of your many and varied blessings. In the name of Thy Son we pray, Amen."

"Amen," I repeated, along with Miriam, Cassandra and Missus Warren.

"Am— ow," Dave cried as Missus Warren's serving fork jabbed his elbow.

"I meant to warn you about that," I said, barely able to stifle a laugh. "Elbows aren't allowed on the table here."

"Thanks for that," Dave groused, rubbing his elbow as he glared at me. "My apologies, ma'am."

"Providing dinner is no excuse for poor table manners," Missus Warren replied.

"Yes'm," Dave acknowledged, and I couldn't hold back my laughter as he received a further lecture on the English language and its proper usage.

After dinner, Dave and I joined Cy for cigars on the back porch.

"How are you, really?" I asked.

"We're fine," Cy assured me. "Things aren't quite so bleak as the appearance of this old place would make you think. Seemed prudent to let things slip a bit so as not to draw attention to ourselves. And, truth be told, the place is a fair bit more than the four of us could tend to anyway."

"What happened to everyone?" I said.

"When the Federals came in, they freed all our slaves. Conscripted the men, and did Lord-knows-what with the younger women. Miriam's the only one left. Thought we'd lose her, too, after they took Timothy. Poor thing — her boys vanished and her man sent off to fight."

"Dave, would you mind giving us a minute?" I asked.

He cocked his head at me, but didn't press his curiosity.

"Sure," he said. "I'll just take me a little look-see at the garden again."

When he'd gone, I told Cy everything about Zeke and Izzy. Of Zeke and Ketty's escape, and my promise to Timothy not to tell Miriam. Of Izzy's death at Nashville, and my murdering his killer.

"Did Timothy tell you where Zeke and Ketty settled?" Cy asked when I'd finished the story.

"No. Somewhere in Indian Territory, I imagine, but there's no telling if they've moved on since then."

Uncle Cy nodded thoughtfully at that.

"I appreciate your telling me," he said. "I'll see what more I can find out, and we'll see to Miriam. Now, then, how long might you boys stay?"

"We don't have any definite plans, if that's what you mean. But I'm a bit anxious to get back home to Britton."

Cy's face clouded at that, but he tried to mask the change with a puff of cigar smoke.

"And — ah — what all have you heard from there?" he asked.

"Nothing since I left for the war," I admitted as my stomach turned to rock, and a chill crept toward my heart. "Why? What's happened?"

Cy waved a hand to dismiss my concerns. "Not to worry. Everyone's fine," he said. "Well, Ben's had a rough go of it, but Charlotte and Angelina are both well. Things got tough for them once the war got underway, and they — well, they moved up to Saint Louis to wait things out."

"I see," I said, though I didn't see at all. Why Saint Louis? And why the feeling that Cy was holding something back from me? No sense pressing the matter, I decided, but maybe Cassandra would be a little more forthcoming.

"Well, if they're not in Britton, I don't

suppose there's much point in heading upriver. By the looks of things," I added as I leaned against a weathered porch rail, "you might could use a hand around here for a little while."

"A couple of pairs," Dave added as he came around the corner from the garden.

"Now, boys, I can't ask you to do that," Cy said. "After all this time, you must be anxious to be on your way."

"That's so," I agreed, "but you and Missus Warren have done more for me than I could've ever hoped for. More than I can ever repay, in fact, but I wouldn't be a man if I didn't at least try."

Over the next two weeks we helped restore the old house to a semblance of its former glory. We closed up broken window panes, replaced loose and squeaking steps, added a fresh coat of paint. Dave even set out a series of snares for Miriam to keep her garden free of rabbits and her stew pot full.

I watched with amusement — and just a hint of envy — as Cassandra's girlish crush on me transformed into a womanly attraction to Dave. Despite his worldly ways, the former scout seemed entirely ill-equipped to deal with a lady's affections outside the safe confines of the Higgins sisters' establishment. He fumbled and stuttered any time Cassandra came near him.

The morning we left, Mister Warren led me into the sitting room. He rummaged through the stacks of books until he found the one he was looking for.

"For you," he said, and handed me a battered copy of *The Age of Fable,* his most cherished book.

"No, sir, I can't."

"Take it," he insisted, pressing the book firmly into my hands. "Lord knows I've read it enough times to have it by heart."

"If you're sure," I said, and got a satisfied nod in return. "Thank you."

"And there's one other matter I'm sure you haven't forgotten."

I grinned sheepishly at that.

"I haven't forgotten," I said. "I just didn't figure there was much point in bringing it up."

Before I'd joined the state guard, I entrusted Uncle Cy with the thousand dollars or so of Gina's dowry, and arranged to have the bulk of my pay — when it was actually delivered on — sent directly to him. After Little Rock fell to the Union — and even more so now that the Confederacy had been dealt the deathblow — I gave up hope of ever seeing my small fortune again.

"Let's see now," Cy mumbled as he searched through another stack of books. "Ah, here it is," he said as he located the copy of Ovid.

He leafed through the oversized volume and pulled out several sheets of paper that had been tucked between the pages. He counted the individual sheets and riffled through the book once more to make sure he'd recovered everything.

"Here you go," he said.

I took the sheets from him and flipped through them. They were all identical, with the exception of a serial number printed on the upper left side of each. Every page was headed by the title, *Union Pacific Corporation, Certificate of Stock.*

"Seventy-three shares of common stock, par value one hundred dollars," Cy read from a ledger sheet, which he also handed to me. "I know it's not good practice to put all your eggs in one basket, but I believe this railroad will be just the ticket, as it were. When Congress passed the Railroad Act last year, I cashed out all our other positions and bought up as many shares as I could."

I stared blankly at the ledger sheet, unable to wrap my mind around the numbers shown there.

"You're free, of course, to do with them

as you like," he said, "but the dividends alone will turn a fair income for you. Frankly, I've yet to see a railroad that can be run worth a damn, but Congress is going to make sure this road gets built. Till then, at least, I don't see this stock going anywhere but up. There's this, too," he added, and pulled a small purse from his coat pocket.

I took the silk bag from him, untied the string and peered inside. The metallic *clink* and ruddy gleam of the contents made my breath stop.

"What's this?" I said.

"The part of your pay I wasn't able to invest I changed out of scrip," he said. "Even if we'd won, the decisions coming out of Richmond weren't worth spit. I didn't figure it'd be long before a dollar wouldn't be worth the paper it was printed on. After the Federals took the city, I managed to find a few . . . businessmen, shall we say, who were willing to take scrip for gold. I only managed about thirty cents on the dollar but, looking at it now, I'd say it was a fair trade."

"I won't argue with you there," I said. "But I still don't know what to say."

"No need to say anything. It's all money you earned — I just piggy-backed it with my own, helped steer it along a bit."

"I can't wait to see the look on Gina's face," I said. "Thank you, sir."

He faltered a little before saying, "My pleasure, son. Godspeed."

I scarcely noted the edge in his voice as I placed the fortune in my bag, then followed him out of the sitting room to the front porch where Dave waited with the ladies. Cassandra spoke quietly and earnestly to Dave as I said good-bye to Miriam and Missus Warren, then she gave me a fierce hug and a kiss on the cheek.

"You two look out for each other," she told us, then handed me a slip of paper with a Saint Louis address.

Dave seemed reluctant to go, but followed me out the gate, down the hill and to the rail depot across the river. We boarded a flatcar on the Memphis train that would carry us to the Mississippi River. From there, we'd find a paddlewheel to carry us up to Saint Louis.

To my dream.

CHAPTER ELEVEN

Saint Louis, Missouri — May 1865

"Vagabond filth."

The angry shout was followed by the sharp slam of a door. Dave and I picked ourselves up from the lawn where we'd been thrown by the house's manservant.

"You sure this is the right place?" Dave asked as he retrieved my crutch and helped me to my feet.

I compared the crumpled, rain-soaked slip of paper with the stone-carved number in one of the columns that framed the ornate veranda.

"Twenty-seven, Lucas Place," I read. "We are in Saint Louis, right?"

"That's what the man said."

Our riverboat had docked less than an hour earlier. We'd trudged up the long hill from the boat landing, through the Missouri Park and under the gated archway that marked the entrance to this neighborhood.

A cold spring rain hampered our progress and dampened our spirits, but my anticipation of the homecoming had driven me on.

Dave sucked at his teeth and shook his head sympathetically.

"Well," he said, "I don't know what to tell you. Maybe it's best to try again in the morning?"

"Maybe so," I agreed reluctantly, then took a lingering gaze at the unwelcoming door and limped heavily after Dave toward the gate.

"Jim?" A tentative voice came from the direction of the house.

I paused and turned to take in the vision as the house lights outlined a form in the doorway, backlit in graceful silhouette. Wide, velvet skirts tapered to hug a slender waist. A heavy shawl hid most of the luxuriant, auburn hair, but what was revealed framed the alabaster skin of a sculptured face, with lips and cheeks glowing red in the chill air. Even from across the lawn I could see the emerald eyes ignite as they met mine.

"Oh, God — Jim," Gina cried, raising her hands to her lips.

She stepped toward me, hesitantly at first, then with rapidly growing speed as she crossed the veranda, leapt down the steps and dashed across the walk. I overcame my own surprise just in time to open my arms to meet her as she threw hers about my neck. I took two or three painful steps back to keep from falling under the force of her embrace, but I easily set the pain aside as Gina clung to me. I folded my arms around her and pressed her body to mine, hungrily breathing in her scent as I buried my face in her hair.

The world stopped. All existence faded away, leaving no other reality than the woman I held in my arms, no notion of the passage of time other than the rapid staccato of our hearts pounding against one another. When I was at last able to draw back from the embrace, it was only to bring my lips to hers. The moist warmth of our mouths was a stark contrast to the cold night air as we fed one another's hunger for an eternity. Only the rough clearing of a throat brought the world's intrusion once more.

"I hate to interrupt," Dave said, "but knowing Jim's social graces, I'm like to melt before he introduces me."

Gina giggled as she pulled herself away from me. She licked her lips as I wiped at my own, blending the last sweet drops of our passion into my rain-soaked goatee.

"I see things haven't changed then," she said, the lilt in her voice a balm to my ears. "His manners never were quite proper. I'm Angelina Bra—" She bit off the word, and more color rushed to her rosy cheeks. "Oh, just call me Angelina," she said, and extended her hand.

"Dave Perkins. Nice to meet you. I've heard a lot about you."

She lowered her eyes and looked awkwardly from Dave to her hands to my feet. The blood drained from her face as she finally noticed my crutch.

"Jim, you're hurt," she said.

"Nothing that won't mend," I assured her, then winced as I shifted my weight. "Of course, it's nothing that standing in the pouring rain is liable to help, either."

"Of course," she said, drawing the shawl more tightly about her shoulders. "I'm already soaked and you both must be chilled to the bone. Come in, please."

She led the way up the walk and onto the veranda. As we crossed the threshold, the same manservant who had ejected us now held open the door for our entry, his steely eyes no more welcoming than before.

"Avery, hang these gentlemen's coats to dry, and put on some tea," Gina instructed him.

"Yes, madam."

The man didn't bother disguising his contempt as he looked up and down Dave and me, then to the growing puddle on the floor. He grimaced as we shrugged out of our soaked coats and more water dribbled from our hats.

"And please bring my father to join us in the parlor," Gina added.

"Yes, madam," he said, then disappeared through an adjacent doorway.

"Chatty fella," Dave observed.

We set down our bags and followed Gina through a set of sliding doors into a brightly lit salon whose fireplace glowed with a welcome blaze. An older woman sat by the fire, white hair covered with a black shawl that matched a plain black dress. For a moment, I thought it must be Gina's grandmother. When the woman looked up at us, I recognized Missus Barnes, aged twenty years in the four since I'd last seen her.

"Mother," Gina said, "look who's come. It's Jim."

The older woman raised a trembling hand to her mouth. Wide eyes shifted from Gina to me and Dave and back again.

"My land," she finally managed to say, then rose shakily to her feet and stepped toward us, her face twisted with emotion.

"Come here, child."

She opened her arms to me with more warmth than I could ever remember from her. I limped forward and wrapped my free arm gently about her.

"My land," she said again. She held me firmly for a moment before patting the damp back of my shirt and releasing me. "But where are my manners? You must be bone-weary. Here, do sit down."

"Yes, ma'am, thank you," I said as she steered me to a chair beside the fire. I fell into the thick cushions, stretched out my stiffening knee and rubbed my hands over the fire. "Please forgive me — this is my friend Dave Perkins."

"Pleased to know you, Mister Perkins."

"Likewise. Thank you for having us in. It's a mite nasty out," he observed as he shook the woman's hand, then took a seat on the other side of the fireplace.

An ornate divan lay next to my chair, and Missus Barnes sat at the end nearest me. Gina sat quietly on the other side of her mother and alternately wadded then smoothed the fabric of her dress.

"I must say, it's quite a surprise to see you," Missus Barnes allowed, "but a pleasant one, indeed."

"Thank you, ma'am," I said. "I'm sorry

305

for not sending word ahead. I wanted to surprise you, but I hope it's not an inconvenience."

"Don't be silly. After all, you're practically family — you were always like a brother to Angelina and Matty."

Her eyes took on a pained look as she said the name. Her son had been lost for more than three years, but the wound to her heart seemed still fresh.

I shot a questioning glance at Gina on being equated as a brother to her. Her eyes were fixed on her hands, now white-knuckled as she bunched up the material of her skirts. The hiss and pop of the fire was the only sound as a queer silence fell across the conversation, until the doors rumbled open and Avery appeared with Mister Barnes.

My heart sank. I struggled to my feet as Avery wheeled Mister Barnes into the room. The butler placed the rolling chair next to Gina, who tucked a blanket snugly about her father's legs and smoothed his hair.

Barnes was only a shadow of the man I remembered. The farmer's powerful, meaty hands — hands that had worked his own fields and provided for his family — now rested limply atop the blanket, his right hand bent and gnarled. The familiar shock of reddish-brown hair was replaced by a sparse patch of white atop a head that lolled to one side. His formerly penetrating eyes were now dull and unfocused. A narrow rivulet of white crust stretched from one corner of his mouth to his chin. Gina moistened a handkerchief and daubed gently to clean his face.

"Daddy," she said softly, and Barnes's eyes wandered in her direction. "Daddy, look who's here. It's Jim."

The man's eyebrows twitched at that. His head bobbed in short jerks as he scanned the room with lazy eyes. I stepped around the coffee table and knelt in front of him to ease his search. His right eye refused to hold steady, but his left eye locked onto mine and glistened in recognition. His lips parted as though he were trying to speak, but all that came out was a wheezing moan accompanied by a trickle of saliva, which Gina dabbed away.

"Mister Barnes, sir," I said, and tentatively laid my hands on his. "It's good to see you."

"Avery, fetch another chair, if you would," Gina said as I winced with the pain of kneeling.

The man stepped wordlessly from the room and returned a few moments later with a hard, straight-backed chair that he placed next to Mister Barnes.

"Thanks," I said.

Avery ignored me and turned to Gina.

"I'll bring the tea along shortly, madam."

"When did this happen?" I asked after Avery closed the doors again.

"Just after you boys left for the war," Missus Barnes answered with a sigh that registered more resignation than sadness. "About a month after you were gone, the raiders came again. They burned the fields and what was left of the barns. Only the house was spared. I'm afraid the loss was more than Benjamin could bear."

"Doc Aubry said there was nothing he could do for Daddy in Britton." Gina took up the telling. "So we moved up here." She glanced quickly to her mother, and the two women shared a moment of silent understanding.

"So that's when Matt joined the Missouri boys?" I said. "I never did see much of him after that, not till Elkhorn Tavern. And when you never wrote," I added to Gina, "I thought — well, I'm not sure what I thought."

A pained look crossed her face, while Missus Barnes went suddenly guarded. Mister Barnes just looked slackly at me, his good eye glinting with reflected firelight.

"I wrote," Gina finally managed to say. "Hundreds of letters. You never got them."

"No," I answered, unsure whether there'd been a question.

"Army probably wanted to make sure you weren't passing secrets to the enemy," Dave chimed in helpfully.

"That must be it," Missus Barnes agreed while Gina resumed the gloomy study of her knuckles.

It suddenly felt like there was some great secret hidden in the room and I was the only one kept out of it. An awkward silence again fell over us, broken only by the fire sounds, Mister Barnes's labored breathing and the grim ticking of the mantel clock.

"Jim," Dave said after several moments, "what's the time?"

The clock was right over his head, and it took me a bit to fathom his meaning.

"Oh, right," I finally said.

I reached into my jacket pocket and pulled out a gleaming, gold pocket watch. Both women gasped as the watch spun on the end of its chain, reflecting firelight in a rippling pattern on the papered walls of the salon. Mister Barnes's eye twitched and fixed on the heirloom and his crippled right hand jerked slightly as he tried to reach for the watch.

"When it wasn't with Matty's effects, we thought it was lost," Gina said as she reached out a trembling hand.

I lowered the watch into her hand, coiling the golden links atop the closed lid. As I placed the fob in her hand, Gina closed her hand lightly and caught my fingers in her grip. I was electrified by her touch and sat motionless, unable and unwilling to break even that slight connection. Missus Barnes broke the spell by clearing her throat, and Gina pulled back her hand, then gave the watch to her father.

"Matt made me promise to bring it home to you myself," I explained.

"You saw him?" Missus Barnes asked, her eyes shimmering in the firelight.

"Yes, ma'am. I was with him when he — when he passed over." I explained about the flanking Union troops, Champion's charge and the sharpshooter's aim. "He didn't suffer," I lied. "I held him, and talked to him until he fell asleep."

"Did he say anything?" Missus Barnes asked, her handkerchief held to her mouth with a trembling hand.

"Just that he was sorry," I recalled. "That, and to bring the watch home." I didn't mention the part about following my dream, who was sitting right across from me.

"And he nearly botched that job," Dave interjected as Missus Barnes retreated behind her handkerchief and sobbed softly.

"True enough," I allowed, glad for the change of topic. "I'd have probably lost it if Dave hadn't been around to keep an eye out for me."

"Oh?" Gina said.

"Well," Dave said, "I don't suppose it was all that much."

"Oh, come on now," I needled him, "there's no need for modesty here."

He shot me a wry glare, then took a deep breath and embarked on an engrossing — if not entirely accurate — account of our meeting. Avery's arrival with tea and cookies gave me a chance to interrupt and correct some of the fabrications. The ladies seemed to prefer the unedited version, particularly when the story benefited at the expense of my dignity. Even Mister Barnes's eyes seemed to sparkle with amusement.

"And that," Dave offered in conclusion —

"Is how he single-handedly put down the rebellion and saved the Union," I finished for him, raising my teacup in salute.

"Something like that," he said with a grin, and took a sip of his tea.

"Well, thank you for that riveting tale, Mister Perkins," Missus Barnes said, and wiped at the tears of laughter that mingled with the earlier ones of sorrow.

"Yes, thank you," Gina added. "For that, and for bringing our Jim safe home to us." She raised her cup and took a slow sip, fixing me with a look of unsettling mixed emotion.

The parlor door slid open and I looked up over my shoulder, expecting to see Avery's scowl. The doorway was empty, though — or appeared to be until I lowered my eyes to where a sandy-haired angel stood shivering in her nightdress. She rubbed at sleepy eyes with one tiny fist while the other clutched a bright-colored rag doll.

Gina glanced at me with a pained expression, then hurried to the door.

"What are you doing up?" she asked as she scooped the girl up and brought her to the divan.

"I heard Grandmama laughing," the child said in a little voice, then eyed the coffee table. "And I smelled Avery's cookies."

"You may have half an oatmeal, then it's back to bed with you." Gina broke one of the soft, brown cookies in half and handed it to the child, who eagerly accepted the treat. "Ginny, can you say hello to our guests? This is Mister Perkins," she indicated Dave, and the girl looked shyly at Dave under long eyelashes.

"Pleased to meet you, miss," Dave replied with friendly formality, and Ginny hid her eyes behind the half cookie.

"And this is your —" Gina's hand trembled as she indicated me. Her eyes took on a tortured expression. "This is your mommy's good friend, Mister Robbins."

The girl took a bite of cookie and stared at me through wide, hazel eyes.

"Are you hurt?" she asked me between chews.

I nodded even before I realized she was pointing at my crutch, for the hurt was now centered a few feet above my wrecked knee.

"In the war?" she said.

She couldn't have seen four years yet, and it seemed tragic that this innocent should know anything of war. I nodded again and managed a hoarse, "Yes."

"My Uncle Matty was hurt in the war, too," she added. "He's in heaven now."

"Yes, he is," I agreed.

I stared into the flames that did nothing to thaw the ice that formed about my heart. When I found the strength to move, it was to grab my crutch and pull myself to my feet.

"It was good to see you all," I said as Dave rose and moved to my side. "I'm glad Matt's watch is where it belongs, and I —"

I scanned the eyes in the room, but Gina's and her mother's were turned away, with only Mister Barnes's good eye and Ginny's wide pair meeting mine.

"Good night." I swallowed hard and turned for the door.

Avery was waiting in the foyer with our coats. I was too eager to escape to mind his scornful, victorious glare, or to mind that the coat was as cold and wet as I'd left it.

"Jim," I heard Gina say behind me, but I couldn't turn to face her. "Jim, please, I —"

"Thank you for the tea," I said, summoning all my strength to keep my voice even.

I pulled the wet coat around me. The ice in my heart flowed through my veins to chill and settle my emotions. I stooped to pick up my bag and turned.

"Good night, Missus . . . ?"

Gina shook her head slowly, painfully, and said, "Jim, please, don't."

I cocked my head and repeated, "Missus . . . ?"

Gina took a shuddering breath and hugged her arms around herself. A pleading gaze held my eyes for a moment, then turned down, away from my cold stare.

"Braddock," she finally admitted.

I snorted in grim understanding as I

314

recalled the pompous captain from Fort Smith.

"Good night, then, Missus Braddock," I said, and stepped into the frigid night's welcoming rain.

The following weeks and months passed sluggishly, as though Time itself were caught in the same frozen grip as my heart. Dave and I took rooms at the Lindell Hotel, and I found a clerking job in the county recorder's office while Dave was hired on at a meat-packing plant. The jobs were anything but interesting, but kept us sheltered and clothed and fed. For me, life had boiled down to just that, only the essentials.

After the first night in Saint Louis, I'd avoided any contact with Gina. I ignored the invitations to dinner — much to Dave's annoyance — and by the time summer rolled around, the offers had all but stopped coming.

"Are you planning to avoid her forever?" Dave asked at one point, as we sat in Missouri Park and I stared blankly at the falling autumn leaves.

"I don't know," I admitted with a sigh. And I didn't.

The answer came, though, on a warm January afternoon, the first thaw of winter.

I returned from the map room to my cubbyhole of an office and was surprised to find a visitor seated at my desk.

"Take me to lunch?" Gina asked innocently.

The diffuse light from the single, small window lit her features and melted my heart like the snow that dripped from the ledge outside.

"Sure," I stammered.

I fumbled to set the maps on the crowded desk before reaching for my coat and cap and cane.

"You need a new hat," she observed as I flipped the worn, red kepi on my head.

"It serves well enough."

I wrapped my hand tightly about the cane and stuffed the other in my coat pocket as I led the way up the flight of stairs to the main level and out the heavy doors of the courthouse. I flinched as we started down the wide marble steps and Gina wrapped her arm through mine, pulling herself close to me as we walked.

I gave an ironic snort and shook my head.

"What is it?" she asked.

"Nothing."

"You don't get off that easily."

"We've never been out in public together before," I said. "Somehow I didn't imagine

316

our first time out to be with you as someone else's wife. Hell, I never thought you'd be someone else's wife, period."

She let go of my arm. Her eyes lost their sparkle, and she kept silent for the rest of the walk. I led her a few blocks up Fourth Street, to a little café where I often had lunch.

"It's probably not up to your standards," I said as I pulled the door open, "but the food's warm and filling."

"I'm sure it'll be fine," Gina said.

We'd beaten the lunch crowd and had our choice of seats. Rather than my usual place at the counter, I steered Gina to a little table in the corner, away from the draft of the door. We sat in awkward silence until the waitress came for our order. Once those simple words were spoken, the rest came more easily.

"We missed you for Christmas," Gina began.

"I know. I meant to thank you for the invitation, but I was —"

"Busy, I know," she finished the lie. "Just like you were busy at Thanksgiving and Independence Day and every other time. May I ask with what, exactly?"

I'd practiced a dozen excuses, but these evaporated in that instant, leaving me with only silence or the truth for an answer. Truth won.

"Trying to breathe," I said. "Trying to keep my heart beating."

A moist sheen came over her eyes at the blunt honesty, and she looked at the checkered linen tablecloth, where she traced a random pattern across the red and white squares.

"I never meant to hurt you, Jim," she said. "And I didn't mean for you to find out the way you did."

"The best laid schemes . . ."

"That's not funny," she rasped, and shot an icy glare across the table.

"Neither is finding the woman I love married to another man, and with his child." I struggled to keep my voice under control so as not to disturb the few other diners. "Did you wait at all, or did you go to him as soon as I left your bed?"

"It's not how you think," she whispered, and a tear rolled down her cheek.

"Well, that's my mistake then," I said. "I thought you'd simply thrown away our six years together, forgotten all our promises and passed over your poor surveyor because you were really in love with some rich cockerel. Clearly I must be wrong."

"I never said I was in love with him," she

318

retorted, her eyes ablaze with pain and anger.

I sat open-mouthed, unable to form a response. The waitress returned and set our food on the table before making a hasty retreat.

"Then why?" I absently picked up my spoon and stirred my soup until I realized I had no appetite.

"What else could I do?" she asked plaintively. "I was alone and Daddy was sick. We needed someone to take care of us."

"I would have done that," I said.

"You left," she said, and the simple accusation slashed through my heart.

"I left to protect our home," I said. "To protect you."

"The best laid schemes . . ."

Gina threw the words back in my face, and it was my turn to study the tablecloth. She reached across the table and laid a soft hand on mine, and I looked up into sparkling eyes.

"Jim, if I could leave Simon, I'd do it in a heartbeat, but it's not that simple."

"Why not?" I asked. "Gina, I can take care of you."

"And Ginny?"

I swallowed hard at that.

"She's a part of you, so how could I not

love her?" I said, half believing it. "Look, I have my savings and a decent job. Given time, I can turn it into a good job. I may not be able to give you Lucas Place, but I can provide a good home for you. For us."

"I know about the dowry you were saving up before the war, and it's sweet," she said in gentle condescension. "But what of my parents? Can you provide for them, as well?"

I lowered my eyes at that, unable to meet her probing gaze.

"We have nothing, Jim," she said. "Nothing. Our crops were all burned out, and we had to mortgage everything when Daddy took ill. You know there's nothing I wouldn't give up to be with you," she insisted, "but I can't make that sacrifice for Mother, and I won't make that sacrifice for Daddy."

"Whatever it takes, we can find a way," I said, my voice faltering as I squeezed her hand and searched her eyes for some sign of encouragement.

"I already have," she stated flatly, and pulled her fingers out of my grip. "His name is Simon Braddock."

"So that's it? You're giving us up, just like that?"

"I have to," she said, "for the sake of my family. And, if you love me — if you really love me — you'll let me go."

"You know I love you," I said, blinking away the clouds of confusion in my eyes, "but I don't know if I can do that."

"That's why I have to," she said, and pushed back her chair. She rose and placed her hand softly atop mine, leaned over me and pressed her lips to my cheek for several seconds. "Good-bye," she whispered in my ear and brushed my cheek with hers, mingling our tears.

Then she was gone.

I stared across the table at the empty chair, stunned and sick at heart and oblivious to anything else around me. When the waitress finally returned to clear the table, I was surprised to find the dining room nearly empty.

"Are you all right, sir?"

I looked up, and the pity in the woman's eyes drove the knife deeper into my heart. I bit my cheek and shook my head.

"What do I owe you?" I managed in a husky voice.

"Don't worry about it," she offered with a gracious smile. "I take it the food wasn't very good. No charge."

I nodded my thanks and struggled lamely to my feet. I gathered my coat and cap from the rack near the door, but lacked the energy to put them on. The morning's warmth had given way to a bitterly cold afternoon. I ignored the chill as a stinging north wind made my eyes water, and shuffled numbly toward my room at the Lindell.

"A package for you, Mister Robbins," the desk clerk told me on the first Saturday of February.

"Thank you," I replied with some surprise.

I took the large box from the counter to a seat in the lobby. The wrapping had only my name on it and gave no clue as to the sender or the contents, but my heart leapt when I recognized the handwriting.

I pulled the string loose and tore away the brown paper to discover a hat box with *Fellini* printed on it. I lifted the lid and was surprised to find a brown felt fedora inside, a bright red feather gaily tucked in the hat band. I set the hat on my head — a perfect fit — and looked again in the box, where I found an envelope and a second, smaller box.

The envelope was blank, and I set it aside to open the box. I instantly recognized Matt's watch nestled in a bed of cotton stuffing. I pulled it out and ran a thumb over the scratched script-*B* on the lid, then depressed the spring to open it. I took a sharp breath as, looking back at me from

within the hollow of the lid, was Gina's image, her graceful features faithfully pre-
served in a sepia-toned tintype.

I balanced the open watch on my knee,
swallowed the lump in my throat, and slid a
finger under the seal of the envelope. I
trembled as I tried to keep a tight rein on
my hopes, and clapped my knees together
as the watch began to slip. I set it safely on
the table and pulled the letter from the
envelope.

*I said you needed a new hat — hope it
fits.*

*Daddy wanted you to have Matty's
watch, and I wanted you to have what's
inside, to remember. And to say good-bye.*

*We leave for New York on the 3rd, sail-
ing on the 10 o'clock steamboat for Rock
Island. I don't know that I would be able to
leave you again if I were to say good-bye
in person, but I do hope to see you once
more.*

*I know my decision has brought you
pain, as it pains me to make it. I can only
pray that a loving Providence will have
mercy for this sacrifice, and that we may
one day find each other again.*

Until that day, I am lovingly and af-

fectionately yours.

G —

I read through the note twice, blinking hard to clear my eyes. As I searched the meaning of each word, I chanced a look at the watch: 9:43.

I shot to my feet, grabbed the watch and hurried to the door.

Hobbling as fast as my lame knee would allow, I hopped-limped the eight blocks from the hotel to the boat landing, where I pressed my way through the queue at the ticket counter. I ignored the angry shouts as I scanned the roster of departing boats, found the one that matched the time and destination, then pressed deeper into the crowd.

Only two minutes remained until the scheduled departure and the *Eurydice*'s stacks already billowed with smoke. Stevedores and porters crowded the area near the aft gangway, and the press of bodies and cargo nearer the passenger ramp made it impossible for me to pass.

The ship's bell rang the hour, and the shrill blast of the steam whistle cut through the air. Deckhands tossed off the lines while the last of the shore crew leapt nimbly from the deck to the pier. The port side paddle began to spin, churning the muddy water as the boat edged away from the dock.

I pushed my way to the edge of the pier and wrapped my arm about one of the stout bollards as I leaned out over the water to watch the departing boat. Scanning the crowd of passengers that lined the aft rail, I spied the telltale flash of bright, auburn hair. I had no breath to shout, and knew the effort would have been wasted over the noise of the engines and whistle. I merely raised the hat in my free hand and waved it slowly over my head.

I was about to give up the effort when I saw Gina raise her handkerchief. She held Ginny in one arm and pointed me out to her. The little girl waved pudgy fingers at me while her mother blew a kiss across the silt-laden water. I held the hat as if to catch the farewells, then dropped my arm to my side. Still clinging to the bollard, I followed the *Eurydice* with my eyes until she turned the first bend in the river.

As she disappeared from sight, the steam whistle loosed a mournful wail that matched the cry of my heart.

CHAPTER TWELVE

Nebraska Territory — May 1866

Dearest Gina,
My heart is broken within me. A pool of sorrow lies stagnant where once flowed happiness and joy. I haven't words to describe the depths of my sadness, yet I must give expression to it or be drowned in the abyss.

All I've known has been taken from me — family, home, the friend of my youth. Everything. I am alone in the world with none who knows me, none who understands me, none to whom I can unveil my heart and mind. None, save you.

Yet, Flame of my Heart, it is you who has taken my last happiness from me, who has dealt the death-blow and placed the final shovelful of dirt on the grave of my joy —

I put down my pen and tore the page from

my notebook, crumpled the brittle paper into a tight wad and pitched it into the flames.

"If you're just gonna burn it, couldn't you at least let me have it for bum wad?" Dave asked from the other side of the campfire. "I'm getting tired of using bark."

I ignored the question. Instead, I capped my pen and ink and returned them with my leather-bound journal to my bag.

"I'm going for a walk," I said, then picked up my hat and cane and struggled up the slope that flanked the riverside camp.

"A walk. Well, that makes sense," Dave said to my backside. "We've only been walking for two weeks."

I didn't answer, but willed myself to the top of the slope and into the high grass where I might lose myself in the rolling waves of wind-swept prairie. Despite a cooling breeze, I soon broke a sweat from the effort. I only managed a few dozen strides before my cane landed in a prairie dog hole. My knee buckled, sending me headlong into the grass.

I cursed and shouted and beat at the ground. My anger quickly turned to frustration, frustration to grief. I lay where I'd fallen, clutched at the thick grass, and shouted my rage and heartache into the earth. It was the first time since Gina left that I'd given in to the pain. In utter isolation — no family or friend or lover or God to comfort me — I plunged into the hell of despair until, completely overcome, I loosed my hold and fell into oblivion.

By the time I came again to my senses, the breeze had died away and the sky had faded from powder blue to a dark-sapphire curtain. Occasional clouds glowed red in the last rays of the sun. The thin sliver of the moon peeked just above the eastern horizon, accompanied by a handful of stars.

Spent, I lay on my back and watched the formation of the night sky. Reason suggested I head back to camp. I couldn't muster the will to move, so remained on the ground even as the cold earth sapped the heat from my body. After what seemed hours, my full bladder provided the impulse I needed, and I stirred myself from my stupor.

I groped about for my cane and found it still standing in its hole. The tip drove itself deeper into the earth as I put my weight on it. I managed to find my feet, and limped toward a row of brush to relieve myself. I sighed with the release and scanned the prairie as my eyes became accustomed to the growing darkness. I breathed deeply of the night air as my own scent mingled with that of the rich soil and plants in a thick, heady smell that cushioned just beneath my nostrils.

My stream suddenly stopped and my spine went rigid as a familiar tingling shot through me like a bolt of lightning in my veins. Even before my mind could make sense of things, I found myself crouched behind the row of brush, fumbling to button my fly while I struggled to keep my balance.

Someone is there, instinct warned me. *Several someones.*

Senses honed to a fine edge, my ears strained for some hint of what lurked beyond the veil of darkness.

It's only the wind, I tried to convince myself.

But there was no wind.

The rustling in the grass — slow, careful, stealthy — might have been lost in even the slightest of breezes, but the deathly stillness of the night gave no cover for whoever or whatever was approaching. The brush and grass blocked my view, and it was only my ears that registered the passage of several sets of heavy footsteps somewhere in front of me.

The rustling had almost faded when I heard one of the tracks falter, sensed the figure turn and look in my direction. I held my breath and willed my heart to cease its pounding against my ribs, lest it give me away. I could feel my adversary reaching out with all his senses even as I tried to meld into the night.

I caught the sound of another set of footfalls approaching — heavier than a man's — followed by a whispered exchange, then more silence as two sets of senses probed the darkness for me. After another round of whispers and what sounded like the rustle of a horse's mane, the pair continued on their way.

When their footsteps faded, I allowed myself to take a shallow breath, just enough to ease the burning in my lungs. The ache of my knee was joined by the sting of cramped muscles as I held my crouched position for another hundred rapid beats of my heart. Then I pushed myself erect and exhaled through clenched teeth to let the tension seep from my muscles and nerves.

I took my bearings and realized the steps had faded in the direction of the creek. With as little noise as possible, I retraced my steps toward camp. As I neared the embankment, I caught the faint glow of a shielded fire and the hiss and crackle of unseasoned wood. I dropped to my belly and crept forward until I could peer down into the camp where the little fire valiantly struggled to hold back the fearsome darkness.

Dave lay on his back near the fire, his head resting on his rucksack, eyes covered by his hat. Wary of the night stalkers, I thought it better to warn Dave quietly rather than to raise a sudden alarm. I felt along the edge of the bank to find some pebbles or clods of earth.

Without warning, the night's stillness was sundered by a string of heart-stopping war cries. The shrill ululations froze me where I lay, but Dave immediately bolted upright. A Bowie knife appeared in his hand as if by magic.

Before he got to his feet, four sets of thundering hooves crashed into the campsite, painted ponies bearing painted men. Other than their decorations, the ponies were unremarkable. Their riders were another matter.

Their faces and bared chests and arms were smeared with ghastly patterns, and the warriors looked as though they'd emerged from the mouth of hell itself. Eyes wide with bloodlust, mouths gaping as they screamed their war cries, the riders' long hair streamed behind them like darkling flames. The riders wore only buckskin loincloths and rode bareback. They gripped their mounts with their knees while their hands wielded fearsome war hatchets that whirled in sweeping arcs, the blood-stained heads gleaming red in the firelight.

Separated from the raiders by the fire, Dave took a defensive posture and made as though to retreat from the flames. His escape was cut off as the band stretched into a column and formed a deadly circle that spun madly about the camp, just at the edge of the fire's light. Dave raced back to the fire, using the flames as a rear guard. He crouched low, his eyes scanning the darkness beyond the riders, looking for help.

Looking for me.

I swallowed my fear and forced the abandoned lover to give way to the warrior I'd tried to forget. I traced the movements of the riders, timed their passage and — when the moment was right — launched myself from the river bank.

My own war cry resounded in my ears.

My target had just enough time to turn his head and show his surprise before our bodies met and my momentum carried us both over the pony's croup. I wrenched the grotesque hatchet from his hand and swung the death tool across his throat, leaving a bloody gash in its wake.

I turned from the fallen man as another rider bore down on me. There was just time to note the twin handprints on the pony's chest before I threw myself out of the way and tumbled across the rough, pebbled ground. No sooner had I righted myself than, from the corner of my eye, I glimpsed a body sailing toward me through the air.

I'd somehow managed to hold on to my cane all this time, and I aimed its tip at the center of the attacker's feral snarl. I fell back from the impact and shuddered at the sickening crackle as tipped wood penetrated the soft flesh at the back of his throat. The howl that had rung out only moments before instantly fell silent.

The cane jerked out of my hands when its tip met the back of the rider's skull, and the man went reeling past me. He came to a stop as the butt end of the cane stuck among the river rocks. The force of the impact drove the cane into the ground, leaving the Indian's body propped almost comically on his knees.

I spun away from the grisly scene and scanned for the next attack. By this time, Dave had felled one of the remaining warriors. The last man — finding himself alone

— loosed a bone-chilling cry before steering his pony away from the bloody scene and back the way he'd come.

For the barest flicker of a moment I thought to let the man go, but he could easily return with reinforcements, and there was no telling how close his camp was. I hefted the tomahawk I'd captured, took aim and flung it after the fleeing rider. Dave's Bowie knife flew close behind and we were rewarded with a dull *thwap-thunk* as the blades found their target. The pony raced on into the gloaming beyond the camp's fire, but the heavy sound of a falling body assured us that news of the raiding party's fate would not reach far.

"You all right?" Dave asked breathlessly.

"I think so. You?"

"Better'n I'd have been if you hadn't showed up when you did. I think it's safe to say these three are out of it," he said as he surveyed the carnage. "I'll check on the other one."

"Good idea. I'll see if I can't corral a couple of these ponies. We'd best put some distance between us and them tonight."

"No argument there," he agreed, then grabbed a fallen hatchet and stalked into the darkness.

Without their riders, the ponies had

gathered together at the edge of the creek, tamely drinking from the cool water and nickering softly to one another. I moved to my rucksack — past the third man, slit belly to bollocks by Dave's Bowie knife — and pulled out a coil of rope and my own knife. I measured out a few arm-spans of rope, cut it off, then repeated the process to make a pair of lariats.

I rummaged through the bag until I found a small apple, which I quartered before sheathing the knife in my boot. I eased sidelong toward the ponies, careful not to make eye contact or any sudden moves.

The ponies watched me through cautious, paint-encircled eyes. The largest one — a striking dark bay — stepped between me and his companions, shook out his mane and sniffed the air as he pawed at the ground. The handprints on his chest marked him as the same one whose charge I'd narrowly escaped. I swallowed my nervousness and approached the beast at an angle, an apple quarter held out in my hand.

I stopped about four paces from the pony, the apple still held out to let him smell the sweet fruit. He was already accustomed to people, so it didn't take much effort to earn his trust — the fate of his previous owner notwithstanding. With a confident tread, the pony came closer, accepted the peace offering and let me slip one of the lariats over his head.

Seeing their companion's good fortune, the other two — both dappled palominos — ventured a few tentative steps toward me, which I encouraged by the offer of two more apple chunks.

As I led the team toward the fire, Dave emerged from the darkness. He didn't say a word as he headed straight for the water's edge, where he knelt to rinse his knife and the hatchet in the pure stream. I let him make his peace while I gathered our packs and lashed them together in a makeshift saddlebag.

The ponies didn't seem to mind the new arrangement, so I chose the bay and the larger palomino for riding, fashioning crude halters from the rope. I put a lead around the third pony's neck and set the bags on her back. By the time Dave joined me at the fire, the pony train was ready to set out.

"Let's get the hell out of here." Dave jammed the Bowie into its sheath on his belt and handed me a pair of tomahawks.

I choked back a gag as I took a last look at the charnel-house scene, then stripped the bodies of their remaining weapons and tucked them into the packs.

"What about your cane?" Dave asked as he swung onto the back of the palomino.

I looked to where the warrior hung from the hickory stick.

"I'll manage without."

Dawn had gathered on the horizon by the time we reached the muddy banks of the Missouri River and turned north. The fourth pony had found us during the night, and it was with two mounts and two pack animals that we rode into Nebraska City just before noon.

The freight town's streets were clogged with people and livestock and wagons, all part of the mammoth effort of moving goods from the industrial East to the burgeoning West. In addition to the household goods needed to settle the plains — and the military supplies to protect those settlements — were tons of steel rails and wooden timbers awaiting shipment upriver to Omaha and the ribbon of track that stretched westward from there.

As we passed through the crowded streets, pedestrians and teamsters pressed against one another to make room for us, their faces mixed with curiosity and horror. I was too tired from the all-night ride to pay much mind, and it wasn't until we reached the livery yard that I chanced a look back toward Dave — and understood the reasons behind the attention.

We'd not stopped along the way any longer than to water the ponies. The war paint was still bright on the animals' breasts and flanks and legs and heads, symbols of power in bold, savage colors. More savage was Dave's appearance, his clothes thickly smeared with black veins of dried blood, smaller spatters on his face and hat. I looked down at myself and, judging from the front of my shirt, my own appearance was no less frightful.

"Sixty for the pair of 'em," the hostler offered for the pack ponies when we reached the livery.

"Seventy-five," Dave countered. "These here are genuine Pawnee war horses. You can sell each one for that price, easy."

The other man scratched at a grizzled jowl and smacked toothless gums impatiently.

"Sixty," he repeated, "and I won't charge you for washing the damned paint off them."

"Done," I agreed before Dave haggled us out of the sale. "And, if you'd point us toward a fair outfitter and a room, we'd be much obliged."

As the liveryman counted out the bills, he

gave us directions to a general store where we'd find a good bargain on tack and supplies, and an honest hotel that offered hot baths and clean beds.

"And, unless you want them for souvenirs," he said, indicating our packs, "I'll give you five dollars apiece for them hatchets."

"Deal." I eased the pack off my shoulder and fished out two tomahawks as Dave did the same.

The man licked hungrily at cracked lips as he eyed the ugly weapons.

"I — I don't reckon you took the scalps, eh?"

A wave of revulsion washed over me, and I threw down the blades at the man's feet.

"Five dollars each," I growled, sickened at taking the blood money.

"Just asking, Chief," he said. "There's plenty enough folks around here that's lost kin to those savages. More still that's heard the stories. I reckon you could turn a pretty penny if you was to pawn a sure-enough redskin pelt."

"We'll just be stabling with you overnight," I said, changing the subject. "See you first thing in the morning."

"Suit yourself," he said. He stooped to pick up the weapons, then thumbed one of the blades, crusty with dried blood.

I turned away and limped out the gate, onto the rough-planked boardwalk and toward the general store. At first taken aback by our appearance, the shopkeeper warmed to us when we showed him our bankroll and gave him the list of supplies and goods we needed. Accepting a deposit of half the total bill, he promised to have the saddles and harnesses delivered to the stables before we left.

"Can you point us to the Seymour House?" I asked after we'd made our arrangements.

"Seymour?" he scoffed. "You fellows don't want to go there. Oh, it's a fit enough place for river rats and farm boys still with shit between their toes. Gents like you — present appearances aside — would be far more comfortable at the Cincinnati House. Brand spanking new, and the rooms are still cheap. Trying to put the squeeze on old Seymour," he added with a conspiratorial wink.

"Corner of Eighth and Otoe," he said as he led us out the door and pointed the way. "This here is Fifth. You go three blocks up and two blocks left. I send my boy up there every so often, so if you need anything, just leave word with Mister Bagley and we'll get you all squared away."

Following his directions, we arrived at the

340

massive, wood-framed building. As we approached, a small black boy emerged from a side door on the alley followed by a man in a long-tailed suit. On seeing us, the boy's eyes went wide. He turned on his heels and scampered down the alley away from us. The man, however, put on a smile and came toward us.

"You must be the gentlemen Mister Naisbitt sent to us. Mister Perkins?" He extended his hand and Dave shook it. "Which would make you Mister Robbins, yes? Splendid. I am Phillip Bagley, *maître d'hôtel*. Please, come this way."

He led us through the alley door to a well-appointed office.

"We are delighted to have you gentlemen staying with us," he said. "You will understand, of course, that your entering through the lobby in your current condition might arouse more attention than you would otherwise wish. Please, do have a seat."

He pointed us to a pair of overstuffed chairs, then tugged on a bell cord and pulled a pair of keys from his desk drawer.

"Your rooms are prepared," he said, "and I have hot baths being drawn for each of you. Also, Mister Dodge has asked that you be his guests at dinner this evening at eight."

"General Dodge?" I asked.

341

"Yes, of course. Word has already spread of your unusual arrival, and the general is eager to meet you. Ah, Master Luke," he said as a young man dressed in the hotel's livery knocked on the door and stepped inside. "Be so good as to take these gentlemen's things to their rooms."

"Yes, sir," the boy replied, taking the keys from the man and not seeming to notice our bloody appearance.

"Master Luke will be at your service during your time with us," Bagley said. "Once you are settled in, we'll see to laundering your clothes. Have you a replacement set?"

We both shook our heads.

"Then allow me to see to that." He closed the door and spoke to us in a lower voice. "Ours is a proper establishment, gentlemen, but we pride ourselves on anticipating our guests' every need. Should you require any . . . shall we say, assistance while bathing, or to facilitate your rest, I shall be happy to make suitable arrangements."

It'd been more than a year since Dave's last visit with the Higgins sisters, so I was surprised when he shook his head.

"That won't be necessary, thank you," he said.

"Very well," Bagley said. "Now, if you'll follow me."

342

The innkeeper led us from his office, up three flights of stairs — which I managed with increasing difficulty — and down a long hallway before stopping at a pair of corner rooms. "The view from these rooms is not our finest but, being above the alley, they will be the quietest at this time of day." He handed us each a key and shook our hands again. "If you have need of anything else, please let me or Master Luke know. Good day, gentlemen."

I shared a questioning look with Dave, then shrugged, stepped into my room and closed the door behind me. I stripped off my bloody clothes and sank into the canvas tub. Steaming water leached the pain from my muscles and joints, but could do nothing for the ache that continued to squeeze my heart.

At length, I rose from the tub, toweled myself off and fell naked on the soft bed. I pulled the watch from my bag and flipped open the cover, then set it on the nightstand. With Gina's smile emblazoned on my eyelids, I fell into a deep, dreamless sleep.

I awoke with a start, and it took several moments to remember where I was. A low-burning lamp had been placed on the nightstand while I slept, and I turned up the wick. The light revealed a new suit of clothes hung by the toilet stand. I was still puzzled by Bagley's hospitality, but would have to save the questions for later. My watch already read 7:30, so I hauled myself stiffly out of bed and hurriedly dressed.

As I looked in the mirror, the image was that of a younger man in a different suit, one I'd worn on my first night with Gina so many years before. I could feel her touch, smell her scent, hear the song of her voice. My heart and mind faltered, and when I came to my senses again, I found myself sobbing on the floor by the bed, rocking back and forth as I hugged my knees to my chest.

A knock sounded on the door, and I checked my grief and wiped my eyes with my palms.

"Yes?" was all I could manage.

"You about ready?" I heard Dave's voice say.

"Sure. Just give me a second."

I eased off the floor, then wiped my eyes and blew my nose on a handkerchief. I straightened my suit in the mirror, and gathered my watch. Gina's image caught my eye again, and I fought to stay in the present. I took a deep, shuddering breath as I stroked the sepia-toned cheek, then pried the thick paper from the lid. I held the tintype in the palm of my hand and studied the features one last time before closing my fist around it.

"If you love me, you'll let me go," I said in a hoarse whisper.

The words wrenched my heart no less than the first time they'd been spoken. I steeled my resolve, straightened my shoulders and dropped the crumpled photograph down the oil lamp's chimney. The paper flared brown and gold, and a thin column of black smoke marked the funeral pyre of my love, my hope.

"How'd you sleep?" Dave asked as I stepped into the narrow hallway.

"I slept," I said. "That's enough."

"I hear that," he replied. "What do you make of all this, anyway?"

"No idea," I admitted as we turned down the stairway.

The answer came as we stepped into the lobby. The room was packed with men and women dressed to the nines.

"Ladies and gentlemen," Bagley addressed the room, "our heroes."

The crowd cheered and applauded enthusiastically, and we were instantly surrounded and pebbled with questions.

"How many were there? Are they truly

red? Did you take any scalps? I hear they ride naked."

"Don't I know you?" a gruff voice boomed, and the pressing crowd parted to make way.

Grenville Dodge no longer wore a soldier's uniform. There was no mistaking his military bearing, though, and his manner still made people jump to obey. He approached us, a burning cigar in one hand and a snifter of brandy in the other.

"Yes, sir," I acknowledged with a grin. "I had the pleasure of sitting in lodge with you back in sixty-two, just before —"

"Pea Ridge," he finished for me.

"At Elkhorn Tavern, yes, sir."

"You came across the creek with the others," he said. "Helped convince us you all were still camped across the way. Mighty fine strategy, taking us in the rear like that."

"I'd like to say it was my doing, sir, but it was all General McCulloch's idea."

"Might've worked, too, if you hadn't run short on ammunition."

His eyes glinted as he took a sip of brandy. I thought back to that second day at Elkhorn Tavern, to the short stores of artillery rounds, the news of the supply wagons being sent back to Bentonville, the Confederate retreat that shortly followed.

"That was my idea," he added.

"This, too?" I asked, indicating the new suits and crowded lobby.

"No, I have to say the credit for all this goes to our host, Mister Bagley." He drew on the cigar and leaned toward us, letting his words float on a puff of smoke. "I daresay he'll make more than enough on drinks and dinner tonight to pay for a pair of suits. Now, then," he said, stepping back and including the entire room in the conversation, "from what I hear, I could have used you men up in the Black Hills. How many savages were there? Eight? Ten?"

"Four," I replied dully.

He raised an eyebrow at that.

"Even so," he said, "two-to-one odds is nothing to buck at."

"Four-to-one, till Jim showed up," Dave pitched in, stepping up to the role of carnival barker. "And, let me tell you, it was none too soon."

While Dave wove his tale, I slipped through the crowd toward the bar.

"Rye," I ordered.

"Same," Dodge said as he joined me. "Your friend is quite the story-teller."

"He is that," I agreed.

"And what of you, Mister Robbins?"

"Jim, sir," I said with a shake of my head.

"I've been a blacksmith, a surveyor, a gunner. A story-teller I've never been. Frankly, I'm not sure what I am now."

Dodge nodded thoughtfully at that and studied me with sharp eyes. Our drinks came and he tipped his glass to me before taking a sip.

"I leave for Omaha tomorrow to start driving that pig of the Union Pacific westward. Tell me, Jim — what do you know about railroading?"

CHAPTER THIRTEEN

Lincoln County, Nebraska — September 1867

I shifted in my saddle and urged Rigel onward, galloping into a night lit only by the half moon and a dozen torches. Scouts had reported a band of Cheyenne camped on railroad lands. Colonel Sperling, General Dodge's right-hand man in charge of railroad security, had sent us to evict the squatters.

I'd wondered aloud why the mission couldn't wait for morning, but the colonel's wilting stare made me bite my tongue.

"I'll take the men, if you need your beauty rest," my second, Charlie Garrett, had generously volunteered.

Veiled insult aside, I'd seen how Charlie dealt with Indians — or blacks or Chinese or Mexicans — before. The troop would ride with or without me, and my being there to draw a rein on the men would give us a better shot at a peaceful outcome.

As we approached the camp of four tipis pitched around a central fire, our thundering hooves brought warning shouts. Men tumbled out of their shelters to line the small defensive barrier of brush that guarded the entrance to the camp. My riders fanned out from double-column to form a single line, twelve across.

I brought them to a stop a dozen paces from the camp and raised my right hand in greeting.

"*Ha-ya-heh,*" I said in greeting.

The men kept their rifles and war hatchets visible and their eyes locked on us, but one called over his shoulder, "*Pok' Ho'nehe, hoa'ha.*"

An old man — the clan elder, I supposed — answered the summons and stepped from one of the tipis, leaning on an attractive young woman for support. I tried to focus on the pair as they approached, but the flickering of the campfire and the wavering shadows thrown by our torches had a hypnotic effect on me.

At once, the scene resolved into something from a nightmare. The nine Cheyenne men transformed into a mix of Union officers and Pawnee warriors, all with faces painted or streaked with blood. Turquoise and buckskin changed to diamonds and silk and, where the girl and old man had been, I now saw Gina and her father, hands and feet bound as a raging fire inched closer to them.

"Gina!" I shouted.

I drew my revolver and spurred Rigel toward the camp. Without waiting for orders, my men drew their weapons, and shots rang out. The gunfire brought me back to my senses, but it was too late.

Four of the Cheyenne fell in a heap at the entrance to the camp. The other five fell back, while the girl half-supported, half-dragged the old man toward the shelter of the nearest tipi. Even as I shouted for my men to cease fire, more shots tore through the night, and the remaining Indians dropped in a tangle, the big-caliber rifle shots adding to the men's momentum to drive them headlong into the ground.

I tried to bring order to the chaos, but a dull *whoosh* flew over my head and I watched helplessly as torches landed among the tipis. The fire quickly spread in the dry buffalo fur, and the skins and support frames quickly took to flame. I shouted again at my men, but there was no stopping the massacre.

Women and children fled from the burning tents, only to be shot down by the riders who now circled the camp like vultures awaiting the next kill. Screams echoed from the tents as the occupants chose the inferno to a bullet.

The horror lasted for what seemed an eternity. One by one, the tipis collapsed as the framing gave in to the flames and turned into funeral pyres for the poor souls left inside.

I drew Rigel closer to the camp, using my hand to shield my face from the raging heat. The horse shook his mane and pawed at the ground as the stench of wood smoke and burning flesh filled the air. The pounding of hooves and the cheers of my men sounded outside the camp, but the only noise that came from within was the rush of the flames.

Bodies lay scattered among the carnage. Some were past recognition as having ever been human. Others — the lucky ones, I supposed — bore little more than a red-ringed hole in their backs to suggest they were anything more than simply asleep.

I scanned the debris for signs of life, moving from one tipi to the next. As I passed the third one, a movement caught my eye and a shape crawled out from the smoking ruin. What had once been a slender, shapely arm was now a blistered, cracked and charred thing that groped to pull the rest of the form from the debris. A silver band on the arm caught my eye, and I recognized it as the one worn by the young woman I'd seen earlier.

Of the long, luxuriant hair, all that remained were a few locks of frayed strands clinging to her charred scalp. Bright red flesh shone through cracks in the blackened skin. The buckskin dress — what remained of it — hung in tattered pieces that fused to her body. A lipless mouth gaped at me, moving in silent speech. Her eyes stared straight at me from a face scorched fleshless.

She reached a skeletal hand toward me, her mouth crying out in silence, eyes pleading. Blinking away tears and ash, I drew back the hammer on my revolver, took aim and put two bullets through her head. Her body jerked and one eye drooped closed. The other eye, its lid already burned away, remained fixed on me.

"Nice of you to put her out of her misery, Jimmy Boy," a rough voice said behind me.

Charlie Garrett reined in his horse beside me, his rifle barrel still smoking. I tried to say something, but couldn't form the words.

"I'd say we're about done here, eh?" Charlie said.

I nodded dumbly and drew my horse

around. Charlie shouted for a couple of the men to round up the Indians' ponies, which had been picketed a little way from the camp.

"Ought to make a nice bonus," he said, "seeing as the colonel's put a stop to counting coup."

I ignored him and the continued hoots and hollers of my men, pointed Rigel toward our base camp at North Platte, and rode away from the smoking holocaust.

I dangle from the tree branch and wave my free hand.

It's the same dream I've had so many times before, and I wonder why it's come to me now.

I look down to see Ma and Pa and Becca, Zeke and Ketty — and a stranger, whom I vaguely recognize as the Cheyenne girl. Her dazzling white smile is made all the more brilliant by deeply tanned skin. Long, loose plaits of jet-black hair frame her face. I lock on to her deep, brown eyes, captivated by the intense gaze that sends a chill up my spine. In a graceful, fluid motion she rises, smoothes her buckskin dress and climbs toward me.

The tree bursts into flame. Slender walnut leaves turn brown and curl in on

354

themselves as a thick, acrid smoke rises from the green wood. From high atop the tree, I can just make out the calm world beyond the smoke and flames, but I can see nothing directly beneath me.

The branch from which I hang is smothered with flames. Even as it sags, a form emerges from the inferno below. First comes a hand, fingers stiff and curled into a death grip by the fire's heat. Clawing at the burning branches, the arm pulls its owner into view. Her hair is nearly burned away, the flesh of her head charred and cracked to reveal the bright red of raw meat beneath.

Her white teeth shine out still, not in a smile but in a ghoulish rictus exposed by lips that have burned away. Her eyes fix on mine as she nears me. She clutches my clothes to draw herself closer, and the stench of her seared flesh overwhelms me. The flames grow higher, wrapping us in a torrid embrace as she draws level with me, her eyes staring into mine. She brushes my cheek with one hand while the other clutches tightly at my shoulder.

"It's all right," she whispers in my ear, somehow forming the words through her lipless mouth.

Even as she speaks, the branch gives in

to the flames, tearing away from the surrounding limbs.

"It's all right," she repeats more emphatically, roughly shaking my shoulder as we plunge into the fiery abyss.

"Mister, wake up. It's all right."

The hand roughly shook my shoulder, then fell away as I jerked up in bed. I stared blindly into the darkened room, my breath coming in heavy, ragged gasps as I tried to find my bearings. Sweat streamed down my back, my naked skin sprouting goose bumps where damp flesh met cool night air.

"Are you all right?"

I jerked around toward the voice and tried to make sense of things as the woman turned up the oil lamp. Her henna-dyed hair was mussed and frazzled, and glowed dimly in the lamplight. Her wide eyes were only slightly brighter, and I recognized in them the vague, unfocused look that comes out of a laudanum bottle. She wasn't quite ugly, but I could see how dim light and a smoke-filled room would favor her. My thrashing around had played havoc with the sheets, which now bunched around her hips to reveal fair, pockmarked skin — almost ghostlike in pallor. Her small breasts bore testimony to the chill in the room.

356

"I'm fine," I lied, and the words rasped through my dry throat and whiskey-swollen tongue.

I squeezed my eyes shut, blinking hard against the nightmarish images that still lingered. When I opened them again, my gaze was fixed on the woman's midsection and a dark tuft of hair that gave the lie to her red locks.

I looked away and took in the drab room. The walls were papered with worn purple velvet, the floor littered with rickety, mismatched furniture. I tried to remember how I came to be here.

There'd been the celebratory gunshots as we rode back into town, Sperling's offer of whiskey all around, and the flash of red hair across a smoky saloon. Things became dimmer after a second round of whiskey and a steamy bath, but I got the gist of how things had gone.

"How long have I been asleep?" I asked.

The woman relaxed as I came back to my senses.

"Can't have been long," she allowed as she leaned against a pillow.

She laced her fingers behind her head, and the twin patches of black under her arms matched the one beneath the sheets.

"I don't usually fall asleep on the job,"

357

she said with a grin that I supposed was intended as lewd, "but you must've wore me plumb out. I'm surprised you had any energy left in you, after such a horrible experience."

"How's that?" I said.

"Your friends told us all about being attacked by those savages," she explained. "It must've been terrible, not knowing if you was gonna live or die?"

The words were spoken in a tone of comfort, but her eyes had the hungry look of a carnival-goer in line for the Hall of Wonders.

I shivered, both from the carnal look and from the events that spawned it.

"There, there," she said as she sidled toward me, wrapped one arm across my chest, one somewhat lower. "Jeanne's here to take care of you. Is it Jeanne?"

"Gina," I corrected her.

"That's right," she said. "Gina's here to take care of you. You just lie back, and everything'll be just fine."

But it wouldn't be fine and this wasn't Gina and I hated myself as I took her again. And yet again.

The sun was just limping over the horizon as I hobbled down the rickety, narrow stairs of the saloon. The stink of the place grew thicker with each step. The pungent blend of tobacco smoke, stale beer and unwashed bodies mixed with the tang of fresh sawdust and the stench of even fresher vomit. I tried to hide myself as I looked for the quickest way out, disappointed to find the table nearest the door occupied by Charlie Garrett and a handful of other men.

"Jimmy Boy," Garrett shouted around the cigar clamped in his teeth. He gestured for me to join them. "You survived, looks like," he said with an obscene laugh as I neared the table. "Here, I saved a seat for you."

He kicked the chair out for me, and I dropped into it. The table sat near the open window, where the fresh morning air held some of the room's foulness at bay. A pot of coffee and some cups sat in the middle of the table, though most of the men still had whiskey glasses in front of them.

"Thanks, Charlie," I said as I reached for the coffee pot. "Colonel." I tipped my hat to the man at the head of the table.

Colonel Francis Augustus Sperling sat with regal bearing as he held court at the small table. Garrett and the others tried to outdo each other in currying favor with the man.

"James," he said in greeting. "I trust you

had a proper debauch."

I wasn't sure how to answer the man, so I just raised my cup of steaming coffee in toast to him and sipped the near-boiling liquid. Blisters instantly rose on my tongue, and the pain served to clear my head.

"I understand you had quite a scrape with those raiders," the colonel pressed me.

Sperling had tracked Quantrill and his men throughout the better part of Missouri during the war, and *raider* was among the vilest of epithets to the career military man.

"I wouldn't exactly describe it that way, sir," I said.

"Really?" he said, and slupped his coffee from a saucer. "Exactly how would you describe being outnumbered three-to-one by a band of Cheyenne warriors?"

"I told the colonel all about it," Garrett chimed in before I could sputter my objection. "How we were ambushed by thirty of the savages while we rode under a white flag. How we fought them back, and they set fire to their own tents — women and children inside, the bloody savages — so their families couldn't see them get whupped. Ugly business," he pronounced, then threw back a double shot of whiskey and slammed the glass down on the table.

"That it was," I managed to say, sickened

as much by the lie as by the truth.

The blood rose in my cheeks and ears, and the pounding of my pulse drowned out the buzz of conversation at the table and the cries of agony that echoed in my memory.

"Excuse me," I said, and moved toward the door, bumping into men and chairs until I made it through the opening and into the fresh air.

The morning's coffee churned a stomach already rebelling against the night's whiskey. I just reached the alley before I spewed my guts onto the boots of some passed-out wretch. I stood doubled over, head between my knees, as I tried to catch my breath.

"Better?"

"I'll live," I said as I turned to face Charlie.

"That's more'n some can say, eh?"

A wicked sneer twisted his lips, revealing ugly, yellowed teeth.

"You and your men made sure of that, didn't you?" I said.

"Don't tell me that's what's eating at you. You were *there*," he said. *There* always meant the war when it was said that way. "You seen people die before."

"Yes, I have," I answered sullenly, and my fingernails cut into my palms as I clenched my fists. "More than I care to remember. I've watched men die before. I've killed before, but this . . . You murdered those people in cold blood, and you made me a part of it."

"It was you started the charge, you damn fool," Charlie said. "The boys and I just backed your play. Besides, the only one I seen you kill was that little bitch, and she was good as dead anyway. You just helped speed her on her way. Pity, though. She looked like she'd have been a bit of fun for a while. Well, before the fire got to her, anyway."

He laughed at his own joke, then folded his thick arms across his chest.

"Now that I think about it," he said, "I'd be mad, too, if I was you. You had to waste two bullets, plus a sawbuck upstairs, when you could've got it for free if we hadn't roasted that little slut."

Charlie's lips kept moving, but the sound of his voice faded beneath the pounding of blood in my ears. Before I had a chance to think, I found myself hurtling through the air. My shoulder drove deep into Garrett's gut as we flew out of the alley and landed heavily in the empty street.

"Boy, you just made a big mistake," he growled.

His meaty paws pried my grip from around his waist. He brought his knee up and caught me in the groin, then threw me over his head and sent me tumbling through the dirt and manure that littered the road.

Rage masked the pain as I picked myself up and turned to face him again. Before I made it all the way around, a sledgehammer fist smashed into my jaw and sent me reeling. A boot rushed toward my head, but I managed to roll away. I staggered to my feet, and Garrett fought against the whiskey and his own momentum to keep his balance.

Seizing the temporary advantage, I rushed him again, only to be brought up short by a vise grip at my neck. Garrett rammed his knee into my stomach once, then again, oblivious to the blows I rained down on his head and shoulders. Still holding tightly to my throat, he stood me upright and delivered another clout to my jaw. Blood flew from my mouth as I fell back under the assault, but I managed to keep my feet under me. I staggered back a few paces and brought myself to a stop just in time to meet another wallop.

The pulse in my head was replaced by an insistent ringing in my ears. My left eye swelled shut and the teeth felt loose in my head. Through my blood-clouded right eye, I saw Garrett say something I couldn't hear. He cocked his arm for a final blow. As his fist sailed toward me, I pivoted on one foot.

A look of surprise flashed across Garrett's face as I spun toward him, rather than away. The surprise deepened as I drove one fist into his thick paunch, the other into his Adam's apple. His momentum gave more force to the blows than I could have managed on my own, and sent me caroming off the big man.

Garrett sagged to his knees as I staggered back to my feet. His hands clutched uselessly at his throat as he tried to draw breath. I limped toward him, rage burning in my breast. Part of my mind argued for restraint, now that the man was down. The louder part reminded me of the screams of pain and horror wrought by his cruelty.

Don't sink to his level, the voice of conscience implored me. *If you strike while he's helpless, you're no better than he is.*

I knew the voice was right.

I also knew that I didn't give a damn.

I spun on one leg and delivered a roundhouse kick to Garrett's head. I watched in satisfaction as blood and teeth flew from his lips. In an instant I was atop the fallen man, clutching at his blood- and sweat-stained shirt as I pounded my fist against his face, switching hands when the first tired from the blows.

"That's enough, Jim." I hardly heard the voice through my murderous rage. "Enough."

Strong arms pulled me off Garrett, hauled me to my feet and pushed me away. I redirected my fury and swung blindly at the new target.

Dave caught my fist in his hand and twisted my arm up behind my back. Taking hold of my collar, he lifted me bodily and hustled me away from Garrett, toward a watering trough.

"I'm not finished," I said, and struggled vainly against my friend, my anger and hatred not yet spent.

"Oh, I think you are." Dave forced me to my knees in front of the trough and plunged my head beneath the water.

"Son of a bitch," I spluttered as he pulled my head from the trough. Long strands of horse saliva mixed with the water that streamed from my face. "What the hell do you think you're doing?"

"You want to make a mess of yourself?" he said. "Fine. But no amount of whoring or drinking or killing will bring Gina back to you."

"What do you know about it?" I spat over my shoulder, Dave's grip still firm on my collar and wrist.

"You self-absorbed prick," he rasped. "You think you're the only person to lose someone? The only person to feel alone in the world, to carry their mistakes around like a stone in their heart? Pull your head out of your ass and look around, Jim. The world's full of walking mistakes, people loaded up with guilt and regret. The best any of us can do is just push through the pain and get on with life."

"And what if I don't want to?" I turned my head toward Dave, and the rage in my heart turned to something colder. "What if I can't?"

"Then don't bother holding your breath this time," he said, and plunged my head once more into the trough.

I take a deep, surprised breath, only to find myself once more leaning against the great walnut tree. I shake off the images I've just seen, knowing full well what's to come.

"I don't want to see any more," I say.

"You always were a weak little cunt." Another figure breaks away from the circle of dancers and steps toward me. Removing the head covering reveals cold, steely eyes, a crooked nose and sneering mouth. "I half-feared you might see this through. Should've known you'd tuck tail."

I look to the first man, the kind one, but he just stares silently at me through calm, green eyes. The newcomer stalks forward. I shrink back as he reaches toward me, but he just throws his arm around my shoulders and draws me aside.

"Am I glad to see you," he says in a conspiratorial voice. "Whatever you do, don't listen to that bastard. You know who he is. You know

*what he done. Shit, you must've told me a
dozen times what a sumbitch he was. All he
wants is for you to go with him to whatever
hell he's made for himself. My own whore of a
mother tried the same thing when I first got
here. But I didn't listen to her. No, sir, not me."*

He draws me farther from the tree, toward
the gap he'd left in the ring of dancers.

"Now you listen, and you listen good." He
stops and grips me by both shoulders. *"I don't
know what they've cooked up for themselves
on the other side, but ain't no use in jumping
through all their hoops to get there, with, 'Oh,
I did this and I did that and ain't that too
fucking bad.' Where I am, it's just like old
times with whiskey and whores and everything
you'd ever want."*

"Is she there?" I ask.

His eyes lose their ravenous glow for an
instant. They flicker away then back to me.

*"Her and a dozen more just like her, if you
want,"* he says. *"I tell you, boy, it's a paradise
for the likes of us. I saved a seat for you and
everything."*

I look up at that. His eyes are wide with
hunger and his tongue flicks out as he licks
his lips. I shake his hands off my shoulders
and feel the scratch of claws raking through
my flesh.

"Get away from me," I say, and back toward

the tree.

"You're coming with me, boy," he says, stalking me as his eyes take on a yellow glow.

I back into the tree, and my old friend looms over me, teeth bared in a demonic grin. I throw an arm over my face and cower against the tree. I feel the hot, wet breath against my sleeve.

And nothing more.

I chance to open an eye, to peek over my arm. The leering face is still there, inches away. Saliva drips from a ghoulish fang. But the eyes have lost some of their glow, replaced by the look of a child who fears his toy might be taken away.

"You have no power," I say, and the realization is punctuated by a whimper from the other. "You can't take me. I have to choose to go with you."

A soft, hollow cry echoes from the gaping maw of the beast.

"No," I say, "I won't. Go back to whatever hell you came from and leave me be."

I turn my back on the demon and the cry turns into a wail, then a shriek that rends the sky, making the leaves and the wind chimes rattle.

Then the air stills again, and the tree resumes its gentle music. I step around the thick trunk to see the first visitor calmly leaning against it, one arm hanging lazily by his side while his fingers drum softly on the tree.

"Show me," I say.

He grins and nods his head.

I close my eyes and concentrate, filtering out all but the tap-tap-tapping of his fingers against the tree.

CHAPTER FOURTEEN

Promontory Summit, Utah — May 1869
Dah-dit-dit. Dah-dah-dah. Dah-dit. Dit.

The telegraph wires buzzed in time with the operator's key as he spelled out the message that marked the completion of the Transcontinental Railroad.

D-O-N-E

Cheers rose from the gathered crowd of statesmen, investors, laborers and curious onlookers. I couldn't help being caught up in the excitement, and I raised my hat and joined in the cheers. The uproar lasted for several minutes before California's governor, Leland Stanford, silenced the crowd to express his sentiments.

The snap of Old Glory drowned out his droning as I surveyed the crowd from my perch atop a telegraph pole. I looked beyond the inner ring of invited guests and dignitaries, their round bellies stuffed in black frock coats, heads topped with stovepipe hats. I searched past the surrounding corps of white laborers from the Union and Central Pacific lines, until I finally spied a small group of Chinese workers.

The men were decked out in broad-brimmed hats and brilliant blue, silk pajamas, but it wasn't these I sought. In their midst, dressed far more humbly than her countrymen but outshining them all, stood the object of my quest.

Nankande.

I had no idea what her name meant — or if it meant anything at all — but it seemed as exotic as its owner. I'd met the woman only once and briefly, barely long enough to learn her name, but I found myself captivated by this vision from the East. The few words I'd heard her speak conveyed all the mystery and enchantment of a distant — yet hauntingly familiar — paradise. The words themselves were mundane, but the voice that breathed life into them resonated with a soft, transcendent tone that stirred to life a part of me I'd long thought dead.

"Brings a tear to your eye, don't it?" Dave mused as I climbed down from the pole after the ceremonial benediction.

"It does indeed," I said, and looked past him, over the crowd toward the now-hidden gang of Chinese workers.

"You, too?"

"Me, too, what?"

"Aw, come on, now, Cap'n, Every man at the dinner table was smitten by that sweet little thing," he said, referring to the dinner hosted by the Central Pacific the previous evening. "But before you go chasing off to Shangri-La, Casement wants to see you."

I gestured for Dave to lead the way and reluctantly followed him to the Union Pacific's engine, *No. 119*. The UP's lack of imagination was contrasted by the brightly painted *Jupiter* that adorned the Central Pacific's engine and timber car. What the eastern line lacked in imagination, though, was more than made up for in the tenacity and sheer iron will of the men who drove the company.

Such a man was Dan Casement. As I approached him — his five-foot-nothing frame dwarfed by the great iron wheels of the engines — the man radiated a supreme confidence. He and his brother Jack had driven the crews that reshaped the face of the American prairie and conquered the Rocky Mountains, laying more than a thousand miles of track in four short years. To have been a part of that effort filled me with a pride I'd never before known.

"Colonel," I said, greeting Casement with

373

a casual salute.

A man might make the mistake of equating stature with ability, and gauging his respect by the same scale. Where the Casement brothers were concerned, no one would make that mistake twice.

"Jim," he welcomed me, and extended his small hand with its iron grip. "You know Jim Strobridge."

"Yes, sir." I shook the other man's hand. "We met at dinner last night. Thank you again for the hospitality, sir."

"My pleasure."

The Californian stood more than six feet tall, his eyes level with mine. Eye, rather. His right eye was covered with a patch, the result of a blasting accident while cutting through the Sierra Nevada range. His left shone brightly enough for the both of them, and bore a confidence that matched Casement's.

"Dan here tells me you're one of his best crew drivers," Strobridge said.

"The colonel is overly generous, sir. I was just lucky enough to have a good crew working for me. No disrespect, sir, but they're the ones who made this possible." I gestured toward the final rail tie where ceremonial gold and silver spikes gleamed under the desert sun. "Men like you and me, we just

374

tugged the reins a bit and tried to keep out of the way."

"What'd I tell you," Casement chimed in. "Lyingest son of a bitch on my crews. Why, Jim here can do every job on the line, right down to cooking up the best damned buffalo stew you'll ever taste. Lets on it's all his crew, but men like these don't follow a man unless they know he's the best among them."

"Just the sort I'm looking for," Strobridge said with a grin. "What do you say, Robbins?"

"I'm sorry? Say about what?"

"Stro's putting together some crews for the lines out in California," Casement explained. "I told him he'd be a fool if he didn't try dragging you out west with him."

"California?"

"It's the new Promised Land," Strobridge boasted. "California is to the East what America was to Europe a hundred years ago. A half million people have come west just in the past twenty years. With the railroad complete, I expect that number'll double before long. All those people are going to need new roads to link them together, to carry their gold and iron and grain and produce. And I aim to build them."

He grinned lustily and clamped a cigar

between his teeth as he set the glorious image within the gilded frame of his ego.

"Makes a right pretty picture," Casement observed.

"That it does," I agreed. "It'd be fair to say you have my attention, Mister Strobridge."

"My friends call me Stro, and I'm glad to hear it." He scratched at the space between his beard and eye patch. "Now, there is one catch. I've three thousand Chinese workers. Every single man on my line earns his pay, but I'll be damned if I ever saw a harder-working bunch than those little yellow bastards. It'd be a shame to lose all that experience, and I mean to hold on to it."

"The catch, sir?" I prompted him.

"I want you to head up a Chinese crew. If you have a problem with that, I might still be able to find a place for you, but . . ." He shrugged.

"I've heard stories of the work they did in the Sierras," I said after only a moment's pause. "If even half of them are true, it'd be a privilege to work alongside men like that." *And a woman like Nankande,* I didn't add.

"Grand," Stro said, his face splitting into a broad grin. "Come by my car this evening. There's a bottle of eighteen-year-old Scotch I've been meaning to open."

"Yes, sir," I said, and shook the men's hands once more.

"Well, how about that?" Dave observed after the two foremen excused themselves to rub elbows with the upper brass.

"Yep — how about that? Now, if you'll excuse me," I said, "I think I'll try to get acquainted with some of my new crew."

I turned toward the group of Chinese workers and floated in that direction.

"You do that," Dave said with a slap on my back. "And good luck."

"What the hell am I doing?" I muttered to myself as I stumbled along sand-blown tracks under a burning sun.

The Chinese crew had disappeared by the time I reached the spot where I'd last seen them. Figuring they'd returned to their camp a few miles west of Promontory Summit — fittingly named Victory — I set out after them. I went on foot, thinking I'd catch up with them in the same time it would have taken to find and saddle Rigel. After only a couple of miles, though, with the heat of the Utah sun and the deepening ache in my leg, my doubts gathered steam and I turned back toward the UP camp.

"Don't look back."

I spun around to find the source of the

words. There was only the hush of the wind and the skittering of sand along the gleaming steel rails. I cocked my head and listened again, unsure whether the words had come from without or within.

When you find your dream, don't look back. You just follow right after her . . .

"And damn the rest," I finished the words, the last ones Matt had spoken to me at Elkhorn Tavern.

At the time, I'd assumed they referred to Gina, and I could make no sense of them. But here, now, with so much behind me that might hold me back from a new dream, they rang out with a new clarity. With renewed energy and hope, I set the brim of my hat against the afternoon sun and pressed on along the westward line.

A half hour later, the track led me between a pair of dunes where a commotion caught my attention. Angry shouts rose from one of the dunes, and I scrambled up the sandy bluff to see what was the matter.

My heart lurched into my throat as I crested the hill and caught sight of Nankande. I was more surprised to see Charlie Garrett. One thick hand wrapped around the young woman's wrist, while the other fended off the feeble attacks of an elderly Chinese man.

378

Most surprising of all was the old man's stance. Between each charge at Garrett — who was easily twice his size — the little man shouted a phrase while gesturing with his arms and hands. I couldn't understand the words, but there was no mistaking the sign he gave.

"What's this, Garrett?" I asked as I stepped over the rise and eased my way down the slope.

One hand still stretched toward the old man, Garrett spun toward me, dragging Nankande around with him.

"Nothing to concern you, Jimmy Boy," he said after a moment's pause. "You just run on along."

"It may not concern me directly," I said, "but I'd say it affects these two. They don't seem any too happy about the whole thing."

"I said move on, Robbins." Garrett glared at me, and the young woman's eyes widened in pain as he tightened his grip on her wrist.

"Let her go," I ordered.

Nankande gasped as Garrett squeezed tighter still. The old man charged again, his rush easily deflected by the larger man.

"We've been here before, Garrett," I said. "As I recall, it didn't end so well for you then. You sure you want another go-around?"

Anger flashed through the steely, blue eyes, followed by just a hint of reason. With a disgusted growl, he flung the woman to the ground. The old man quickly rushed to her side and Garrett stalked toward me.

"She ain't worth it anyway. But this ain't over, Jimmy Boy," he rumbled. "Not by a long shot."

I braced for an attack, but the thug just brushed roughly against my shoulder before retreating over the bluff. I watched him pass out of sight before turning my attention to the pair behind me. The old man knelt beside Nankande and gingerly examined her wrist. He spoke to her rapidly, but lightly, with what I gathered were words of comfort.

"Are you two all right, Miss Nankande?" I said.

They both looked up as I pronounced the name — one in curiosity, the other in alarm.

"Yes, thank you," replied the curious one. Her eyes narrowed at me as she tried to place me.

"I had the pleasure of meeting you at dinner last night." I took off my hat and self-consciously smoothed my hair.

"Yes, of course. Mister Roberts, is it?"

"Robbins. Jim Robbins."

"Mister Robbins," she repeated in a soft,

heart-rending tone. "Thank you for your help."

"My pleasure, ma'am. I'm only sorry it was necessary."

The old man followed the exchange with a mixture of confusion and suspicion. He interjected a Gatling fire of words to which Nankande listened attentively.

"My father says to thank you for your aid," she interpreted, "and to ask that you leave now and let us be on our way."

I recoiled at the rebuff, but kept my temper in check.

"I'd feel better if you'd let me see you back to your camp," I said.

Nankande translated the offer, which was answered by another agitated stream of words.

"Thank you, Mister Robbins," she said as the tirade continued, "but it will be better that we see to ourselves. We —"

She stopped as her father rattled on and concluded with an insistent gesture in my direction. When Nankande hesitated, he repeated the final phrase with an even more forceful gesture.

She lowered her eyes and the color rose beneath her fair skin.

"My father trusts few white men. He says that, while you act as a rescuer, you will try

381

to take by good will what the other tried to take by force."

The brunt of the charge hit me like a slap in the face, despite the charm of the messenger and her attempt to soften the blow. I bit my cheek against the anger that welled up in my breast as I glared at the man, then at his daughter.

"Tell him," I spat through gritted teeth, "I didn't do this for myself. You tell him I —" I pointed my finger straight at the man, fixed his eyes with mine. "Tell him I did it for the sake of a widow's son."

With that, I turned on my heels, limped up the rise with as much dignity as I could, and followed the tracks back to camp.

"My father wishes to speak with you." The words were accompanied by a gentle tug on my sleeve.

I'd ridden out to Camp Victory with Stro to meet the crew I'd be accompanying back to California. After a brief introduction by Stro and a few words of my own — all translated by Nankande — the men of the crew filed past, alternately shaking my hand and bowing in greeting as they sized up their new *gongtou*. The ranking member of the crew was Nankande's father, whom she introduced as Zhang Shu. He'd been first in line and coolly bowed without shaking my hand, then wordlessly moved on.

That he now wanted to talk caught me by surprise.

"More assaults on my character?" I instantly regretted the harsh tone.

"I apologize for my father." Nankande lowered her eyes. "He means well, but distrusts strangers and is very protective of me."

"I understand." My resentment quickly melted in the warmth of her presence. "Of course, I'll be happy to speak with him."

Nankande led me through the crowd of workers. I tried to keep my eyes from wandering, but couldn't ignore her figure as she glided across the ground. With conscious effort, I managed not to be staring directly at her as we neared her father.

The older man bowed again, and I awkwardly returned the greeting. To my surprise, he then extended his hand. As I accepted it, he slid his fingers into a familiar grip. Whatever enmity I still held toward him fell away.

"My father welcomes a — a companion in the art," Nankande said hesitantly as she translated her father's words. "He invites you to join him —" She interrupted herself to clarify his meaning, the exchange as brief as it was unfathomable. "He invites you to join in the work this evening."

I grinned broadly at the invitation, and Zhang Shu returned the smile.

"Please tell him I'd be happy to accept," I said.

Nankande translated the time and place before I was forced to excuse myself to rejoin Stro for the trip back to camp at Promontory and dinner in his personal rail-car.

I spent the balance of the afternoon in anxious distraction as the seconds grudgingly gave way to one another. I had to apologize to Missus Strobridge several times as I picked at my meal, asked for questions to be repeated and otherwise made a poor guest of myself. It was with great relief, then, when the clock chimed seven and I was able to excuse myself for the evening.

"Thank you, ma'am," I said. "I'm sorry I wasn't better company."

"That's quite all right," she said. "I imagine you've a great deal to wrap your mind around, and Stro isn't in the habit of giving folks much time to reflect on things."

"Yes, ma'am, I'm learning that," I said. "Night, Stro."

"Good night, Jim," he said. "Have a good evening, and get some rest. We'll start loading up the cars at first light."

"Yes, sir," I replied and shook his hand.

He patted me on the shoulder and gave me what might have been a wink — with the patch over his right eye, I could never be sure. I stepped down from the car, swung into the saddle on Rigel's back and started toward Camp Victory. I set Rigel on an easy pace, enjoying the warmth of the evening sun while I whistled some nameless tune until I reached the edge of the Chinese camp. I was surprised to see Nankande waiting there alone.

"Good evening," I greeted her with a tip of my hat, then swung down from the saddle.

"Good evening," she said in turn, and the sun seemed to dim in comparison with her smile. "Father asked me to meet you and take you to him when you arrived."

"He wasn't worried for your virtue?" I regretted the familiar tone as soon as the words were spoken.

Nankande didn't seem put off.

"I asked him the same thing," she said. "He seems to think that my honor is safe with you."

"I'll do my best not to disappoint him."

I gestured for her to lead the way and walked alongside, leading Rigel by his reins.

We walked in silence. For my part, it was as much due to a natural comfort as to the inability to think of anything to say. After too short a time, we arrived at a cleft in a rock outcropping where a solitary member of the Chinese crew stood watch.

I recognized him as Shan Chang, one of the men I'd met earlier that day. He stood a full head above his countrymen and rivaled the bulk of many of the Americans who'd worked the line westward. He'd been cordial enough at our earlier meeting, but his bearing was now stern and forbidding. His feet were spread and firmly planted beneath a coarse leather apron. His facial expression implied he was not about to step aside for anyone. Speaking even more clearly than his stance was the large pickaxe he bore at port arms across his broad chest.

Nankande exchanged a few words with the man, then turned to me.

"He says that I must not go any farther with you. He says my father commands you to give him a . . ." Her eyes narrowed as she sought the proper word. "A symbol of your skill?"

I nodded my understanding.

"Thank you," I said. "Would you mind?"

I held out Rigel's reins to her, and felt a thrill as her fingers brushed against mine.

She looked back at me once as she led the horse toward camp. I was still grinning as I extended my hand to the man-mountain. He took my hand and stared at me expectantly, then raised his eyebrows as I adjusted my fingers within the grip. He matched the gesture, followed by what I assumed to be a question.

"The grip of an entered apprentice," I said.

We traded gestures and questions and responses, neither of us understanding the other but, I hoped, following a common ritual that transcended language and culture. When we reached what should have been the exchange of the password, I was relieved to hear him speak the letter I was expecting.

"A," he said.

"B," I replied, and we both smiled in recognition.

We passed through the signs and words for the next two degrees. When we finished, he released my hand, dropped the head of the pickaxe to the ground and rapped the heavy iron against the stony ground.

Ping. Ping. Ping.

The sound rang through the still night and echoed from the darkness beyond the sentry's post. After a short pause, another set of notes answered the summons and a second man stepped out of the gloom bearing a pry bar. The newcomer exchanged a few words with Shan, then disappeared the way he'd come. After a short while, three raps rang out from the beyond, which Shan duly answered.

Pry Bar reappeared and, after another brief exchange, Shan moved the pickaxe to his shoulder and gestured for me to pass. I stepped by him, only to be stopped short by Pry Bar, who spoke a few words to me. I stared back at him blankly, shrugged my shoulders and shook my head. The man repeated himself — slowly and more loudly this time, as though that would help — then indicated the lambskin apron tied around his waist. I finally nodded my understanding, pulled my own Masonic apron from my coat pocket and tied it around my waist.

Satisfied, Pry Bar led me deeper into the outcropping, which formed a sort of winding, narrow corridor. Eventually, the trail opened into a natural amphitheater and I stared in wonder. The upper room of Elkhorn Tavern might have been carved into stone and carried out to the desert, so closely did the layout of the space match the lodge I'd known. But, whereas the former lodge room had its ceiling painted to represent the canopy of heaven, this lodge was roofed over by the starry night itself.

I saluted the east, where Zhang Shu presided as master, then took a seat among my newfound brothers. While the language of the ceremony was foreign to me, I was soon caught up in the familiar rites. Before long, the ritual began to serve as its own interpreter and, by the close of the meeting, I'd picked up a handful of words in the strange tongue.

I'd sat in lodge before with Englishmen, Scots, Irishmen, Germans, Poles — even Yankees. The commonality of religion and skin color and language, accents aside, had made the fraternal bonds easy to accept. Here, I finally began to understand brotherhood beyond the ties of Nation or Race or Creed, one based on a shared humanity under the One God, by whatever name He might be called.

After Zhang closed the lodge, several of the younger men filed by me to shake my hand and exchange a few words of greeting. I noticed a group of older men talking animatedly among themselves and gesturing in my direction. Zhang spoke firmly to the men, who stopped their squabbling, but stormed angrily toward the exit.

Zhang approached me then, took my hand

in both of his and spoke warmly to me. He nodded toward where the other men had disappeared and shook his head, as though to dismiss their objections. I smiled and followed him out the passage, past Pry Bar and beyond giant Shan, where a pleasant surprise stood waiting.

"I hope the meeting was not uncomfortable, Mister Robbins," Nankande said in greeting after kissing her father and handing me Rigel's reins.

"Not at all," I said. "Please express to your father my deepest gratitude for including me."

"Father says that you are welcome to take part at any time. He also says that, as you have proven yourself a worthy brother, you may——"

The color drained from her face, the starlit glow of moments before replaced by a sickly pallor. She turned to Zhang and spoke to him in a harsh whisper.

The old man gave the serene smile of a sage, quietly repeated himself and gestured toward me with an open hand.

"What is it?" I asked, and my heart fluttered with the sudden change in tone.

Nankande's mouth opened as if to speak, then clamped shut again as she turned her gaze toward the stars, the ground — any-

390

where but at her father or myself.

"Zhaquei, zhaquei," Zhang said to her, then tucked his palm under her chin and raised her eyes to his.

She gave a submissive nod, lowered her gaze again to the ground and resumed the translation.

"He says that, as you have proven yourself worthy, you — you may court his daughter, if that is your wish."

The flutter in my chest took on a different character at that.

"I'm honored," I managed to stammer, "but . . ."

I looked to Zhang, whose eyes beamed with the glee of a boy who had pulled off the perfect prank. Then I looked to Nan-kande who had the look of a frightened doe. I fought the urge to reach out to her, for fear she would bolt. I took a deep breath to settle my nerves, and spoke as evenly as possible.

"What does his daughter wish?"

"She —" A flush of color restored the vitality to her cheeks, and her eyes rose by a fraction. "I do not object."

CHAPTER FIFTEEN

Washoe County, Nevada — September 1869

"What is that he calls you?" I asked.

The train rocked southward along the spur line toward Carson City. Nankande and I enjoyed the breeze from a flatcar. Nearby, her father sat around a cotton bale with three other elders, smoking long pipes and playing a table game with ceramic tiles.

"Ching Ting," Nankande said.

Her eyes were closed, her face turned into the wind, and the sunlight limned her graceful features. Her silk blouse rippled in the breeze to hug her slender form.

"It is Father's pet name for me," she said. "It means 'dragonfly.'" She took a deep breath, and her face softened as she opened her eyes and looked at me. "When I was a child, I would chase dragonflies in the fields of our village. Father would tease me and say that he could not tell me apart from them when I ran about so."

"Does he never call you by your given name?" I asked. "It's very pretty."

She lowered her eyes at that, and a look of sadness replaced the happy one of moments before.

"No," she said. "He does not wish to disgrace me further. He calls me only Ching Ting."

"Disgrace?" I said. "I don't understand."

She took another deep breath, as though to rally her strength.

" 'Nankande' means 'ugly one,' " she said flatly. "It is the name my father chose for me when I was born. Though he will not choose a different name for me, he does not wish to hurt me further, and so he uses only his pet name for me."

I stared at her in disbelief.

"That's terrible," I said. "Why would anyone give such a name to a child?"

"My father is of the old ways. My mother was very beautiful, I am told, and —"

"You're told?" I said. "You don't remember her?"

"She died giving birth to me," Nankande — the name now seemed shrill and cruel to me — explained. "Father says that it was because of her beauty that the gods took her from us — or perhaps because of her pride. He gave me my name so that the gods

393

would pay no attention to me, so that they would leave us in peace."

"That must have been very difficult as a child," I said, and reached out to smooth an errant strand of hair behind her ear.

She smiled up at me and I let my fingers linger on her cheek.

"Father did his best," she said. "But, yes, it was difficult when the other girls' fathers told them how pretty they were, and he never would. When he began to call me Ching Ting, it made things easier."

"Well, I certainly can't call you by your given name anymore," I said. "It would be a lie. And I don't want to take away from your father by using his name for you." I mulled over the problem for a moment before asking, "Do you share your father's concerns?"

"His superstitions?" she asked with a wry grin. "No."

"Good," I said. "In that case, what is your word for 'beautiful'?"

"It — it is *mei*," she said, as the color rose in her cheeks.

"Mae," I repeated. "I like it."

"Mind if I interrupt a moment?"

I tore my eyes from Mae and looked up to where Stro stood over us. "Not at all."

"Forgive the intrusion, ma'am," he said, "but I need to steal Jim for a bit."

"Of course," she agreed, and went to join her father at his game.

The train slowed as we entered a track-side town whose sign read *Toiyabee City*. Despite the lofty designation, the burg was little bigger than the dozens of hell-on-wheels towns we'd passed along the way, settlements that grew up like weeds beside the rail line. Stro pointed out a row of shanties whose shaded lamps glowed red through curtained windows.

"Y'know, Jim," he said, "there's a lot simpler ways of sampling those Asian delicacies than by going through with this damn-fool courtship."

Jim Strobridge was a big man and — like most big men — was unaccustomed to being manhandled. So it was with surprise that he glared at me when he found himself dangling over the edge of the flatcar. He struggled to keep his boots in contact with the car's deck as I gripped his collars to hold him out over the passing landscape. The shock quickly turned to good humor, though, and a mighty roar of laughter echoed across the Nevada plains.

"Just checking," he said as I pulled him back from the brink and set him on his feet again.

A dozen pairs of shocked eyes — including Mae's and her father's — stared at us in wonder before quickly returning to their games or letters or naps.

Stro threw an arm across my shoulders and led me back toward Mae.

"Remind me never to get on your bad side."

The happiest day I'd ever known was a rather miserable one by other standards. Cold rains had blown in from Lake Bigler for the past several days, turning the streets of Carson City into a miry mess. Clouds hung low in the sky and cast a damp pall over the earth.

"Have you ever seen a finer day?" I asked Dave.

"Mm-hmm," he grunted, then spat a stream of tobacco juice that disappeared in the mush at our feet. "Pretty much all of them." He fixed me with a cool, cynical stare before breaking into a brown-streaked grin. "But I ain't never seen me such a lousy day made so nice by what happened on it."

I gripped his shoulder and turned to watch the approach of the wedding party. The ceremony would follow the traditions of Mae's people, but some allowances had been made for her foreign groom. Since I had no family, I'd appointed Dave to fill the role, which he happily accepted — especially the duties that involved drinking large amounts of sweet plum wine. The previous night's festivities had made this morning hard to face, and made the ceremonial breakfast of raw eggs harder still.

I couldn't be sure how much of the ritual I'd had to endure was based on custom, and how much was invented to entertain the crew at the expense of the hapless groom. But it didn't matter, for the prize that awaited me at the end of this day was worth whatever trials I might need to face. The hardest test had already been won, after all — that of earning Mae's trust and love.

I waited with Dave at the Strobridges' personal railcar, alongside Stro and his wife and the *buzhang* — the elder next in line to Zhang Shu — who would perform the ceremony.

The wedding party neared, singing a festive song. The past few weeks had been spent crafting the bright-colored robes and *papier-mâché* animal masks that now spun and dipped and swirled brightly in the grey Nevada gloom.

At the head of the group came Zhang Shu. The hem of his brilliant purple robe was soiled with mud, but his face was radiant behind a solemn mask. I eagerly scanned the crowd for a glimpse of Mae, but she was hidden in their midst. As the party approached, Shu took his place beside the *buzhang* and the rest of the party peeled off to either side until, emerging from the wrapping paper of the gaily dressed attendants, my priceless gift was revealed.

The red veil and white ceremonial makeup could not diminish her beauty, which shone through the coverings like the sun through a light mist. Mae was draped with a heavy, silk robe of red brocade, but the tent-like covering could not disguise the lissome grace of her movements as she drew near. Dave's sharp elbow in my ribs reminded me to take a breath.

When Mae reached my side, we turned to face the *buzhang*. I strained to hear over the ecstatic buzzing in my ears as Mae softly translated the man's words. The entire celebration would last out the day, but the ceremony itself was surprisingly short. After a few words of introduction, the man confirmed our intent. He then offered us two cups of wine tied together by a red string, from which Mae and I drank at the same time.

A murmur of approval rose from the crowd as we interlocked our arms and drained the cups. The *buzhang* instructed me to take Mae's right hand in mine, if it was indeed my intent to take her as my wife. He placed his wrinkled hands around ours to pronounce the blessing.

"Now there is no rain," Mae translated the words, "for you are shelter to each other. There is no cold, for each is warmth to the other. No longer is there darkness or pain, for you are light and comfort to one another. Two bodies, but your hearts are joined, and you are now one person."

I lifted Mae's veil and found myself lost in her deep, black eyes as I bent toward her. She leaned into me in welcome, and her breath was warm and sweet and filled my lungs with new life as I breathed in her scent. I drew her into my arms and found the rapid pounding of my heart matched, beat for beat, by hers. Dave, Shu, the Strobridges, everyone around us disappeared, and we were wrapped in a soft, warm glow that created for us a world apart as our lips met in a sublime, magical kiss.

Chapter Sixteen

Ormsby County, Nevada — February 1870

I awakened slowly and kept my eyes closed as I savored the feminine scents and the taste of lingering kisses, the whispered sound of gentle breathing, and the wondrous feel of the soft, warm body nestled against me. After assuring myself I was truly awake, I chanced to open my eyes.

The canvas panels of the tent were still dark at this early hour, but a lantern cast a soft amber glow throughout the space. Mae's head lay against my shoulder, and the fan of her thick, black hair cascaded over my chest. I took a deep breath, then crawled out from under the covers, taking care not to disturb her. I quickly dressed, then stepped into the cold morning air.

Following the wedding, the balance of the crew had continued east from Carson City to lay the track up to Virginia City. Stro had complained that the proposed route would make the Virginia and Truckee Railroad the crookedest line in the world, but Dave was confident the crew could get it done. The boss had sent Dave east, while he ordered me west with Mae, into the mountains for some time alone.

I blessed the crusty foreman for the hundredth time as I came out of the tent and looked down the slope from our campsite. Lake Bigler — some of the locals called it Tahoe — was a yawning black gulf in the predawn darkness, but the snow-covered peaks on the other side were beginning to glow with the first hints of sunrise.

Bracing myself against the cold, I set about the morning chores of checking on the horses, spreading their fodder and gathering the day's water from a small spring. Along the way, I looked for signs of any unwanted guests. There wasn't another human soul for miles around, but a series of paw prints at the edge of camp hinted at an occasional visitor's passage during the night.

"You are not getting up so early, are you?" Mae asked as I reentered the tent and buttoned the flap.

She propped herself up on one elbow and hugged the buffalo skin blanket around her.

"Just getting some water." I set the bucket

next to the small stove in the center of the tent and poked the fire back to life. "Shall I put on some coffee?"

Mae sat all the way up, pulled the tresses of her hair over one shoulder and let the buffalo skin fall around her waist. "I think coffee can wait, don't you?"

I tried to catch my breath as I looked at her in wonder, taking in each curve and contour. She must have mistaken my silence as hesitation. To give unneeded encouragement, she folded open the blanket and beckoned me to her.

"Yes," I finally said. "Coffee can wait."

By the time we were ready for breakfast, the day shone brightly through the tent walls. I built up the fire and put on coffee while Mae prepared a breakfast of venison, porridge and dried berries. We took our time eating, savoring each bite and each moment. Then we lingered over coffee and tea. Mae sat with her feet tucked under her, draped in one of my green flannel shirts. Neither of us spoke the words, but we both knew our getaway must soon be over, and we'd have to rejoin the world.

After breakfast, we followed a trail to a nearby mineral spring whose warm waters raised a plume of steam that filled the air with heavy mist. The morning's clear sky had given way to low clouds pregnant with snow, so we wrapped our clothes in an oilcloth before slipping into the heavy water of the salt bath.

"So you really believe in it?" I asked, picking up our conversation as I settled against a smooth rock ledge.

"Reincarnation? Certainly." Mae waded through the waist-deep water and joined me on the rock.

These conversations had played a big part in our courtship, and continued into our marriage. Mae's education in a Jesuit mission school far outstripped my humble learning, and I had to venture far beyond Missus Warren's nearly-forgotten philosophy lessons to keep up.

"Nature is filled with cycles of death and rebirth," Mae continued her line of reasoning. "The seed dies, then is reborn in the flower it produces. We are but another part of nature, and it is only fitting that we be subject to the same laws. Our bodies may die, but our souls are the seed to a new life that grows out of the old."

"But scripture says it's given to a man once to be born and once to die," I said. "Isn't that a contradiction?"

"No more a contradiction than Lazarus,"

she said.

"How's that?" I asked as snow began to fall, the flakes dancing on the rising mist of the pool.

"The Gospels tell us that he died and was raised," she explained. "Surely he must have died a second time. If that is possible, why not a second birth as well? Besides, in reincarnation it is not the man who is reborn. Jim Robbins has not lived before and will not live again, but the spark within him may find life in a new form, many years from now."

She raised a slender arm from the water to catch the falling flakes.

"Take this snow, for example," she said. "Each flake is distinct and has an existence of its own. It lives for a time, then melts and is absorbed into the pool. It evaporates, blends with the steam and is drawn back into the clouds. After a time, it again falls as rain or snow and begins the cycle anew."

I let the thought sink in as I drew Mae into my arms.

"Well, I just hope it's so," I finally said.

"Why is that?"

"Because I want another chance at this." My voice was husky as I wrapped an arm around her waist and stroked her hair. "I want to find you when we're both young. I want to grow up falling in love with you, and grow old falling in love with you even more. I want a life I can look back on and not remember a single day that didn't have you as its best part."

Mae turned to face me, and we shared a lingering kiss.

"I'm not picky," I said, when she at last pulled back from me, hands cupped on my cheeks. "It doesn't have to be right away — next life, the one after that. I can be patient. But, one of these lifetimes, I want this." I placed one of her hands over my heart. "And this." I placed my hand over hers. "Every waking moment for a hundred years."

"Hello, the camp."

The greeting came from the darkness as we settled down for dinner. We jumped at the sound of another human voice, but recognized it immediately.

"What the hell are you doing here?" I asked as I stepped outside and waved the traveler in.

"Is that any way to greet a friend?" Dave said as I took his horse's reins from him and led him to the tent. "I ride through the cold and dark, and that's the welcome I get?"

"Pretty much," I said. "Get inside and thaw out. I'll take care of your horse."

He stomped his boots and ducked under the tent flap while I led the horse to the makeshift stable under a spread of pine boughs. I put out fresh fodder while the other horses made room for the newcomer and gathered around him to share their body heat. Satisfied he was in good company, I turned back toward the tent.

A light scratching in the snow stopped me in my tracks as I looked for the source of the sound. My blood ran with ice when my eyes met the steely gaze of a grey wolf who stood poised midstride a few yards behind the horse pen. He stared at me and his nostrils flared as he picked my scent off the breeze. Satisfied I was no threat, he set his ears forward, sat back on his haunches and opened his mouth in a wide yawn.

"Hey there, fella," I whispered, and stepped gingerly toward the beast.

The wolf loosed a nervous whine, but let me come a few steps closer before his raised hackles and bared teeth brought me to a stop. I squatted as best I could on stiff joints, and made myself appear as harmless as possible.

The wild thing cocked his head and studied me a few moments more before he limped toward me, one rear leg cocked up. He sniffed my outstretched hand, sat in front of me and locked his eyes on mine. I found myself lost in the glowing, amber orbs, at one with the animal.

I sensed — knew — the loneliness of isolation from the pack, the pain of forced separation from his mate. I felt the pain of his solitary existence, alone in the world, no companion for warmth, for help in the hunt, for security or affection. My heart recalled the ache of loss, of the need to go on without any desire to do so. Misery welled up between us until it found expression in a great, mournful howl.

As quickly as it came upon me, the spell was broken. I blinked my eyes and looked around, but the wolf was nowhere to be seen. Only a fresh set of tracks in the snow suggested he'd been there at all. I took a moment to catch my breath and gather my wits, then rose and limped back toward the tent.

"Are you all right?" Dave asked, bursting through the tent flap as I approached.

"I think so."

"That wolf sounded awful close," he said, and strained his tracker's eyes into the surrounding darkness.

"Yeah, but he's gone." I led him back into

the tent, where Mae had a stew simmering on the stove. "Now, you mind telling us what brings you all the way up here?"

Dave accepted a serving of stew from Mae, and shoveled a couple of spoonfuls into his mouth before answering.

"Much as I hate to interrupt your little honeymoon," he said around a mouthful of cornbread, "I figured you'd rather take the train to California than walk."

"The line's done?" I said.

"First car rolled into Virginia City two weeks ago. The crew's all buttoned up, and we're getting ready to head west. Stro cabled from Sacramento — he's got a line for us to lay out of a place called San Wakeem, or somesuch." Dave wiped his hands on his shirt front and fished a yellow telegram out of his pocket.

"Looks like it's back to the world," I told Mae after I scanned the sheet. "But we won't be going anywhere tonight. Best turn in and get a jump on it first thing in the morning."

By daybreak, we'd polished off the last of the stew and started breaking camp. The horses were soon loaded, and it was just past noon when we started down the eastern slope of Carson's Range. I looked back toward the mountains that had been a heavenly retreat, not knowing the hell they would soon become for me.

CHAPTER SEVENTEEN

Stanislaus County, California — June 1872

My love — Thank you for a most exquisite send-off. Find me as soon as you can. Ever — Mae.

I reread the note before folding it and tucking it in my shirt pocket. Mae had left before sunup to join the crew in celebration of *Duan Wu,* the Dragon Boat Festival. Most of the crew had left the day before, loaded down with picnic baskets and bundles of fireworks for the four-mile trek to the banks of the Stanislaus River. Mae and a handful of others had spent the night in the rail camp and set out first thing this morning.

My advance survey crew was camped some eight miles farther down the line and, with the Chinese gone as well, the empty camp had a funereal air. Even though I knew the reason for the silence, I was haunted by the shadow of a fear, and shuddered as a chill ran down my spine.

"Everything all right?" Dave asked as I swung into Rigel's saddle beside him.

"Fine," I said, shrugging off the icy hand of dread. "Just a little chilly this morning."

"It'll warm up soon enough," he said. "All the more reason to get a move on. I don't want Thomson using the heat as an excuse to hold us up."

Stephen Thomson — chief of my survey crew and nephew of one of the officers of the Stockton & Visalia Railroad — had created more than his fair share of problems during his six months on the line. The most recent had been a three-mile stretch of road over hilly ground that required several tons of earth to be moved from the tops of the hills into the vales between them.

"They say the damn Celestials can move mountains," the arrogant young man had said. "Let's see how they do here."

A detour of only a few hundred yards would have set the line on smoother ground. Dave and his grading foremen, however, were eager to put the brash young surveyor in his place. They'd finished the work two days ahead of schedule.

"Y'know, Jim," Dave said as we set out from camp, "you really don't have to ride up. I'll take care of Thomson. You go join

411

Mae for the party and catch up with us tomorrow."

Thomson normally chafed at our constant looking over his shoulder, but had taken the unusual step of asking us to review his proposed route for the final approach to Oakdale, our destination for this part of the line.

"Nah," I said regretfully. "We've kept little Stephen waiting long enough as it is. I need to be the one to say 'yea' or 'nay' on his route. Besides, this is a day for the crews. A lot of them still haven't accepted me. I'd just as soon let Mae and Shu enjoy the day with their people, without my getting in the way."

"You are a dumbass, you know that?" Dave said, gracious as always. "You're their people now."

I just shrugged at that as I nudged Rigel into an easy trot and set out along the line, marked every thirty or forty yards by a red-flagged stake. After less than an hour, the smells of coffee and ham welcomed us, and the survey camp appeared from behind the crest of a shallow hill.

Unlike the Transcontinental, the short line afforded the forward crew the relative luxury of the main camp. Most of the surveyors, though, were men accustomed to wide-open spaces and could only take a night or two of sleeping in the tent city before making their escape back to the field. This did not at all suit the lead surveyor, and Thomson's large tent stood conspicuously apart from the other men's bedrolls spread around the campfire.

"Morning, gents," Paul Kimball greeted us in his deep, booming voice as we rode into camp.

Paul was an old hand at surveying, and about as even-tempered as they came. I'd assigned him as Thomson's assistant, hoping the boy might learn something from the railroad veteran. Kimball also made the best coffee west of the Rockies, two cups of which he had ready for us by the time we dismounted.

Dave and I each took a cup and joined the men around the fire, absent their chief.

"How's the boy coming along?" I asked after a couple sips.

"Oh, he's coming," Kimball allowed.

" 'Coming' means not quite there, don't it?" Dave said.

"Well, I ain't yet seen me a man that ain't got a bit farther he can go," Kimball said. "And, truth be told, he's actually made a couple of good decisions over the past few days. Won't be long till he's able to take a piss without getting his trousers wet."

Dave and I joined in the laughter that rumbled around the fire.

"Goddammit," squawked a petulant voice from the tent. "How many times do I have to tell you oafs to keep it down while I'm trying —"

The voice broke off as puffy, bleary eyes came into focus first on Dave, then me. They opened wide enough for me to see the red rims around bloodshot eyes that told of at least one sleepless night.

"Jim," Thomson stammered when he again found his voice.

"Stephen," I replied. "You were saying?"

"Hmm? Oh, I — uh — no, it's just that I . . ."

The color drained from his face and he ducked back into the tent. The sounds of retching soon explained the hasty retreat.

I glanced at the faces around the fire. Dave seemed as bewildered as I was, while the others shared looks of amusement, tempered with a touch of embarrassment.

"What the hell's going on, Paul?" I demanded.

"Aw, Jim," he drawled, "he's still just a kid. We all had to work out our own kinks along the way."

414

"How long's he been on the bottle?" I said.

Paul bit his cheek and lowered his eyes to the fire. The other men stared at the same bit of nothing.

"How long?" I demanded.

"A couple weeks," Kimball finally said. "I mean, he'd usually have a drink at night, to take off the chill. Past couple of weeks, though, he's been hitting it pretty good. But it ain't hurt the schedule," he insisted.

I struggled to keep my temper in check, tried to remember if any bad news had come along that might explain the change. I could think of nothing, so — with a compassionate response ruled out — I steeled myself to deliver a little lesson.

"You men start breaking camp," I ordered, and tossed the remainder of my coffee into the flames. "Dave, lend them a hand."

"Jim —" he started, before I cut him off with a glare. He took a deep breath and nodded his agreement.

I stalked toward the tent, the weight of five pairs of eyes heavy on my back. The stench of cheap liquor and vomit almost made me gag as I stepped through the flap. A half-dozen empty bottles were strewn about the floor, even though the men had only camped here for two days. Thomson had stopped retching and was now rinsing his mouth from a seventh, half-full bottle.

I slapped the bottle from his hand, and some of the contents spilled down his chin onto a sweat- and filth-stained shirt.

"What's going on here?" I said.

"Jim, I'm sorry," he slurred. His eyes bobbled as he tried to focus on mine. "I didn't think they'd really do it. I didn't think they'd really hurt anyone."

"What are you talking about?" I said. "Who did what?"

"Isn't that why you're here?" He hiccupped and belched a foul cloud in my face.

"I'm here because you asked me to review your survey route. Now, what the hell are you babbling about?"

"Well, if nothing's happened, then I guess it doesn't —"

I cut off the words as I grabbed the stinking shirtfront in my fists and bent Thomson backward.

"Answer me, you little shit," I said, "or I'll rip your tongue clean out of your mouth."

"Charlie," he managed to squeak through the tight grip at his throat. "Charlie Garrett," he added as I released some of the pressure. "He and his boys were planning some kind of trouble for the Chinks — I-I mean, for the Chinese crews — while they

416

were having their festival." He swallowed hard and his Adam's apple pressed against my knuckles. "They were gonna do it last night — that's why they wanted me to call you up here, get you out of the way —"

"Where are they?" I said, my words nearly inaudible.

"But, if there hasn't been any trouble yet, maybe they changed their minds," Thomson continued, talking past me as though he'd forgotten I was there.

"Where are they?" I shouted, shaking him roughly.

A cold, sober look cleared the blurry eyes that now stared straight at me.

"Dunno," he slurred. "I only wish they'd done what they said they were gonna do. Wish I could've had a hand in teaching those filthy Chinks a lesson — showing me up the way they did. No one should've been able to make the schedule through that kind of terrain, no one. They're devils — have to be. And you," he hissed, crazed eyes fixed on mine, "you're practically one of them now, speaking their gibberish, fucking their women —"

Before I knew what had happened, I found myself alone in the tent, fire coursing through my arms and legs, and a lingering roar echoing in my ears. It took a moment before I recognized the sound as my own voice. I stepped through the swinging flap to find Thomson crumpled in a heap, his animal eyes staring fiercely up at me.

"You men," I said to Kimball and the others, "shut him up and tie him up. He doesn't leave here until you hear back from me, understood?"

A dirty sock was stuffed into the captive's mouth before I'd even finished speaking.

"Jim, what's going on?" Dave asked as I whistled for Rigel.

"Garrett," I said, and leapt into the saddle.

"What about —" He cut himself off and pointed back along the survey route. "Jim, look."

I looked where he pointed, scanning the line until I spied a running figure dressed in a bright-blue *chenshan* and with a long, black braid streaming out behind.

"Keep him here," I said, indicating the bound Thomson. "If he tries to run, shoot him."

I kicked Rigel into a gallop and raced to meet the messenger. In less than a minute, I drew rein and jumped down before the horse had come to a complete stop. I wrenched my bad knee and hopped the last few paces toward the runner on one leg.

"Ninyang," I greeted the boy as he all but

collapsed in my arms. "What is it?"

"Trouble," he panted. "At the river."

"Take care of him," I told Dave as he caught up to me, then climbed back into the saddle.

"Jim, what's going on?"

I owed him that much of an answer, and held the reins tight.

"Garrett and his men are making trouble at the river," I said. "Get Ninyang up to the camp, then come after me."

Without waiting for an answer, I pointed Rigel toward the river and let loose the reins.

The California countryside flashed by as seconds blurred into minutes, minutes into hours, hours into days, weeks, a lifetime. After an eternity, I reached the river where the crew held their celebration. Bright paper lamps and pennons and other decorations hung from the trees by the banks of the river, but the mood was anything but festive. The Chinese gathered into several clusters, some stunned and mute while others shouted and gestured angrily.

I yanked Rigel to a halt and climbed down next to an old man. Belatedly, I recognized him as the *buzhang* who had performed our wedding. His knees were pulled up to his chest and he rocked gently back and forth.

"Shue-fu," I said as I knelt beside the old

419

man. "Uncle, what has happened?"

The old man kept rocking and beating the sides of his head with his open hands. I shook him until he looked at me, and his eyes slowly dawned in recognition.

"Mae?" I said.

"*Zai na bian.* Over there." He pointed toward the heart of the crowd.

I helped him up and handed him Rigel's reins. The old man dragged himself out of his self-pity as he saw the panting, sweating, bloodshot-eyed beast that had flown me across the countryside. He led the limping horse toward the river's edge while I pressed through the crowd.

The people stood aside as I passed by, until I reached a cluster of men huddled in a loose circle.

"What's happened?" I demanded, drawing blank stares until I repeated myself in broken Mandarin.

The men averted their eyes and stepped aside to reveal several figures lying on the damp grass. Ugly wounds glistened brilliant red in the dappled light that filtered through the leaves. I instantly recognized Zhang Shu, and hurried to kneel by his side.

"*Yuefu,*" I said, taking his hand and pressing my handkerchief to the gash in his head.

"Old father, what has happened? Where is Mae?"

"Nyishu?" he said, his eyes unfocused, pupils uneven. "My son, is that you?"

"Shi, yuefu, it's me," I said. "Where is Mae?"

"Yi-di," he cried, seized with pain and rage. "Barbarians. They violated the *Duan Wu.* We tried to make them go, but they would not. Ching Ting tried to talk to them, but they would not listen. The chief, he —"

The old man tensed with pain and squeezed my hand in a feeble grip before going on.

"He insulted my Ching Ting," he said. "He tried to shame her. She fought back, scratched his face. I tried to pull her away and someone did this to me."

He put his fingers to the wound on his head, and I saw that his other hand had been crushed in the fight. He began to ramble and drift, and I tried to keep him with me just a bit longer.

"Where is Mae, Father?" I said. *"Yuefu, dao na Ching Ting?"*

"Ching Ting?" he repeated.

His eyes danced about, then locked into place, focused on something behind my shoulder. I turned to look, and his good hand gripped mine as another wave of pain

421

overcame him. As quickly as it began, the seizure ended and the old man's body went slack. His grip loosened and his head lolled to one side, eyes still fixed on the point behind me.

"Shu?"

I cupped the slack jaw in my hand and shook gently, trying vainly to get him to look at me.

"Yuefu," I demanded, and roughly shook his shoulders — still with no response.

I bent my head to his chest and mouth, searching for some sign of life, but finding none. I swallowed my grief, bit back my rage and folded lifeless arms across the still chest. I closed his unseeing eyes and pushed myself unsteadily to my feet.

"Where is she?" I asked a man who stood nearby.

He looked mournfully down at Shu, and I grabbed him by the shoulders, nearly lifting him off the ground.

"Answer me, God damn you," I cried. "Where is she?"

His eyes went wide with fear. Several of his compatriots rushed in to help, but he stayed them with a word and a look.

I set him back on his feet, and compassion replaced the fear in his eyes. He took my hand and led me toward the river bank, where a group of women moaned and wailed. I expected to see Mae's soft profile and delicate features, but saw only a tangled litter of banners and pennons lying on the ground, shaded by the overhanging branches.

As I moved closer, the shadows began to resolve. I could make out shapes beneath the paper and fabric — human shapes. The man led me to the far side of the mourning circle, knelt by one of the shapes and pulled me down beside him. He pulled back the shroud and my heart stopped.

Mae's eyes were softly closed, her lips slightly parted as in sleep. The sleeves and front of her dress were torn, exposing her fair skin to the dappled light, the moving shadows the only sign of life in her face. I could see no wounds, though. I was sure there'd been a mistake. Perhaps she had merely swooned. Surely she was otherwise fine.

I shook her shoulders gently and whispered her name, trying to wake her. When that failed, I took her hand in mine, but the cold, sallow flesh gave no response. Finally, I wrapped an arm around her and eased her body against my chest, cradling her head with one hand.

A damp, sticky mess met my hand. I

pulled it back to find it covered in blood and bone and gore. I swallowed the gorge that rose in my throat, unable to breathe or think. Or see.

Or be.

When my breath returned, it was in choking sobs that I released in a fierce roar that echoed across the shady grove as I rocked Mae in her final slumber.

Morning dawned cool and clear. The sky was a flawless blue unmarred by a single cloud. A gentle breeze swept down from the mountains, bringing with it the fresh scent of a place untouched by human hands.

The Chinese cemetery in Oakdale was situated just south of the Stanislaus River, between the stagecoach road and — fittingly — the railroad grading. Atop rough-sawn planks stretched between pairs of sawhorses, ten figures lay wrapped in gauzy, white grave clothes. Shu's body was distinguished by the white lambskin apron tied about his waist, and by the smaller body that lay beside him. Mae and her father would share a common grave, together in death as they had been in life.

Several dozen crew members gathered around, along with members of other crews who, like Dave and me, wore the white gloves and leather aprons of Shu's brother Masons.

"The last respects given to the dead are useful as lessons to us who remain. From them, let us gain instruction." The new elder spoke the words in Mandarin, but I knew the English version by heart. "Death has established dominion over all the earth, yet in our folly we fail to remember that we are born out of death, and to death we must return. May our thoughts be raised from sorrow to the heights of that divine light, that we may prepare ourselves for the great transition that awaits us all. Let us seek the will of Almighty God, whose grace and power are unbounded, and before Whose judgment seat each of us must stand."

I turned away from the graveside while the master recited the benediction, and stalked toward the open gate.

"You're not staying till it's over?" Dave asked as he came alongside me.

"I've said my good-byes," I said as evenly as I could manage, and stripped off my gloves and apron. "No sense kicking my heels, waiting to throw some dirt."

"Ceremony's still going on, though," he said. "They're still paying their respects."

The singsong lilt of the Mandarin benediction floated on the early summer air, a serene contradiction to the storm that raged inside me.

"I know," I said after a deep breath. "But you know what comes next."

Dave shook his head. "I've never been to a brother's funeral before."

"The master is invoking the brethren to be true and faithful," I said. "To speak what is good."

"Sounds nice."

"And he's charging them to live in love and, when the time comes, to die in peace." I shook my head. "I can't accept that charge yet. He'll quote Job, 'The Lord gave and the Lord hath taken away.' I prefer Moses: 'I will render vengeance to mine enemies.'"

Dave weighed the words, then nodded and gave a heavy sigh.

"I've set up a meeting with the marshal and Thomson's uncle," he said. "It seems Stephen had a fit of remorse and might be able to give enough information for an indictment against Garrett and the others."

I snorted at that.

"And just what do you think the odds are of that happening in this county?" I said. "In this state?"

Dozens of Chinese had been killed in race riots over the past few years. The only charges to stem from the murders had been for creating a public disturbance.

"Look, Jim," Dave said, "we have to do this within the law. That's the way it's got to be, and it's the way Mae would want it. You know that."

"Don't you dare talk to me about what she'd want." I spat the words, inches from Dave's face.

He didn't flinch.

"If we do this," he said, "we have to do it legally. Otherwise, we're the ones who'll swing, while her killers go scot-free. Is that what you want?"

I had no answer.

"I know you need vengeance, Jim. So do I. So do all those folks up there." He gestured back toward the grave site. "But, if we're gonna do this, we have to do it by the rules, if at all possible."

"And what if it's not possible?" I said.

The Yankee's eyes narrowed at that, and the look on his face was one I hadn't seen since the war.

"Then we by-God change the rules."

We mounted our horses, and I took a last, dry-eyed look toward the cemetery. Fate had already stolen so much from me. Now, as the first shovelfuls of dirt were tossed into the hole, it robbed me of the ability to cry over my wife's grave. I wanted to curse at the sky, to pray — like Job — that I'd never been born. But all I could manage was a prayer for Mae's safe passage, and a plea that I might soon be with her.

As I turned Rigel away from my heart's grave, a dragonfly darted at me from a bed of wildflowers. I looked at it from the corner of my eye as it settled on my shoulder. Its iridescent wings sparkled blue and green in the sunlight. It rested there for several seconds, wings flicking slowly up and down before it again took flight. It hovered a moment by my ear, and the gentle whisper of its wings left a soft kiss against my skin.

"I'll find you as soon as I can," I whispered.

Then the dragonfly was gone, darting across the river to be lost against the western horizon.

CHAPTER EIGHTEEN

Alpine County, California — February 1875

I stared through the brass-bound tubes of the binoculars, toward a telltale column of smoke. The thin plume rose from a cleft among the jagged eastern slopes of the Sierra Nevada range. The smoke might have been lost in the cloud cover, but its cut against the grain of the sky was like a jagged scar that caught my eye.

"What do you think?" I handed the binoculars to Dave, who scanned the bit of sky.

"Not a big fire," the former Union scout judged. "Probably just a couple of men. Looks to be in a pretty good position behind that bluff, so there's no way to say for sure." He gave the binoculars back to me and rubbed his eyes with gloved fingers. "But this ain't exactly the kind of weather to be going out for a nature walk. There's no mines in these parts, and no game to be found this far up. So if they ain't mining or hunting, chances are pretty good it's our men."

I nodded my agreement, and nervous anticipation twisted my gut.

"All right. Let's make for that grove of trees," I said, and pointed toward a thin stand of pines. "We'll work our way down from there."

Dave nodded and led off. I clucked my tongue for Rigel to follow, and the two other men — Paul Kimball and Tuck Foster — fell in behind. I rubbed a glove on the eagle-crested shield that hung from my coat. The tin badge still felt unnaturally heavy after more than two years.

With Stephen Thomson's help, indictments had been brought against Charlie Garrett and a half-dozen other men. My fears were borne out, and the men were charged simply with creating a public disturbance and destruction of private property — for the railroad's axe handles they'd damaged while using them on Mae and her father, I supposed.

Justice looked certain to be miscarried until Charlie and his band failed to show up for their trial. The judge was a founding member of the Stanislaus Asian Exclusion League and no friend to the Chinese. Deeper than his intolerance of Orientals, though, was his hatred of disorder and indifference toward his court. He'd declared the men fugitives, added murder and conspiracy to the list of crimes, and had the local US marshall swear Dave and me as deputies.

Since then, we'd tracked down — and brought to some semblance of justice — five of the men. Only two remained: Charlie Garrett and his little brother, Pinky.

"Looks like they're staying put," Dave said as we tied our horses to the skinny pine trees and tromped through the snow-packed slope above the sheltered camp.

"Yep, but if they've run this far, they must know we're still on the trail, so don't anyone go getting careless." I checked the action on my rifle to drive the point home. "You men tack on around the left side," I said to Foster and Kimball. "Dave and I'll go right."

Nervous nods acknowledged the order.

"Look," I added, sensing the tension in the air, "we've been here before. Not in these conditions, granted. But there's no difference between what we're about to do and what we've done a half-dozen times before. We go in, we tell them to throw down and we go home. Simple as that."

"But this is different," Tuck Foster said, his eyes fastened on the toes of his boots. "The others might get fined, might do some time. But Charlie? He's the only one up against a murder charge — ten of them, in fact. He's got real skin in the game, and he knows it."

"True," I said. "He's smart enough to know he might have a rough go of it if he stands trial. He's also smart enough to know I'm not about to let go of the scent."

I scanned the other men's eyes, and only Dave returned my gaze.

"One way or another," I said, "it ends today."

"We ain't had to deal with two at once before," Dave observed, breaking an uneasy silence. "How best to go about it?"

Kimball snorted at that.

"Pinky Garrett ain't but a snot-nosed, wet-behind-the-ears pup," he said. "He's like to be scared out of his wits by now — what wits he had to start with, that is. Probably throw down as soon as he sees us coming."

"Maybe," I allowed. "But a scared man's unpredictable. He doesn't reason rightly. And, depending on what Charlie's filled his head with, Pinky might be more scared of a jury — or even Charlie himself — than he would be of four men with guns. I say we find cover on either side of them and call out. Give them a chance to throw down and come out easy. We might be able to talk them down, but I don't want anyone exposed."

Heads nodded as the men stamped their feet and blew into their hands. I pulled my oilcloth duster tighter about me.

"All right, then," I said. "You two head on down that way. You'll probably be in place before us, so just find cover and hold steady. I'll call out once we're in position. We take it good and slow and, with luck, we'll be heading down the other side by noon."

It took twenty minutes for us to get into position. The hip-deep snow was made nearly impassable by a deep ache that seemed frozen in my bad leg. When we finally took cover in the brush at the left-hand approach to the camp, it took another five minutes for me to catch my breath. I strained my ears to pick out any manmade noise over the whisper of the mountain breeze and the hum of running water in the deep ravine below, but could hear nothing.

I looked over to Dave, and took a deep breath when he gave me a nod of agreement.

"Charlie Garrett." My voice seemed strangely muted by the thin air and thick snow cover.

A flurry of activity answered the summons

—— a scuffle of feet, the clatter of tinware falling to the ground, and the distinct *clack* of rifle hammers being drawn back.

"Charlie and Pinky Garrett," I shouted again. "We're here to bring you in. Throw up your hands and come on out."

"Well, Jimmy Robbins, is that you?" Charlie's voice rang in that deadly, comical lilt I'd learned to hate.

"This ain't a social call, Charlie," I hollered back. "We're here to take you in, same as Carson and Jenkins and the others."

"They got Robbo?" a younger, shakier voice cried out.

"That's right, Pinky," Dave shouted back. "And they all came along real peaceable, just like you ought to do. No need to make things any harder on yourself."

"But they're gonna hang us," Pinky protested, panic in the edge of his voice.

"Not necessarily," I answered, sickened by the truth of my own words. "Charlie's the only one up for murder. You and the others will likely be free before springtime."

"But you said . . ." Pinky's voice dropped to hushed tones, answered by a growling rumble.

I took advantage of the exchange and signaled Dave. I inched out from the thin cover, dragging myself by the elbows toward

434

the rocky hollow. From my new position, I could just make out Kimball and Foster, crouching on the other side of the encampment. I motioned for them to move up even with me.

"Pinky," I called again, using my voice to mask the men's movement, "there's no point in running any farther. Come back with us nice and easy, and it'll go better for you. It all ends here, today." I tried to make the words sound more like a promise than a threat. "Just throw down your guns and come out."

A moment's hesitation.

"They ain't gonna hang me?"

"They won't hang you," I promised, and breathed a little easier at the thought of at least one surrender.

Another rumbled exchange hinted at the threats of the older brother.

Pinky's plaintive argument was punctuated with a sharp, "Dammit, Charlie, I'm going."

The crunch of snow approached the opening to the hideaway.

"I'm coming out," Pinky shouted. "Coming out."

The tentative steps grew more and more confident as they neared the edge of the camp, and the younger fugitive toddled toward the waiting arms of the law.

He stepped into sight, a shotgun held by the barrel in his left hand, both arms stretched away from his body. He saw me, and I nodded for him to come all the way out.

Tuck rose from his place.

"Come on this way, Pinky," he said.

The boy froze and his eyes changed to those of a cornered fox, casting about to see how many hounds had him hemmed in.

A shot rang out, the sound amplified to a deafening roar as it echoed off the stone walls of the hideout.

A spray of red puffed out from Pinky's chest, sprinkling the fresh snow in front of him with a rose-shaped, crimson-dropped pattern. His eyes went wide with shock and dim understanding, and the shotgun fell from his hands as he sank to his knees and pitched facedown into the blood-spattered snow.

The shotgun fell with the body and landed butt first on a solid patch of snow. The hammer dropped with the impact and a second shot rang out. The recoil kicked Pinky's feet out, twisting the cruciform figure into a crooked snow angel. I followed the direction of the gun's barrel to where Tuck Foster lay in the snow, clutching at his gut and writhing in pain.

"Tuck!" Kimball cried out, and rushed to the fallen man, pressing his hands against the blood and steam that rose from the younger man's belly.

In that same moment, an unearthly groan and rumble shook the ground. A slight hiss stirred the air around us. Looking around, I saw a plume of white powder rise from the direction of the peak above the camp.

Avalanche.

The thought echoed in my head even as my tongue froze to the roof of my mouth, unable to form the word.

"Avalanche!" Dave shouted for me. "Move, move."

He grabbed me by the collar and half dragged, half lifted me to a standing position and pushed me toward the entrance of Garrett's shelter. Kimball abandoned Foster to his fate as we rushed toward the protected rear wall of the bluff, heedless of the armed fugitive within.

Garrett seemed not to notice the world crashing in around him. He crouched behind his fire pit, shotgun raised against the three men who now charged his position. The single-barrel gun would only give him one shot, and he aimed for the easiest target.

My knee buckled as the shot echoed off

the rock walls, and I collapsed in a tangle. Even as I fell, the *whiz* of pellets flashed past my ear, and I felt the bee sting of several pieces of bird shot biting into my right shoulder. I twisted with the impact and caught a glimpse of Garrett rushing toward me. He carried his shotgun like a club, oblivious to the huge wall of white that chased after him.

As he reached me, the frozen tidal wave swept over us and we were entombed in the cascading blanket of snow. The slide carried us farther and farther down the slope, toward the cliff I knew lay somewhere beyond the whiteness. The ground gave way beneath me and I felt an odd, weightless sensation.

Pain shot through my wounded shoulder as my fall stopped, and the solid wall of the cliff emerged from the whiteness to slam into my body. Pain and shock threatened to overwhelm me, but I managed to cling to consciousness.

"Still with me, Jimmy Boy?"

The voice came from somewhere above. I craned my neck to look, but the pain of just that little movement sent jolts of lightning down my spine.

"Jimmy, you still with me?" the voice called again.

"Yeah," I managed to grunt.

My right wrist was caught in a firm grip, but started to slip until another hand added its strength to the first.

"This puts us in a bit of a fix, now, don't it?" The deadly humor was unmistakable in Garrett's voice, the danger underscored by a coarse chuckle.

"Charlie," I gasped against the pain as I tried again to look up, "pull me up and we'll get all this sorted out."

"Oh, but everything was already sorted out," he said, "until you stuck your nose into things. You couldn't just leave it be. You couldn't let it go."

"Let it go?" I shot back, my anger overcoming the pain. "You murdered —"

"What? Your slanty-eyed cunt?"

I looked up into hate-blinded eyes set above a bone-chilling leer.

"Y'know, it's true what they say," he pressed on. "I'd about had my fill of killing those Chinks, but an hour later I was hungry for more. I only wish I'd gotten me a better taste of your sweet little dish, maybe dipped my chopstick into her sauce for a little stir-fry."

Fear, grief, even pain fell away in that instant. Only rage remained as I tightened my grip on Garrett's arm and pulled myself upward. I swung my left arm up and groped with my hand until I found a hold in his thick, oily hair. His eyes went wide as I pulled my face to within inches of his. He tried to loosen his grip as he slid closer to the edge of the cliff.

"You crazy son of a bitch," he said. "You'll kill us both."

"You did that when you killed Mae," I spat back.

He tried again to loosen my grip, but only sped his slide toward the edge. His eyes flashed from panic to rage, rage to acceptance, acceptance to cold-blooded determination.

"If that's how you want it, Chink lover," he said, saliva dripping like venom from his bared teeth, "I'll see you in hell."

I tightened my grip and pulled myself up until our noses touched.

"Save a seat for me."

With that, I drew up my legs, planted my feet against the cliff wall and pushed.

Garrett's eyes went beyond fear as he joined me in the void. He let go his grip, and I released mine as the air moved past us faster and faster.

Something hit the side of my leg and raked up the side of my body until it lodged painfully in the pit of my wounded arm.

Garrett rushed past me and I fought through the pain to keep my eyes on his. A part of my mind counted out a childish *One-Mississippi, Two-Mississippi . . .* until, at the count of *Four-Miss—*, his body plunged into the remains of the avalanche.

"Jim?"

The voice called from above, and I looked up into a shower of snow and ice. Through the thin, white cascade, I could just make out Dave's head, poking over the edge of the cliff.

I tried to answer but couldn't find my voice. I waved, then clutched at the pine bough that had saved my life, growing straight out from the steep rock face.

"Hold tight," Dave said. "Kimball's run to fetch some rope."

"I'm not going anywhere," I managed in a raspy voice.

"That's good to know."

Part of my mind noted that Dave kept speaking, but the last bit of consciousness I could muster was focused solely on holding firm. No Dave, no pain, no rage, no grief. Only my arms wrapped tightly about the miracle pine.

I felt a tickle against my cheek, and opened an eye to see the rough braid of a rope dangling next to me. The end was tied into a loop, which I tucked over my head and under my good arm. I tugged twice, and instantly the weight came off my wracked shoulder. Foot by foot, I rose out of the void, spinning like a watch on the end of its chain.

When I reached the top, strong hands stretched out to pull me back onto solid ground. Heedless of my injuries, Dave tugged on my right arm, and the pain finally had its way.

I let out a scream, and part of my mind feared I might set off another avalanche. A cocoon of oblivion soon held at bay any conscious thought. I was only dimly aware as Dave and Kimball reset my dislocated shoulder, wrapped my arm in a sling, carried me up the slope and propped me up on Rigel's back.

The fallen — friend and foe — could only be abandoned to the graves the mountain had made for them. Buried with them was all thought of justice and vengeance, and the survivors — or the part of us that still survived — rode down from the mountain to take our place among the living.

CHAPTER NINETEEN

SS Hardesty, *Pacific Ocean — April 1876*
I leaned over the rail and spat out the bile that remained in my mouth. A full day at sea, clinging to the deck rail, had left my stomach empty and my head dizzy. I took a pull from my flask to rinse my mouth, then swallowed, loath to waste the precious drops.

It'll be in the ocean soon enough, I allowed. *Might as well enjoy it while I can.*

"Do I even want to ask how you're doing?" Dave said from a safe distance upwind.

"I'm still breathing," I said. "Whether that's a good thing or not, I'm not so sure."

"Looks to be a squall coming on," he judged. "We'd best get you below decks."

"You mean it gets worse?"

Dave laughed.

"You see the big yellow glowing thing in the middle of all that blue? If you see that, it means smooth sailing. Now that," he added, pointing toward a massive stack of clouds on the horizon, "could make for a rough ride. You really need to come in."

"To that death trap? No thanks. I'll take my chances up here." I took another pull at my flask and savored the liquid burn as it coursed down my throat. "If it's my time to go, I'd just as soon be able to see the sky — whatever color it is. Hell, maybe a wave will come along and put me out of my misery."

The humor left Dave's eyes.

"I didn't drag your ass off a battlefield," he said, "or down a mountain for that matter, just so you could drown in the middle of the ocean. Or in a God-damned bottle of whiskey."

He stalked toward me, cocked back his arm and let fly. The move caught me by surprise, and his blow sent my flask pinwheeling over the rail. The precious amber liquid spiraled out behind it.

"What did you do?" I cried.

"Look," he said. "Whether it matters to you or not, there's people who care about you. People for who it actually makes a difference if you live or die. So you had your heart broke — that's a hard thing. But do you know how many men would give their right arm to feel the kind of love you had, even if they knew it was gonna be taken away?"

I glared up at him, and his return gaze was ice cold.

"Shit," he went on. "You want to cash it in, there's the rail. Don't worry about the rest of us. We've all lost folks before. We got over them, and we'll get over you."

With that, he turned on his heels and stomped toward the hatch that led below-decks.

"Wait," I called after him.

He either ignored me or my voice was too weak for him to hear. Crewmen scurried about the deck, doubling the tie-downs on the flapping sails, fastening loose rigging and clearing the decks of anything that couldn't be secured. I grabbed the deck rail to pull myself up but, as I stood, the ship pitched sharply. I briefly saw the stanchion as I lunged toward it, then all went mercifully black.

"Easy now," a soft voice cautioned me.

My head ached and throbbed as I came to, making me wish I could pass out again. The whiskey that had numbed my mind and dulled my senses for the past year was already withdrawing its insulating blanket, leaving my spirit bare, exposed to life's cruel coldness. That coldness was palpable now, and seemed to wrap about me from head to foot.

As my mind cleared, I realized the coldness was no illusion, but a very real sheet wrapped about me and soaked with my own sweat. Whiskey leached through my pores, and the stench of it made my stomach churn.

"Take this," the voice said, and the genteel drawl was like a salve to my soul.

A wooden spoon pressed against my lips, and I parted them to let warm liquid trickle into my mouth and run down my throat. The taste was of broth and — something else.

"It's ginger root," the voice replied to the face I must have made. "It'll help settle your stomach."

After a few more spoonfuls, the bowl was set aside and the cool cloth lifted from my eyes. The cabin was dimly lit. Shadows danced wildly across the walls as the single lantern rocked and swayed with the motion of the ship. A small brazier burned in the corner of the room. It added to the soft glow but did little to hold back the chill from wind and waves that roared on the other side of the bulkhead.

As my eyes grew accustomed to the dim

and shifting scene, they settled on the figure that sat beside my bed. The face was masked in shadow, but the coppery red hair captured every spare bit of light to glow with a warm radiance.

"Gina?" I rasped the word in little more than a whisper.

The figure leaned nearer and the features resolved into the warm, freckled face of another.

"No, silly. It's Cassandra."

She dipped the cloth into a basin, wrung out the water and placed it on my forehead.

The soothing touch did little to clear my mind, but did help me find my voice.

"What are you doing here?"

An impish grin creased the thin lips she'd inherited from her mother, and her eyes sparkled with her father's good humor.

"I suppose Dave enjoys his surprises a mite too much," she said. "He didn't tell you we were sailing with you?"

" 'We'?" I said. "You mean your folks are here, too?"

The humor in her eyes dimmed a bit.

"Papa's here," she said. "Mother passed on, a year ago Christmas."

I sank a little deeper into the thin mattress.

"I didn't know," I said. "I'm sorry."

Cassandra managed a smile and picked up the bowl once more.

"Nothing to be sorry about. You couldn't know. Besides, you had enough to deal with at the time." She paused her ministrations, and looked me in the eye. "I was truly sorry to hear about Mae and her father. I wish I'd had a chance to meet them."

I struggled to swallow a spoonful of broth past the lump that rose in my throat.

"You would have liked them," I managed after another slurp. "But you still haven't told me what you're doing aboard the ship."

Cassandra shook her head as she tipped more broth between my lips.

"I can't believe Dave didn't tell you," she said. "Papa's been named director of the Western Australia Railroad."

I blinked in surprise, the coincidence too great to accept. Not long after our final run-in with Charlie Garrett, Dave had left me in Truckee, California. He gave no explanation, only saying he'd be back after a month or two. Just a week ago, he'd shown up out of the blue, dragged me out of a saloon, thrown me on the flatcar of a west-bound train, and produced a recruitment flyer for the Western Australia Government Railroad.

"You've gone west to start your life over

before," he observed. "It doesn't get much more west than this."

Two days later, I was emptying my stomach into the Pacific Ocean.

"But Cy doesn't know anything about running a railroad," I objected as I tried to wrap my mind around Cassandra's words.

"No, but he knows how to invest in them. The day-to-day he'll leave to his foremen." She arched a conspiratorial eyebrow.

"Foremen?"

She rolled her eyes and groaned in exasperation.

"You and Dave," she explained. "He didn't tell you any of this?"

I shook my head.

"Honestly, that man will be the death of me."

I came to his defense as best I could.

"He's really not all that bad, once you get to know him."

Cassandra's eyes sparkled as her brow softened, and her cheeks glowed with a fresh blush.

"I know that, JD," she said. "I married him three weeks ago."

"So you've had a rough go of it," Uncle Cy observed as I replaced the pawn he'd moved into my king's row with a queen piece.

449

He could have meant anything from the chess game to the voyage to my whole damned life. I crafted my answer for the easiest choice.

"Game's not over yet," I said, and slid a knight into a blocking position.

"That's very true," he said. "I've seen games that last for ages, while some seem to end even before they get started. Check."

I studied the board as Cy plucked my knight from the field, set a bishop in its place, then lit a fat cigar. I pulled my blanket tighter about my shoulders even as the older man wiped a trickle of sweat from his brow. Under Cassandra's care, I'd mostly recovered from my year inside the whiskey bottle, but I was still wracked by alternating bouts of fever and chills.

"Feel like giving up?" Cy asked, his words accented by a cloud of blue smoke.

"Sometimes," I admitted, and it wasn't because of the queen and bishop that hemmed in my king. "How do you go on?"

Cy's bushy eyebrows arched over brown eyes that glistened in the equatorial sunlight.

"Some days, I really don't know," he said. "Helen may not have been perfect, but she was the best part of my life for nigh on forty years. When she passed, I found myself lost, alone in a way I'd never known before. If

450

not for Cassandra, I mightn't have been much longer for this world." He took a long drag on the cigar and leaned back in his deck chair. "Then there was Helen herself."

"How do you mean?" I asked.

The older man grinned sheepishly.

"She came to me in a dream a couple of months after," he said. "Told me I'd moped around plenty long, that grief is a vain luxury of the living and I'd pampered myself enough. As usual, she was right."

I blinked at him a couple of times.

"How can grief be a luxury?" I said.

"Pretty simple, really — so simple we can't even see it when we're in the midst of it." He took a deep breath, and the air filled with his blue-tinged sigh. "There's nothing wrong with mourning a loved one. Dead or alive, when they leave they take the part of us that joined with them. It's only natural we should feel the pain of their loss. But, when we live in that grief, we turn love into self-centeredness."

I opened my mouth to object, but Cy waved his free hand to silence me.

"When I mourned Helen," he said, "it was because her time had been cut short, because Cassandra had lost her mother. When I let the mourning turn to grief, though, it became about my loss, about how alone I was. It didn't matter that Helen had given me years of more happiness than I deserved, or that she'd given me a beautiful daughter. All I could see was my own pain and how my life was now something less than it had been."

I nodded my understanding, but Cy shook his head.

"I couldn't have been more wrong," he said.

I looked at him, stunned, but he pressed on.

"If Helen's life really made a difference for me, if she really added a value to my own life, then that value couldn't evaporate just because she was gone. Cassandra wasn't her only legacy to me. I was a part of her legacy, the man I became because of her. If I wanted to honor her memory, grieving was not the way to do it. I'd best honor her by being the man she'd made me, by becoming an even better man."

"But you were a good man to begin with," I objected, and Cy's raised eyebrows invited me to go on.

I did.

Though the telling was haunted by the ghosts of Pawnee warriors, innocent Cheyenne, a red-headed whore and a hate-filled roughneck, when I finished speaking my soul felt lighter. The pain of dozens of old wounds reopened, though, nearly took my breath away. I had no more tears to shed, and I sat in uneasy silence with Uncle Cy until he reached across the chess board, tipped over his king and picked up a bishop.

"You know," he said, "in medieval times the bishop was known as the ship. Its moves were seen as similar to a ship's as it tacked against the wind. Funny thing about sailing — a contrary wind might blow you off course but, if your sails are set right, the same wind can drive you closer to your goal."

He set the chess piece back down and fixed me with a hard stare.

"Every choice you ever made brought you closer to Mae," he said. "Good or bad, every step led you to her. Now, from what Dave tells me, you brought real love and joy into her life. There's not much better a man can do than that."

He stood and laid a heavy hand on my shoulder.

"What's done is done," he said. "There's no changing that. Where you go from here, son, is entirely up to you. I know Helen wouldn't let me sit about, so here I am starting out on a new life in a new country. What would Mae have you do?"

He patted my shoulder and set off about the promenade deck, while I huddled deeper into my blanket and turned my face into the crisp sea breeze. The thrum of the steam engine, the churn of the propellers and the hush of the wind all seemed to whisper the answer to me.

Go on.

CHAPTER TWENTY

HMS Shalimar, *Southern Ocean — August 1876*

"The Geraldton-Northampton line has been under construction for more than two years, and they've already spent the full budget."

Uncle Cy described the line that Dave and I would be taking over. We strolled along the main deck with Dave and Cassandra, enjoying a rare breeze in this part of the Great Australian Bight. Following the voyage from San Francisco, we'd boarded another ship at Sydney and would arrive at the Western Australia port of Fremantle in a few days.

"Must be a long road," I said.

Cy shook his head. "Thirty-five miles."

I stopped mid-stride and turned to look at him.

"We've laid that in less than a week," I said. "Rough terrain?"

Another shake of the head.

"A couple of rocky stretches," he said, "but mostly flat plains from sea level up to about four hundred feet. They're giving us four years and another two times the original budget to get it done."

I stared at Cy open-mouthed, unable to believe what I heard.

"The government wants us to finish a road at three times the cost and three times the schedule originally planned, and they'll be happy with that?"

A nod.

"And they're backing that up with bonuses if we meet the new timeline."

I looked to Dave, who gave me a nod and a wry grin. I shrugged my acceptance and turned back to Uncle Cy.

"I think I'm going to like Australia," I said.

We continued our walk about the deck and I leaned heavily on a new cane, which I'd found to be a help in acquiring my sea legs. I stopped as we passed a vent stack, and cocked my head to listen to a sound that caught my attention.

"Do you hear that?" I said.

Dave joined me at the bellmouth opening and closed his eyes to listen. Out of the inky blackness of the hold came a haunting echo.

"Lord God Almighty, ain't there no one

to help a poor widow's son, a-wandering alone in this cold, dark world?"

My eyes opened wide as the meaning of the words sank in, and I flagged down the nearest crewman.

"Where does this vent lead?" I asked.

"The forward hold," he replied in a coarse English accent, "but passengers ain't allowed there."

"Take me," I ordered.

"Sir, I can't."

I fixed the young man with a heavy glare.

"Maybe you didn't understand. I'm not asking. I'm telling you to take me to that hold. My friend here," I indicated Dave, "will go find an officer to give the order, but you're going to take me there right now."

"Y-yes, sir."

The sailor actually saluted, then led me toward a nearby deck hatch. I balked a little as the man climbed down into the darkness. I screwed up my courage, swung stiff-legged into the opening and followed him down the ladder while Dave went to find someone in authority. The crewman led me along a low, narrow passageway until it widened into a small open area lit by a pair of lanterns. The forward bulkhead held a stout, wooden door while another passage led toward the rear of the ship.

"No passengers allowed, huh?" I said as I looked around the space.

The sailor swallowed loudly, then turned tail and scampered back the way we'd come.

Five large, rough-looking men sat around one of the lanterns, in front of the door that was barred by a thick timber set in sturdy iron brackets. As one, they looked up from their playing cards to stare at me through dull, brutish eyes. A thin shadow flitted across the men's faces and I turned to see a much slighter man who rose from his place by the second lantern.

"Am I glad to see you," the small man said with a Scot's burr as he pumped my hand in greeting. "Seth's been without water or food for at least a day."

"Excuse me?" I said, releasing the young man's hand.

"Aren't you the doctor?" he asked as he stared wide-eyed at me through thick spectacle lenses.

A rumble of laughter came from the seated men, and the Scot looked from me to them and back again.

"Doctor ain't coming," one of the toughs said in a thick Irish brogue as he rose to join us. "Leastways, not today."

The man carried a solid frame on tree-trunk legs, his arms larger than most men's thighs. Broad, square shoulders supported a thick neck that cocked to one side to avoid the low deck joists. A bristle of dull-red hair crowned a head decorated with jug-handle ears. Thick, smirking lips, a crooked nose and narrow eyes gleamed with arrogance and disdain.

"Tim Sullivan," he said as he extended a meaty hand.

From the look in Sullivan's eyes, I could see the gesture was not one of courtesy, but of challenge. The game about to be played was one I hated, but there was no getting around it with a man like this. The game had one rule, and a simple one: the strongest wins.

I took Sullivan's hand and tried not to wince as I met the force of his iron grip. I locked my eyes on his, and watched with satisfaction as confusion replaced some of the big man's arrogance. His eyes flashed with anger as I continued to hold his grip, and I could see the muscles of his jaw tighten. Finally, he released my hand and slapped it away.

"Seeing as you're not the doctor and not part of the crew," he said, "what brings you to our little corner of the ship?"

"Sounded like someone was hurt down

here," I said. "I reckoned I'd best look into it."

"You'd do better for yourself by turning around and going back the way you came," Sullivan growled, then looked to his men who stood and grunted their agreement.

"It's Seth," the slight man told me. "These ruffians beat him and bound him, tossed him into that hold and now won't let me look in on him."

"Is that true?" I asked Sullivan. "Are you holding a man in there?"

"Aye, and what if it is? The captain's not said a word against it, and I don't see it's any business of yours. Besides, that rot in there," he jerked a fat thumb toward the door of the hold, "is no more than a murdering piece of filth."

"That's a lie," the Scot said.

"Hold your tongue, little man," Sullivan warned, looming a foot taller than the other man. "Better yet, take your scrawny arse and your fancy surveyor's books and head back topside with this one."

"Surveyor?" I asked.

"Aye," Sullivan said with a laugh. "The wee one thinks he can become a railway man just by reading books."

"Better a man with a book than a brute with a hammer," the Scot said.

460

"See here, laddie," Sullivan said, his voice rumbling in the small space. "My patience with you is wearing thin. Why don't you run along back to where you belong? And take this one with you."

The smaller man was about to reply, but I laid a steadying hand on his shoulder.

"Do as he says."

He glared at me through the thick lenses and started to sputter his objection, but I steered him toward the passageway and turned to follow him.

"There's no sense trying to reason with the ignorant piker bastard," I said.

I'd met many Irishmen over the years, most of them decent men. Good or bad, they'd all shared certain characteristics. Chief among them was a heightened sense of pride in their intelligence, nationality and certain patrimony. To question any one of those virtues was to invite a storm of Hibernian wrath. To attack all three was sure to unleash a hurricane.

I wasn't disappointed.

I watched the walls of the hold as a huge shadow raced toward my own. I tightened my grip on the cane and spun as the shadows met, catching Sullivan square in the Adam's apple with the head of the cane. His momentum carried us a few steps

461

farther. As his hands clutched at his throat, I jabbed the cane brutally into his belly, then swung it up into his jaw. The big man lurched back and smacked his head into a deck joist.

The sound of the impact echoed in the small space, and a glaze clouded the fury in the man's eyes. Without giving him a chance to recover from his daze, I kicked at his knee and swung the cane at his head. The wooden handle connected with Sullivan's temple and the man's eyes rolled back in his head.

The other four men watched their leader slump to the floor, and I backed into the narrow passageway to keep them from attacking all at once.

"Aw, hell, Jim," I heard a voice say from the rearward passage. "You couldn't wait till I got here before getting acquainted?"

I ventured back into the open area, casting a watchful eye on Sullivan to make sure he was down. The young surveyor crept out behind me, his wide eyes filling the thick spectacles.

"We were just getting started on the introductions," I said as Dave stepped into the hold and came to my side. "That one there is Tim Sullivan, and I'm afraid I didn't catch the rest of your names."

"Bannon — Jeffries — Roarke — Grant,"

came the jumbled reply from the four big men, lost without their ringleader.

"Which would make you Andrew Fraser," Dave said with a nod toward the young surveyor.

"Andy, aye," came the reply.

"How'd you know that?" I asked.

Dave fixed me with a crooked smile. "Meet our new crew."

I looked dumbly back at him but, before I could respond, a uniformed sailor stepped into the crowded space.

"All right, you rot, back above decks," he ordered.

The large men — those still standing — looked to me and I nodded.

"Get him out of my sight." I indicated Sullivan, and a pair of the men unceremoniously hauled him upright, slung his arms over their broad shoulders and dragged him through the aft passageway, followed by the others.

"Ship's doctor?" I asked Dave as I hefted the beam from its place at the door of the hold.

"On his way."

Ignoring the sailor's protests, I tossed the beam aside and wrenched open the door on its screeching hinges. A stench rolled out of the cramped hold and threatened to bowl me over. I grabbed one of the lanterns, took a deep breath, then steeled myself as I stepped through the doorway.

The small space was tucked up into the bows of the ship. I had to hunch over to keep from hitting my head on the deck joists, and I doubted I'd be able to stretch out across the floor if I had a mind to. The man that lay on the floor was larger still — at least as big as Sullivan — and fit into the cramped hold only by curling up into a ball.

The lantern did little to brighten the space but, as my eyes adjusted, I saw that the man's posture was not of his choosing. Thick ropes bound his arms and legs, and his wrists were tied together beneath his knees. The man's back was to me, and I stepped around him to get a better look.

His dark face was a mask of even darker dried blood that had come from his nose and mouth and several cuts on his head. One eye was swollen shut, the other merely a slit. One ear glistened with fresh blood, and I recognized in the series of small gashes the bites of rats that infested the hold. His breathing was ragged and shallow, and a slight gurgling sound told me a lung had been punctured.

"Andy, would you fetch me some water?" I said through clenched teeth, fighting back my revulsion.

When no reply came, I looked up to see the young man's ashen face.

"Andy," I barked, and the lad blinked his eyes and turned his focus on me. "Water," I said more gently.

"Aye, water."

He stepped through the doorway, and I knelt by the fallen man, pulled open my jackknife and hacked away at the ropes that bound him.

"My God," Dave muttered as the man — Seth, I recalled his name — moaned and began to unfold.

Dave held a handkerchief over his nose to filter out the stench. Seth stank of sweat and stale blood, and — held captive for a day or more — had soiled himself at least once.

I cut away the last of the ropes from Seth's wrists. His fingers were purple and swollen from lack of blood flow, and the tips were rat-bitten. I took a meaty hand in mine and rubbed it briskly to restore circulation. As I reached across to take his other hand, Seth's torn shirt fell open to expose his chest and stomach, the black skin dotted with ugly bruises. I started to look away, but a strip of leather about the man's neck caught my attention.

At first I feared he'd been choked, but, as I tugged on the leather thong, I found it looped through a small pendant. The carved wood was decorated with a familiar pattern of lines and curves, and my hand moved to the talisman about my own neck as Andy returned with a bucket of water.

"Thanks," I said as he set the pail on the deck.

I laid the pendant gently back on Seth's chest, and pulled a blue bandana from my pocket. I doused it in the water and squeezed a few drops onto Seth's swollen, parched and cracked lips. The water restored the man's senses and must also have stirred his memories. His body jerked and his hands covered his face as he cried out hoarsely.

"It's all right, Seth," the Scot said. "It's me, Andy."

The big man relaxed a fraction, but his hands still protected his head.

Gently, carefully, I placed a hand atop his head and said, "Easy, brother. We're here to help you," then whispered a word in his ear.

At the sound of the syllables, his struggling ceased and he slowly lowered his hands. His good eye opened a fraction wider and he whispered, "Who . . . ?"

466

"Just another widow's son," I said, "come to lend a hand."

CHAPTER TWENTY-ONE

Perth, Western Australia — October 1876

". . . and teaches us all that we are traveling upon the broad level of time, from whose bourne no traveler returns."

Seth leaned back against his pillows and raised a glass of water to his lips with a trembling hand. Uncle Cy, Dave and I looked at one another and shook our heads in amazement. Over the past two hours, the young man had recited his part of the Masonic catechisms more flawlessly than I'd ever heard. From the looks on the other men's faces, they were similarly impressed.

"How was it?" Seth asked after draining half a glass of water.

Cy patted the man's shoulder — the one not wrapped in bandages — and said, "Perfect. You've learned your lessons well."

Seth's dark cheeks flushed to a bronze hue. "I've had some good teachers, is all."

"Without a doubt," Cy agreed. "Be that

as it may, there's still the question of —"
He bit off his words and looked to Dave
and me for some support.

"Seth," I stepped in, "you know the rights
and benefits needed for acceptance into the
lodge."

"Yes, sir," he said, then quoted from the
catechism. " 'By being a man, freeborn, of
good repute and well recommended.' "

Silence hung thickly in the room as the
three of us avoided Seth's eyes. Dave cleared
his throat, then stood to open the transom
above the door. He noisily crossed the
wooden floor and raised the sash on the
window.

An early autumn — *spring,* I reminded
myself — breeze washed through the room,
renewing the air but doing little to ease the
tension.

"You think I ain't a regular Mason." Seth
broke the awkward silence. "You think I
ain't freeborn, so I couldn't rightly be made
a Mason."

"As far as we're concerned, you're a
Mason through and through," Cy assured
him, "a true fellow of the Craft. But there
are some that may think it . . . irregular for
you to have been initiated in the first place."

"But that ain't right."

"We know it's not, Seth," I said, "but

that's just how some men — even some brothers — are."

Seth waved his good hand in dismissal. "No, I mean it's not correct."

He looked from one of us to another, his deep-brown eyes boring into each of us until we had no choice but to meet his gaze. He propped himself up against the pillows as best he could with one arm, and his chest swelled with pride, straining against the bandages that bound his cracked ribs.

"What I mean to say is, I am freeborn. Ain't never been no man's slave all my born days. Now, don't fret, brethren," he reassured us when we all looked away, shamed by the base assumption. "Most nigras my age back home was only made free after the war. Them that never wore the yoke are mostly from up north, and probably a lot more fine and educated than me. All the same, every breath I've taken has been as a free man, from the day I was born."

He breathed deeply, as though to emphasize the fact, but fell into a wracking cough as he strained his battered lungs.

"My mama and pappy were slaves," he explained after a sip of water, "and their mamas and pappies before them, back some five or six generations. But, when Pap learned Mama was expecting with me, why they run off to Indian Territory, met up with some Choctaw folk who took them in as they own. Pap took the name Freeman, and that's how I was born. Free."

The glint in his eyes faded and he sagged against his pillows.

"Now I've thrown all that away."

"What do you mean?" Dave asked as he pushed himself off the window sill and returned to his chair.

"What Sullivan and the others been saying, about me being a murderer." Seth looked nervously at each one of us. "It's true. We all got a little drunk the night we left Sydney, and I let slip what I done. I reckon they was fixing to turn me in here at Perth, ship me back for whatever reward money they might get. You good brothers stepped in, but I can't see that makes no difference. I still got to pay for what I done."

"Tell us what happened," Cy ordered gently.

Seth took a deep, shuddering breath, sipped once more at his glass and unfolded his tale. He told us of his wife, Lydia, daughter of one of the Choctaw elders. After marrying, they'd gone west to California, where Seth had found work with a large mining interest and Lydia had set up a school for the miners' children.

"The boss man had me working late one night," he explained. "I traded chores with one of the other fellas and went by the schoolhouse on my way home, to see if Lydia was still there. Sure enough, the light was burning, but when I went to try the door it was locked. I jiggled the latch a bit, then heard something muffled from inside."

The blood drained from his face, and his features sagged as he went on with his tale.

"Pap always tried to teach me to mind my temper, but there was no minding anything that night," he said. "I bust that door clean off its hinges, and there they were — Lydia on her desk, her dress half tore off and the boss on top of her."

He shuddered at the memory.

"I don't remember moving," he went on. "Don't recollect anything that happened right away, but a loud snapping sound brought me back to my senses. I had the man laid out across a bench, my hand on his throat and his neck right on the edge of the bench. Broke. Damnedest thing I ever saw. His eyes was still moving around, and he made noises like he was trying to say something. Then he looked straight at me. Then he stopped twitching."

Silence filled the room. I chanced a look at Seth, but his eyes saw nothing of me, nothing of Australia. The far-off look — one with which I was all too familiar — saw only the horror his mind mercilessly rehearsed.

"I found Lydia out back," he went on, "trying to wash herself out. I picked her up and carried her home. We packed a few things, and before daylight, we was gone from there. She'd helped out teaching the orphans at a Spanish mission not far from the camp. The *padre* there offered to take her in, but thought it best I get away from California soon as I could. See, another nigra fella had got himself hung some time before for killing a white man in a knife fight the white man started. I didn't reckon I had much more of a chance than he did. The *padre* drove me down to San Francisco, to the harbor. First billing I saw was for hands on the railroad here, passage paid. That night I was at sea."

Silence drowned out the street noises from beyond the window as, his story told, Seth slumped back into his pillow. His stove-in chest moved in time with his rapid, shallow breaths. Dave, Cy and I sat silently except for the creaking of our chairs as we shifted uncomfortably.

"Killing a man is no easy thing," I said, finally breaking the silence. "It's something that stays with you for a long, long time —

maybe forever. But what's also forever," I went on, reaching out a hand to clasp Seth's shoulder, "is the fact that he won't harm your wife ever again — nor anyone else, for that matter."

Seth chanced a look toward me, his eyes glistening with grief and regret, tempered with hope.

"Law doesn't always serve justice," I said. "Sometimes, taking the law into your own hands — or running from the law when it's been corrupted by small men — is the only way to see justice done. Have no fear, brother," I assured him. "You were born free, and a free man you'll stay. All we have to do now is get word back to Lydia so she can come join you."

The big man cocked his head, his eyes glistening.

"You — you'd do that for me?"

A knock sounded on the door and Dave patted Seth on the shoulder and spoke lightly.

"What are brothers for?" he said, then crossed to the door and pulled it open.

"Visiting hours are over, gentlemen. You, too," Cassandra told Dave with a wink and a kiss. "Our patient needs his rest."

"Yes, ma'am," Dave said, and led the three of us from the room while Cassandra laid out a small meal for Seth.

The house Cy had taken in Perth sat on Saint George's Terrace, not far from Government House. More important to the moment, it lay close to the marketplaces that supplied fresh daily fare. Uncle Cy had quickly taken to the local custom of ale and cold mutton sandwiches for lunch, and a pail of the amber brew and a platter of meat sat on the kitchen table.

"Poor boy," Cy muttered as he spread horseradish on a thick slice of bread. "Can you imagine, living with guilt over sending someone into the hereafter, knowing full well the bugger had it coming to him?"

"Hard to fathom," Dave said around a mouthful of tender, stringy meat.

"Uh, I'm sitting right here, and I get what you're saying," I chimed in. "I appreciate what you're trying to do, but — please don't take this wrong — you don't know what you're talking about."

"No?" Cy said.

"Not unless you can tell me how many lives you've taken," I retorted.

"Four," the older man replied without hesitation. "At least, that I can distinctly recall. Three were in the Sabine War, and there may have been more. The other was just a few months before you boys showed up on our doorstep — some no-good drifter that broke into the house."

"I never knew," I admitted, surprised to learn Cy's coup count nearly matched my own.

"Why should you?" he said around a mouthful of mutton. "A man has no need to rehash his battles, nor to let them rule over him. War's an ugly thing, but it's war. And if someone breaks into a man's home, threatens his security and that of his family, that person has broken the bonds of civility and abandons all right to civil treatment. More to the point," he went on before I could fathom what he was saying, "how many lives have you saved?"

"One," Dave said, raising his hand. "At least. If any other Reb had come across me that night, I doubt I'd be sitting here."

"And one more upstairs," Cy added promptly, "plus Zeke and Ketty, and who knows how many more of your fellows during the war. The point is, it's not just the good or bad a man does that defines him. Everything he does, every choice he makes, makes him a new man every day, every moment. It's what he does with that next moment, and the next one and the one after that, that defines who he is. Without the bad, there's no drive to make the good better. It's like a checkerboard —"

"Or a quilt," I interrupted, and Cy and Dave both stared at me across the table.

I traced my fingers around the floral patterns of the yellow damask tablecloth, trying to smooth the rough weave as I gathered the memories.

"I remember Ma making patchwork quilts to sell," I said, startled by the recollection. "She'd fashion all sorts of designs, sorting through the pieces of material in her sewing basket until she found one with just the right shape and color to fit the pattern. Every scrap of fabric in that basket had a history, and she'd tell each one's story as she sewed it into place, even the sad ones. I asked her once why she kept the pieces that made her sad, like from her mother's funeral dress and such. She said it didn't matter whether the pieces were bright or dark, whether their stories were happy or sad — once they were part of the quilt, they all worked together to make the pattern."

I took a sip of ale and snuffled noisily.

"She said the quilt's purpose was to keep a body warm, but it was how the bright and dark colors worked together, how their stories blended, that made it unique, made it special. Otherwise, it'd just be a blanket."

CHAPTER TWENTY-TWO

Mines Road District, Western Australia —
May 7, 1878
PING-tink.

I stood on the dusty plain and stared blankly, past the telegram in my hands, to where a wildflower stood as a splash of red against the drab landscape. The twin blossoms of the flower danced in the late morning breeze, dipping and bowing to one another.

PING-tink.

A gust of wind upset the smooth motions and sent the flowers crashing into one another. I frowned at the harsh notes, so at odds with the delicate grace of the petals.

PING-tink.

I shook my head and stirred myself from the trance of the flowers, then turned to look toward the true source of the noise. Along the crest of Hundley's Pass my hammer crews pounded their heavy drill bits

478

into the rock outcropping, driving the bore-holes for the dynamite that would soon shave off the peak.

The telegram burned in my hand, and I turned my attention back to the message I'd received that morning.

We arrive at Geraldton on the 7th. Long-ing to see you. G —

"Nice stroll?" Dave asked as he ap-proached me, clouds of dust rising about his boots with each step.

"Mm-hmm," I grunted absently.

"Any news from town?" A wry grin tugged at the corner of his mouth, and I looked up at him and folded the telegram.

"Probably nothing you haven't heard about already. Cass and Cy coming up, too?"

"Yep," he said. "Boat should put in to Geraldton before noon. If we've done our job right, the train should reach our end of the line by two or so."

I nodded and rubbed sweaty palms on my shirtfront.

"It'll be fine," Dave assured me with a slap on the shoulder.

"Things are so different now." I took off my fedora and wiped the sweat from my brow through thinning hair. "What if I'm not the man she wants anymore?"

Dave's look turned serious and he chewed on his lip for a moment.

"I see what you mean." A stream of tobacco juice shot through his teeth. "If that's that case, I reckon there's plenty of other fellas for her to choose from. It's a right good-sized crew."

I looked up at that, and my nervousness evaporated.

"Bastard," I said with a grin.

"Maybe Coombs — he's seems a mite lonely."

The company cook was a good man, but about as wide as he was tall, with cauliflower ears and a pock-scarred face that even a mother would be hard-pressed to love.

"If it comes to that, I'll leave the matchmaking to you," I said with a laugh, then led the way up the slope.

As we neared the summit, the ring of hammers on drill heads was punctuated by the heaves and grunts of the men on the hill. My attention was drawn to the lead crew where Seth Freeman and Tim Sullivan outpaced the others by a good four or five strokes a minute.

At Cy's suggestion, I'd paired the men together once Seth had recovered from his injuries. What started as a fierce battle between the two giants soon settled into an uneasy rivalry and, now, had become something of a friendship. I watched the pair as they worked, their bared chests and arms rippling with power. Sweat glistened in the sunlight and attracted the dust that rose from their work until each was plastered the same shade of grey.

"You want them to push on through or go ahead and break?" Dave asked.

I pulled my watch from its pocket, and a chill ran from my hand to the message that rested over my heart. I shook off the feeling and snapped open the lid to check the time.

"Go ahead and call them off," I said. "We'll start fresh after dinner, and should be ready to blast by the time Cy gets here."

"That'll make Kincaid happy," Dave said, then spat a stream of tobacco juice on the ground.

I looked down the slope toward the field camp, where Leslie Kincaid sat fanning himself under the awning of the staff tent, while Andy Fraser kept him out of my way.

"I can't tell you how much his happiness means to me," I said drily. "Call dinner."

Dave put a pair of fingers in his mouth and blew a shrill whistle. The drilling sounds slowly faded and the hammermen and drillers shouldered their tools and headed down the slope.

"Good job, men," I offered as they passed by in dust-caked indigo dungarees. The men nodded and grunted their thanks, not daring to open their mouths until they'd had a chance to wash away the grime.

"You coming?" Dave asked as he headed toward the chow wagon.

"I need to talk to Kincaid first," I said, "but I'll be along in a bit."

"Enjoy."

"Yeah," I said, and headed toward the staff tent.

"The plunger spins the dynamo, creating an electric current," Andy Fraser was saying as I approached, "which passes along the cables to detonate all the charges simultaneously. Oh, there you are, Jim," he said, visibly relieved as I rounded the corner.

"Andy, would you run and find Dave?" I said. "I need you to help him with some of the blasting prep."

"Yes, sir," he said immediately, a grateful look in his eyes as he made his escape.

"I must confess, Mister Robbins," Kincaid lisped in Queen's English, looking at me through beady eyes as his wispy mustache twitched beneath a long, thin nose, "I have reservations about these new methods.

This is not how we have done things in the past." He wiped a drop of sweat — perspiration — from his brow and slicked back his oiled hair.

While the directors of the railroad had given Cy — and, therefore, Dave and me — a relatively free hand in restructuring the operations, they had insisted on having one of their own men assigned to observe and report back to them, independent of the American interlopers. For the most part Kincaid stayed well out of the way, but he provided just enough of a nuisance and a distraction that I half suspected his real job was to keep us from making our schedule, and thus deny any performance bonuses.

"It is exactly by doing things as they were done in the past that this line fell so far behind schedule," I pointed out. "If we're to make up the lost time, we need to take advantage of every new opportunity we can."

"Be that as it may, I have notified the board of my concerns." Kincaid puffed out his slender chest and pulled a sheaf of telegrams from the pocket of his khaki jacket.

"And?" I said.

The little man deflated a bit.

"And they agree that operations are to

proceed as planned. But the director himself is coming up to observe this afternoon," he hastened to add, "and I am to inform him of any further concerns."

"Naturally," I said, then pushed past him into the tent.

"Are you sure this thing will work?" he pressed, lugging the Smith Exploder into the tent behind me. "After all, the ink is barely dry on the patent."

"Look, Leslie," I said with a tired sigh.

The man bristled at the familiar use of his name.

"If it doesn't work," I said, "we have plenty of safety fuses to fall back on. Worst case, we blast tomorrow instead of this evening, which still leaves us right on target. I wouldn't do that —" I added as Kincaid moistened his fingers, touched them to the detonator's terminals and pressed on the plunger, "— if I were you."

He screamed and jerked his hand back, waving it as he tried to cool his fingers from the electric shock.

"You might want to avoid that in the future," I suggested, then steered him toward the tent flap. "Why don't you go see Coombs at the chow wagon. Some lard should take the sting right out."

Finally alone, I took a deep breath and sat

down at my camp desk to sort through the new stack of orders and telegrams. The courier had come up from Geraldton this morning, but I'd ignored the official communiqués as soon as I discovered Gina's telegram. Unable to put off the work any longer, I forced myself to set aside her arrival, and plunged into the pile of forms. Midway through the stack, a head poked through the tent flap.

"Were you planning to eat today?" Dave asked.

I looked up as I dropped another telegram in the *Later* pile.

"I completely forgot," I said, and accepted a plate of stew and biscuits.

"That's what I'm here for. Someone has to keep this line on track."

I grunted as I shoved a gravy-laden biscuit in my mouth.

"Maybe Cy should've put you in charge of this outfit," I said. "I could have stayed back in Perth."

"Nah," Dave said. "You're better at dodging the bullshit than I am. You just keep pushing that little pencil of yours while I push the crews, and we'll see this line finished yet."

"Did Andy find you?" Another biscuit.

"Yep," Dave said. "I let him hide out in

my tent, making up the last of the blasting caps. Should be ready to go as soon as we've finished drilling."

"Good. Let me get through these papers, all right? And maybe find a hole for Leslie to fall into."

"Accidents have been known to happen," Dave said with a grin as he turned to leave the tent.

"Thanks for dinner," I said, then started on the next telegram. The next ten minutes saw three more interruptions, and I began to think I could drill back to the States before I managed to dig through the stack of papers.

"What?" I demanded as the fourth interruption was announced by a light knock on the tent post.

"I'm sorry, Mister Robbins," Seth said, his hat bunched up in his enormous hands. "I'll come back later."

"It's all right, Seth," I said, and waved him into the tent. "What can I do for you?"

"Nothing," he said, his eyes brightening. "I just wanted to let you know — Lydia's had a boy. I'm a papa."

We'd arranged for Lydia to join Seth about a year earlier. She'd shared a small cottage with Cassandra in Geraldton until a month or so ago, when the women had rejoined Cy in Perth, in expectation of Lydia's delivery.

"That's great news," I said, and came around the desk to offer Seth my hand. "Did you settle on a name?"

"Sure did," he said as he ignored my hand and pulled me into a fierce embrace. "Ezekiel Jade Freeman — for my father, and for the man who set him free."

I'd never spoken with Seth about the totem he wore or about my almost identical one. All thought of coincidence was now gone, replaced by the certainty that both had been carved by the hand of my old friend Zeke.

Before I could say anything, the camp bell rang, and Seth released me from the bear hug.

"I got to get back to work. I just wanted to let you know," he said, then disappeared through the tent flap, wiping his eyes on his sleeve as he went.

I sat back down at my desk, but old memories kept claiming my thoughts until I finally gave up. Setting the work aside, I returned to my tent and pulled an envelope from between the pages of *Age of Fable*. The pages of the letter were creased and crumpled and stained with grime and sweat and tears. I read the letter again, mainly to see the familiar handwriting, for the words were long since etched in my mind.

My Dearest Jim —

Cassandra will have told you already of Daddy and Mother's passing. God forgive me, but it was a relief to see his spirit at last freed from the body that had so long held him prisoner. Poor Mother had been strong for him for so long and, when he finally passed, it seemed he took that strength with him. She followed him to Heaven two days later.

I write, though, not to tell you of them, not to look back, but to look forward. My obligations here are ended, and I, too, am free of the life that was. I have left Simon and am coming to Australia, taking with me only what I brought into his home: a few possessions, a long-held hope, and my darling treasure, Ginny.

Or might I say, our *treasure.*

For you and I created her, and, in taking her into Simon's home, I took a part of you. She has been my comfort these years. In her eyes I have found your strength, and in her smile your humor. I pray you might find a way to forgive me, my love, for keeping her from you all this time. Fear and uncertainty can make a young woman take a path on which she would never otherwise have set foot. Once on that path, there can be no turning back — only ever forward, praying and hoping against hope that one day, somehow, another path might appear to lead her to where her heart is.

That path is now open, my Heart, and it leads westward. We will take the train to San Francisco, and Ginny is eager to see the railroad that her father built. I expect to reach Perth by Easter, where I will await word from you.

I cannot expect your forgiveness. I cannot expect you to wish to see me. I can only beg you to see Ginny, that she might know her father, know what a good man truly is. And, if by some miracle you can again open your heart to me, I vow — to my final breath — to repay every hurt with joy, and every tear with kisses.

Till then, I am as I ever have been, and ever shall be — Yours. G —

An hour later, drilling finished, I stood atop the summit of Hundley's Pass and surveyed the week's work while I soaked in the westerly breeze. I squinted my eyes against the wind that tickled my nose and stung the back of my throat with its dust. A thin column of smoke rose from the southern horizon, where the company train steamed up from Geraldton. I swallowed a nervous flutter then turned at the sound of boots scuffing over the rock, accompanied by the soft *whirr* of the cable spool's unwinding.

"About time they finished up here," Kincaid griped, idly wringing his hands as he led Dave up the slope.

"We're still half a day ahead of schedule," Dave reminded him, then set down the cable spool.

I took the heavy blasting kit from his shoulder while he spun out a few arm-lengths of cable.

"Are you sure that's safe?" Kincaid asked as I set the crate on the ground and pried off the lid.

"What, this?"

Dave picked up one of the brown sticks of dynamite and waved it at the Brit.

Kincaid reeled back as Dave fumbled with the stick. The little man screamed and crouched into a ball, clapping his hands over his ears as the dynamite fell from Dave's hand and rolled harmlessly across the ground. The Englishman winked open a fearful eye, then stood when he realized he still had legs.

"Well," he stammered, "I see you have the

490

situation well in hand here. I'll head back down to greet the director when he arrives."

He turned and hurried down the slope toward the barricade that had been set up at the railhead to protect the crew from the blast. He stifled a curse as he slipped on some scree and took the next several yards on his backside.

Dave laughed aloud as he cut the cable from the spool and stripped the insulation from the ends. I stabbed the blasting caps into the sticks of dynamite, then twisted the ends of the cables together to create a web of explosives that would reduce the hilltop to rubble. We'd nearly finished setting the charges when a quick glance south suggested the train would reach camp within a few minutes.

"I can wrap up here," I suggested to Dave, knowing he was as eager for the train's arrival as I was. "Why don't you go on down to meet them?"

"No, I can help finish," he offered weakly.

"You haven't seen Cass in over a month. We're almost done, and it's nothing I can't handle while you go wash up — which you really need to do," I added, wrinkling my nose. "Besides, I could use a little time alone before . . ." Dave didn't need to hear the words to know my thoughts.

"Fair enough." He started down the slope, hands in his pockets and hat pushed back on his head, before he stopped and turned back toward me. "Life's good, you know that?"

I nodded and gave a small laugh. "Yeah, I do. Now go."

He scuttled the rest of the way down the hill while I turned back to the remaining bit of work. Before long I had the last hole loaded. I pulled off my hat and wiped my forehead on my sleeve. A sudden gust of wind jerked the fedora from my grip and the hat sailed downward, floating on the breeze toward the barricade.

As I followed the hat with my eyes, I noticed Kincaid flapping and strutting around the barricade like a mother hen, fretting over every last detail before Cy's arrival. He stopped at the detonator, and my eyes widened when I saw the cable ends already screwed to the terminals. I watched helplessly as he pulled the handle up into the armed position, thought better of it, and began to press it back down.

I cupped my hands to my mouth and yelled for him to stop. Kincaid cocked his head at the shout and spun around. As he twisted, one knee sprang out at an odd angle and the man tottered. Kincaid released the handle of the detonator and flailed his arms as he fought to keep his balance. The effort was wasted, though, and he toppled over, catching the plunger in the crook of one arm and driving it inexorably, fatally down under his weight.

So this is what it is to die, I managed to think before my life flashed before my eyes in a blaze of light.

EPILOGUE

My eyes blink open against the glare of tent walls glowing in the midday sun. Grief and concern are etched on the faces of those gathered around. Seth, Uncle Cy, Dave and Cassandra. I turn my head as far as the pain will allow and look into my own eyes set within a face graced by Gina's features, and I blink away the tears that blur the vision of my daughter, Ginny. I force a smile, then turn my attention back to Gina, to the emerald eyes that have so long haunted me, eyes filled now with pain and regret.

I feel my hold on life slipping. My body trembles as though to shake my spirit loose. The air sears my throat and lungs as I take a deep breath, then rasp out a final word.

"Forgiven."

That last breath carries me with it, and I feel the rattle more than hear it as I pass from the body. I watch fondly as the images of my loved ones fade away, to be replaced by the dancers and my guide and the tree.

"What now?" I ask.

"What you always wanted to do," he says. "What I wouldn't let you do anymore for fear you'd be hurt again."

I look into the man's eyes, my father's eyes, clear and filled with a vigor that I never saw in life.

"Climb," he says.

I grin and place a hand on the familiar bark. I trace my way around the trunk until I come to the burled root that has always served as a mounting step. I step up, balance myself against the trunk with one hand, then push off to reach the first branch just beyond my arm's reach. I catch the limb, bring up my other hand, swing my feet up.

And I climb.

I rise through the branches as easily as climbing a set of stairs. The earth drops away and I hear Pa's voice repeat the words I'd long ago forgotten.

"That's the way to climb. That's my boy. Reach for it."

As I near the top, the world is only leaves and branches and the rustle of the wind and the sound of chimes. From below I hear a faint "I'm proud of you, son," and I am through the leaves.

The world spreads out below me like one of

Ma's patchwork quilts, the land a checker-board of varying shades and shapes and styles. Rather than crops and landholdings, I recognize each one as a living, breathing soul, the patterns blending together to form a whole more beautiful than any one piece could ever be.

I hear a loud snap, and my foothold gives way. For a bare moment I dangle by one hand, then the tree limb evaporates and my hand grips nothing but air. A flutter of panic rises in my stomach and I brace myself for the rush of branches and leaves and twigs to tear at my skin and clothing. I look toward the ground only to find that I am racing farther and farther away from it.

Heavenward.

I soar beyond the leaves. The green canopy of the tree grows and spreads beneath me, stretching its branches toward the horizon until the entire earth is hidden by the shim-mering sylvan veil.

With a jerk, I stop rising, my ascent checked by a shining silver thread that stretches between me and the center of the leaves. I smile as I pluck it loose and continue my race toward the sun, even as the thread spirals down, down, until it disappears from sight.

I look up. In the midst of the brightly glowing sky, I see a point of light that glows brighter even than the sun. I will myself toward it and the light begins to separate into distinct figures. Clusters of forms appear, then individual shapes from among the clusters. As I draw nearer, I recognize each one by nature, if not by form.

First to come into focus is Becca, her smile warm and welcoming. Ma and Pa stand behind her, alongside Matt and Izzy, Zeke and Ketty. Missus Warren, Mister Barnes and a host of others are on hand to greet me. Eager as they seem for my arrival, they all step aside to allow me to pass, until I come face to face with the one I've ached to see.

"What took you so long?" Mae asks sweetly as I draw near.

"Just some business to finish up," I reply, and joy floods my being as I stand on the threshold of the place I've yearned for and from which I've so long been kept apart.

"Welcome home," Mae whispers, and reaches out to me.

I take her hand and fix my gaze on those eyes that once and fully captured my soul. She wraps her arms about me, and the others circle around to embrace us. I melt into the oneness of that embrace.

As I cross Death's threshold and enter into the wondrous bliss of eternal light and love, I finally know what it is to live.

AUTHOR'S NOTES

I first discovered Jim Robbins's story in the winter of 1999. During the course of an hour, I experienced a few brief scenes from his life. Over time these expanded into the story presented here. While there is no historical evidence to suggest Jim actually tramped through the backwoods of Arkansas or laid rail across the Great Plains, I'd like to think the spirit of those who did so inform his journey.

I was made a Freemason in Virginia, in 1996. Where Masonic rituals and allusion are presented, they are derived from works in the public domain, and differ from those I was taught. No oaths have been broken in the telling of this story.

Jim's hometown of Britton appears on an 1891 map of Arkansas, near the confluence of Frog Bayou and the Arkansas River. The town has since disappeared, but Van Buren remains the seat of Crawford County.

The Battle of Elkhorn Tavern (also known as the Battle of Pea Ridge) was one of the costliest engagements of the American Civil War west of the Mississippi. Fighting took place March 7–8, 1862, near Bentonville, Arkansas. The upper room of the tavern was used as a Masonic lodge, but the meeting on the night before battle is my own creation. This is based in part on another pre-battle meeting (perhaps apocryphal) between Union and Confederate brethren at Mason's Hall in Richmond, Virginia, on the eve of the Union assault on that city. Both Grenville Dodge and James "Wild Bill" Hickok took part in the fighting at Pea Ridge, though it is debatable whether either was a Freemason.

The improbable charge of Champion's company in support of Guibor's artillery battery — wherein fewer than two dozen riders charged several hundred infantrymen — is as true as any eyewitness record of battle. The account, including the verbal exchange between Captains Champion and Guibor, is derived from an article originally printed in the *St. Louis Republican* by Hunt P. Wilson, who served under Guibor. For an excellent examination of this pivotal battle, see *Pea Ridge: Civil War Campaign in the West* by William L. Shea and Earl J. Hess.

Likewise, the recounting of the Battle of Nashville is based on contemporary reports and personal accounts. This battle effectively ended Confederate action in the western theater, and it is perhaps fitting that it included one of the largest concentrations of United States Colored Troops (USCT) in the war. Indeed, this was the first combat most of these regiments saw, having previously been assigned to garrison duty or guarding railway lines. Notably, the taking of Peach Orchard Hill was accomplished by the 13th Regiment USCT, who suffered a forty percent casualty rate.

The building of the Transcontinental Railroad, fast on the heels of the war, represented another fundamental shift in a rapidly changing nation. Despite the staggering degrees of graft and corruption associated with it, the significance of this achievement, and the determination and commitment of resources that made it possible, rival those of the space program initiated a century later. Stephen E. Ambrose provides a detailed and engaging look at this great undertaking in *Nothing Like It in the World: The Men Who Built the Transcontinental Railroad 1863–1869.*

Despite the uneasy peace between North and South, and the steel rails that linked

East and West, America remained a nation deeply divided. Those who had recently been made free, and others who willingly came to this country in search of opportunity, faced hatred and violence. Equality under the law was a concept still foreign, as the justice systems of California and other states and territories barred minorities from giving legal testimony against white men.

While a few hundred Chinese immigrants had settled along the Pacific Coast before that area became part of the United States, thousands more began to arrive following the annexation of California and its subsequent statehood. The discovery of gold and the burgeoning settlement in the West provided tremendous opportunities for people fleeing from civil war and foreign aggression against their homeland.

Despite the industry and ingenuity that had made the Central Pacific Railroad possible — or, perhaps, because of these — Chinese immigrants were subjected to physical and legislative attacks. In 1853, the California Supreme Court declared the Chinese to be an inferior race, of limited intellectual development. This decision overturned the murder conviction of a man whose guilt had been based, in part, upon the testimony of Chinese witnesses.

With the economic slowdown that followed the Civil War and the completion of the Transcontinental Railroad, jobs were at a premium. Hardworking Chinese immigrants, who routinely earned far less than their white counterparts, were often viewed as stealing work from white men. As early as 1867, labor organizers led attacks against Chinese workers. In 1871, a mob of several hundred men attacked Los Angeles's Chinatown, resulting in the deaths of nearly two dozen Chinese. The 1882 Chinese Exclusion Act barred further Chinese immigration to the United States, and remained in effect until World War II.

Given the large amounts of federal land granted to railways, and the interstate nature of the lines, the US Marshal Service played a significant role in law enforcement along the steel roads. While the murder of a few Chinese workers would not be enough to spur justice into motion, it is conceivable that the destruction of railroad property would do the trick.

The Geraldton–Northampton Railway was authorized by the government of Western Australia in 1873. The road was completed in 1879, the year after Jim's death.

ABOUT THE AUTHOR

Marc Graham is an actor, singer, bard, engineer, Freemason, and whisky aficionado (Macallan 18, one ice cube). When not on stage, in a pub, or bound to his computer, he can be found traipsing about Colorado's Front Range with his wife and their Greater Swiss Mountain Dog.

marc-graham.com
facebook.com/marcgrahambooks
@Marc_Graham

The employees of Thorndike Press hope you have enjoyed this Large Print book. All our Thorndike, Wheeler, and Kennebec Large Print titles are designed for easy reading, and all our books are made to last. Other Thorndike Press Large Print books are available at your library, through selected bookstores, or directly from us.

For information about titles, please call:
(800) 223-1244

or visit our Web site at:
http://gale.com/thorndike

To share your comments, please write:
Publisher
Thorndike Press
10 Water St., Suite 310
Waterville, ME 04901